# Praise for Candace Calvert

"Candace Calvert's *Rescue Team* had me intrigued by page 1, laughing by page 2, and in love with the hero by page 3. If you love inspirational romantic suspense and haven't yet discovered Candace's books, you need to go to the nearest bookstore and pick up a copy of this book—*stat*."

**—JORDYN REDWOOD,**
author of *Proof* and *Poison*

"Head nurse Kate Callison finds herself pulled in many directions at Austin Grace Hospital—ethics, loyalties, and love drag her in deeper as she struggles to escape her darkest secret. Rescue volunteer Wes Tanner wants to help her but has his own demon from the past. A multilevel morality play in a modern hospital with a rich and varied cast of characters."

**—LYN COTE,**
author of the Northern Intrigue series

"*Rescue Team* is a great story with great characters on a realistic journey through a tough few days. Candace brings the hospital routine alive with believable people and situations."

**—JANICE CANTORE,**
author of the Pacific Coast Justice series

"Full of memorable characters and guided by Calvert's own experience as an ER nurse, the first novel in her Grace Medical series evokes a realistic and intriguing world readers will definitely want to return to."

**—*BOOKLIST* ON *TRAUMA PLAN***

"Candace Calvert has crafted another gut-grabbing medical thriller. . . . The faith message was clear, the medical traumas heart-stopping, and the romance heart melting. . . . A great read and one for your keeper shelf."

—**LYNETTE EASON,**
award-winning, bestselling author of the Women of Justice series

"Candace Calvert paints an exciting story on a canvas she knows very well—the world of medicine and the people who inhabit it. *Trauma Plan* is a novel that will grip your heart and keep you turning pages."

—**RICHARD L. MABRY, MD,**
author of the Prescription for Trouble series

"[*Critical Care*] flows well and keeps the reader's attention. . . . Characters find not only psychological healing, but also spiritual renewal."

—*CHRISTIAN RETAILING*

"If you like *ER* and *House,* you'll love Logan and Claire and their friends at Sierra Mercy. Give me another dose, and soon!"

—**SUSAN MAY WARREN,**
award-winning author of *Happily Ever After* and *The Shadow of Your Smile*

"If you need an infusion of hospital drama, *Code Triage* is just the prescription."

—**IRENE HANNON,**
bestselling author of the Heroes of Quantico series

"*Code Triage* is an adrenaline high, ripped from today's headlines, with enough romantic tension to spike your pulse."

—**JULIE LESSMAN,**
award-winning author of the Daughters of Boston series

GRACE MEDICAL

# RESCUE TEAM

GRACE MEDICAL

*Candace Calvert*

Tyndale House Publishers, Inc.
Carol Stream, Illinois

Visit Tyndale online at www.tyndale.com.

Visit Candace Calvert's website at www.candacecalvert.com.

*TYNDALE* and Tyndale's quill logo are registered trademarks of Tyndale House Publishers, Inc.

*Rescue Team*

Designed by Stephen Vosloo

Edited by Sarah Mason

Published in association with the literary agency of Natasha Kern Literary Agency, Inc., P.O. Box 1069, White Salmon, WA 98672.

*Rescue Team* is a work of fiction. Where real people, events, establishments, organizations, or locales appear, they are used fictitiously. All other elements of the novel are drawn from the author's imagination.

**Library of Congress Cataloging-in-Publication Data**

Calvert, Candace, date.
  Rescue team / Candace Calvert.
    pages cm. — (Grace Medical ; 2)
    ISBN 978-1-4143-6112-3 (sc)
1. Nurses—Fiction.   2. Medical novels.   3. Christian fiction.   4. Romantic suspense fiction.
I. Title.
  PS3603.A4463R47 2013
  813'.6—dc23

Printed in the United States of America

19   18   17   16   15   14   13

7   6   5   4   3   2   1

*For the very real heroes of search and rescue,*

*whose courage, skill, heart, and selfless*

*dedication offer a lifeline of hope to so many.*

# Acknowledgments

Heartfelt appreciation to:

Literary agent Natasha Kern—for more than a decade of blessings.

The amazing Tyndale House publishing team, especially editors Jan Stob and Sarah Mason—it's a joy to work with you.

Critique partner and fellow author Nancy Herriman—you're the best and I'm grateful.

Patti Pearson, former training officer, Sacramento County Sheriff Search and Rescue (mounted), and Brian M. Brown, president, Travis County Search and Rescue—for your generosity in answering endless technical questions and for giving me a strong sense of the heart that drives you and your courageous volunteer teams. Any inaccuracies, or changes to accommodate fictional portrayals, are mine alone.

Tess Calvert—for your expert insight into special-needs character Dylan Tanner and especially for being such an extraordinary mother to Vin and Drake.

My wonderful family, especially husband and real-life hero, Andy—your loving encouragement means the world to me.

And with deep appreciation to my readers—it is an honor to bring you these stories of hope.

*I once was lost but now am found,*

*Was blind but now I see.*

JOHN NEWTON, "AMAZING GRACE"

**1**

**"THE GULLY, BELOW THE WATER TANK**—I see something." Wes Tanner pocketed his radio and plunged downhill through tinder-dry Texas cedar and darkness, his cowhide boots scattering limestone gravel like stray bird shot. Logic argued that he could be wrong, that what he'd spotted might be no more than a sack of trash. Or a poacher's deer bag sent soaring by the November wind. But hope was wearing spurs tonight.

He pushed his stride. *I'll find you. I'm coming.*

The blue-white beam of his headlamp flickered as branches slapped his helmet and rescue pack; he hated to think of the damage they'd do to the parchment skin of an eighty-year-old. Or of how this woman, battling Alzheimer's, would fare dressed only in a nightgown. With dawn minutes away, the air temperature couldn't be more than fifty degrees. There was no way of knowing what time the former piano teacher had wandered away from the old ranch house she shared with her sister-in-law. She could have been out here for hours, confused, frightened, cold . . . injured? Wes's jaw tensed. He'd find her in time.

He halted, took a deep breath of air made musky by cedar and oak, then swept the light along the shallow gully. "Mrs. Braxton? Amelia?"

The beam lit a stand of prickly pear cactus, a rotting tree stump, and a mound of dirt more than a little suspicious for a nest of stinging fire ants. Wes refused to imagine that cruel scenario and scanned farther, growing increasingly impatient to—

His heart stalled. There, beneath the brush.

The beam focused on a body sprawled in the leaf-strewn gully. Flowered nightgown, snowy-white single braid. Face pale, eyes closed, mouth slack. Breathing?

"Subject located," Wes huffed into the radio, jogging the remaining few yards. "Can't tell yet if . . ." He swallowed the rest of the sentence, hoping he wouldn't have to report back with the team's code word for a deceased body. *Don't be dead. Please.*

"Copy, Wes. We're right above you. On our way down."

"Good."

There was a yelp in the distance—Gabe's chocolate Lab signaling human scent—then voices. One deep, the other feminine. His "hasty search" team, assembled within minutes of the 5:30 a.m. callout by the sheriff's department. Wes was grateful but wished his rural volunteers still included a nurse or paramedic. As an EMT, he carried basic medical supplies, but . . .

"Ma'am?" He dropped to one knee beside the woman and grasped her thin shoulder, shook her gently. "Are you awake?" *Alive?* He held his breath, nudged her again, watching for the rise and fall of her chest that would confirm breathing, a blink of her eyelids, a small grimace—anything. "Amelia?"

"Unh . . ." Her muffled groan was the sweetest thing Wes had heard in a long, rugged week.

"Hello there." Relief threatened to choke his voice. "It's okay. You're not lost anymore."

She blinked and he averted the light.

"You're . . ." Amelia swept her tongue across her dry lips, then stared at him for a long moment.

"Wes Tanner, ma'am. I'm here to help you," he explained, doubtful she recognized him, though he'd seen Lily and Amelia last week, Amelia's ever-present doll propped in the elderly ladies' grocery cart. But his appearance right now would seem intimidating at best: shadowy bulk, dark beard stubble, equipment dangling from his search-and-rescue vest, squawking radio—and every square inch smelling of rode-hard horse. On the white-knight scale, Wes was a notch above Sasquatch.

He lowered his pack to the ground. "Miss Lily asked me—"

"Asked *us*," Gabe Buckner corrected. A headlamp lit his face like a jack-o'-lantern as he stepped into the clearing. He snapped a leash onto his dog's collar and walked closer. A few yards away, the team's newly certified member—a coffeehouse barista by day—said a few words into her radio before following him.

"Deputies are guiding the medics in," she reported, first-rescue excitement making her voice climb an octave.

"See?" Wes smiled down at Amelia as he lifted the foil rescue blanket from his pack. "Plenty of help tonight." He patted her shoulder as she tried to sit up. "Don't move yet, Mrs. Braxton. Let's be sure you're okay."

"You're . . . ?" Her gaze moved over Wes's face again, her chin trembling.

"Wes Tanner," he reminded. "My family takes care of the wells around here. And over there is Gabe. His family . . ." Bad time to mention that they owned the local funeral home. "His family lives right down the road. The pretty one is Jenna. And that four-legged guy is Hershey, the best rescue dog in the county."

As if on cue, the chocolate Lab whined and wagged his tail.

"We're your neighbors. Come to help you back home, ma'am."

"Oh . . ."

Wes watched as she looked from face to face, her expression as wide-eyed and incredulous as Dorothy's in the black-and-white aftermath of Oz.

"Yes. I remember now." She returned her gaze to Wes, beginning to smile. "You're Lee Ann Tanner's boy."

Gut-punched, Wes managed a nod.

"Let's get you warm, ma'am," Gabe offered, moving forward to help.

They had Amelia wrapped in the blanket moments before law enforcement and the medics arrived. And in less than ten minutes she'd been moved via rescue litter to the waiting rig. An initial assessment concluded that, beyond some scrapes and mild symptoms of exposure, the piano teacher had survived her unexpected adventure fairly well. Considering she'd made the trek in an ancient pair of men's cowboy boots—worn on the wrong feet.

"They're taking her to Austin Grace ER?" Gabe asked, watching as they loaded the woman into the ambulance.

"Right." Wes scraped his fingers through his hair, loosing some twigs left from his scramble through the underbrush. "I'm going to follow along after I get my horse settled. I'll give Miss Lily a ride into the city and let the granddaughter take over from there. I'm supposed to meet with the hospital social worker later this morning anyway. We're doing that emergency department presentation on critical incident stress this week."

"Oh yeah." Gabe stooped to pat his dog. "The media's all over those 'new details' on our missing nurse—has to stress those folks in the ER. Even after this long." He sighed. "Now there's a rescue we all wanted to see happen."

"Yeah."

Gabe was quiet for a moment. "Must have been a surprise when Mrs. Braxton mentioned your mother."

Wes hated the way his stomach sank; he should be long past that. "Not unusual for Alzheimer's. Can't remember what a toothbrush is on most days but then can clearly recall the name of a woman who's been gone for twentysome years." *Twenty-seven, come January 3.*

"Right." Gabe glanced away as the ambulance engine leaped to life. "Sure you don't want to catch some breakfast before driving into Austin? Hershey's got his mind set on apple-smoked bacon. I'm buying." He raised his brows. "Jenna's coming too. I get the feelin' she'd be pretty happy to see you show up."

"You're reading things into that one. Thanks, but I'm going to grab something to eat at the hospital."

Gabe shrugged. "While you're there, find us a few volunteers, would ya? I'm willing to share this opportunity for an early morning hike."

"You mean recruit the one remaining nurse who isn't working extra shifts to pay the mortgage and put gas in her car?" Wes frowned at the truth: their community search-and-rescue team was shrinking in this tight economy. He'd proposed a horse-mounted team and a long list of equipment he wanted to add to their incident command trailer, but donations were down and grant money was drying up. Fewer team members, less overall support. Still, today they'd had a live find. And it felt good.

"Hey, thanks for coming out, buddy." Wes clapped his friend's shoulder. "For a funeral director, a latte maker, a well digger, and a dog that still smells of last month's skunk chase, we didn't do half-bad."

Gabe grinned, snapped an exaggerated salute. "You call; I'm here. Count on it. It's more than worth crawling out of a warm bed to find someone alive."

"Nothing beats it."

Wes headed down the road to his horse trailer as morning lit the hill country cedar and prickly pear cactus—golden as the yolks in Gabe's favorite breakfast. He glanced back at the gully, remembering the moment he'd found Amelia Braxton. *It's okay. You're not lost anymore.* His favorite words in the world. Being able to say them and offer that lifeline of hope to another human being had become as important to him as breathing. It was the reason he'd answer any callout—anytime, anywhere. Even if he had to do it alone. And sometimes he did that . . . hours, weeks, even months after other searchers called it quits.

Because he understood how it felt to be lost, cold, terrified, and desperate for help. Despite a lifetime spent trying to forget, he still remembered it as if it were yesterday: the January night that Lee Ann Tanner left her seven-year-old son in the woods. Then drove her car into the river.

- + -

Emergency department director Kate Callison hugged her scrub jacket close and crossed the employee parking lot, watching dawn's attempt to erase the bruise-dark shadows that shrouded the entrance to the Austin Grace ER. With every step she fought an almost-suffocating urge to jog back to her car, gun the engine, and drive away to . . . anywhere else. Somewhere without media, lawyers, patient complaints, and a sullen and dwindling—and quite possibly mutinous—nursing staff. The last few weeks had been miserable enough to make Florence Nightingale jump ship, and there was no guarantee today would be any better. There was already a rescue rig parked in the ambulance bay.

Her gaze followed the empty sidewalk to the visitors' tables, and an unexpected sliver of hope lightened her step; at least the night shift patient load hadn't spilled outside. It was almost a miracle. Maybe—

"Oh, excuse me," Kate apologized, stepping aside at the doorway. "Sorry; I didn't see you there."

"Uh . . . no problem."

A girl, wrapped in an oversize sweater coat as dark as the shadows, had appeared out of nowhere. As if the building itself simply spit her out. No more than a teenager, she had oily and lank hair, her face thin and far too pale. Even in the chill air, her skin glistened with perspiration.

"Hey . . ." Kate tipped her head, trying to catch the girl's gaze. "Are you all right? You look like you're feeling—"

"Okay," the girl whispered, eyes downcast. Her fingers moved to clutch the front of her sweater. Chipped black nail polish, a silver ring shaped like a Celtic cross. "I'm fine."

"Are you sure?" Kate asked gently. She glanced through the glass door panel and saw that the waiting room was indeed packed. "I can have someone look at you. That's why we're here. To help."

The girl's eyes met Kate's at last. Watery blue, lashes sodden, dark pupils dilated. Pain? Worry? Then Kate saw it with sudden certainty. *She's afraid.*

"You would do that?" the girl whispered, her trembling hand on Kate's arm. "You'd help me? Even if I—"

"Kate!"

Kate glanced toward the sound, then back at the girl. "I'm Kate Callison, the emergency department director. That nurse is waiting for me, but I meant what I said just now. We're here to help. With whatever you need. Go sign in at the registration desk. Tell them you spoke with me."

"I have to go," the girl said, backing away.

"But . . ."

As fast as she'd appeared, she was gone. Skirting the corner of the building, heading—

"Kate?"

The nurse in melon-pink scrubs held two Starbucks cups aloft, hot brews merging with cool sunrise in a fragrant cloud. Kate smiled, her uneasiness replaced by a rush of gratitude. ICU nurse Lauren Barclay was the only real friend she'd made in the months since she'd moved to Austin. Their prework coffees had become the best part of her day. Lately, the best part of *anything*.

"What do you think?" Lauren asked, glancing at the vacant visitors' tables. "Sit out here?" She raised her brows, one of them disappearing beneath the flowered surgical cap she'd tied over her hair. Another attempt to tame the thick blonde mane, as wavy and long as Kate's was dark and wispy-short. "I realize cool mornings are nothing special to a California girl," she teased in the familiar drawl, "but in Houston, we'd call this a flat-out miracle."

She handed Kate her coffee and settled onto a chair. "That poor mother was out there on the boulevard again. Did you see her?"

"Yes." Kate winced. A young woman had been stationed at a busy intersection for two days now, holding a huge poster of a bright-eyed and chubby toddler. Below the photo, in heavy and uneven strokes of marking pen, she'd printed a heart-wrenching plea: *Need money for my baby's funeral.*

"One of the cafeteria ladies said she's from out of state. They were visiting here when the baby got sick. So sad." Lauren peered at Kate over the top of her mocha. "How'd things go yesterday with the boss?"

Kate rolled her eyes at the reference to her meeting with the chief nursing officer. "I think Evelyn's exact words went something like 'Your team's morale is sinking.' She was being polite. It's more like I'm captain of the *Titanic* and instead of a band playing, there's one endless Willie Nelson CD." She sighed. "I never intended to be interim director of the emergency department. It's not what I applied for. And I had no idea I'd be stepping into the shoes of a saint."

Lauren nodded. "Sunni's disappearance has been hard on a lot of people. And if there really is new evidence, another search, and they find conclusive remains . . . I know you're skeptical about it, but I do think the social worker's right to present the critical incident stress information again. There's been more staff coming to the chapel lately. Several from your team."

"Hmm." Kate knew her friend was talking about an informal fellowship she led for hospital personnel, designed as a support system. Fortunately she'd figured out there was no point pressuring Kate to join in. Fellowship and hand-holding were the farthest things from her mind.

"When's that supposed to happen—the CISM refresher?" Lauren asked.

"At the staff meeting on Friday." Kate watched as an elderly woman made her way toward the doors to the ER. She was accompanied by a man in a faded denim jacket. Tall, with broad shoulders, dark hair, and considerable beard shadow. Wearing cowboy boots, of course—apparently a state requirement.

Kate turned her attention back to Lauren. "It's not that I'm exactly opposed to peer counseling or debriefing after a specific traumatic incident." For some reason, she thought of the too-pale face of the girl she'd met in the shadows. "I think it may have some benefit in isolated cases."

"But . . . ?"

"It's been six months since Sunni disappeared. I'd be blind not to see how respected she was. I understand that her loss left a big hole. And I don't kid myself that the things I've tried to do have helped much. But in my experience, dwelling on the past—resurrecting it—doesn't help either. At some point, you have to steel yourself and move on."

Lauren stared at her. "You're not quitting?"

"No," Kate said quickly, glad her new friend couldn't know about her recent conversation with the travel nurse recruiter in Dallas. Lauren wouldn't understand that a fallback plan was a necessity. Thankfully she'd never asked how long Kate had worked at Alamo Grace and, before that, the Mercy Hospital in San Jose or any of the other hospitals in California and elsewhere. Places where she'd joined the staff only to find that something didn't fit, wasn't quite right. Plan B was a lifeline for someone like Kate. "No, I'm not planning to resign. In spite of my teasing about big trucks and bigger belt buckles, churches on every corner—" Kate smiled—"and that there are actually places you can buy Texas-shaped tortilla chips, I like it here. It doesn't make any sense, but it's growing on me."

Nuts as it seemed, it was true. Kate wouldn't say this city felt like home—nothing ever had, including home—but . . . "Maybe it's because Austin feels a little more like California."

"Whoa, girl. Don't say that out loud," Lauren warned in a stage whisper. "You'll be run out of town." She checked her watch and stood. "We should head in."

"Right." Kate followed her toward the entrance to the ER. "I'll probably be run out regardless. Interim director is a temporary position. No guarantees. I came in on the heels of a lawsuit against the hospital that's still being settled. Patient-satisfaction surveys are at an all-time low. And last month I had to suspend that nurse."

"For drugs—you had no choice."

"The rumblings are that Sunni would have handled things with far more compassion. I'm working my tail off to prove myself, Lauren." Kate plucked at her scrubs. "I wear these instead of a suit so I can pitch in alongside the staff. All shifts, I come in to see what I can do to help. Ask Vicky who offered to give that soapsuds enema she groused about. I even baked red velvet cupcakes for the last staff meeting. But . . ."

She looked toward the doors of the department. The man in the denim jacket was standing there, using his cell phone. He glanced up as they approached.

Kate lowered her voice. "My performance review is coming up. At this point, only one of the full-time clinical coordinators supports me. I can probably count on a few of the docs to put in a good word. But if I want to stay, I've got to make a breakthrough with my nursing staff. Get them behind me somehow. Any way I can. Or at least prevent any more ugly PR catastrophes from happen—"

"Nurse!" A man from the waiting room forced his weight against the half-open automatic door. He gestured at them wildly. "Hurry! We need help in here!"

"I've got the door," the man in denim said, hitting the button to open it fully. Kate lunged into the waiting room with Lauren following. People were on their feet, shouting.

"Let them through!" the man in the denim jacket ordered, forging past Kate to clear the way. What was going on?

"Over there," someone pleaded, grabbing at Kate's arm. "That janitor—something's wrong. Please hurry."

Lauren pointed toward the far side of the room: a hospital janitor stood against the wall, eyes wild and face as gray as his uniform shirt. In his quaking hands were wads of blood-soaked paper towels.

*Laceration? Bleeding ulcer?* Mind whirling, Kate wedged through the space created by the man in denim, Lauren close behind.

"It's a baby," the janitor moaned, staggering toward them, his face even paler. "It was on the floor . . . the hallway bathroom. Oh . . . help . . ."

Kate's heart climbed to her throat. *No . . .*

"He's gonna pass out!" A woman's shout rose above a frenzy of panicked voices. "Somebody catch him! Don't let him drop that poor—"

Kate lurched forward a split second too late.

The janitor's legs gave way. In his last conscious effort, he thrust the tiny, motionless newborn into the denim cowboy's arms.

2

+

"I'M AN EMT. Show me where to go," Wes said, feeling the impossibly fragile weight in his hands. The look in the eyes of the dark-haired nurse confirmed his thoughts: *No time for protocols or even a pass off.* The only hope was to start running.

"To the code room. Follow me."

In seconds there was an open door, a flurry of scrubs beyond, and then a doctor jogging alongside Wes down the corridor toward the ER.

Overhead, a page blared. "Code purple, ER. . . . Code purple, ER. . . ."

Beige walls, yellowed vinyl floor—Wes's boots thudded down the hallway toward the resuscitation room, a short distance made agonizing by the stillness of the tiny body in his hands. He tried to tell himself it didn't feel cold through the sticky and congealing paper towels; he wanted to believe there was a gurgle, a gasp, a barely discernible shudder. *Please, don't let this baby be lost.*

He dove through the doorway to the code room, met immediately by lights, a hiss of oxygen, beeping machines, a chorus of voices—some giving orders, some asking questions—all of them focused on the bundle in his hands.

"Put the baby here," the dark-haired nurse instructed, and all at once Wes's hands were empty. He stepped back. Before a sea of multicolored scrubs filled the void, he managed to get a glimpse of the infant he'd carried into the room. A boy, achingly small. Hair and scalp still covered with membrane. Eyes closed, tiny lips parted, limbs fragile and limp, skin . . . *too blue.*

In an instant, a translucent resuscitation mask covered the infant's face. The dark-haired nurse's gloved hands slid beneath his tiny body, her thumbs over his breastbone, ready to start cardiac compressions. Wes tilted his head and caught a look at the young woman. Short hair, waiflike features, big eyes. Yet despite the fact that she'd run down the hall ahead of him, her face looked pale and her expression almost—

"Sir, this way, please." A man in a security uniform gestured to Wes. "I'll show you where you can wash up; then I'll need you to return to the waiting room."

Before Wes turned, the nurse glanced his way and their eyes met. The expression in hers was more than professionally focused and intense. It seemed . . . *grief-stricken.*

- + -

"Wait." The neonatologist slid his stethoscope beneath Kate's hands. "There's no brachial pulse. Let me listen. He's extremely preterm. Do we have any estimate on the time of birth?"

"No." Kate struggled against a wave of dizziness. "The janitor found him on the bathroom floor." She glanced at the clock. "It's been less than five minutes since then . . ."

"Here, let me," a NICU nurse offered, stepping close to relieve Kate. Someone else moved in with an Isolette.

Kate watched the physician's face, her stomach sinking when he frowned.

"No heart tones." He nodded as a nurse offered him the equipment for an umbilical line. "Start compressions. We'll need a dose of epi. Let's tube him, oxygenate him—get him warm. Give him a reasonable trial. I'll always try, but . . ." He looked at Kate. "No sign of the mother?"

"No, sir," the chief of security reported from the doorway. "We're watching the doors, doing an in-house check, OB and all the floors. PD's been notified." He looked at Kate. "They'll want to talk to the ER staff that has been here. In case they saw her. We shouldn't let anyone go off shift."

"Of course," Kate agreed, her voice emerging in a thick whisper. "I need to talk with the triage nurse myself." *To see if that laboring woman was signed in as an ER patient and didn't get care in time. Don't let it be true.*

"I'll go do that now." She forced herself to leave the code room, knowing the infant was receiving the best care possible. As department director, Kate's responsibilities were elsewhere. She should check on the janitor who fainted; Lauren was with him. Make sure the other patients were still being taken care of. And then she'd talk with the registration clerks and triage. But first . . .

Kate groaned softly. First, she needed to step away from here. Only for a minute. To get some air, stop herself from shaking. *And . . . oh, please.* To stop thinking of that baby boy's face, imagining his mother's anguish as she wrapped him in a nest of paper towels. Because if Kate didn't stop, the next step would be to start remembering the details of her own lonely moment of desperation. Merciless pain and guilt would flood back. She'd worked too hard, come too far, to risk having that shameful darkness swirl again.

- + -

"Such a shame on all counts." Cynthia McConnell dropped a crumpled butterscotch wrapper on her desktop and looked up at Wes. The social worker's expression said she was already weighing the emotional impact Baby Doe's death might have on emergency department staff.

"Want to bet how long it takes the media to start swarming?" Wes knew his question sounded bitter, but the blame game would soon begin. The hospital staff would become a target. Fingers pointing like they had at that Dallas search-and-rescue team during a high-profile murder last spring. Unpaid, dedicated volunteers accused of incompetence and shredded on the witness stand by attorneys for the defense. It had left Wes more than a little wary of lawyers. "If the emergency department staff wasn't already stressed by Sunni's case, this could do it."

"I've asked Lauren Barclay from the ICU to do some one-on-one contacts with staff. She's been recently trained as a peer counselor."

Wes nodded. "I co-taught that class."

"She feels her limited involvement this morning won't keep her from being objective." Cynthia's eyes showed concern. "It had to be tough when the janitor gave you that baby."

"I'm okay." Wes knew the social worker was taking his emotional pulse. He scraped a hand over his beard growth, remembering the weight of that tiny body in his hands. And then thought of his relief at finding Amelia Braxton alive just before dawn. *Found . . . lost.* Barely 9 a.m. and it had been a full day already.

"It was a shock," he continued, knowing Cynthia needed to hear more. The "I'm okay" badge of courage was brandished too quickly by first responders and medical personnel. It led to stress and serious burnout. "There wasn't much I could do but run him to the code room. I'm glad I could."

"I'm glad too, Wes." There was kindness in the social worker's eyes. "And then?"

"I was only there a few seconds but long enough to see he was going to need all the help that team could offer." He shifted in his chair. "We'll go ahead with the presentation we have planned for the staff meeting?"

"Depending on Lauren's concerns after talking with staff individually, we'll either offer a brief review of critical stress management or do a specific debriefing of the Baby Doe incident. Either way, the goal will be to bolster these folks' coping skills. They've had some problems in the past six months that have sort of . . ." She hesitated as if carefully choosing her words. "Shaken their sense of teamwork. That's why I'm especially glad that you'll be helping me with the presentation." Cynthia smiled. "I happen to know that *team* is your middle name, Mr. Tanner."

Wes smiled back at her, recalling what he'd said to Gabe. *"For a funeral director, a latte maker, a well digger, and a dog that still smells of last month's skunk chase, we didn't do half-bad."* Gratitude warmed him. He was proud of his team.

"So—" Cynthia checked her watch—"I'll give you a call after I touch base with Lauren and the emergency department director."

"Who did they finally hire for that position?" Wes stood, reaching for a butterscotch.

"A nurse from Alamo Grace, via California. Kate Callison. You probably saw her this morning. Late twenties, petite, short brunette hair?"

"Ah, right." *And sad eyes.*

- + -

Kate glanced at the trio of police cruisers in the parking lot, then shot Lauren a pained look across the pebbled visitors' table. "If I cut and run—right now, real fast—will you cover for me?"

Lauren held out a peanut butter cookie. "Eat something first." She waited until Kate finally took it. "Rough morning."

"Rough? Rough was finding that first scorpion in my shower or being compared to Sunni Sprague every single day. And finding that note on my car: 'Go back, California Girl.' Today makes *rough* look like a picnic." Kate shook her head, the events of the last two hours choking like her first taste of Texas humidity. "You saw our back hallway. Crime tape across the bathroom. Police uniforms outnumbering scrubs. They dusted for prints, questioned my staff, and took the tapes from the security cameras."

"I heard they asked for the name of every patient who sat in the waiting room during the night. To see if anyone could identify the mother of the baby."

"Yes. As if we didn't have privacy laws to consider." Kate groaned under her breath, knowing she'd be talking to the Lyon firm, the hospital's lawyers. "And—" Kate fought a shiver despite the sun on her shoulders—"as if what happened in there wasn't completely awful enough to deal with the first time around."

Lauren was quiet for a long moment, the distant sounds of

traffic on Ben White Boulevard filling the void. She brushed cookie crumbs from her lips. "It was awful. And it happened so fast. When did you realize what the janitor was holding?"

"I saw those paper towels and how pale Albert's face was. I thought he'd cut his hand somehow. Or was having a gastric bleed. When he said *baby*, I didn't think I heard it right; then he started to faint and that man was there catching the baby." Kate stopped, stared at Lauren. "Hold on. Are you interviewing me? Did the social worker ask you to do that?"

"No." Lauren swiped at a wavy strand of her rebel hair. "Not specifically. I did talk to the night nurses, registration clerks, and poor Albert. I'm a peer counselor; that's what we do." She smiled at Kate, sincerity in her expression. "I'm here now because you're my friend, Kate. I care how you feel."

Kate regretted that she'd sounded so accusing. "Thank you. I know that. I guess right now I feel like I just want things back to normal. Such as that is."

Lauren glanced toward the parking lot. "Well then, here comes part of your normal now. Right on cue. Isn't that your ever-loyal volunteer reporting for duty?"

"Judith. She's here more than I am." Kate watched as the middle-aged woman in a pink Ladies Auxiliary uniform walked between two of the police cars—not easy with the huge tote bag she carried. It was undoubtedly stuffed to the brim with wooden puzzles, magazines, and a bottle of iridescent bubbles to make the children smile. The woman was amazing; she'd even headed an autumn fund-raising event specifically for the emergency department. And best of all—unlike paid employees—Judith Doyle went cheerfully about her work without complaining. If only Kate could clone her.

Kate started to wave, then lowered her hand and frowned. "Look who else has arrived."

"First of the news vans. Better freshen your lipstick."

"Better move my car," Kate grumbled around the last bite of her cookie. "I'm not going to get ambushed in the parking lot. Again."

Wedging her Hyundai into the last remaining visitors' parking space was about as easy as the first few hours of her day. Two huge vehicles flanked her, barely contained within the painted lines. Her playful jabs about "big trucks, bigger belt buckles" held more than a measure of truth. Vehicles this size should span two spaces . . . in the overflow lot. She peered through her window at the late-model Ford pickup beside her—a dually. Because, of course, four massive tires weren't enough. A business slogan on its side, above eye level from her vantage point, read:

**Got Water?**
Tanner Wells—Drilling, Repair, Rain Catchment

Kate slid from her car, thinking that at least the reporters would never spot her between these high-testosterone vehicles. She turned sideways and began shuffling toward the walkway, trying not to brush the truck's dusty door.

"Sorry! I shouldn't have—"

Kate jumped at the deep voice in the distance, yelping as the back of her head connected with the truck's side mirror. Then before she could blink, the man hurried forward and took hold of her arm. He led her to the walkway, offering an apology for his oversize truck and another for startling her.

"Are you okay?" His dark brows scrunched as he peered down at her. "I have an instant ice pack in the—"

"I'm fine," Kate interrupted, vaguely aware that his fingers still encircled her arm. She studied him for a moment: nearly black hair, beard stubble, wide jaw, dark-lashed blue eyes. No Levi's jacket, but . . . "You're the one who held the waiting room door open. And carried the baby to the code room."

"Right." He let go of her arm. "I followed an ambulance in. A woman we found in the woods this morning. My team," he added quickly. "Search and rescue."

"Oh yes. The Alzheimer's patient." Kate gingerly touched her fingers to her scalp, noticing the Got Water? logo stitched on his polo shirt—over a broad, muscular expanse of chest. Only the awful chaos of those moments in the lobby could have kept her from noticing how good-looking this man was.

"You sure you're all right?"

"Yes," Kate insisted. "I have to get back to the department. But thank you for helping this morning, Mr. . . ."

"Tanner." He offered his hand. "Wes Tanner."

She accepted his handshake, telling herself a small rush of dizziness had more to do with the impact of a Ford dually than a denim cowboy. "I'm—"

"You're Kate Callison. Director of the emergency department," Wes finished the introduction for her. "Cynthia McConnell told me."

Kate grimaced. "The social worker interviewed you? Did she make you go through one of those awful debriefing sessions?"

Wes hesitated as if choosing his words. "That would be called a *defusing*, which is done the same day as the event. To assure a person that feelings of stress are normal. The social worker told me your name because I'm helping with the CISM review at your staff meeting this week."

"I see." Kate's lips tensed. "I expect Cynthia also told you that I'm not exactly excited about the idea."

"No. She only said that there have been some problems, and now might be a good time to touch base—remind your team of some coping skills. Today, with the baby, couldn't have helped the situation."

"Look . . . it's been a horrible day. In a miserable couple of weeks . . . that really started months ago. Before I was even hired. But I'm doing everything I can to pull this department together, to keep staff working, patients safe and cared for. And to keep bad PR at bay. I'm going to continue doing that." Kate crossed her arms and lifted her chin. "I told our CNO that I'd go along with Cynthia's plan. But in my experience, dwelling on tragedy— overanalyzing these things—doesn't help anything. I appreciate your help today, Mr. Tanner. And I think it's great that you found that woman in the woods . . ."

"But?"

"I should make this clear: no one here needs to be rescued."

Kate aimed her key-chain remote at her car, and when the horn sounded an answering beep, she gave Wes a curt nod and left.

- + -

Wes watched her walk toward the ER door, her stride surprisingly long for her height. Eager to get away.

Not any more eager than he was.

He glanced at her clown-size car. A hybrid, of course— probably ran on recycled alfalfa sprouts. Then he thought of what the social worker had said earlier. That the Austin Grace emergency department had problems that had shaken their sense of teamwork.

It was obvious now that the problem was Kate Callison. The small nurse with sad eyes. And a giant chip on her shoulder.

# 3

**AVA SMITH.** *Reason for visit: Food poisoning.*

"You think she could be the one?" Kate shifted her gaze from the computer screen to the nurse sitting on the other side of her desk. "Baby Doe's mother?"

"I guess it's possible." The night shift triage nurse, Dana Connor, pressed a hand to her midsection as if she had a sudden case of salmonella herself. "I told the police . . ." Her eyes, shadowed with obvious fatigue, focused somewhere beyond Kate. "I went over this with two detectives and then I had to talk with that nurse the social worker sent. Do we have to do this right now? My husband's caregiver won't stay past—"

"Yes," Kate insisted, "we do." She tapped her finger against the triage note on the screen in front of her. "This Ava Smith arrived shortly after 3 a.m.?"

"If that's what it says."

"It does," Kate confirmed, wishing it didn't. She was already dreading the media slant: *Mother of dead baby waited hours in hospital emergency department.*

"She didn't answer when they tried to room her for an exam," Dana explained.

"After nearly three hours. The ER staff called her at 5:47." Kate couldn't keep the edge from her voice. She'd had to wait in line to interview this nurse, and getting her cooperation now felt like pulling teeth. "What this doesn't say is what happened with this young woman after you triaged her. Hospital policy requires follow-up notes on patients having extended waits. There are none here."

Dana's teeth scraped across her lower lip. "I remember looking for her a couple of times. I thought she was probably in the bathroom. She said she had cramps. From diarrhea, I figured."

"You didn't ask the date of her last menstrual period?"

"I'm sure I did, but . . ."

"If it's not documented, it didn't happen, Dana."

The nurse changed position in her chair. "It was a busy shift. The staff in the back was dealing with a ruptured aneurysm; then that COPD patient deteriorated and had to be tubed. Plus there were still those patients from the p.m. shift waiting for beds in the ICU." Her teeth tortured her lip again. "The waiting room was packed but people kept coming in. I tried hard to keep up, get them to beds in the ER. The staff couldn't take them; the patients were complaining—it's like being caught in gunfire." Her eyes shone with sudden tears. "I didn't get a chance to sleep before my shift. My husband needs round-the-clock care since his motorcycle accident last year. We have a little boy. I need to work if we're going to keep the house." She reached for the Kleenex box Kate nudged forward. "Do the police think Ava Smith is the mother of that baby?"

"I believe they're pursuing that possibility." Kate hated this conversation and her role in it. She'd been under the gun in triage countless times in her career and knew it could be incredibly rugged. And thankless. Still . . . "Apparently the information she gave during registration was false. The detectives are looking at the security tapes. Were you able to give them a physical description?"

Dana twisted the tissue. "Young. Nineteen, she said, but she seemed younger. Dark hair. Straight and not very clean, about shoulder length. Thin. Wearing a long sweater that looked two sizes too big on her—dark colored, maybe navy blue."

*Black nail polish, a silver ring. Pale and perspiring, eyes filled with fear.* The realization hit Kate in a dizzying wave. The girl in the shadows. She'd talked with her.

Stunned, Kate tried to focus on what the triage nurse was saying. Her tears had welled again.

"I mean," Dana continued, voice dropping to a ragged whisper, "do you think if I'd done things better, the baby would be alive?"

- + -

"No thanks." Wes smiled at the emergency department volunteer holding a small stack of magazines. "I appreciate the offer, though . . . Judith," he added, noting the name tag on her pink smock. "I won't be here much longer. I'm waiting to drive someone home."

"The sister-in-law of an elderly patient who came in by ambulance. You're part of the search-and-rescue team." The woman nodded and her earrings, embossed silver angels, swayed as if taking flight. Her smile brought tiny lines to the outer corners of her smoky-blue eyes, the only clue that indicated her age. Midfifties, Wes guessed—close to his stepmother's age. Well-cut blonde hair, tasteful makeup, manicured nails, and a kind expression. A star in the crown of the Austin Grace Hospital Ladies Auxiliary, he'd be willing to bet.

"Your friend should be out any moment," the woman said. "The patient's being admitted upstairs."

"You're certainly on top of things."

Judith smiled, sliding a small spiral notebook from her pocket. "My cheat sheet. No names, of course, to respect privacy. But I make notes." Her discerning gaze took in the dozen or so people seated in the chairs, from the man in a wheelchair to twin girls— one with a gauze square taped to her chin—to the elderly couple signing in at the registration window.

Wes imagined Judith with a rescue pack and a GPS. She was sharp.

She turned back to Wes. "Waiting isn't an easy thing when you're sick, hurting, or worried. And the staff has their hands full. I try to help where I can. Run some interference for the patients, be a bit of an advocate." Judith chuckled. "Without appearing to be too pushy, if you know what I mean."

"I do," Wes acknowledged, the image of Kate Callison rising without warning. No doubt she thought his advocacy for her staff was pushy. Not that Kate wasn't completely capable of pushing back. Or even arm wrestling. He'd seen the determined look on her face in the parking lot. And again a few minutes ago when she'd walked by with the triage nurse in tow. Wes didn't envy that obviously exhausted woman. He made a mental note to thank Gabe and Jenna again; mutual respect was strong glue when teamwork mattered. He didn't take their dedication for granted.

"I should go check on that young lady." Judith glanced toward the far side of the waiting room, where an African American woman sat with a toddler on her lap. "Her husband's deployed, so she's handling things alone. She's worried about her son, and they've been waiting awhile."

"I'm sure she appreciates your help, Judith. The hospital's lucky to have you—especially today." Wes shook his head. "Their morning got off to a rough start."

She leaned in, lowered her voice. "I couldn't help but overhear that you're the man who rushed to help with the newborn."

"I only did what little I could, ma'am. Right place at a tough moment."

"Well, thank you," she said, extending her hand. "If more folks took the responsibility to help where they could, this would be a healthier community—and a kinder world."

"Amen," Wes agreed, taking her hand.

- + -

"Did the police talk with you yet?" Lauren sank into the desk chair across from Kate.

"No." Kate minimized the computer program. *But I am going to tell them I saw that girl. Aren't I?* "So far they've only asked me to point them in the direction of the night staff. You?"

"They wanted to know what I saw in the waiting room. Which, beyond the horror on Albert's face, wasn't much. Except the backside of your hustling scrubs and that blur when Wes Tanner sprinted by."

"You know him?"

"Wes helped teach my CISM classes. And he was here after Sunni went missing—for the staff debriefing." Lauren caught Kate's frown. "What?"

"I got an earful in the parking lot," she explained, resisting the urge to once again check the back of her head for a lump. "He's teaming with social services to give that refresher at our staff meeting."

"Um . . . things have changed some. Cynthia said she called you."

"I haven't listened to my messages. What's going on?"

Lauren spread her hands on the desk. "Friday's going to be a debriefing instead. Small, voluntary of course. For those directly involved in the Baby Doe incident. It will be offered to the clerks, the janitor, and the nursing staff. Anyone who feels affected by this tragedy."

"Why the change?" Kate asked, certain Wes Tanner was responsible.

"Because your team's feeling more than a little shell-shocked, Kate. They need to know they have our support." Concern flickered across Lauren's face. "Albert is sure that if he hadn't changed his routine—if he'd cleaned the bathroom an hour earlier—the baby would still be alive."

"I heard the doctor say there's a chance the baby never took a breath," Kate said solemnly. "He was so premature. But we won't know the official cause of death until the medical examiner's finished."

"Meanwhile, Albert's blaming himself. And the clerk who opened the door when you and Wes were rushing the baby to the code room has a daughter with a high-risk pregnancy. She cried when she told me about it. Everyone's been affected in some way."

Kate thought of Dana's whispered question. *If I'd done things better . . . ?*

"Because Wes was directly involved in the incident," Lauren continued, "he'll take part the same as the others. Like you and—"

"Wait." Kate held up her hand. "You said *voluntary*. I agreed to the dispensing of stress information at a staff meeting. I never said I'd volunteer for a debriefing. Besides," she added, determined to make Lauren understand, "I don't think the staff would be comfortable talking about their personal situations and feelings in front of their department director."

"Rank is set aside at a debriefing. It's not a fact-finding mission or a critique of an event," Lauren explained. "It's human beings coming together to get through a tough situation. Cynthia and the chaplain will facilitate. Wes and I will offer what we can in a supporting role. And I think," she added gently, "taking part could go a long way toward getting your team behind you. It could show them that you care." She smiled. "Even more than making cupcakes."

Kate squeezed her eyes shut. "Please swear to me you're not going to follow that jab by saying, 'Now is the time to ask yourself: What would Sunni do?'"

"I guess I don't have to. But really, I mean this: I'm on your side, Kate. And I'll admit a huge part of that is selfish. Because I like you and I want you to stay."

*Stay* . . .

Lauren stood. "And now I get to spend my evening doing another assignment for our CNO. Someone needs to take the 'Let's get Lauren to do it' sign off my back."

Kate smiled weakly, realizing she was tired. Bone-level exhausted. Half an hour and she was out of here, regardless. "And what's that assignment?"

"She wants me to pull together some information on the Baby Moses law."

"Sounds suspiciously religious."

"That's the original Texas name," Lauren told her. "We were the first state to adopt the law. You probably know it as Safe Haven."

Kate's stomach lurched.

"The legislation that allows a mother to surrender her newborn baby without legal penalty—at designated facilities like hospitals and fire departments," Lauren clarified.

*Oh, please, no.* Why was this following Kate? How far away was far enough?

Lauren continued, "Austin Grace is on that list. Though we haven't had an infant surrender in years. What happened with Baby Doe brings up some serious questions." She turned as a man in uniform arrived at the office door.

"Kate Callison?"

"That's me," Kate managed despite the fact that her heartbeat was pummeling her ears.

"Police department, ma'am. We need to ask you some questions."

It was dusk when Kate finally unlocked her car, no longer wedged between two massive trucks. She wondered for a moment how Wes Tanner's elderly passenger had managed to climb into the cloud-scraping seat of the Got Water?–mobile. Maybe he had a red cape stowed with his search-and-rescue gear and had scooped her up like Superman. The man apparently did everything well—a masculine counterpart to Sunni Sprague.

Guilt jabbed at the unkind thought. There was no excuse to be that way except that today had been awful. Finding temporary respite was the only thing on Kate's mind. Especially since administration and her only friend planned to steamroll her with a touchy-feely debriefing session. It was the last thing in the world she wanted. No, the last thing Kate wanted would be—

"We're outta here, pal." Lauren grinned from the lime-green convertible VW Beetle braking to a stop behind Kate's car. "Gonna hit the gym, then give the family a call and see where I fit on Mom's long task list for our Houston turkey day. And maybe try to get a handle on how things are going with my sister. If she's in a talkin' mood, that is." Concern clouded Lauren's expression for a second. Then she tilted her head, the smile returning. "I never asked—are you traveling home for Thanksgiving?"

*Home.* Kate made herself shrug casually. "We'll see. I'll be calling Dad tonight, so . . ."

It was the truth. She did call on Wednesdays, sometimes Mondays or Fridays. Between 7 and 8 p.m. The hour her father attended the Presbyterian church AA meetings—or at least when he'd let voice mail pick up so she'd think he was at the meetings. It was a painful dance they'd perfected as flawlessly as the stars waltzing in the finals on that sequin-studded TV show. She'd call and leave a quick, always-chipper message saying that work was great and she was fine. He'd forward e-mails that featured heartwarming images of animal antics—horses and puppies, his favorites. They posted happy birthday cards on each other's Facebook pages. Texted once in a while. But they hadn't actually spoken, really talked, in nearly a year. And the very last thing Kate wanted in the world was for that to change.

"Have fun at the gym," she said as Lauren put the VW into gear. "I'm making a request for a better day tomorrow."

"You and me both."

Kate climbed into her car and headed for the highway, glad for the distracting chaos of Austin's commuter traffic, everyone eager to put the workday behind them and enjoy the live-music capital of the world. University students, politicians, arts enthusiasts, aspiring musicians with guitars strapped on like turtle shells, foodies—Kate's stomach rumbled. Dinner.

Chuy's Tex-Mex, definitely. It was in Barton Springs, not far from the small guesthouse she rented. She'd get a to-go order: green chile chicken taquitos with creamy jalapeño sauce, pico de gallo, and a side of refried beans. She braked, waited for two bearded cyclists—one in tie-dye, the other in a faded purple *Keep Austin Weird* T-shirt—to weave through traffic. Then she rounded the next corner, and—

*Oh* . . . Kate's heart cramped. The mother. Standing on the busy corner with a long scarf draped over her hair. And that sign with the beautiful baby's face. *Need money for my baby's funeral.* The light from a single candle flickered on the face and downcast eyes of what could have been a likeness of the grieving Madonna.

Kate's foot found the brake and she reached for her purse. But at the sudden blare of car horns behind her, she drove on, all thoughts of dinner extinguished. All she wanted was to get home and close the door, blot everything out: that poor woman on the street corner, the girl in shadows this morning, the tearful triage nurse . . . and a baby born on the bathroom floor.

By some miracle, Roady had been home. Raspy meow, scabbed ears, swaggering pet-me-while-you-can attitude. Filled to bursting now with canned albacore, he lay sprawled on the couch beside Kate.

She'd rescued the cat in San Antonio after he fell asleep under the hood of an ambulance. And lost most of his tail in the fan belt. Not that the trauma, or a subsequent neutering appointment, had curbed the orange tabby's wanderlust. She smiled, thinking of what she'd said to Lauren about wanting to "cut and run"—Roady had that skill in spades.

Kate stroked his striped belly, felt his rumbling purr. She was grateful for his company. And thankful, too, that she'd found a measure of peace after all. She'd shed the day like she had her scrubs. Showered, pulled a Pilates tunic over leggings, and reheated some leftover Annie's mac and cheese. Then opened a celebratory can of tuna for her prodigal cat.

Kate glanced toward Roady's food bowls in the tiny blue-tiled kitchen. "Do you have water?"

*Got water?* She was caught off guard by the sudden image of Wes Tanner. Those blue eyes and dark lashes, that broad chest . . . the warmth of his skin when he shook her hand. And the memory of his concern and quick action when she'd bumped her head. She squeezed her eyes shut for a moment, reminding herself that he was part of the plan to further derail her staff with psychobabble. Even more importantly, that her instincts regarding men had brought her nothing but trouble all her life. Her last real date, months ago in San Antonio, had been a no-show. Which turned out to be merciful, considering the man was now doing prison time. It proved her point: Kate made bad choices. But tonight, right now, was comfortable. Her cat, her home—such as it was.

She glanced around the one-bedroom guesthouse, set on a vine-tangled hillside lot near Zilker Park. Close enough to a creek to hear it through the screen at night, once the cicadas stopped their deafening jungle hum, and lit by magical fireflies in summer. The house had come complete with bleached muslin curtains tied back with brown raffia and dried flowers. Leftovers from the last tenant, a college student who'd also hung a hammered-tin cross near the front door. Kate left the cross there for a few days, then carefully wrapped it in newspaper and tucked it in the closet. She spoke to God even less than she spoke to her father. And had no doubt that God preferred it that way.

Kate took a slow breath, telling herself that this place was as much a home as she needed. A place to run to, a door to close when painful reality crowded in. It had worked today, hadn't it?

She drew her legs under her cotton tunic and pushed the button on the TV remote. She froze as the news camera zoomed in on the emergency entrance to Austin Grace Hospital.

"The premature baby boy," a reporter continued, "was found on the cold tile floor of an emergency department bathroom early this morning. The time and circumstances of his birth are unknown. It is speculated that the mother may have intended to surrender her infant under Texas Safe Haven law. This can be done without legal penalty against the mother."

Kate hugged her knees, feeling them tremble.

"However, since the law requires that the infant be placed directly into the hands of a Safe Haven provider, the mother, if located, may face criminal charges in this tragic case. The police have few leads but are—"

Kate jabbed the remote before it slipped from her shaking fingers. She squeezed her eyes tight. It didn't help; she still saw the face of the girl in the shadowy entrance to the ER. The fear in her eyes. The desperation. Kate knew without a doubt that this girl had spent months in lonely denial. Then labored in hiding before wrapping her sticky-warm baby in brown paper towels . . . to abandon him. Kate knew the pain of that final act was like ripping out your own beating heart. She knew it. But she hadn't told the police. Because . . .

*No.* Kate wrapped her arms around her stomach, struggling against the sob that had threatened to rise for a decade. Along with a collage of memories too painful to bear: overwhelming grief at her mother's death, angry confusion in running away, rape by someone she'd trusted . . . crippling panic and then desperate denial after the positive pregnancy test barely three months after her seventeenth birthday. Running, hiding—wishing she could die. Failing at it once. And then the night she wrapped her son in a ratty sweatshirt and left him crying in the darkened doorway of a Las Vegas fire station. She'd walked away with an empty womb and a hole in her soul.

Kate hadn't been able to tell the police about that girl today any more than she could tell anyone about the guilt she'd carried all these years. But maybe . . . maybe now it was finally time to . . .

*Daddy.* Somehow the phone was in her hands, the speed-dial number pressed. She glanced at the time on its display, her tears blurring the numbers. Almost 8:30 in California.

If she finally did it, told him . . .

"Matthew Callison. I'm not home. Please leave a message."

"Daddy . . ." The merciless sob threatened to strangle her. *I threw your grandson away.* "I . . . Everything's okay. I'm fine. Work . . . is great."

Kate disconnected, willed herself to stop trembling. This wasn't going to happen. Not now, not ever. She'd meant what she said to Wes Tanner that morning. It didn't help to dwell on tragedy. Especially her own.

**4**

+

"SO THIS NEW ER DIRECTOR . . ." Miranda Tanner peered at Wes over a mug of morning coffee, the rising steam making her face look a little hazy. With the faded bandanna, deep-auburn hair, and silver hoop earrings, she could have been a gypsy who'd wandered onto the porch of this limestone ranch house. A world-weary vagabond stopping long enough to tell a colorful fortune and collect a fast fee. Except that she was wearing a Got Water? polo shirt, and everyone knew Wes's stepmother was as enduring as the decades-old pecan trees shading this home. Fiercely loyal, firmly rooted in her devotion to her children and husband, this community—and her faith. Her Bible lay on the table beside her, next to her laptop and a tidy stack of well-drilling invoices.

She chuckled as a fat-cheeked squirrel chattered from a tree branch above, then fixed her gaze on Wes again. "Kate Callison. What's she like?"

"She's . . ." Wes frowned, at a loss for how to explain his encounter with Kate, even to the woman who'd become Mom. And unsure why he was suddenly battling the memory of how Kate's hand had felt in his. Small, soft, warm . . . "She's about as friendly as brushing up against a cactus."

"Prickly?"

"You could say that. After she found out that I'm part of the critical stress team, she pretty much dismissed me." Wes shook his head, remembering Kate's crossed arms and the stubborn lift of her chin. "I quote: 'No one here needs to be rescued.'"

"Ouch." Her expression was both wise and gentle. It was the same way she'd looked at him when he was a motherless ten-year-old, still furious at the world. "It can't be easy stepping into Sunni's shoes. Or coping with this sort of thing." She tapped the screen of her laptop. "In the online edition of the newspaper."

"Something about the baby?"

"Yes, there's a short article. With an anonymous comment by 'Waiting for Compassion,' the person who's been writing those letters to the editor."

Wes nodded. The letters had appeared sporadically in the *Austin American-Statesman* over the last year. Written by someone who claimed to be reporting from the waiting rooms at several city hospitals and was obviously on a personal mission to depict local medical systems as disorganized, dispassionate, and sometimes dangerous. Recently Jenna had seen copycat posts on the social networks, one with an obviously fabricated photo of a waiting patient with an ax blade buried in his skull. No medical, rescue, or law enforcement personnel should be the target of that kind of harassment. Prickly attitude or not.

His mom traced her finger down the screen, reading aloud. "'One has to wonder if this precious life could have been saved if the (reportedly) skilled staff of a hospital system that claims, "providing safe, quality health care is our number one priority" actually practiced what they preached. Then, perhaps, a woman in labor wouldn't be waiting for compassion . . . on the floor of a hospital lavatory.'"

Wes grimaced, recalling the terror on the janitor's face and the too-still, too-cold feel of the baby's body through the paper towels. And the grief in Kate's eyes.

"I'm glad you'll be taking part in the hospital debriefing," Miranda continued, her expression showing concern for Wes as much as the others. "It had to be awful finding a child who's been abandoned like that."

*You're Lee Ann Tanner's boy.* Wes quickly dismissed the idea of telling her what Amelia Braxton had said yesterday morning. There was no point in bringing that up. Just like there was no way to understand why a mother would pull her sleeping son from bed at 3 a.m. and load him into the car only to abandon him in the woods. The incident with Baby Doe only added to the bad memories Mrs. Braxton's confused comments had stirred. He had to let all of that go.

Wes glanced toward his parents' shop and barn, buildings that had stood there for three generations. He drew in a breath rich with familiar scents: oak, earth, and hay mixed with a faint trace of motor oil and morning coffee. Though he rented a town house with closer access to the freeways, he would always feel that this ranch was home. As deeply as his initials carved in the weathered barn siding.

Wes downed the last of his coffee, then nodded at his mom. "I'm going to check the equipment for the Masons' pump install and make sure our men have everything they need; Dad has it on the schedule for this afternoon. Then maybe I'll take Duster out for a while. Let him eat grass down by the creek." He smiled, remembering the big sorrel's groan as he'd lumbered from his stall to the waiting horse trailer before dawn yesterday. "He's gonna go sour if all he gets to do is the occasional early morning search-and-rescue call."

"Oh, I forgot." His mom handed him a sticky note. "Lily Braxton called last night. She wanted to thank you again for finding Amelia. And she wondered—" it looked like she was trying not to smile—"if you might have a few minutes to help her with another search."

"Someone's missing?"

"I'm afraid so." His mom shook her head, yielding to the smile. "Nancy Rae. The doll Amelia carries with her everywhere—that poor plastic creature with the matted hair and the polka-dot apron. You've seen her."

"Nancy—" Wes groaned, set the note down. "You're kidding."

"I'm afraid not. Miss Lily's frantic."

Wes sighed. "Does she think the doll's in the gully?"

"She's looked everywhere else. Of course she can't climb down that hill. She tried to phone her renter—that hermit who has the trailer down in the grove—but he didn't answer. Amelia will be home from the hospital today, and she's been asking and asking."

"Okay." Wes raised his palm. "If you promise that word doesn't leak out about this."

"About helping your neighbors? Now that's compassion worthy

of a letter to the editor." She laughed at his expression. "I won't. I prom—" She stopped short as Wes's cell phone rang.

"Hey," Wes said after seeing Gabe's ID. He walked down the stone steps of the porch. "What's up?"

"Maybe some news on Sunni Sprague's case."

Wes's breath caught. He'd spent so many hours over the past months reviewing the reports and phone tips. "What did you hear?"

"Unofficial. I was talking with one of the deputies. An inmate may be trying to make a deal, trade some information about the location of . . . evidence."

The tone in Gabe's voice sounded too much like he was talking about human remains. But even then, it would be better than never finding anything. "When do they expect to know something more concrete?"

"Not sure. But I'm thinking it's possible that teams will be called out to do a grid search." A muffled whine told Wes that Hershey was sitting beside Gabe. "Hey, do you have time to grab some coffee?"

"Sure." Wes smiled at his mom, raising a thumbs-up signal. "After you help me with a search."

- + -

"It's okay; you can pick Harley up. It won't hurt anything." Kate smiled to reassure the observably anxious young mother. And because the infant girl, two months old and wearing a pink headband, shared the name of a motorcycle.

"I . . ." The mother's eyes, magnified by dark-framed glasses, traveled from the sensor taped to her daughter's heel up the cord to the pulse oximeter unit's blinking digital display. "Are you sure?"

"I'm sure." Kate pointed to the current oxygen saturation reading. "Your baby's oxygen level is 99 percent on room air. That's perfect. It's been normal ever since you brought her in. Even though," she added, careful not to dismiss the mother's concerns, "you noticed that difference in her breathing at home."

"She looked sort of blue when I leaned over her crib."

Kate stroked the baby's cheek, pinker than her headband. She was glad she'd offered to roll up her sleeves and help with patient care this morning. Not only because they were short staffed— Dana, the triage nurse Kate questioned yesterday, had called in sick—but because this new mother needed some TLC. And maybe because today . . . *I need to touch a living, breathing baby.*

"Harley's getting a thorough exam," Kate continued. "Labs, X-ray, monitoring. The ER physician will discuss everything with your pediatrician. Right now, though—" she glanced down as Harley began to fuss in her infant seat—"I think Mommy's the best medicine. Go ahead; pick her up. If the monitor comes loose, I'll fix it. No problem."

"That's okay." The mother jiggled the seat. "I can wait. She likes her pacifier." She pushed her glasses up her nose, then reached for the diaper bag. "I brought two, and—" She stopped, stared into Kate's eyes. "You don't think they'll keep her tonight? Maybe that would be better." Her fingers moved to the strings at the neck of her hoodie. "Safer, you know?"

Kate saw the anxiety on her face. "I don't know yet what the doctor will recommend, but he'll discuss everything with you. And answer all your questions. Harley won't be released unless your pediatrician agrees that it's completely safe."

"I'm back," the staff nurse announced, arriving at the exam room door. Behind her, sounds of voices, beeping equipment, and a short volley of indignant grumbles indicated the emergency department patient census was rising. "Thanks for giving me a break," she added, connecting briefly with Kate's gaze. Then she smiled warmly at Harley. "Looks like you're still behaving yourself, angel girl."

Kate left the exam room after one more glance at the worried mother. And at her staff nurse, too. The nurse had been there yesterday when Baby Doe was rushed to the code room.

*"Your team is shell-shocked."* Wasn't that what Lauren had said after doing some peer counseling? Kate frowned, scanning the rooms as she made her way through the department. Physicians, nurses, technicians, clerks. All busy, a little understaffed and maybe grumpy about it—Kate understood that. Sure, there had been TV news about Baby Doe, and a few reporters had bothered some folks in the employee parking lot. There was another of those miserable Waiting for Compassion diatribes in the online edition of the paper. But no one looked shell-shocked.

She slowed to check the staff assignment board, then headed down the corridor toward her office, confident she was right. The triage nurse could have needed the day off for any number of reasons. She'd be back, ready to work. Harley's mother would recover from her new-mom jitters, reassured that her daughter was safe enough to go home. Things would return to status quo here in the ER, the same way Kate had pulled herself together last night. *"I'm fine. Work is great."*

She thought of what she'd said to Wes Tanner in the parking lot and told herself it was still true. *"No one here needs to be rescued."*

"Oh, thank you." Kate smiled with surprise as Judith Doyle set a Starbucks cup on her desk and pulled paper napkins from the pocket of her volunteer smock. "Did I look like I needed a caffeine jolt? And may I please reimburse you for this?"

"No and no." Judith lifted her own paper cup. "I'm using

you as an excuse to feed my own shameless habit. Pumpkin spice latte—don't ask how many I've had since September." Her expression grew almost wistful. "There's something about the scent, like family gathered around a holiday table. Home. You know?"

"Mmm." Kate nodded, thinking of Lauren's question about Thanksgiving. She reminded herself to send a harvest-themed e-card to her father. "Dare I ask the status of our waiting room?" She tapped the census screen on her desk computer. "It looks like we had a rush about an hour ago."

"Fourteen. A woman with emphysema was taken straight back to a room; she's a regular, and the triage nurse recognized her right away. No problem. And . . ." Judith set down her cup to tick one manicured finger against the others. "A man with gout, a kindergartner who cut his chin at recess, a young woman with a headache—she's had them before; no stiffness in her neck—a high school football player with his ankle wrapped in ice . . ."

Kate glanced at the computer to confirm the list Judith was reciting from memory. She never ceased to be amazed at the dedication of this volunteer; Judith had even been here on Sundays and holidays.

*"Family gathered around a holiday table."* Kate had never thought to ask Judith if she had any family in the Austin area. Though her beautiful wedding ring set would indicate as much.

"And the longest wait time is only around forty-five minutes," Judith finished. "No complaints yet. Though I forgot my puzzle stash today. So if we get a backlog of toddlers, I may be forced to tap-dance and juggle tongue depressors."

Kate laughed, then felt a wave of regret. She had no doubt that her own mother would have been much like Judith Doyle. Kind, funny, compassionate, young for her age. Full of life.

"I saw that Harley Forrester was discharged home." Judith's

eyes showed concern. "The baby brought in after trouble breathing at home?"

"Yes."

"I've gotten to know her mother, Trista, a bit over the past couple of weeks," she explained. "Harley's grandfather goes to outpatient rehab in the afternoons. Trista drives him. She doesn't feel comfortable sitting in that waiting room—and we have the big TV in ours."

"And you." Kate smiled. "We have you, Judith. That's why she waits here."

Judith's cheeks flushed. "I do try to keep a certain distance. We learned that in volunteer training. But until today, Trista's baby wasn't actually our patient. She's so young and inexperienced. So I—"

"Kate?" The registration clerk leaned through the doorway. "Mr. Lyon's here to see you."

"Which Mr. Lyon?" Kate asked, hoping it wasn't—

"Barrett."

Kate suppressed a groan.

"I'll go." Judith retrieved her latte.

"Thank you again. For everything." Kate had an irrational urge to ask the selfless volunteer to trade places with her. Stay here, meet with the hospital attorney, and let Kate handle the crowded waiting room. Right now, juggling tongue depressors sounded a lot more appealing than another rendezvous with legal. Especially with Barrett Lyon.

Much more of this and Kate might need rescue after all.

In less than twenty minutes, she was almost convinced of it.

"I'm not sure I understand what you're suggesting," Kate said, stomach churning. She leaned forward in her chair, staring across the desk at the youngest partner of the Lyon legal firm. "The police are trying to locate the mother of that baby. It's only been one day. No one's blaming the hospital."

"Except for our self-appointed community health care vigilante." Barrett Lyon's eyes, gray as his well-cut jacket, narrowed a fraction. "This person, Waiting for Care—"

"Compassion," Kate corrected, suspecting the attractive attorney had none whatsoever. "Waiting for Compassion. But the letters and online posts have only alluded to medical settings. No specific hospitals have been named."

"Correct. And any number of Austin-area facilities could have discovered a newborn infant on a bathroom floor yesterday." Despite the obvious barb, Barrett's eyes softened. He sighed, splaying his hands on the desk. "Kate, I know this is the last thing you need on your plate right now. Yes, it's possible that the police will locate the mother who abandoned that baby and prosecute her. That would be good."

*Good?* Kate tasted bile.

"But we have to be prepared if someone who may have standing in the case comes forward and accuses the hospital of wrongdoing. We need to look at the possibility of shared liability."

"Meaning the triage nurse." Kate thought of Dana Connor.

"If she initiated care of that mother and accepted professional responsibility." Barrett nodded. "It helps things that this nurse isn't regular staff; given that she's contracted with a nursing registry, she may be covered by outside insurance. We'll be looking into that. And at the chain of command within the emergency department."

Kate swallowed. "Including me."

Barrett was quiet for a moment. "Again, this is all necessary preparation. On the whole, designed to protect the hospital and the staff. I'm here for you, too, Kate." He slid back his sleeve to check his watch. "It's nearly lunchtime." The gray eyes met hers and Barrett smiled, perfect teeth against a flawless tan. "We could discuss this further, say at the Shore View Grill? Been there yet?"

"No," Kate answered, uncomfortable on a whole new level. "I can't leave. We're short staffed. I really should go check on things out there."

"Of course." Barrett stood. "I'll be in touch, and—oh, one last question?"

Kate waited.

"The man in the waiting room yesterday, the one who accepted the baby from the janitor . . ."

"Wes Tanner?"

"Yes, that's the name. He's an EMT, isn't he?"

"He was here as a visitor," Kate explained, beginning to have a bad feeling. "And a volunteer for search and rescue. But I think he did say he was also an EMT."

"Which, of course, implies training, certifications. Hmmm." Barrett reached for his briefcase. "Perhaps Mr. Tanner should have done more. I'll see what I can find out about him."

Kate opened her mouth, closed it. Pushed papers around on her desk until the hospital's attorney was safely out the door. Then propped her head in her hands. Lunch? The only thing on Kate's menu today was a handful of antacids.

- + -

Wes halted Duster along a deer trail that disappeared into dense cedar, waiting as Gabe came up alongside. His friend was riding the Tanners' three-year-old Appaloosa mare, Clementine. She nickered at Duster, then stood quietly. "How'd Clem do when you crossed the creek back there?"

"If I say, 'No problem,' are you going to trot out a llama, then set off a string of firecrackers? Fire up a chain saw, maybe?" Gabe pulled off his orange Longhorns ball cap and wiped a beefy arm across his forehead. "You call me out for a missing person that ends up being a plastic toy, then expect me to train your horse along the way? You're gonna owe me, Tanner." He smiled. "I see Salt Lick barbecue in my future."

Wes grinned. "When I get the green light on adding a mounted detail to our team, we'll be that much more ready. You'll appreciate riding, not walking."

"*If* we get that grant for equipment, train some more volunteers, and—"

"We'll do it." Wes checked his watch. "Hey, I don't know about continuing with this. We've been out here for nearly an hour and a half. Nothing. And it's not like the old girl walked off."

"Could be something dragged her off. Dog, coyote. That doll sits at more diners than I do. She probably smells like fried chicken." Gabe squinted downhill. "There's a renter down there?"

"In the trailer under the trees." Wes lifted his field glasses, scanning the grove less than a quarter mile away. "No truck, though. Gone somewhere. Not that he'd answer the door if he was home, I hear." He shook his head. "Look, I've got a pump to install and you've probably got . . ." Wes gave an exaggerated grimace, never missing a chance to bait his friend about his family's funeral home. But Gabe knew the respect Wes had for the compassion that guided that business. And Wes could easily imagine the satisfaction this good man felt in being part of a team dedicated to finding people alive. "Don't tell me what's on your schedule today."

"My lips are in rigor." Gabe glanced at the stand of trees in the distance. "How 'bout we give it twenty more minutes? You follow that sorry deer trail while I make a quick pass around the renter's trailer. One last shot at putting a smile on our piano teacher's face. If we come up empty, we'll make up a story about Miss Nancy Rae taking the Greyhound bus to SeaWorld. Then con your mom into searching the thrift shops for her identical twin." He shrugged. "It'll give me a chance to take your mare over that creek again."

"Sold. Meet you back here in twenty."

But in less than ten minutes, Wes's radio crackled to life with Gabe's victorious whoop. "Guess who I found in the grove?"

"You're kidding."

"Swear." Gabe laughed. "She's sorta grubby, but I'd still call it a live find." The radio was breaking up. "Got her tied . . . my saddle. And we're headed—" Gabe smothered a curse. "What the . . . What's . . . wire? Blast it, Clem's tangled up in . . ."

"Gabe?"

A single, gut-wrenching blast echoed up the shallow gully— the unmistakable discharge of a shotgun. Clementine's panicked snorts were followed in less than a heartbeat by Gabe's shout: "I'm shot!"

5

+

*"HEEYAAH!"* Wes urged Duster into the gully, the horse's hooves scrabbling on loose rocks and chest-high cedar branches flogging them both. No time to find a trail, no time to waste. *Shot? Hunters? Drug operation?* Wes carried a concealed Springfield pistol but had never had to use it. He'd given what little he knew to 911 dispatch before spurring Duster, but he sure wasn't going to wait.

The ground dropped from under them and Wes grabbed a hunk of Duster's mane as gravity pitched him forward.

"Gabe?" he huffed into the radio clipped to his vest. "I'm almost there. Answer me."

*Oh no.* Clementine trotted by a few yards below, riderless except for the doll tied behind the saddle. Then the terrain leveled out and the grove loomed not far ahead. He spurred Duster on.

"Gabe?" Wes's lips met the radio again.

"Here . . ." There was a groan. "My leg . . . Shotgun rigged in a tree . . . Trip wire. Not a shooter. Can't see one, anyway."

*Thank you, Lord. He's alive.* "I see you now, buddy. Hang on."

In seconds Wes had reined Duster to a skidding halt and vaulted to the ground. He looped the lead rope over a branch, grabbed his rescue kit, and ran toward where Gabe lay sprawled in the dirt. Pale as a fish belly, face contorted with pain. And on the ground beneath him . . . too much blood.

Wes dropped to his knees beside his friend, grateful for the faint sounds of sirens in the distance. He scanned the clearing around them, what he could see of the rusty trailer. Gabe was right; no sign of anyone else.

"I think I'll be . . . okay." Gabe tried to raise himself on one elbow.

"Don't—don't try to sit up. Stay down. Let me get some pressure on that." Wes's gaze moved over Gabe quickly. Head, neck, chest, belly, all without obvious injury. But all that blood . . .

"It caught me in the hip and leg." Gabe's face glistened with sweat. His expression was anxious. "Clem bolted. Don't know if she got hit."

"She's walking. You're first." Wes pulled the rescue blanket and medical pouch from his pack. "I'm going to get some pressure on that wound while I update the police and medics. They need to know what they're walking into here. Meanwhile, I'll keep one eye on that trailer. We don't need any more trouble." Wes spread the foil blanket over his friend. "I'm sorry, buddy. You wouldn't be out here if I hadn't—"

"It's okay." Gabe smiled weakly. "Just promise you'll get that doll to her mama."

"Promise." Wes tore open several heavy wound pads, pulled on some gloves. "This is going to hurt."

In ten minutes the scene was secured, several armed deputies providing watchful cover while fire department paramedics attended Gabe, getting vital signs, starting oxygen and two large-bore IVs. Twenty minutes later, they hauled him uphill on a rescue litter to a waiting ambulance. Wes waited as they loaded him, his arms full of Gabe's gear—including a very dusty Nancy Rae.

"I'm not gonna ask," a deputy assured Wes, eyeing the doll with an amused look. "But don't worry about the horses. Gary's a posse member; he's getting them watered and he'll make sure they're okay until your dad can get here to trailer them back." He glanced downhill, where fellow law enforcement investigators swarmed, radios squawking. "We'll be on scene awhile. At least until we locate Mr. Let's-Jerry-Rig-a-Gun-to-an-Oak-Tree. Doesn't even look like he had anything to protect down there. No pot farm or weapons arsenal." The deputy shook his head. "There's all kinds of crazy in this world. Glad your friend wasn't hit worse."

"Right." Wes glanced at Gabe. His face was partially covered by an oxygen mask, eyes closed and color improved. Far more relaxed after a titrated dose of morphine. Wes shifted his grip on the doll, and a thought struck him with sickening clarity: it wasn't only Gabe who'd been at risk. Amelia had dropped her doll in that grove, an old woman lost, confused, and stumbling in the dark. She could have tripped that lethal booby trap.

"Which hospital?" the deputy asked as Wes climbed into the ambulance beside Gabe.

"Trauma center's packed," Wes told him, reporting what he'd heard from the fire department a few moments ago. "Gabe's vital signs are fairly stable, so dispatch will direct them to the closest hospital that can have a surgical team ready and waiting."

An EMT jogged toward the rear of the idling transport rig. "Got our destination. Austin Grace ER."

*Austin Grace.* Wes glanced down at his clothes and forearms, sticky with drying blood despite the gloves. Second time in two days he'd be at that hospital in this condition. He thought of Kate Callison. *"No one here needs to be rescued."*

He wished that were true.

- + -

Lauren sat down opposite Kate at a table outside the ER. She eyed Kate's paper plate. "What on earth is that?"

"Muff—*mmph*, excuse me." Kate swallowed a couple of times, dabbed at her lips. "Sorry. Whole wheat English muffin. Peanut butter, cream cheese, and orange marmalade—as much as I could scrape out of the last little foil package in the staff refrigerator. I needed . . ." *Peanut butter . . . and peace.* She smiled sheepishly. "Comfort food. Don't judge."

"Cross my heart. I've seen the bottom of a few Blue Bell ice cream cartons myself." Lauren tipped her head. "I figured things were bad when you asked the ICU if they could spare me for a few hours."

"You can't know how much I appreciate you helping out. And being the one friendly face in my hostile world." Kate frowned. "Legal came to see me."

"Can I assume that means Barrett Lyon?"

"He had the nerve to ask me to lunch minutes after describing his plan to defend the hospital from any possible litigation that might happen as a result of Baby Doe. Which could include pointing the finger at individual staff. Throwing any or all of us to—"

"The Lyons," Lauren finished. "Pun intended. That man sure

does seem intent on proving my mom's advice that good-lookin' isn't nearly good enough."

Kate glanced around the tables, lowering her voice. "He even implied that Wes Tanner could have some responsibility for what happened. Because he was there. And because he's an EMT. Lyon said he was going to see what he could find out about him."

"Unbelievable." Lauren's eyes narrowed. "That completely fries me. A decent man steps up to help and . . ." She reached over and dabbed her finger at some muffin crumbs. "Maybe we should share that comfort food. I was in the waiting room too, if you recall."

"He didn't mention you. And he thinks that if the mother's found, blame could fall on her. Even as far as prosecution." Kate's throat tightened unexpectedly as she recalled what she'd said to the young woman who was almost certainly "Ava Smith." *"That's why we're here. To help."* What kind of help was this?

"Lyon could be right about the mother." Lauren pulled several sheets of paper and a stack of brochures from her tote bag. "I've been doing that research on Texas's Baby Moses law—Safe Haven."

Kate's stomach quivered as Lauren nudged the brochure toward her. On its cover was a photo of an obviously distraught young woman. Below, in bold red letters, it read, *No one ever has to abandon a child again.*

"The statistics will break your heart," Lauren continued. "Out of a hundred babies abandoned each year, sixteen will be found dead. In parking lots, Dumpsters . . . bathrooms." She tapped a sheet of paper with yellow highlighting. "Texas adopted the law in 1999—after thirteen babies were abandoned in Houston in a single year. *Thirteen* in one city—my city. Now all fifty states have similar laws to protect unwanted babies. And their mothers. Of course, the ideal situation is to assist the mother earlier, arrange for adoption. There's contact information for all that in the brochure. But with the Safe Haven law, a woman can anonymously surrender her infant after birth, no questions asked." Lauren pointed to the brochure. "But it says right there that the baby has to be placed in the care of a designated Safe Haven site. Handed directly to a *person*. At a hospital, child welfare agency, EMS provider . . ."

*Fire department . . . Oh, please. Stop.*

"So," Lauren sighed, "leaving a baby unattended on a bathroom floor, even in a designated hospital—"

The wail of sirens squelched her words.

Kate glanced toward the approaching ambulance, grateful for the first time in her career for incoming trauma. "Is that the shooting victim?"

"Thirty-four-year-old male. Shotgun blast to the hip and thigh. Relatively stable vitals after IV fluids. We've got everything ready to go. Surgery's standing by." Lauren stood and began stuffing papers into her bag. "Go ahead and keep that brochure," she said as Kate tried to hand it over. "I'm going to run back to triage so my lunch relief can help in the trauma room."

"Good." Kate crumpled her paper plate, resettled her stethoscope around her neck. "Tell them I'll be right there too."

As Lauren jogged away, Kate tossed her garbage—and the Safe Haven brochure—into the trash can, then watched as the rig with lights still flashing backed into the ambulance bay. Followed by two sheriff cars. And a van with a TV news logo printed on the side. She grimaced. At least Barrett Lyon was gone, Lauren was here, and miraculously, Kate had a moment to sit down and eat something. A slice of peace slathered with peanut butter. Right this minute she'd even go so far as to hope that despite these lights and sirens, her day could actually be turning around.

Then the doors of the ambulance opened. And Wes Tanner climbed out.

- + -

"Tanner, hold on."

Wes turned and saw the medic gesturing from the ambulance. "Yeah?"

"You can follow us to the doors, but then you'll have to go to the waiting room." The young man attached Gabe's oxygen tubing to a portable tank. "Security's really strict. Nobody but staff goes in there, unless you've got some serious pull with someone. The doc or . . . ?"

*Department director?* Wes almost laughed. "No. No pull."

"I'll let the ER staff know you're waiting," the medic offered, guiding the stretcher from the rig. The wheels dropped and locked into place. In seconds they were hustling toward the hospital doors with Wes alongside.

Gabe's eyes were half-lidded above the oxygen mask. A portable monitor registered his vital signs in digital red. Blood pressure 106 over 48. After nearly a liter of normal saline. *How much damage did the gun blast do?* Heart rate 102. Respirations 20, oxygen saturation 100 percent. A telltale spot of blood, dark as a moonless search, seeped through the white sheet in the vicinity of his right hip.

IV tubing dangling, Gabe raised a hand toward Wes.

Wes clasped it. "Hang in there. I'll be in to see you as soon as they let me," he promised, hating the clammy feel of his friend's fingers. "And I'll keep an eye out for your family."

"Thanks." A faint but familiar smile appeared on Gabe's pale face. "Though the last thing a man in my condition should want is a visit from a mortician."

"Right," Wes managed, his voice trying to crack. "And don't start dictating some cheesy eulogy. You're going to be fine."

"I know . . .'s a long way from my heart." Gabe's eyes closed for long enough to make Wes's breathing stall. But then he opened them again. "You promised. Nancy Rae—don't forget."

"I won't."

They stopped the stretcher at the ambulance bay doors; a security guard hit the button from inside and they all disappeared down the corridor toward the ER. Out of sight.

Wes leaned against the cool stucco of the hospital wall and hunched over, his legs suddenly weak. He thought of his best friend wanting to search a little longer at the Braxton ranch. *"One last shot at putting a smile on our piano teacher's face."* So typical. No man had a bigger heart. And Gabe wouldn't have been there—wouldn't be here right now—if Wes hadn't asked for a favor. *Please, Lord. Don't let him die.*

"Mr. Tanner?"

"Yes." Wes looked up to see a woman in pink, the volunteer he'd met in the waiting room. The woman with the kind eyes. Judith.

She smiled. "You're here with Gabriel Buckner."

Wes nodded. "I was just going to the waiting room. The paramedics said they'd tell the staff I was here. And maybe I should—" he glanced down at his arms and shirtfront—"wash this off."

"This way." Judith pointed toward the doors Gabe had just entered. "I'll show you where you can wash up. After I get you a scrub top." She gave him an assessing glance. "Large, I'd say."

"Uh . . . yes." He followed her, not about to argue, thinking of what the medic had said about not getting past the ambulance doors unless he had "pull." Who'd have thought this volunteer was his ticket in?

"After you change," Judith continued, keying in the door code, "I'll check and see if the team will allow you to visit with your friend for a few minutes. Not more than a peek because they're getting him ready for surgery. But I know you want a chance to wish him well. It's important for a patient, too. Even with so many people bustling around, without a family member or a friend, a person can feel almost abandoned. That shouldn't ever happen." For a mere instant there was a look of sadness in her eyes. Then the doors opened and she led the way in. "Of course, I'll need to check the timing with our department director."

Wes's hope vanished. He might as well go back to the waiting room. "Kate Callison."

"Yes. She sent me out here to get you."

- + -

"Where do things stand?" Kate asked, catching the clinical coordinator outside the trauma room doors. She glanced inside and saw Wes Tanner crouching low to speak to his friend amid an organized tangle of IV lines. The concern on his face was obvious. "Ready for the OR?"

"Anesthesia's already been here," the nurse told her. "Lungs and belly looked clear on the portable films, but there's a lot of swelling in that thigh. Blood bank is sending the first unit straight to the OR. Catheter's in, antibiotics infusing. When surgery gives the green light, we'll roll."

"Good." Kate had almost said, "Good job," but she wondered how the nurse would take it. *Good job* as in *better than you usually do* or . . . Ugh, she hated second-guessing what she said to her staff.

Everything Kate did was measured against Sunni's perfect leadership. "I'll be out in triage if you need me," she added, certain she saw a look in the nurse's eyes that said, *"Dana called in sick because you harassed her."*

Kate's current prescription for peace and comfort was beyond a peanut butter muffin, even with the last packet of marmalade. Far beyond. What she needed was a kind word, a human connection devoid of political ramifications.

On second thought, scratch the human connection altogether. Maybe the wayward Roady cat would be home again tonight. Maybe—

"Let's go!" the technician directed from inside the trauma room. Gurney brakes released and wheels rolled. IV bags swayed. There was a communal *swish-swish* of hustling scrubs. And in seconds, the space was empty. Not a person in sight—nurse, physician, lab or X-ray tech, or visitor. All gone. Only the inevitable clutter remained, those empty husks of lifesaving effort: depleted bags of IV fluids, discarded medicine vials and tourniquets, a lead apron from radiology . . . and a drying puddle of blood on the floor.

- + -

Wes was grateful for the quiet of the hospital chapel. And that he'd heard from both Gabe's parents and his own. They were all on the way, even Wes's seventeen-year-old brother, Dylan, who'd called Gabe "my good pal" for most of his life. It was a rare and important connection for someone with Dylan's special needs and limited social skills.

Wes smiled. Wait until Dylan found out that his good pal's dog, Hershey, would be staying with the Tanners for a few days. *Only a few days. Gabe's going to be all right.*

He glanced from the simple cross above the chapel's altar to the clock on the wall. The surgical technician had said Gabe would be in the OR at least an hour. Now would be a good time to get that other thing done. He'd promised.

With reluctance, Wes rose from the chair and walked back toward the door, where he'd stowed the hospital-issue bag holding Gabe's belongings. And the item that wouldn't fit in it. He shook his head, bent down to grab the bag, and—

"Hi."

Wes stood, surprised to see Kate Callison outside the door.

- + -

"There's a decent surgical waiting room with coffee and crackers and a TV," Kate told Wes, feeling immediately foolish. He could have gone to the chapel to pray. *Not everyone wraps a cross in newspaper and hides it in the closet.* "It's there if you want it."

"Thanks." Wes glanced back into the chapel. "What I really could use is a sort of . . . big . . . garbage bag." His blue eyes, Kate noticed, were the exact shade of his scrub top. "For some of Gabe's belongings."

"A trash bag?" she asked, needing to break the gaze because of the ridiculous way her pulse was suddenly behaving. No more Starbucks Doubleshots. "Oh, you mean a patient belongings bag. I'll grab—"

"No, a trash bag. Garbage-can size. It's for . . ." He turned and reached down behind the door. "This."

Kate's eyes widened at the toddler-size doll with tangled hair, fading rouge, and a frilly dotted apron. But mostly at the ludicrous image of this ruggedly handsome man struggling to grapple with such a completely girlie thing. "That's—"

"Nancy Rae," he said, balancing the toy awkwardly in the crook of his arm. "But you can call her Nancy." He looked from the doll's well-worn face to Kate's, amusement erasing his earlier discomfort. "It's my turn to be surprised: you *do* smile, Kate Callison."

"It's just . . ." A laugh rose, more wonderful than any marmalade. Kate pressed her fingers to her mouth, unable to stop it. "You look so . . ."

"Idiotic, I know," he agreed. "But I've got to get this to someone upstairs."

"The Alzheimer's patient you rescued in the woods yesterday," Kate guessed. *The same day you carried that dying baby.* The merciful laughter disappeared as quickly as it had come.

"The doll's important to her. She's had it for years—'rescued' from a church garage sale. Gabe wanted to make sure she got it." His eyes met hers again. "Judith said you gave the okay for me to be in the trauma room. I want you to know I appreciate that. Thank you."

"No problem." Kate willed her heartbeat to slow. "I should thank you—and Nancy—for the laugh just now. I needed it. It's been . . ." She let the words trail off, wary of being too honest. "If you'll wait a minute, I'll get that trash bag."

"Thanks." Wes's smile returned, making the corners of his eyes crinkle. "Nancy Rae likes to travel incognito—paparazzi."

Kate chuckled, unexpected warmth spreading again. "Be right back."

By the time she managed to locate a janitor's cart and snag a trash bag, Kate had convinced herself that it would be a sincere gesture of Austin Grace hospitality to show Wes to the surgery waiting room. Or maybe the cafeteria. Join him there for a few minutes.

She hurried back. Then heard the voices, even before she reached the chapel. A discreet peek from the doorway confirmed that other people had arrived. A man nearly as tall as Wes, with silver-shot black hair and similar good looks. A woman wearing faded Levi's and an expression of motherly concern. And under Wes's protective arm, a gangly young man shifting his weight from foot to foot. He wore an oversize blue football jersey stenciled with the number 1 and white block letters that spelled out *Team Tanner*.

Wes's family. Kate would have known it without the personalized jersey. She could tell by the way they looked at each other and moved together in a palpable attitude of loving support. She felt it even from where she stood. On the outside looking in. Always.

Kate tucked the trash bag inside the chapel door and headed back to the ER. She took a deep breath, let it go. It had been crazy and pathetic to let fatigue, frustration, and a much-needed laugh—and that incredible smile—fool her into hoping things could change. It was a dangerous combination that could make her lose sight of the truth. She had a long history of bad choices. Getting personal with Wes Tanner would have been more of the same. They couldn't have less in common. She had no team. No real family. And tomorrow they'd face each other at the critical stress debriefing. Something he believed in and she most certainly didn't. Analyzing the emotional impact of Baby Doe's death was the last thing Kate needed.

Her heart cramped as she remembered her conversation with Lauren. And the brochure she'd tossed in the trash. Abandoned babies, terrified mothers. A Safe Haven?

Kate shook her head, sensing another soul-deep truth. *There is no safe place.*

**6**

+

**JUDITH DOYLE MOVED DOWN** the emergency department corridor, each brisk stride marked with a swish of her pink uniform and a *squeak-scrunch* from her SAS sneakers. And the occasional twinge of her arthritic knee. She'd probably already trekked a dozen miles through the vinyl-paved, fluorescent-lit, bustling maze that was Austin Grace Hospital.

After nearly two years, she knew every square foot like it was home. The humid, grease-scented engineering department on the basement level. The laughter and food-tray clatter of the cafeteria. The cool, blue-green, capped and masked inner sanctum that was the OR. She knew the route from the bright finger paint– and balloon-festooned halls of pediatrics to the blanket-soft, milk-and-miracle atmosphere of the newborn nursery. Judith had covered it all in the last four hours. Delivering interdepartmental mail, pushing wheelchairs, guiding visitors, making coffee, and . . . making a difference. Yes. She believed that with every fiber of her being. But of course, it was much more than that.

"Judith!" The ER registration clerk, Beverly, poked her head through the office doorway. There was an orange speckle of cheese puffs on her chin, and her eyes were etched with fatigue—single mother, working two jobs. *No sleep, again.* "Can you restock the information pamphlets in the waiting room? I think the last cold-and-flu sheet just sailed by my window. As a paper airplane."

"Happy to." Judith made a mental note to double-check the patient sign-in list against her most recent head count in the waiting room. Beverly was a department veteran and a hard worker, but fatigue took its toll and that's when mistakes happened. "And how 'bout I bring you some coffee?"

"Thanks, Judith. You're a real lifesaver."

"I . . ." Judith hesitated, a lump rising in her throat. *A lifesaver?* Her fingers played with her angel earring as she glanced through the registration window at the patients in the waiting room. The woman with swollen ankles, a college student with a scratch from his contact lens, a carpet layer with lower back pain, and several more. Judith knew their names, their faces, how long they'd been waiting. She'd offered magazines, cups of water, Kleenex, a listening ear. And her own private, ongoing assessments. Because even if right now everything was "same old, same old," as Beverly liked to say, things could change at any moment. The woman with swollen ankles might develop breathing trouble. The carpet layer's chronic back pain could be the symptom of an undiagnosed aneurysm—a bulging vessel shredding itself, ready to explode in a massive hemorrhage. The possibilities were always there, endless and frightening and so easily found on the Internet. Insomnia was providing Judith with an unexpected medical education.

"Wes Tanner, please call 7674. Wes Tanner, 7674." The overhead PA system crackled, went silent again.

Judith suspected the young man was being paged by the family of the gunshot victim. She'd seen them gathered in the chapel, a room used by visitors for respite and prayer, and by staff during Lauren Barclay's fellowship gatherings. It was the one room in the hospital that Judith never visited. Never would. She had no use for chapels, church, or God himself. Not since he'd allowed a medical mistake to steal her husband's life. A good, loving man who would never know grandchildren or toast a golden anniversary. Judith battled the familiar snarl of anger and pain, tamped it down. Then she grabbed a fresh stack of brochures and strode toward the waiting room, the angels beating silvery wings against her neck.

God had allowed human error to make Judith a widow. She couldn't change that, but it also left her determined that the senseless tragedy would never happen to anyone else. *Not on my watch.*

Her throat squeezed at the thought of the tiny baby left to die in the bathroom. It shouldn't have happened.

She'd check the census statistics and the staffing schedule. All she had left was time waiting to be filled. There was no reason she couldn't volunteer on the night shift too.

- + -

"I heard your friend's doing better." Lauren joined Wes Tanner at the cafeteria table. Though he'd managed to get hold of some clean clothes, he still looked emotionally rumpled. "So now how are *you* doing? Peer counselors—we have to ask, right?" Lauren tried not to imagine what Kate would think of that. But then, this might be a good time to feel Wes out about the debriefing. If he was still planning to be there.

"If I say, 'I wish it was me full of shotgun pellets,' will you rat me out to the social worker?" He dragged his hand along his jaw. "I feel bad. But a whole lot better now that Gabe's out of surgery and there were no complications. No damage to the major vessels or the hip joint. They'll be watching for infection, of course."

Lauren nodded. She couldn't count the number of times she'd wanted to trade places with her younger sister, spare Jessica pain. "They arrested the man who rigged that gun?"

"Right." Wes half groaned, half laughed. "He's been feuding with his brother for, like, ten years. Over something he can't even remember. But he sure wasn't going to let him come 'poking around' his property. Can you believe that? Gabe got shot—could have been killed—because this lunatic can't forgive his brother?"

"Don't get me started." Lauren shook her head. "Last summer one of the ER techs got in a phone argument with his ex, put his car in reverse, and backed over a pharmaceutical rep in the parking lot. Fractured leg—and the lawsuit that welcomed Kate to her new job."

Wes's brows drew together.

"She got you past security to see your friend before surgery?"

"Yes." Something that looked like a smile played across his lips. "And helped me with another problem—long story. I'm surprised, considering all she had to say against what we're doing with the ER staff tomorrow."

"You're still planning to be there?"

"Yes. Gabe will be upstairs, so it works on all counts. Do you know how many people will attend the debriefing?"

"About nine, I think. Counting the facilitators, you, and me. And Kate."

Wes's eyes widened. "How'd you manage that? Hypnosis?"

Lauren weighed her response. "I told Kate it might score points with her team. It hasn't been easy to take the lead after Sunni. They have different styles of leadership, and—" She stopped, catching a glimpse of scrubs in the distance, then waved her hand. "Kate. Join us."

- + -

Wes could tell by the look on Kate's face that joining them wasn't something she wanted to do. Even less when Lauren got paged and had to return to the ICU within minutes. He had a quick, irrational wish that Nancy Rae were here to mediate. He tried to remember how Kate's face looked, transformed by that unexpected smile in the chapel. Not possible.

Kate cleared her throat. "Horses?"

"Beg your pardon?"

"You and your friend were on horseback when he was shot?"

"Right." Why did he have the feeling Kate was about to add tetanus exposure to his growing list of Gabe guilt? But her eyes softened instead. Big, dark, vulnerable . . . *beautiful.* He'd be laughed out of the county if anyone knew he'd just thought of Bambi.

"My father and I used to ride," Kate told him, voice as soft as her eyes. "Summer vacations when I was little. We rented a cabin near Donner Lake in the Sierra mountains. He bought me fringed chaps with my initials made to look like a brand. Mom didn't ride, but she'd pack us a lunch, and . . ." Kate swallowed, glanced across the room. When she met his gaze again, the vulnerable softness was gone.

"Duster and Clementine," Wes offered. "My sorrel gelding and my father's young mare. Gabe was helping me put Clem through some field training. For a search-and-rescue demonstration we're doing Saturday—*I'm* doing—on my folks' ranch." Wes took a chance, stubbornly holding on to the image of a little cowgirl with her daddy. "If you'd like to come by, the horses will be there. Saddled and ready to go." He hoped she heard a shrug in his voice—and couldn't tell he was holding his breath.

"I don't ride anymore," she said abruptly, checking her watch.

"Does your father?"

Kate frowned, pushed her coffee away. "I don't know. We don't talk."

Wes thought of the hermit and the rigged shotgun.

"So," Kate said, standing, "I suppose I'll see you at the debriefing tomorrow." She looked at him like she was imagining a scorpion in her shoe.

"Yep."

Her shoulders rose and fell with a sigh. "I guess it won't be only the baby they'll talk about. With all that news coverage this afternoon."

"News?"

"About Sunni Sprague."

Wes's pulse quickened. "I heard there might be a new development, but I didn't see that report. What's going on?"

"The sheriff said there could be a break in her case. And that there would be more information coming soon. I got the impression they thought they'd be locating a body." Kate's eyes clouded. "I think not knowing is worse."

Wes wasn't sure if he nodded. But finally they agreed on something.

His mother's body hadn't been found for nearly a year. Not knowing—searching, struggling to hope against worsening odds—was far worse.

- + -

"You're still here?" Kate asked, spotting Judith in the hospital gazebo. "You're making me feel like a slacker. I'm on my way home."

"Me too." Judith's smile was warm. "I was sorting through some photos I took of Harley a few minutes ago."

"But she was discharged hours ago. She's having trouble again?"

"No. Her grandfather's rehab appointment," Judith reminded. "Trista drives him here every weekday. Harley's fine. But when Trista told me that she didn't have a camera and hadn't had any photos done since her baby was born . . ." Judith's earrings swayed as she shook her head in obvious disbelief. "Of course I took some. And said I'd e-mail them. Want to see?"

"Sure." Kate sat down beside her, scrolled through the digital photos as Judith narrated. "These are great. She's such a cute baby." She kept going and found shots of lush foliage, hills, and water. "These landscapes are nice too. Where is that?"

"I took these along the Barton Creek Greenbelt. It's beautiful along there and it goes all the way to Zilker Park. Which is quite lovely too. There's a botanical garden, an outdoor theater, so many great things for families."

Kate nodded. "I'm embarrassed to admit that I live within walking distance. Lauren's been badgering me to jog with her at the park. I think you've convinced me." She scrolled back to the baby photos, smiled. "This was really nice. You're completely amazing, Judith. What would we do without you?"

"You'll never have to find out," the volunteer promised as if she were making a sacred pledge.

"Good." Kate noticed the sun glinting off Judith's wedding ring set. "Though I would think your family might object if we abuse your generosity."

The woman's barely perceptible wince was enough to make Kate wish she could take the words back. "I'm a widow. Three years this month. My daughter's in San Antonio; Molly and her husband are attorneys. They've been trying to make me a grandmother for nearly two years. Now they're talking about adoption. . . ." Judith lifted her chin, the smile returning. "So you see, I have plenty of time on my hands."

"Maybe the next time I need an espresso Doubleshot and you get a yen for a pumpkin spice latte, we should walk over to Starbucks and have it there. Away from the hospital. Where we can really talk."

Judith's gaze held Kate's for a moment. "I like the idea."

"Me too." Kate glanced at her watch. "I'd better get going. I need to hit the computer at home, do some planning. We have a meeting tomorrow."

"That critical stress debriefing. Beverly told me. It's not my place to say so, but I think it can only be good to foster a cohesive team. Taking care of yourselves—and each other—is part of that. Healthy staff, happy patients."

"I . . ." Kate hesitated, then decided to go ahead. "Did you know Sunni Sprague?"

Judith's expression clouded and Kate felt certain she was struggling with a polite way to say what everyone else had. *You'll never compare to Sunni.*

"I'm sorry," Kate apologized. "I can only imagine how awful it was—still is—for everyone. She was probably a personal friend."

"No." Judith sighed. "You don't need to apologize. I know how difficult your position is in light of that situation, Kate. No person is perfect. No place is perfect. But we all have to try to be the best we can be."

Kate was halfway down Ben White Boulevard and starting to think about dinner when she noticed that the young woman was gone. The corner empty. No grieving mother, no candle, no heart-breaking poster with its painful plea for a funeral. She wondered if the woman had finally accomplished that—buried her baby. Gone home.

Then Kate remembered what she'd told Wes Tanner about the break in Sunni's case. That she thought it meant they were close to finding a body. And that finding out something awful was better than . . . *not knowing*. Her heart crowded her chest and she wasn't sure if the sudden ache was for the young mother or Sunni or . . .

She glanced at the empty corner and let herself imagine for just a moment—like Judith's camera capturing baby Harley—an image of a happy ten-year-old boy riding a horse alongside his very proud grandfather.

**7**

**"OW—HEY!"** Wes jerked upright in the lumpy visitor's chair and retrieved the hurled Kleenex box. He grinned at Gabe. "You're obviously feeling better."

"And you slept here all night?" Gabe shook his head. "Call the nurse. I'm having a fatal flashback to Scout camp." He lifted a container of green Jell-O. "Except the food was better there. You can't call it breakfast without bacon."

Wes chuckled, relief washing over him again. "Don't complain. Looks like you're down to one IV, and you've traded your oxygen for coffee . . . and a *Statesman*?" He glanced at the newspaper open on the tray table.

"Yeah. And we're in it." He lifted the paper. "'Local Businessman Victim of Shooting.' Could have been worse: 'Funeral Director Escapes Coffin.'"

"Did they mention search and rescue? We don't need that. Hard enough to recruit volunteers already."

"Nope." Gabe tapped the paper with his plastic spoon. "Far more interest in details of how our crazy hermit rigged the shotgun."

"No mention of why we were out there?"

"You mean Nancy Rae?" Gabe peered at him over the paper. "Thank you, by the way, for getting her back to Mrs. Braxton."

"No problem." Wes remembered Kate's smile. "Who told you?"

"Nobody. I read it in the paper."

"You just told me the article didn't say any of that."

"It didn't. But . . ." Gabe refolded the paper and held it out. "This one did. Complete with pictures."

"Gimme that." Wes grabbed the paper, eyes widening at a close-up shot of Lily and Amelia Braxton. Smiling bookends to a doll's face. The caption below read, "Grateful ladies laud local heroes—Nancy Rae is found."

Gabe clucked his tongue. "Apparently our newest 'live find' offered plenty of human interest."

"Great." Wes was quiet; the faint hum of the intermittent compression device on Gabe's legs filled the short stretch of silence. "Did you hear that the sheriff made a statement about Sunni Sprague? It sounds like you could be right about evidence from an inmate. Though I got the impression his statement was more to stop rumors from spreading at this point. He said he wasn't prepared to make anything public yet, but that they were 'hopeful to have some new information soon.'"

"He wouldn't have come out at all if they didn't have something." Gabe pushed his hands against the mattress, grimacing as he slid higher in the hospital bed. "Looks like I won't be there for the callout when they organize a search."

"They'll need help at the command trailer with search management. You're certified. And we don't even know that this so-called information will point to anything local."

Gabe pinned Wes with a look. "I know. You know." He glanced toward the doorway. "Every staffer at this hospital knows it. Sunni disappeared after leaving a shift right here. Her car was abandoned in Barton Springs, only a few miles away. If there's something to find, it's close by." He raised his brows. "Hey . . . you're doing that debriefing today."

"Right." Wes frowned, remembering what Kate Callison had said the last time he saw her. *"I suppose I'll see you at the debriefing tomorrow."* There had been no smile on her face that time. "I'll tell you the truth: it's the last thing I feel like doing."

- + -

Kate peeked into the conference room. The chaplain and social worker were already seated. She turned back to Lauren. "I see you're providing Kleenex."

"Tissues, water, an opportunity to feel heard and supported."

"Even if we have nothing to say." Kate stopped herself from crossing her arms.

"Even then. I never thought to ask—have you ever attended a critical stress debriefing?"

"No." Now Kate's arms crossed of their own volition. "Or had teeth pulled without anesthetic or set myself on fire." She dredged up a smile, reminding herself of her upcoming performance review. She needed staff morale to improve. Or else she'd be scheduling a plan B interview with that Dallas recruiter. "First time for everything."

Lauren squeezed her arm. "No worries. No one's going to put you on the spot. I'll be there with you. And so will Wes."

Kate decided Lauren didn't need to know that having Wes Tanner anywhere close created critical stress of its own. She was still kicking herself for telling him about riding horses with her father. How had she let that happen? Never again.

She checked her watch. "This will take an hour?"

"Approximately." Lauren smiled to acknowledge the arrival of Albert the janitor and one of the registration clerks. Neither of whom made eye contact with Kate. "Well, I think I'll find a seat since folks are starting to arrive. Are you—?" Lauren's brows pinched together. "Heads up; Lyon on the prowl." She escaped into the conference room.

"Kate, glad I caught you."

Kate turned to see Barrett Lyon's ingratiating smile. "I only have a minute. Meeting." She pointed at the conference room, suddenly eager to join the group. There were worse things.

"Yes. The debriefing. About the Baby Doe incident." Barrett's smile stretched wider, gray eyes almost glittering. "I just heard about it. It's why I wanted to catch you." He glanced toward the doorway, then took hold of her elbow and guided her a few steps away.

"What?" Kate slid her arm from his grasp.

"It could help," he said, lowering his voice, "if you let me know if any staff member mentions feeling personally responsible."

"Are you serious?" Kate felt blood rush to her face as Barrett signaled for her to keep her voice down. Several employees filed by. She backed toward the doorway and Barrett followed.

"I'm completely serious," he told her, stepping close enough that she could smell his citrusy cologne. "I believe I told you that our preference would be the prosecution of that teenage mother. But so far there have been no leads on her identity. And if the hospital incurs—"

"No. This is a confidential meeting. For mutual support," Kate emphasized, surprised to hear herself parroting Lauren. "If you think I'm going to be some sort of spy—"

"Kate, Kate . . ." Barrett grasped her shoulder, flashed his smile. "I'm—"

"Excuse me." Wes Tanner's deep voice interrupted. "I just need to get through." His gaze swept past Kate to Lyon, eyes narrowing a fraction.

Barrett stepped away from Kate.

"Best not to be late," Wes said tersely, moving into the doorway.

"Right," Kate agreed, grateful for the reprieve.

Wes stepped aside for Kate, followed her in, and took the last seat at the table. Directly across from her. She reached for her bottled water, wishing it were coffee. Then started to consider which was the worse fate: being asked to be legal's snitch or finding herself trapped in a room with a mountain of Kleenex.

Someone closed the door and the chaplain rose from his chair. "Let's get started."

- + -

Wes studied Kate covertly, deciding that though the smile in the chapel had almost changed his mind, *prickly* was still the perfect adjective for her. Even her hair seemed at odds with the world. Like right now, with the short, dark tufts sticking up. If she were a cat, her ears would flatten and she'd hiss. Apparently no one had explained to her that crossed arms sent a distinct message—after nearly half an hour, her muscles had to be cramping. Wes looked down as she glanced his way.

"And now we begin the third phase of our debriefing." Cynthia McConnell's expression was warm, compassionate, as she glanced around the table at the gathered staff: the janitor, the registration clerk, a NICU nurse, a respiratory therapist, Lauren, and Kate. "I remind you once again that we've gathered together for mutual support. That no one has any rank here, and everything we say will remain completely confidential."

Kate's lips pressed together in a tight line.

"As we go around the table this time," the chaplain explained, joining in, "we'll ask you to share your first thought after you stopped functioning on autopilot."

Wes knew the question well; it would be a tough one for the staff. Their first thought when they stopped doing and started *feeling*.

Kate fidgeted, swallowed, and reached for her water bottle.

"I'm not sure it really hit me how tragic it was," Lauren began, pressing her palms together, "until after I'd done what I could to help Albert." She turned to meet the man's gaze, empathy in her eyes. "And saw—really saw—the blood on your hands."

"I . . ." The janitor cleared his throat. "I surely did appreciate your helping me. And . . ." He glanced at the chaplain. "I remember handing that babe to Mr. Tanner, thinkin'—right before I passed out—that I shoulda been checking that bathroom an hour earlier. I always do the cleaning in emergency about 4:30 a.m., you see." He pressed a trembling hand to his forehead. "I changed up my routine that night. For no good reason changed it."

Lauren put her hand on Albert's arm as a tear slid down his face.

"I'm a grandpa, nine times. I keep thinking, why didn't I find that precious baby boy sooner?"

"I thought of my daughter," the registration clerk, Teresa, offered, barely above a whisper. "I opened the door for Mr. Tanner and Kate so they could rush that baby back to the ER. I did it without thinking. But then, afterward, I saw a trail of blood drops. Little splashes going past my office and all the way down the hall. There was one on my shoe." She clutched at a small cross on a chain around her neck. "My daughter's lost three babies. The one she's carrying now still has four months to go. I'm so afraid she'll lose this one too—it would kill her." Her face contorted. "How could a mother leave her baby and walk away?"

Wes thought of his mother, then saw the color drain from Kate's face.

"Wes?" Cynthia said gently. "Your first thought?"

"I thought, *He's so small.* I needed him to breathe because—" his throat tightened—"we'd found him. Given him a chance. And it would be so wrong to lose him after that." He swallowed, glanced across at Kate. *And I noticed how you looked with your hands around that little body. The same way you look right now.*

- + -

Kate struggled for air. *I need to get out of here.* She closed her eyes, but all she could see was the desert night made garish by neon casino lights. Then the abandoned car wash near the firehouse. A cash machine broken open, obscenities and gang graffiti sprayed across the cement walls. Cigarette butts—and worse—on the cold cement floor. Her pink sweatshirt spread over it all like a picnic blanket. Kate squirmed in the chair, reached for the water bottle . . . remembered the agonizing contractions, uncontrollable trembling. Then her baby's first cry and her own desperate wail. *"God . . . please, help me. . . ."*

"Kate?"

She choked and felt the water run down her chin. "I'm sorry . . . What?"

"Did you want to share your first thought?" the chaplain asked.

"No," she heard herself say. "No, I . . ." She glanced across the table, seeing Wes Tanner's blue eyes clouded with concern. She couldn't look at Lauren; there'd be no fooling her. She had to leave. Now. "I need to run to the restroom for a minute."

"You're okay?"

"Fine. Sorry. Too much water. I just have to . . ." She feigned a grimace of personal need.

"Of course." The chaplain glanced at the clock. "Hurry back. We're going to be moving on to specific symptoms of stress and offering valuable coping strategies. I don't want anyone to miss that."

"No problem." Kate made it to her feet and across the room that now stretched like an endless Nevada desert. Out the door, down the hall, and past Judith Doyle, who was towing a gigantic blue stork balloon. She finally reached the bathroom across from her office—mere seconds before her stomach heaved.

- + -

Wes was surprised that Kate came back, considering how grim she'd looked before she left. But she returned to the debriefing after the sharing phase, in time for the review and presentation of stress-survival strategies. She slipped into the chair across from him again, arms crossed and expression just shy of prickly once more. He had to admit that given a choice, he'd take it over that pale, stricken look.

She glanced at Wes, then turned her attention to the social worker.

"Again, when a critical incident involving a child occurs, approximately 85 percent of affected staff will develop some symptoms of stress. People who try to handle everything alone take longer to process it. On the other hand, people who talk about the incident eat better, sleep better, remain healthier, and have fewer problems at work, home, and in their relationships. Most reactions to stress—the symptoms we discussed and that you'll find in your packets—are normal. But remember that your employee benefits include counseling services if you feel the need."

The chaplain pointed to a list on the conference room's dry-erase board. "This is all in your packets as well, but some tips for dealing with stress include things to avoid, like alcohol and too much caffeine. As well as things we have found to help: eating regular meals, exercise, staying busy, listening to music . . . doing the things that feel good to you."

What felt good to Kate Callison? Wes thought of what she'd said about riding horses with her father. Then how she'd immediately turned down Wes's invitation to his search-and-rescue demo tomorrow. "We don't talk," she'd said when he asked about her dad. Had to be a story there.

"Any questions?" Cynthia asked the group.

Teresa raised her hand, then looked at Wes. "It's about Sunni. Is that okay?"

"Sure," Wes said, catching the chaplain's nod. And what he thought was a faint frown on Kate's face.

"On the news, we heard that there might be new information. Will you start searching again?"

"When they have something official, when we're called out, absolutely we'll search."

"Sunni did my daughter's pregnancy tests for the last three babies, let her come in anytime and listen to the heartbeat with the Doppler. And sent her beautiful cards when she miscarried."

Albert added, "She came to our house to visit when my wife was so sick from the chemo. Helped me wash her hair. She stayed and painted Irene's toenails—gave her spirits such a lift." He shook his head. "Miss Sprague made everyone feel special somehow."

"I hear you," Wes said, noticing for the first time that Kate had chosen a seat on the opposite side of the table from her fellow staff. "I can only imagine how bad it would be to lose a teammate. Actually, right now one of my guys is upstairs. The truth is I thought I was going to lose him." He splayed his hands on the table, glanced from face to face. "I promise you I'll keep searching."

- + -

"Roady? C'mon . . ." *Please?*

Kate hugged her robe close, padding in sock-monkey slippers along the darkened driveway to peer into the tangle of shrubs and vines. An acorn, one of the scant number not devoured by deer, rolled under her foot.

She sighed. All she'd hoped for after a miserable day at work was the company of the scruffy, stump-tailed cat. Not a visit from Prince Charming, not a call from the Texas Lottery. Not even firefly magic—they were long gone now. She'd settle for fur under her fingers, a simple purr. Was that too much to ask?

"Roady?" Kate bent low to inspect the driveway's trailing rosemary hedge without success, then stood upright again and caught a glimpse of her landlord's window a few yards away. The property's main house was gabled and built of hill country lime-stone with hunter-green trim, a steep metal roof, and multipaned windows throwing light into the darkness. A home completely foreign with its elk-antler chandelier and cactus door wreath, yet still so achingly warm with life and love. *Family.*

She stood on tiptoe to peer farther. Her landlord and his wife, their grown children, and grandchildren, too. Laughing, putting something into the oven while fending off an exuberant springer spaniel. Hugging. She caught a glimpse of a young boy. Then a toddler girl lifted onto her grandfather's shoulders.

Kate stiffened, angry with herself. What on earth was she doing? Looking for a cat that couldn't be bothered to stay put and now peeping? Proving, pathetically, what she already knew: she was on the outside looking in. That would never change.

She walked back to the guesthouse, thinking of what the debriefing team had suggested today—to do things that felt good. She'd heard that advice before at Alamo Grace Hospital in San Antonio. From her friend, nurse and chaplain Riley Hale. And she'd thought then what she was thinking now. What if nothing did? Would she always be an outsider in a life that . . . *never feels good?*

Kate padded into the kitchen, reached for the teakettle. Even if her cat wasn't going to cooperate, at least the day was nearly over. A run-in with Barrett Lyon and that nightmare debriefing complete with tearful, eulogizing memories of Sunni Sprague. Horrible all round. But she'd survived, and tomorrow started her weekend off and—

Kate glanced at the oven clock: 9:10. Two hours earlier in California. If she was going to leave a message for her father—and not run the risk of catching him—she'd better do it now. She sighed, thinking of what she'd said to Wes Tanner in response to his question about her father: *"We don't talk."* She was sure it was something he could never understand, but it worked for Kate. She cleared her throat, waiting for the last ring and the switchover to voice mail so she could leave her generic, cheery message. A final salute to a day that couldn't have been worse.

"Kate?"

Her stomach sank. "Dad—you're there?"

"No. I'm *here*. In Texas. I'd like to see you, Katy."

8

+

MATT CALLISON WATCHED HIS DAUGHTER study the lunch menu and wondered if coming to Austin would prove to be a big mistake. Thirty minutes into it, he couldn't tell for sure. But in her phone message Wednesday, Kate had sounded troubled, sad, her voice completely at odds with her words: *". . . okay . . . fine . . . great."* He'd replayed it half a dozen times, hearing the ache in her voice and the way she'd slipped and said *Daddy* instead of *Dad*, then tortured himself with memories of times she'd been hurt and inconsolable. A broken collarbone in soccer. That rainy day her cat, Pookie, was struck and killed by the car. And those awful last weeks with her mother in hospice. So Matt had asked a neighbor to pick up his mail, fired up the GPS, and headed for Interstate 10.

*I'm here now, Katy. Whether you like it or not.*

"Catfish maybe," she said at last, peering at him with her mother's eyes. Audrey Hepburn eyes. How many times had Juliana heard that comparison? And now Kate was the spitting image of her with that dark hair, sharp chin, and long lashes. The smile, too. When and if it ever happened.

"Fish?" Matt asked after her brows furrowed at his inattention. "Is that what's good?"

She shrugged. "It's a Shady Grove favorite. Tortilla-fried queso catfish. I haven't had it, but I love their beef brisket—that's on a tortilla too. With pickled red onions." The Hepburn eyes met his. "I had you meet me here instead of my place because you've been traveling. I figured you'd be hungry."

*And because you didn't want me too close.* Matt's chest tightened. Despite what the map said, the real distance between him and his daughter was a lot farther than 1,700 miles. How did he begin to close that now?

"It's a great spot." Matt glanced around the bustling patio of Shady Grove. Green umbrellas, stonework, wagon wheels, huge pecan trees strung with lights, and that "hippie trailer" in the parking lot, a vintage aluminum Airstream surrounded by a garish picket fence and tacky clutter, used for overflow waiting. Jukebox music blended with laughter on air spiced with fried onions and jalapeños. He met Kate's gaze again. "And I *am* hungry. Good plan."

Kate was quiet for a moment. "A road trip? I wouldn't have pegged you for that. Taking all the time away from work, I mean."

"I . . ." *Was downsized after nearly thirty years with my engineering firm. Laid off.* Matt still couldn't say the words out loud. He wasn't even close to a solution for dealing with it. Except for the Sold sign pounded into his lawn—a transaction that put a huge crack in his already-fragile nest egg. After forking over thousands on unexpected repairs, he'd finally sold it for a net loss. But that was over, and right now all that mattered was Kate. "I wanted to see you. Talk. Most of the time it's like we're playing phone tag. And the other night, your voice . . ." Matt sensed he was about to make a mistake. "You sounded like you'd been crying. So I—"

"Start you off with margaritas?" the Shady Grove waiter interrupted, arriving beside them.

"Iced tea for me," Matt said in a hurry, reading the anxiety on Kate's face. She was worried he'd order beer. And follow that beer with three more . . . then back the car over her cat. But the medallion in Matt's pocket said it all: *One day at a time.* Twelve steps and now 1,700 miles. He had to do it. All of it.

"Tea for me as well," she told the waiter. "Not sweet."

They added their food orders—his catfish and her campfire veggie plate—and Matt weighed the wisdom of broaching the subject of the phone call again. But Kate beat him to it.

"I wasn't crying," she said, lifting her chin. "It was . . ." Her lashes fluttered in the same tell he'd read all her life. When she'd denied bending the brass angels on the Christmas tree or taking her mother's lipstick to school . . . Had he missed some signs that she was planning to leave home? "Allergies," she explained. "Cedar fever. Another Texas thing I have to get used to."

Matt nodded. Kate had her mother's looks, but that stubborn streak was 100 percent paternal. He wasn't wrong that she was in trouble. One way or another, he was going to do something about it. Matt wasn't going to let her run away this time.

- + -

How soon could she get out of here? And more importantly . . .

Kate took a sip of her iced tea, tried to make her voice casual.

"How long can you stay, Dad? In Austin, I mean. This is such a surprise."

Which put it mildly. Her father's call had kept Kate awake half the night, wondering what she'd say, where they should meet, and what on earth she could do to entertain him. *How can I keep him from seeing what a wreck I'm becoming? I can't do this.*

Now panic was giving way to a growing sense of irritation. Since when had her father ever taken time off to talk? Even in those final days with her mother—her last precious, lucid moments—he'd buried himself in work.

"I have that college buddy in Fort Worth," he said, flipping the corner of his napkin between his fingertips. "You met Phil. Way back."

His eyes connected with Kate's, and she noticed small signs of aging that had appeared since she saw him last. He was still handsome, compelling even. But there were new lines around the hazel eyes, more gray in his hair. And something different in his expression. *What do you want from me?*

"You're going on to Fort Worth?" Kate asked, hoping the relief didn't show on her face.

"Thought I would. Unless you don't have plans for tomorrow. I know I sprang this on you, but—"

"I do," Kate heard herself say. And knew with a wave of guilt that he'd caught the mistruth the way he always had. *Except that day I stuffed my clothes and a photo of Mom into a backpack and told you I was staying overnight with a friend . . .* "I need to be somewhere tomorrow. But I thought of something we could do today—outdoors. We're both dressed for that. And it's such a pretty day."

"Despite cedar fever." One corner of her father's mouth tugged toward a smile.

"Yes. Thank heaven for antihistamines." Kate sighed with relief as the waiter arrived with their steaming plates. "Anyway, there's a search-and-rescue demonstration today. Dog training, swift-water experts, a helicopter, equipment displays . . ." Kate spread her napkin in her lap, trying to remember all she'd read in a desperate 2 a.m. web search. "I know the man who is heading it up, and he'll have his horses there. It sounded kind of fun. They'll be on-site until three, so we could still catch some of it."

"Sure. I'm game."

Kate smiled at her father, thinking she might have just set a record for telling multiple fibs in a short span of time. She didn't have cedar fever, she had no plans for tomorrow, and the search-and-rescue demo sounded like anything but fun. She'd suggested going for the same reason that she met her father at Shady Grove instead of home: more distractions and less opportunity to talk. Her father's new interest in her life was the last thing she wanted to encourage.

So, in that respect only, she was willing to let Wes Tanner rescue her today.

- + -

"Imagine," Wes explained to the group of assembled Scouts, "someone lost a toy soldier and thought maybe it fell into a playground sandbox. When you start looking for it, you scrape the sand around hoping it will show up. Your probability of finding it might be 25 percent. When that doesn't work, you dig a little deeper, look harder, but still have no real plan. Or established routine." He smiled as Dylan passed by, walking Hershey on a leash. "Now you're 50 percent sure the toy isn't in the sandbox. So you search a third time. But this time you plan it out. You draw lines in the sand to divide it up, run your fingers through each 'grid' in a planned manner. When you come up empty, you're—"

"You're 75 percent sure it isn't there," a Scout offered, shielding his eyes against the sun.

"That's right."

"I'd get my mom's noodle strainer," another boy suggested. "Start shaking the sand around in it. Like you do at the beach for seashells."

"Bingo!" Wes grinned. "You got it. Divide the area into smaller blocks and refine the search. Sift each block. And then you find the soldier that was there all along."

"Is that how you found Mrs. Braxton?" one of the mothers asked.

"No." Wes thought of the excitement on Gabe's face that morning and wished he were here now. "We found her using what we call a hasty search. Because time was of the essence—it was dark and cold and Mrs. Braxton is elderly and in fragile health. And especially because my searchers lived close by and could get there in minutes. The idea of a hasty search is to move quickly through an area, first checking the most obvious places and biggest hazards. For instance, on Mrs. Braxton's property there's a barn, a ditch, an old cistern, and an abandoned well." He was grateful no one mentioned the shotgun lashed to a tree or the vengeful lunatic in a trailer. "We'll move over the area listening for sounds, checking for footprints and broken branches. Those kinds of things."

"Tracking signs."

"Exactly," Wes agreed, lengthening the rope on Duster's halter so the gelding could nip at the Tanners' pasture. He rubbed the horse's soft ear, then turned back to the group. "Which is why it's important to use trained searchers. The goal is to bring a quick end to a search. If the missing person is just wandering in the woods, they'll be found. Or if the team comes back empty-handed, there's about a 70 percent chance that a conscious and uninjured victim isn't there."

"Have you ever found a kid who was lost?" an older Scout asked. He nudged a smaller boy who looked suspiciously like a younger brother. "I mean a squirt like this who couldn't find his way out of a sandbox?"

"Hey . . ."

Wes smiled despite the sudden quiver of his stomach—the younger boy was about the same age as he was when he'd been left in those woods. "A few times. Children with developmental challenges are most at risk."

Wes pointed toward where Jenna and several of the Travis County team members were working with the dogs. "We're going to do some field exercises with our K9 crew. We call it a live find drill. It will give you a chance to meet the dogs and learn what to expect if responders ever have to search for you." He added with a rush of pride, "My brother, Dylan, is going to help with that chocolate Lab, Hershey." Wes chuckled. "And if you're wearing even one crumb from Mom's oatmeal cookies, I dare you to find a place to hide from that dog."

He watched as the Scouts headed toward the dogs, a few breaking into a jog to get a first chance at the training exercise. He'd actually done his first rescue when he wasn't much older than many of those boys. At the same abandoned well he'd just mentioned in his talk. But that was a long time ago, and right now Wes was glad the day was winding down. He enjoyed sharing his interest in search and rescue, but he kept thinking of Gabe lying in that hospital bed. And he couldn't help but notice that despite the turnout of schoolchildren and Scouts, there had been only one adult who'd signed up with interest in volunteer training. It made Wes eager to put it all aside and return to the day job. Dig a well, install a new pump . . . stop remembering that look on Kate's face before she escaped from the debriefing.

She'd made it clear that she didn't welcome Wes's concern or share his interests. He wasn't sure which bothered him more—that obvious dismissal or the fact that she seemed to be on much friendlier terms with Barrett Lyon, the hospital attorney. It was clear he'd interrupted a personal conversation when he arrived at the conference room yesterday.

Wes frowned. He didn't want to think about it anymore. All he wanted was a drilling project, and—

*Thwoop, thwoop, thwoop . . .*

He watched as the county helicopter rose from the pasture, flattening clumps of native grasses, scattering leaves, making bystanders stop and point. He tilted his head, thinking he'd heard someone shout through the roar. He decided against it, reached to untie Duster, and—

"Wes!"

There it was again.

Wes shielded his eyes from the sun, scanned the thinning crowd of visitors, and saw her. Wearing jeans, a khaki thermal T-shirt, and boots. Striding purposefully toward him in aviator sunglasses, waving her hand, with an older man closely in tow.

Wes shook his head, remembering what he'd told the Scouts about percentages, probability, and chance. Against all odds, Kate Callison was here.

**9**

+

"AND SO," KATE EXPLAINED, suspecting her breathlessness had little to do with the trek across the Tanners' pasture, "I thought Dad should see some of the Texas hill country, and . . . we're here." Had she ever done this? Introduced her father to a man who—

To Kate's horror, she felt her face warm. *A man who . . . what?* She crossed her arms, glanced toward the sprawling stone ranch house. "Quite a spread."

"The sign said, 'Well drilling.'" Her father accepted Wes's handshake. "Is that your business?"

"Three generations of us. Of course today—" Wes gestured toward the Scouts and K9 teams in the distance—"is about a whole different kind of community service. Rescue." He glanced at Kate, a smile playing on his lips. "For folks who need that sort of help."

*Touché.* Kate decided to let him have that one. "And that's

Duster, I assume," she said, seeing that her father was already beside the muscular quarter horse, extending his palm toward the rusty-red muzzle. Her heart tugged unexpectedly as she recalled his words from so long ago. *"Put the carrot in the flat of your hand, punkin, and keep your fingers out of the way. That's right. See there, he likes you already."*

"Valiant Duster officially, according to his papers," Wes answered, "but I don't let it go to his head. He's passed all the qualifications for search and rescue. And now . . ."

Kate stayed back as Wes and her father talked, her father nodding and running a hand over the horse's shoulder, listening intently as Wes described horsemanship skills like clearing water obstacles, dragging an object, and log jumping. She took a slow breath of country air, glad for an opportunity to collect herself for the first time since her father's arrival. Her gaze swept what she could see of the acreage: rolling hills and live oaks, outcroppings of rock and clumps of the ever-present Texas cactus. A big barn and what looked like a workshop, pecan trees near the house, chairs on the front porch, and—she inhaled with appreciation—a barbecue going on somewhere.

She turned at the sound of the men's laughter, noticed they were wearing similar boots. Wes was taller, his shoulders a bit broader in the orange search-and-rescue shirt, and the cut of his faded Levi's—

"You didn't tell me that Wes was an engineer too," her father said, looking at her.

An engineer? She walked toward them, wondering if this had been a mistake after all. She'd already discovered that Wes had an uncanny knack for getting under her skin. Now her father—who'd been safely mute almost two thousand miles away—had shown up wanting to talk. Putting them together probably wasn't at all smart.

"He said you met at the hospital," her father added, stroking Duster's nose.

*No . . .* Kate's eyes met Wes's. He told her father about the abandoned baby?

"Because I was there after a rescue," Wes clarified, the earnest look in his eyes promising Kate that he hadn't breached any privacy. "In fact, I was hoping to interest a few of the Austin Grace staff in volunteering today. Kind of thought Lauren might show up."

"She wanted to, but she couldn't." Kate hugged her arms around herself. The distant voices and laughter of children seemed to intensify. Happy kids, close-knit families. "She's working an extra shift in the ER."

Kate knew this because she'd called Lauren last night. When she was pacing the house, frantic for ideas about how to deal with her father's visit. And scared witless that seeing him would bring back the same black misery she'd felt at the debriefing. She'd been right.

- + -

"You sound . . . busy," Lauren told her sister, hating the word that had really come to mind. *Manic.* This wasn't clinical. This was Jess . . . being Jess. That's all.

Lauren leaned back in the triage office chair and cradled the phone to her ear. "School's good?"

"Great, easy, aced my physiology midterm. I'm like the star of the lab when everyone else says it's so hard, whines, complains, yada yada: the class time is too early; they're tired, overworked. I say, what's the big deal? Ha! Sleep is highly overrated—you can sleep when you die, ya know?"

*Oh, Jess* . . . Lauren bit her lip, reminding herself not to give advice. Her "suffocating, impossible, mother-hen, preachy" concerns had threatened their close relationship too many times in the past. It was the biggest reason Lauren had taken the job in Austin. Space for Jessica and a cushion against her own inevitable worry. Not that the worry disappeared with distance.

Lauren took a slow breath. "Will you be at Mom and Dad's for Thanksgiving?"

"Sure. Probably—maybe. Haven't thought it out. It's a long weekend and there's this guy I met. He wants me to sign up for the Turkey Trot. I'm jogging every day now—can't seem to stop. Anyway, he's really cute—you'd drool—kind of Johnny Depp but more *Benny & Joon* than Jack Sparrow—"

"I love you, Jess," Lauren broke in. "I'd better go now." She nodded, tried to say good-bye, and finally hung up while her sister was still talking. Easier to capture a hummingbird.

Lauren was glad she'd taken the extra shift today, no matter what went down. If she were off, a rambling conversation like that would have her putting the VW in gear and heading to Houston. For no good reason . . . *because Jessica is fine. She is.*

"No new patients out there?" Lauren asked after walking the short distance to the registration office. She peered over Beverly's shoulder toward the waiting room.

"No. Only the girl with the baby. But I think she just hangs out here." The clerk frowned, leaned toward the office window. "Where'd she go? I see the baby's car seat, but—"

"I'm on it."

Lauren strode into the waiting room, spotted the car seat at the rear of the room, near the door. The baby was in the seat, unattended. *Where's the mother?* She hurried to the sleeping baby and stood with her hands on her hips, scanning the few remaining people in the waiting room. *Where on earth . . . ?*

She turned her attention to the double doors and connected immediately with the gaze of a young woman standing outside. The woman's eyes widened. She glanced toward the parking lot, then hit the button for the automatic door and scuttled inside.

"Is this your baby?" Lauren asked, incredulous.

"Yes, I was just . . ." The woman pushed her dark-framed glasses up her nose. "I was making a call. The sign on the wall says you have to go outside to use cell phones."

*And you didn't take your baby with you?* Lauren bit back the rebuke, reminding herself that the baby was fine and that some people simply didn't think. Then she noticed how very young this mother was. *Don't judge. She's probably doing the best she can.* "Are you signing up to be seen in the emergency department?" she asked gently.

"No. I drive my father to the clinic next door for therapy," she explained. "Sometimes I wait here until he's finished."

"Ah." Lauren saw that the young mother was clutching several of the brochures offered by the emergency department. "And catching up on your reading material. That's good." She cocked her head, trying to see which ones the woman had gathered. "There are some good brochures," she offered, "from the pediatricians' offices. That one on top won't be any help. It's for pregnant women—about the Baby Moses law."

"Baby Moses?"

"It's called Safe Haven now," Lauren explained. "Assistance for women who can't keep their newborns. It was called Baby Moses after a Bible story about a baby who was left by his mother at the river's edge because she was afraid he was in danger at home. Anyway . . ." She stepped closer to the sleeping baby, dressed all in pink. "If you or your beautiful little girl . . . What's her name?"

"Harley."

Lauren smiled. "If you or Harley need anything while you're waiting for your father, let me know. I'm Lauren. You can ask for me at the desk. And if you need to go outside, take Harley along, okay? It's safer."

"Okay."

Lauren went back to the registration office, talked with Beverly for a few moments. Then took one last look around the waiting room before returning to the triage office. Harley and her mother had disappeared. She'd probably gone to pick up the baby's grandfather. Then Lauren remembered it was Saturday. The offices were closed. She headed back to triage, deciding the young mother had simply wanted to escape from the house. How many times had Lauren done that when she and her sister butted heads? Families, regardless of love and good intentions, were never without their troubles.

- + -

Wes nudged Clementine forward through the shallow stream, following Duster, thinking that his gelding had never looked better. Not only because the quarter horse was fit, sure-footed, and shiny as molten copper in the late-afternoon sun, but because . . . *Kate's riding him.*

He smiled, not sure what he was enjoying more—the way her hips and legs moved with Duster's stride or the fact that he'd managed to talk her into climbing up on that saddle, double-teaming her with the help of Matt Callison. It hadn't been easy, and Wes knew—as well as he knew Clementine was prone to shy if a deer came crashing through the brush—that Kate would be riding with her arms crossed if she could handle his horse that way.

But Wes had seen the look on Matt's face at the prospect of taking the horses out, remembered Kate's wistful childhood memory of fringed chaps and trail rides at a California lake. As well as her subsequent insistence that she and her dad didn't talk anymore. It was no way to handle a team, let alone a family. He hoped that big chip on Kate's shoulder, regardless of what had caused it or how long it had been there, would get jostled off somewhere along the trail. And Wes knew some fairly bumpy terrain.

"Hold up," he called to her as Clem cleared the water and climbed the low embankment. "Let's give your father a minute to catch up. Levi's a plodder."

Duster halted and Wes trotted the mare forward until he was alongside Kate.

Her hair was mussed even more than usual from the breeze, and the sun had coaxed a sprinkling of freckles across her nose. She'd removed the sunglasses, pushed up her sleeves. There was lace at the neckline of her T-shirt. No-nonsense khaki thermal . . . and lace? For some reason, it suited Kate perfectly. She couldn't have looked more beautiful.

"How's your backside?" he asked, glancing at Duster's Australian saddle; then he scrambled to rephrase as her dark brows pinched together. "I mean . . . saddle okay, stirrups the right length?"

"You meant, can I handle it?" Kate's eyes narrowed a fraction. "This big horse, the ride, being bullied into it. All because I made the mistake of telling you I'd done this before with my dad. As a kid. In a life that has no relation to my world today." Her lips tensed in a way that said she was seconds from yanking the chip from her shoulder and hurling it at his head.

"I . . ." Wes rose in his stirrups and turned to check the trail. Matt and Levi were clearing the stand of brush just before the stream. "Okay," he admitted, "maybe I pushed you. But I thought it was a good idea at the time."

"You thought." She looked down at the braided leather reins in her hands and then met Wes's gaze again, surprising sadness flooding her eyes. "Have you ever thought that not everyone is like you? Or Sunni? Some of us aren't 'team' people, the kind that Scouts rally around and old ladies call heroes. Or that hospital staff puts up on a pedestal. Some of us can't even spend a random Saturday with family without risking . . ." Kate took a breath. "I came out here because I didn't have a clue how to deal with a visit from my father. I didn't know where else to go. I needed help with this *one* day. Putting me on your horse won't change anything." She shook her head, her eyes suddenly shiny with unshed tears. "Please don't meddle in my life, Wes. Don't do that."

"Uh . . ." Wes held Kate's unblinking gaze, forcing himself to say nothing. Do nothing. Though everything in him wanted to pull her down from that saddle, shake her. Hold her. Until she stopped fighting and he could somehow convince this prickly woman that she was wrong. No matter what her circumstances, there was always hope. Wes believed that. It was the reason he searched ditches in the dark, shouted a missing person's name for hours against wind and freezing rain. Why he never gave up on stubborn horses . . . or people. He'd lowered ropes to the bottom of dozens of cliffs and never once had someone refused to grab hold because he was "meddling" in their lives. Kate was wrong. And maybe it wouldn't happen now, but Wes swore he'd—

"Caught up with you two," Matt said, bringing Levi to a halt beside them. He wiped his brow and grinned. "This is great. Can't thank you enough, Wes. Right, Kate?"

"Absolutely," she said, sliding her sunglasses on before gathering her reins. "I was just saying the same thing."

*In a pig's eye.*

Wes pointed toward a fork in the trail, suggested to a very enthusiastic Matt that he and Levi lead the way. It was the least Wes could do, considering the man had driven all this way to spend time with a woman who wanted nothing to do with him. Wes was starting to understand how that felt.

- + -

Lauren leaned forward, attempting to make eye contact with the teenager. Not easy as the girl slouched in the triage chair, tucking her chin down to let dyed raven hair obscure her face. But Lauren had already caught a glimpse of red in the whites of her eyes and thought she smelled alcohol on her breath. "I asked your mother to step out for a minute so we could talk more easily, Olivia."

The girl shifted in the chair, crossed her arms, and gave a soft grunt.

Lauren glanced at the monitoring equipment, the vital signs the patient had grudgingly allowed her to obtain. BP 98 over 44, pulse 56, respirations 14. Oxygen saturation 96 percent. The reason for the visit—offered by a worried mother—was *"sleeping too much, not eating."*

Depression, substance abuse . . . both?

"I need you to be truthful with me," Lauren said. "Have you been drinking today?"

The girl shrugged. Then met Lauren's gaze at last. Red-rimmed eyes, very slight nystagmus, pupils . . . constricted?

"Please, Nurse . . . just leave me alone."

"I can't do that, Olivia," Lauren told her, not comfortable with the girl's rapidly developing slur. She'd walked in but was looking much groggier now. "Your mother brought you here because she's worried about you. She thinks you need help."

"Don't . . . need anything . . . nobody. Jus' let . . . me be." The girl pressed a hand against her forehead, and her long sleeve slid back, revealing rows of scarring on her forearm, some blanched with age and several freshly scabbed.

Lauren's stomach sank. "Olivia, I need to know: have you had any alcohol, taken drugs of any kind?"

"I . . . feel . . ." The girl's head lolled sideways; she pulled in a breath that sounded more like a snore. Then she rallied just enough to peer at Lauren with half-lidded eyes.

Lauren stood. No more questions. Olivia was meeting an ER stretcher. Now. And it would be a team effort. She hit the button under the desk, heard the alarm start to trill—just as the girl's mother shoved open the triage door, her expression frantic.

"Look! Her brother found this in the bathroom." She held out an empty amber bottle. "My husband's prescription cough syrup. It was full this morning!"

"Need a gurney here," Lauren told a tech as he peered in through the other door.

In mere moments the team converged on the triage office, lifted a weakly resisting Olivia onto a gurney, and hustled toward the resuscitation room. Lauren jogged alongside, eyes on her patient—and her heart in Houston with her sister. But she was nothing like this troubled girl. One bout of depression didn't mean she had a serious problem. Jess was fine.

# 10

**"WHAT HAVE WE GOT?"** the physician asked as they slid Olivia's gurney into place in the resuscitation room. Two techs began the process of coaxing her into an exam gown.

"Sixteen-year-old, 'sleepy' today per mother," Lauren reported, bringing the triage screen up on the bedside computer. "No significant medical history—here you go. Weight, vital signs." She handed him the empty bottle provided by the mother. "She didn't admit to taking anything, but I thought I smelled alcohol. And this was apparently full this morning. Her father's cough syrup."

"Hydrocodone/homatropine. Thanks." He set the bottle down, watched as the girl's heart rhythm began to appear on the digital display screen of the monitor. Then he signaled to the assigned nurse. "Get her on two liters of oxygen and let's have Narcan standing by. I'll examine her now, but I'm going to want an IV and a Foley catheter. Urine HCG, blood alcohol, full toxicology screen. We'll lavage her. Get a chest film, EKG, and—whoops, she's vomiting. Let's protect that airway, folks!"

Olivia gagged again as the technician turned her head to the side and a rigid plastic tube sucked vomit from the corner of her mouth. She tried to reach toward her face, but the reflexive movement was deftly intercepted by another technician.

"Easy, Olivia, let us do what we need to do," he told her. "We'll explain everything, but we need your help."

Lauren saw one of the nurses setting up the lavage—quarts of fluid to wash any pill fragments from her stomach, followed by a charcoal-and-laxative slurry to prevent further absorption of drugs into her system. All via a garden hose of a tube inserted through a bite block between her lips. Beyond obnoxious. Lauren hoped the girl cooperated and swallowed the tube down. Regardless, it would happen. Even if she had to be restrained. *You need help whether you believe it or not, little girl.*

"I'll check with the family," Lauren told the clinical coordinator. "Tell them what to expect." She glanced at the latest set of vital signs: BP 90 over 52. Heart rate 62, sinus rhythm. Oxygen saturation 100 percent with the two-liter flow. She caught a glimpse of Olivia's face—color pink, eyes smudged with mascara and wide with fear. Lauren thought of the scars on her arm, wondered how long she'd hidden them from her parents. She reminded herself to ask the family about clergy and offer the hospital chaplain. Social services would be involved too. Helping this girl would take a well-rounded and compassionate team approach. Starting with the support of her family. It was clear that Olivia had tried to go it alone. And look where she'd landed. Family was oftentimes an unappreciated resource. DNA close, but not always nurtured the way it deserved to be.

It made Lauren think of Kate. And the edginess in her voice when she'd called last night about her father's surprise visit. She wondered where her friend had finally decided to take him today.

Lauren shook her head, thinking how often Kate had teased her about Texas. Which Austin restaurant was closest to California cuisine? That's where Kate Callison would eat tonight.

- + -

The air smelled like barbecue.

Kate walked alongside Duster toward the barn. All traces of the search-and-rescue demonstration, Scouts, and schoolchildren had vanished. And here, closer to the Tanner ranch house, the air was thick with the scent of mesquite smoke and slow-cooked brisket. Her traitorous stomach rumbled to mock the Shady Grove vegetable plate.

Kate's gaze followed the sweep of pecan boughs sheltering the roomy porch and caught an inky-blue and orange swallow swooping low under a branch to careen onward toward the barn. She sneaked another whiff of barbecue, then encouraged Duster forward, enjoying the hollow clop of hooves on the dirt path. Though her inner thighs had begun to whine about their first contact with horseflesh in more than a decade.

"Is this where you live, boy?" she asked aloud, trying to recall if Wes had said to take his horse inside to unsaddle. She stopped at the entrance to the barn, noticing the letters carved in the weathered wood. Bold and childishly uneven, and . . . She traced a fingertip over the carving: *W. T.*

"Wes," a woman verified from Duster's far side. She peered at Kate from under the gelding's jaw. Then swept a lock of coppery hair away from her face. Her silver hoop earrings glinted in the sun.

"When he was eleven. Dulled my best paring knife." Her warm smile crinkled her eyes. "I'm Miranda Tanner. And I'll bet you're Kate."

"Yes," Kate said, easily recognizing her from that day in the hospital chapel. She returned Miranda's smile, trying to find some resemblance between Wes and his mother. "It's nice to—" She groaned as Duster dipped his head, bumping the top of hers. "I'm sorry. Trying to talk under a horse's chin is a little awkward."

"Of course. We'll fix that. Ah—" Miranda turned to glance down the path—"here comes the rest of the team now."

Kate backed Duster a few steps to see that her father and Wes were headed toward the barn, leading their horses. Accompanied by the handsome man who was quite obviously Wes's father. And the lanky adolescent Kate had also seen in the chapel, with a huge chocolate Lab still wearing a search-and-rescue vest. The four men were engaged in animated conversation. If they stayed any longer, her father would be wearing a Team Tanner jersey.

Her throat tightened unexpectedly. She had no clue why. Kate only knew that the nerve-racking day was finally winding down. And she was glad about that. Wasn't she?

- + -

Kate was wearing the poker face again, at least in the glance she'd just tossed Wes's way. Though she was all smiles as he made introductions outside the barn, Wes would bet that getting out of here as quickly as possible was her only goal. And far be it from him to meddle again.

Dylan obviously had other plans.

"Easy, pal, take a breath," Wes told him as his brother continued the nonstop stream of facts and details related to Hershey's training. "Let the lady get a word in. That's good manners."

"Uh-huh, okay," he agreed, shaking his head several times before peering at Kate again. The eager, dog-with-a-bone look returned to his expression. "Hiding or searching?"

Kate looked from Dylan to Wes in confusion.

"Dylan's talking about the K9 training demo today." Wes clapped a hand affectionately on his brother's shoulder. "'Live find.' Where volunteers play the roles of being lost or being a rescuer. He helped with that today. Right, buddy? Hiding and searching."

"Oh." Kate smiled, managed to capture Dylan's gaze, the kindness in her expression beautifully obvious. "I wish I'd known. I would have liked to join in."

"Cool." Dylan grinned. "Hiding or searching?"

"I . . . don't know."

*Hiding.* Wes knew it, even if Kate didn't.

"Of course you'll stay for dinner," his mom said as his father followed Matt into the barn. She smiled at Kate. "I'm sure the main dish is fairly obvious. But there's also ranch beans, coleslaw, and Dylan's favorite, creamed corn." She raised her brows. "Buttermilk pie?"

"Oh, I . . ." Kate glanced toward the barn.

"I'm sure Kate and her father have other plans," Wes gambled, certain this one last meddle was something Kate would approve of. "In fact, I was just going to offer to unsaddle Duster and Levi so they could get going, and—"

"We'd love to stay for dinner," Kate said, cutting him off. "Thank you, Miranda."

- + -

Kate made the hasty decision to stay for dinner knowing it would spare her another uncomfortable meal alone with her father. But she hadn't imagined that accepting the invitation would have her bowing her head as Wes's father, Paul, said a simple blessing at an alfresco dinner table. One of her hands had been joined with her father's and the other with Wes's. She felt awkward for a moment, couldn't remember the last time she'd done such a thing. But in truth, it felt natural somehow too. A few thankful words and six lowered heads around a rustic picnic table made country elegant with bleached muslin and a tall jar filled to brimming with flowers: native purple lavender, yellow chrysanthemums, and a reckless spray of burnt-orange berries. It was a comfortable, makeshift dining room under an ancient spreading pecan tree—and a Texas sky gone van Gogh mad with pink and gold. Dining serenaded by the faint chatter of a squirrel, chirping barn swallows, and an occasional contented nicker from a horse eye-deep in sweet alfalfa. Plus the soft whine of a dog named Hershey stationed well within brisket-pitching distance.

The host's thankful prayer was followed instantly by laughter and lively conversation, sprinkled with oohs and aahs over the plates of food, a clatter of eating utensils, and the tinkle of ice cubes in tall glasses of tea. There were distant strains of music from a CD that Kate had come to recognize as George Strait. She didn't think she'd ever again dine anywhere so memorable.

And neither had Kate expected that a small squeeze from her father's fingers would affect her the way it did, sending her heart and mind cartwheeling toward places and times she'd left behind long ago. She swallowed against a sudden lump in her throat, tried to push aside another flood of memories of a smaller table in Sunnyvale, her mother before the cancer, and her father before—

"Brisket?" Wes offered, holding the platter so she could select a piece of the spicy-sweet–scented beef. He cast a brotherly eye at

Dylan across the table. "Cut that meat. I know it's tender, but you still can't eat those slices whole, bud. There you go. Good job."

Kate helped herself to the side dishes, noticing Miranda and Wes giving the occasional direction to Dylan, encouraging him to stay in his chair. To chew his food carefully. From what she'd observed, Kate could tell that the young man had developmental issues. Her respect for the Tanners grew, knowing the loving commitment that challenge required.

"Of course," Paul Tanner was saying, "at Christmas, this house will be bursting at the seams. Second grandbaby due mid-December."

"My sister," Wes explained, holding a forkful of corn in midair. "She and her husband live outside Dallas. He's a podiatrist, prefers bunions to well digging. More than you ever wanted to know, I'm sure."

Kate smiled over her glass of tea. *Better than talking about my family.*

"I'm hoping to have that one day," her father said beside her. "Not bunions—I'd love to have grandchildren."

Kate's breath stuck in her throat. She gripped her glass, certain she'd spill it.

"Any prospects?" Paul asked, then politely amended his question. "I mean, do you have other children besides Kate?"

"No. She's it."

Kate tried to smile, impossible with every eye at the table on her. And the painful guilt of what she'd done making her want to leap from the table and run to the car.

"Dylan? Hey, guy . . . ," Wes said suddenly, alarm in his voice. "Are you—?" He pushed away from the table.

"Oh, dear," Miranda breathed, leaving her chair. "Is he choking?"

"Dylan . . ." Kate set her glass down, eyes riveted on the obviously struggling young man across from her. She forced her voice to remain calm. "Can you talk?" she asked, hearing a faint whistle as he tried to breathe inward.

He shook his head, sucked in again in a futile attempt, his face going from red to dusky blue.

"Cough, Dylan," Wes instructed, standing. "Try to cough."

Hershey barked.

Dylan's eyes grew wide as he stood, his hand circling his throat. Wes and Kate bolted around the table to his side.

"Try one more time to cough," Wes said, his hand on Dylan's shoulder.

"I don't think he can," Kate whispered, protocols tumbling in her brain. "He's obstructed. And he's going to lose consciousness unless—" She shot Wes a look. "You or me?"

"Got it." Wes's face paled a shade.

"Okay, Dylan," Kate reassured as Wes stepped behind his brother. "We're going to help you. Wes is going to grab on to you from behind. Let him do this. It's okay—he's going to help you cough that food out."

She nodded as Wes positioned his hands under his panicking brother's diaphragm. "Good. Thumb side under the rib cage. Quick upward thrust—good. Again." *Oh, please, let this work.* "Another one."

"I've got my cell phone," Kate's father offered, his voice raw with concern. "Give the word and I'll—"

"Again, now." Kate watched Wes's hands and his brother's still-conscious face. "Again, and—"

In a merciful instant, the meat dislodged, popping out like a celebratory cork. Dylan gagged, coughed, and then drew in a deep, ragged breath, his color instantly returning to normal. "I . . .

choked," he sputtered, a tear sliding down his face. He struggled toward a sheepish smile. "I should've . . . chewed better. Sorry."

"You betcha, and . . . ah, come here." Wes pulled Dylan close, hugging him as tears welled in his own eyes.

"Oh, thank God." His mother's relieved cry began a barrage of grateful murmurings. "And thank you, Wes . . . Kate. Oh, thank heaven you were here."

Wes's eyes met Kate's over the top of his brother's head. His expression made her heart ache as he mouthed, *"Thank you."*

- + -

Matt stood with Kate beside her car in the Shady Grove parking lot. Nearly nine and the place was hopping, its sign lit in neon, strings of bulbs over the patio, sounds of laughter and music. He thought of suggesting that they join the crowd again—have a Coke for the road—but knew Kate would say no. For the same reasons she still hadn't suggested he come to her place, even after spending the day together. She wanted to keep him at arm's length. He wanted much more, but arm's length was infinitely closer than what he'd had. He'd take that for now.

"You think Dylan will be okay?" he asked. "No complications from choking on that meat? I can't remember the last time I saw anything so scary." *Except when I found you gone, Katy.*

"He didn't pass out or have any breathing problems afterward." Kate hugged her arms across her chest. "I'm glad they got his doctor on the phone. And Wes plans to stay the night. I think that reassures Miranda."

"Quite a family," Matt said, wondering if Kate had felt it too— a strong regret . . . *that we weren't more like that. Our little family.* He thought of the Tanners at that table, hands linked and heads bowed. If Matt had learned anything in the last year, it was that a person was wrong to think he could make it through life alone. And to believe—through arrogance, fear, self-loathing, or any combination—that he really was alone. No one was alone. The comfort and hope in that beautiful truth still staggered him. All was not lost. He wished he knew how to share his hope with Kate, really change things between them.

"I should go," she said, pulling her car keys from her purse. "You're driving on to Fort Worth in the morning, and I . . ." She shrugged, not quite meeting his gaze. "I should soak in the tub before I go to bed. Don't tell anyone, but my muscles are already complaining."

"Mine too. But it was fun," Matt added, wanting to hold her. Remembering the first time he had. Tiny, squinting, squalling, black hair standing on end—a feisty miracle in a pink blanket. His daughter, his only child. "Today meant a lot to me, Katy." *You mean the world to me.*

"Me too." There was no clue in her voice whether or not that was true.

He stood there watching the neon dance on Kate's hair. Telling himself to let her go, then arguing that he could be in a fatal collision on the way back to the motel, choke on a pork chop in some diner along the interstate. Life was short and uncertain, and—

"Bye, Dad." She stepped close, rose on tiptoe, and kissed his cheek. Then flitted away as quick as firefly light. "Drive safely."

"You too." *I love you. . . . I'm sorry.* "I'll call you when I'm leaving Fort Worth. Maybe I could swing back through Austin on my way home."

"We'll see."

He watched Kate slide into her car, fasten her seat belt. The headlights came on and she drove away.

Matt realized he was holding his breath. He reached into his pocket for his car keys, and his fingers found the AA medallion. He glanced up at the dark Texas sky and nodded. *One day at a time. I hear you, Lord.*

- + -

Kate averted her eyes from the landlord's lit windows as she walked to her porch. The last thing she needed to see was another Hallmark family scene. Especially after leaving her father standing in a parking lot. What kind of daughter did something like that?

She pressed her palm to the shadowed door as the answer intruded, dark and undeniable as those pecan branches over the Tanners' table. *The kind of daughter who abandons her baby.* Her father's statement—*"I'd love to have grandchildren"*—had struck Kate like a physical blow. And confirmed what she'd feared all these years: her father would have welcomed the opportunity to be a grandpa to her son.

She shoved open the door and stepped into the darkened living room, trying to reknit the mesh of anger she counted on to protect her heart. From questions, truths, scars. She asked herself how an emotionally distant and work-obsessed alcoholic could have dealt with a pregnant teenage daughter. A husband who'd worked overtime and slept at the office more than once to avoid a vigil at his dying wife's bedside. And then couldn't be bothered to comfort his grieving daughter after she died. A man who reached for a bottle instead. How long had it taken him to even realize that Kate ran away?

She switched on the kitchen light, checked Roady's food dishes, then turned the flame on under the teakettle. She hugged her arms around herself, thinking of the way the Tanner family bowed their heads around that table. Hands joined . . . *my hand and Daddy's.* An ache spread across Kate's chest despite her armor. Had he felt what she had? That everything missing from their family was right there in the Tanners'? She sighed, remembering the look on Wes's face as he hugged his brother close. Love, faith . . . hope, served up like a sustaining meal. She wasn't sure the Callisons had ever had that. Which made it impossible to understand why she felt the loss of it now. How could she miss something she never had? Something she didn't deserve?

The only thing Kate knew for sure was that an out-of-the-blue road trip and a hill country trail ride weren't going to change things. Her father was gone, and though he'd said otherwise, she doubted he'd come through Austin again. If he did call, she probably wouldn't answer. Their painful history—sealed by Kate's unforgivable mistake—was etched as deeply as Wes Tanner's initials on the side of that barn. It was there to stay. In a week she and her father would be playing phone tag again. She'd send a Thanksgiving e-card. He'd text her from his firm's holiday party. Everything would return to normal as if today never happened. It wouldn't feel good, but at least it wouldn't hurt. Kate smiled ruefully. Like her aching legs.

The kettle whistled and she poured the steaming water over a Sleepytime tea bag. Tea, then a bubble bath. And a plan for something to do tomorrow so that the excuse she made to her father didn't feel like one more lie.

Her cell phone rang on the counter and guilt pricked. It had to be her father.

But it wasn't. Her stomach did a ridiculous quiver.

"Wes." She glanced at the time display. Nine thirty. They'd exchanged phone numbers in case there was anything to report about his brother. It seemed only natural after they'd teamed up for his rescue. "Is Dylan okay?"

"Better than okay." Wes chuckled, despite the fatigue in his voice. "Mom gave permission for Hershey to sleep in his room. Which means I get to listen to that skunk chaser snore. I'm assigned to the other twin bed."

Kate smiled, easily imagining it. "I'm glad you're there."

Wes was quiet for a moment. "I'm glad you were here."

"I didn't really do anything."

"You kept my brother calm. Not easy. And kept me thinking straight too. Training, protocols—it feels different when it's personal. Anyway, I wanted you to know how much it meant, Kate."

"Your mother thanked me. Over and over. And I have a huge slice of buttermilk pie wrapped in foil."

"I meant *I* want to thank you," Wes insisted. "Your father said you had plans for tomorrow."

She winced, tried to think of something to say, but Wes continued.

"After church, I'm going to the hospital to see Gabe. But if you're free in the afternoon, I thought maybe we could—"

"Wait." She laughed despite an uptick in her pulse. "If you're about to offer me Duster again, I'll have to beg off. I wasn't going to admit it, but I'm not sure I'll be able to sit down tomorrow, let alone ride."

"No worries, not riding," he said, voice rumbling with obvious amusement. "I can do civilized things too. I thought we could walk around South Congress, visit the galleries, catch some music. Maybe find a good place to eat. It's too late for the bat boats, but—"

"Excuse me?"

"Bat boats. They take tourists along Lady Bird Lake to see the free-tailed Mexican bats. One and a half million of them nest under the Congress bridge." Something in Wes's voice made Kate think of Dylan eagerly sharing the information on the K9 training. "Austin has the largest urban bat colony in the world. People come from everywhere to watch them at sunset. You never heard about that?"

"No," she told him, tempted to say she was still getting used to the idea of Texas-shaped tortilla chips. "But I'll take your word for it." Kate was surprised to hear herself add, "And all I have planned for tomorrow afternoon is paperwork. Staff schedules, budget reports, and legal papers to review. Sounds like fun, right?"

"No. So will you let me—?"

"You're not going to use the *rescue* word, are you?"

"Never gave it a thought. Pick you up around three?"

"Uh . . ." Kate hesitated, unsure. The only thing she had in common with Wes Tanner was a choking incident. Spending an afternoon with him made as much sense as saying yes to the visit from her father. And climbing onto that horse. Both had hurt.

"Sure," Kate told him despite frantic, whispered warnings in her head. "I'll give you the address."

**11**

+

**JUDITH USED A PAPER TOWEL** to scoop the remains of an Egg McMuffin from the floor—Sunday brunch in the ER. She surveyed the waiting room. Seventeen people signed in. The elderly woman in an elaborate hat was the only potentially serious case. Indigestion at church, "reflux problems." Judith knew from her reading that female heart attack symptoms often presented differently than men's. Subtle, but equally worrisome. This gracious and apologetic lady told the triage nurse her discomfort was gone, but Judith would keep an eye on her. ERs were busier on weekends and staff often ran thin, increasing the waiting times. And the risk of dangerous error. Yesterday's incident at the Northside ER more than proved that.

Judith caught a glimpse of a familiar face outside the ER doors. Trista with baby Harley. On a Sunday?

"Trista?" she called as the door whooshed open. "Is the baby having troubles?"

"No, no," the young mother said breathlessly, shifting the weight of the baby's carrier in her arms. "I'm going to the pharmacy. I forgot to pick up Dad's prescription on Friday. He needs it." Her teeth pinned her lower lip.

"I'm glad it's not the baby," Judith told her, then noticed a swollen and discolored area along Trista's cheekbone. "Ouch. Is that a bruise, dear?"

"Huh? Oh, this." Trista touched her cheek. "Tripped over the dog. It doesn't hurt. . . . I should go. Dad really needs his medicine." Her brows lifted. "Do you think you could watch Harley for a few minutes while I get it? I'll be real fast."

"I'd be delighted."

"I'll hurry," Trista promised, relief in her expression as she handed over the sleeping baby's car seat.

"Take your time. She's fine here." Judith watched the woman make a beeline for the main entrance, realizing she'd forgotten to ask if Trista received her e-mail with the photos Judith had taken a few days ago. The day the young mother admitted she had no recent pictures of her baby because her phone camera did a poor job and she didn't own a regular camera. No photos. Hard to imagine. Judith thought of the multiple thick albums dedicated to her daughter Molly's first year. How much money had her husband spent on rolls of film? They'd been impatient waiting for even the one-hour prints. But then Trista was a single mother, and—

"Hi, Judith." Lauren Barclay started to pass by but did a double-take as she looked at the infant. "Is that Harley?"

"Sure is."

"What on earth . . . ?" Lauren glanced around, then back at Judith. "Did she lose her mother again?"

- + -

"It's Stevie Ray Vaughan." Kate blinked at the enormous bronze statue of the famous Dallas-born musician. Hat, poncho, electric guitar, bouquets of fresh flowers strewn around his heavy sculpted boots. On the lawn nearby, a young man in a frayed jean vest and a knit cap picked a battered guitar in fame's shadow. A woman nursed her baby beside him, her eyes closed and face lifted toward the afternoon sun.

"Quite a statue." Kate rested her shoe on the low stone wall, felt an immediate twinge in her thigh, and lowered it again. She glanced sideways at Wes, dressed Austin casual in faded Levi's and a tan chino shirt. "And tribute to a legend."

"You like blues guitar?" He raised his voice over excited barking from the nearby dog area. Then stepped aside, making room for a trio of joggers.

"My father, mostly. Huge fan." Kate scanned the Austin skyline across Lady Bird Lake: the upscale residential Austonian tower, waterfront hotels, and the crystal crown facade of the clock-embedded Frost Bank skyscraper, constructed of blue low-E glass. It was a stunning panorama of both historic and edgy architecture, made front-porch welcoming by a profusion of greenbelts and parks. She clucked her tongue, turned to Wes. "I cut my teeth on Stevie Ray. 'Pride and Joy'—Dad and I played a mean air-guitar duet to that one." Kate mimed an impressive stringed crescendo to prove it. "See?"

Wes laughed. "I can imagine the two of you. Matt seems like . . . a great guy."

Kate noticed that he sounded tentative, careful. The way he'd been when he picked her up today—making very few remarks about the leased house, mentioning only its proximity to great eateries like Chuy's and Shady Grove and to Zilker Park. He'd said nothing about her remaining unpacked boxes and the bare fireplace mantel that all but begged for family photos. He hadn't even questioned why Roady—amazingly present—had only a pathetic stump of a tail. Wes made none of the personal observations Kate had dreaded. Probably because of her trail ride remark about meddling or maybe for the same reason folks hesitated to ask the source of a dubious black eye. Fear of intruding, finding out more than they really wanted to know. What if Wes knew she'd taken the previous tenant's cross from the wall and banished it to the closet? *Or that I've done far worse things?*

"Right," Kate agreed at last. "Dad can be sort of cool."

She drew in a breath of autumn-scented air, reassuring herself that this unexpected day offered a respite from all pressures: memories stirred by her father's visit, work, and the frustrating uncertainty of the upcoming performance review. She looked forward to exploring Austin despite the fact that she'd awakened miserably saddle sore, inches from embarrassingly bowlegged. Pulling on jeans had been torture, stretching her short legs to scale Wes's mountain of a truck a Herculean feat. She'd had to tilt sideways on the drive to spare her aching backside.

"I'm enjoying this," Kate said, surprising herself more than a little. But it was true. And simple. She was here because Wes wanted to thank her for helping his brother and because she needed a day off. Past relationship mistakes had no bearing on today. As long as Kate stuck to the plan of keeping Wes Tanner physically and emotionally at a safe distance.

"Good. I'm glad. And I'm starving. I know some great places where you can eat without having to sit down." His grin crinkled his eyes. "Not that I noticed anything, cowgirl."

Before Kate could think of a comeback, Wes's hand found hers. Strong, sure, warm. She thought about sliding hers away, but this unexpected connection felt too good. Just for now, these few minutes. Even if it meant her plan for keeping him at a distance had shortened by a few risky inches.

- + -

Lauren glanced across the visitors' table and reminded herself that even on lunch break she was still a peer counselor. Right now that meant hearing an employee vent about her friend Kate Callison. This triage nurse wasn't mincing words.

"That's why you didn't come to the debriefing?" Lauren asked. "Because Kate was there?"

"Mostly." Dana sighed, pushing her sandwich away. "I don't understand why she went anyway. Albert said she didn't share anything and that she skipped out halfway through." She pressed her fingers to her brow. "She's been powwowing with the hospital legal department. Everyone knows that. And believe me, nobody's happy about it."

Lauren chose her words. "Kate came to the debriefing because she was part of the incident with Baby Doe." She saw Dana's eyes widen at the mention of the dead infant. "And because she wanted to show support for her team. That kind of tragedy affects us all." Lauren waited. *Don't push . . .*

"I couldn't face triage today. They still don't know if that mother came through our department." Dana breathed through her nose, exhaled. "Did you read the article in the *Statesman*? The comments from that Waiting for Compassion person?"

"After the Baby Doe incident?"

"Yes." Dana squeezed her eyes shut for a moment. "I know he was pointing a finger at me. Saying I'm responsible for letting that baby die."

Lauren knew it would do no good to tell this nurse it wasn't so. Or to point out that another waiting room vigilante letter had surfaced online today, about another ER across town—or at least that was the hint. This was an ongoing agenda. Not aimed at any one specific person. But she doubted Dana would believe that right now. "That letter must have made you feel really bad."

Dana's eyes shone with sudden tears. "I became a nurse because I care. I know that sounds corny, but it's true. I've always tried my best. But it's getting harder all the time. Sicker people, fewer staff, more regulations and compliance requirements that pull time from patient care. All that computer time required for records . . . I'm not telling you anything you don't know." She swiped at a tear before it could fall. "I keep going over that night in my mind. Wondering if I missed something in the waiting room, asking myself if there was some way I could have stopped what happened. It was a horrible shift. I tried to tell Kate what it was like . . ."

"And?"

"She didn't want to hear it." Dana's lips compressed. "Talk about no compassion."

Lauren winced. "I sometimes think of things I wish I'd said in certain situations. If you could do that meeting over again, what would you want to say to Kate?"

"I don't know. Maybe . . ." Dana's chest heaved in a sigh. "I'd just ask her if she's ever made a mistake in her life."

- + -

Wes watched with amusement as Kate devoured her meal. Or tried to. "How you doin' with your first taste of SoCo trailer food?"

"Ah . . ." Her expression was a comic mix of bliss and frustration. Coleslaw dribbled from a tortilla stuffed with chicken and fried avocado and shoved sideways into a paper snow-cone cup. She brushed at a sprinkle of crumbs on her clingy navy-blue cardigan. "This is fabulous. The chicken's coated in sesame seeds, almonds, cornflakes, and . . . chili powder, I think." She raised her voice to compete with a boisterous group of college students at a nearby table and lively bluegrass fiddling from somewhere across the street. "Messy, but incredible."

"And merciful." Wes pointed at the rails along the large mobile food cart, providing holes to hold the cones for diners who preferred to stand. "I kept my promise."

The Mighty Cone, one of many trendy food carts on South Congress, also offered red-painted picnic tables and strings of globe bulbs to add light and romance to a gravel parking lot with construction zone ambience. Upscale food, no frills. He'd gotten a kick out of seeing Kate's reaction to the fleet of carts and trailers boasting names like Wurst Tex, Coat and Thai, and Austin Frigid Frog. And the girlish delight on her face when she spotted Hey Cupcake!, a shiny aluminum Airstream with a huge pink cupcake hoisted atop. Kate had nearly squealed; apparently pink frosting was a counterbalance to her natural tendency toward prickly. Wes was determined to find more ways to make that happen.

"It's hard to believe—" Kate dabbed her lips with a napkin— "that this craziness is all within walking distance of that impressive state capitol building." She glanced toward the street, where lights and neon signs began to preen in the deepening dusk.

"That's Austin. Politics, arts, film, music—opera to Dixie Chicks—technology, business, ecology." Wes shrugged. "Weird. And determined to stay that way." He finished off the last of his venison cone dog.

"Austin has the university too." Kate nodded toward the table of students.

"UT. Got my degree there." Wes wiped his fingers. "Interesting that your father's also an engineer."

He doubted pink frosting would ease the immediate discomfort in Kate's eyes.

She was quiet for a moment, fanfolding her napkin and smoothing it out again. "I guess you could tell Dad and I aren't close. He was obsessed with work when I was a kid. Gone a lot." Kate dredged up a meager smile. "Except for the dude ranch vacations." She glanced down at the napkin again. "When my mother got sick with cancer, he started drinking a lot. So even when Dad was there, he wasn't really . . . *there*. Then she died and it was just the two of us. In this oppressive silence." Her eyes were huge in the dwindling light. "You probably can't imagine that. Not with your family."

*I can.* Wes wanted to tell Kate he'd lived it. In those long months after his mother drove into the river. During a search that seemed endless . . . hopeless. All those nights he pretended to be sleeping and heard his father choking on grief. Wes wanted to say he understood that wounded silence. But he couldn't think of a way to begin.

"Anyway," Kate continued, "I do appreciate your helping me entertain him yesterday. I know I gave you a hard time about that trail ride." She shifted her hips, grimaced. "But you more than got your revenge, I'd say."

She smiled, the string lights reflecting in her eyes. Wes was grateful; the earlier sadness had him fighting an urge to put his arms around her. Hold her close and offer any comfort he could. She wouldn't welcome his attempt even if she needed it badly. "Dylan made me promise to tell you hello. And to say he thinks you're really pretty."

Kate laughed; then her expression grew thoughtful. "Is he on the spectrum? For autism?"

"Yes. Mom and Dad have worked really hard for years, made sure he got every possible kind of help. Dylan's made huge strides considering that he wasn't diagnosed until he was four. After he came to live with us." Wes read the confusion on Kate's face. "He's adopted. So is my sister." He realized he'd backed himself into a corner, regardless of his earlier hesitation. "Miranda is my step-mother. My mother was killed in an accident when I was seven." The empathy in Kate's expression touched him. "Anyway, Miranda discovered she couldn't have children. So they decided to adopt." Wes smiled. "And foster. We had fourteen foster kids through that house before I moved out. More afterward. The patter of little feet in Justin boots." He shook his head. "If our Baby Doe had lived, he probably would have found his way to the Tanner ranch."

Wes wasn't sure in the fading light, but it looked as if Kate's face had gone pale.

- + -

Kate made herself smile. "That explains why no one looks like anyone in your family. Except your father. You look just like him." She was grateful the daylight had gone and was relieved to hear the growing swell of music beckoning from doorways along South Congress. She didn't want Wes to see her face, hear the ache in her voice. Or ever discover the ugly irony: his family rescued babies . . . *and I abandoned mine.* This man had gone to church with his family this morning. While she had a cross hidden away in her closet. Kate and Wes Tanner couldn't be more different. Why was she here with him?

"Kate?" Wes leaned closer, the strings of lights illuminating his face. "You okay?"

"Fine." She scurried to change the subject. "So you went to UT Austin?"

"Yep."

"Longhorns." She raised her fist, waggled her thumb and pinky in an enthusiastic UT hand sign.

"Um . . ." Wes appeared to be struggling against a burst of laughter. Someone at a nearby table hooted. "What's that supposed to be?"

"Hook 'em horns." Kate lowered her hand a fraction. Shot him a *duh* look.

"That is 'hang loose' in Hawaiian." He gently repositioned her fingers, the warmth of his skin sending tingles clear to her shoulder. "This is hook 'em horns."

"Oh." She met Wes's gaze, far too aware that he hadn't let go. And that the foolish tingling had reached her ear.

"Are you finished with your chicken cone?" he asked, barely above a whisper.

"Mmm . . . yeah."

"Good." Wes captured her hand and gave it a tug. "Then let's find some music. But no ukuleles, aloha girl."

# 12

**IT HADN'T TAKEN WES LONG TO REALIZE** that Austin's historic Sixth Street music epicenter—Antone's, The Parish, Emo's, The Continental Club, even Stubb's Bar-B-Q—wasn't going to work for his "let's find some music" impulse. Too loud, too crowded, too . . . not Kate Callison. Despite a bass-heavy atmosphere reverberating with excitement and Kate's own memorable history with air guitar, she hadn't looked at all comfortable there. Not to mention there was no place to sit that didn't require shouting like a cattle auctioneer in order to talk. It didn't fit what he had in mind. Wes had caught a glimpse of Kate behind her prickly exterior and he wanted more. He was eager to know who she was apart from being a nurse. And he wanted her to know him beyond his involvement in search and rescue. Kate Callison and Wes Tanner getting to know each other in a do-over. Far removed from the regrettable way they'd first met. Maybe this place . . .

Wes watched as Kate enjoyed the panoramic vista from the coffeehouse's huge lower deck; the tree branches overhead were already strung with the first thousand lights of what would be an incredible annual holiday display. A view of Lake Austin, air rich with the aroma of roasting beans, tabletop candles, a three-man combo offering a "smooth gospel" blend of acoustic guitar, flute, and drums. Yeah, Wes finally hit it right. Especially because—

"Heaven." Kate's tongue caught a smudge of pink frosting on her lower lip. "A genuine Hey Cupcake! I've been craving one of these since I saw that Airstream trailer. And this—" she glanced at the hills and water again—"is wonderful. Austin is so different from San Antonio, all these lakes and greenbelts and parks." She shook her head. "It's funny; people always think of Texas as flat and dry. I sure did. Not that it's the Sierra mountains, but there's some fairly rugged terrain here." She reached for her coffee. "Which I'm sure you've seen on searches."

"Yes." *So much for who I am apart from search and rescue.* He chewed the last bite of his chocolate cookie. "Swift water, canyons, vast tracts of cedar, and—" Wes grimaced—"cactus. Up close and far too personal. But a fair amount of our callouts involve urban searches for missing children and adults. Door to door and in parks." He frowned. "I volunteer with Travis County Search and Rescue, too. They're a much bigger organization, very involved in the search for Sunni Sprague. Her car was abandoned not far from Zilker Park."

"Zilker?" Kate's eyes widened. "I live within walking distance of there."

"Right." Wes kicked himself. *Cupcakes and crime. Smooth, Tanner.* "We searched it several times. Hasty search, K9, grid . . . nothing. Then searched up and down Barton Creek, Shoal Creek Greenbelt, and along the adjacent Colorado."

"Do you think there really is new information coming on her case?"

"Maybe." Wes thought of his visit to Gabe this morning and how convinced his friend was that a search for evidence would begin soon. "But tips from inmates are notoriously misleading. I heard this one's secondhand, from a guy with a serious drug history."

Kate folded her cupcake paper into a square. "I'll bet my staff will trample themselves to volunteer if there *is* a search. You heard them at the debriefing."

"Yes." He knew he should probably stop there. "A few of them joined in when she first went missing. But if there's anything to uncover now, it would be—"

"Remains," Kate said, wincing. "Oh, horrible. Still, I suppose even that would provide some closure."

"Yes," Wes agreed, thinking once again that *closure* was such a poor word. Finding his mother's body after that long year hadn't really brought a close to the pain of losing her. *Or the questions I still have.* "Finding someone alive is what we all hope for. Locating a body or identifiable remains is at least something. A find. But when you search and search and there's nothing—" he shook his head—"it's like leaving someone lost."

"Did you know Sunni?"

"A little. She was on duty when Dylan broke his wrist last year; she stayed over into the next shift to sit with him while it got casted. I talked with her a few times when I followed ambulances in." He shrugged. "I didn't know her that well. But it was still a shock when she went missing. Everyone felt it."

"I could see that from the first day I was hired. Impossible shoes to fill."

Wes thought of the debriefing. Kate choosing to sit apart from her team. "You haven't been there long. Give it time." He regretted the platitude even before she frowned.

"Unfortunately I don't have that luxury." Kate flicked the cupcake wrapper with her fingertip. "My performance review is coming up. I can hear the Munchkins chanting, 'Ding-dong, the witch is—'" She grimaced. "Considering what we just talked about, I suppose that remark proves I'm a poor choice for emergency department director." She summoned a rueful smile that did nothing to dispel the hurt in her beautiful eyes.

"C'mon," Wes said, standing. He held out his hand. "People are dancing. Help me pretend I know how."

- + -

Before Kate could think of an excuse, she was in Wes's arms. Confirming something that until this moment she hadn't realized she'd wondered about: *We fit perfectly.* His height, her lack of it, didn't matter at all. Slow-strumming guitar, light-strung deck, night air. And one of Wes's hands against her back, the other holding hers. They were close enough that Kate could smell the soap-fresh scent of his skin, feel the solid muscles of his shoulder under her palm. And that warmth . . . The earlier unexpected tingle multiplied a hundred times.

"How am I doing?" he asked, dipping his head closer. "I get far more practice with drill rigs, water pipes, and windmills." His chuckle warmed her ear. "Bad enough to be sore from riding without the risk of stepped-on toes."

"So far so good," Kate managed to say as he drew her closer. *Way too good.* She tried not to think about the last time she'd danced. What a fool she'd been and how badly it had all ended. Right now she needed to think that this dance, this man, could be different.

She wanted the slate wiped clean, if only for tonight. She wanted to believe in honest blue eyes, in the magic of a pink cupcake, and—

"Careful there," Wes said, guiding her a little sideways on the darkened deck. "Raccoon."

"What?" She stepped away from him, warmth replaced by confusion. A woman dancing next to them squealed. Kate stared down at the deck. "Where?"

"There." Wes pointed, raising his voice as a dog on the pet-friendly deck began to bark. "Under the table now. I think he has your cupcake paper."

"Really?" Kate shook her head and then laughed out loud. Magical cupcakes? Tingling insanity was more like it. When Wes slid his arm from her waist, she'd be rational again. The raccoon had disappeared into the darkness; the dance was over.

"Grab your purse," he said, taking her hand. "It's getting crowded here. I know where we can walk along the lake."

Walk? It was the right time to say something about ending the evening, needing to work on the department budget before tomorrow, check on her cat. Still . . . "I suppose that's part of the whole thing. Lakes . . . 'Got Water?'"

"Absolutely." Wes's smile crinkled his eyes. "Family crest."

*So* . . . Roady cat wouldn't be home. The paperwork could wait. Kate wanted to pretend just a little longer. Believe things could be this simple, warm . . . safe. Tomorrow's reality would always be there, eager to steal happiness as fast as that raccoon grabbed her cupcake paper.

"Okay," she said, smiling at him. "Let's go for a walk."

- + -

Lauren cradled the phone, tucking her knees up under her fleece bathrobe. "You didn't meet the family for brunch either?"

"Forgot." Jessica's tone was 180 degrees from yesterday, slow and sluggish. "I needed sleep. Like that Rip van Winkle guy. Except twenty years isn't long enough. And—" she yawned—"impossible with all the noise in this apartment complex. Someone always running up and down the stairs, moving furniture, playing music too loud."

*Careful.* "Maybe," Lauren suggested, twisting a length of her shower-damp hair, "that would be easier at Mom and Dad's. No neighbors coming and going or—"

"No."

Lauren knew to back off. If things sounded worse, she'd have to consider calling Eli. Like it or not, he usually knew what was going on in Jess's life.

Lauren fought a familiar, uncomfortable confusion. Talking to Eli Landry was the last thing she wanted.

No. The last thing Lauren wanted was for her sister to have serious problems. *Please, Lord, don't let that be true. . . .*

"Gotta go," Jessica told her.

"Okay. Text me tomorrow from school?" Lauren held her breath.

"Sure. Fine."

"I love you."

"Mm-hmm . . ."

Lauren disconnected, held the phone to her chest, weighing actions she could take. And the problems each could cause. Take a day off work, drive to Houston. Risk that her sister would use the intrusion as an excuse to disappear again? Not good. Maybe—

The phone buzzed against her chest. *Thank you, God.* But it wasn't Jess. She didn't recognize the number.

"Hello?" Lauren asked tentatively.

"Hello, Lauren. Barrett Lyon—sorry to disturb you."

"Is there some problem?"

"A concern, perhaps. I wanted to run it by you."

Lauren didn't like the sound of this.

"I've had the opportunity to view the hospital security tapes," he explained. "The police retrieved them the day of the Baby Doe incident. You were aware of that?"

"I heard about it." *What on earth?*

"You had coffee with Kate Callison before your shift that day." It wasn't a question.

"Yes, sure. We do that a lot." Lauren's stomach went queasy.

"Before you sat down with her, do you remember seeing her in conversation with anyone?"

"No." Lauren's memory tumbled, her caution increasing. "It was still dark. What's this about?"

"A police question, which naturally causes me some concern as well. The security tape shows Kate talking with someone outside the doors to the emergency department. A young woman."

"They think . . . ?" She bit off the thought. Prayed he hadn't heard.

"Think what?"

"Nothing."

She heard him sigh. "Lauren, I need to know. Did Kate tell you she might have spoken to the mother who abandoned Baby Doe?"

- + -

"Seven," Wes said, answering Kate's question as they walked the shoreline trail. "Seven Highland Lakes, reservoirs formed by dams along the Colorado River. Starting eighty-some miles north of here. Lake Buchanan, Inks, LBJ, Marble Falls . . ." He chuckled. "Sorry. Nothing as dry as an engineer tour guide. Don't let me bore you."

"Not bored." Kate stepped off the trail to walk closer to the water. The scant moonlight danced over her dark hair in shades as blue as her sweater.

"Look," Wes said, catching up with her at the water's edge, "I didn't mean to sound like I was blowing you off earlier when we were talking about you taking over as director. I'm sorry if I did. You're seriously concerned about that performance review?"

"I wish I weren't. But I stepped into trouble with both feet from the very first day I started at Austin Grace. One of the nurses backed over someone in the parking lot, I had to suspend another for drugs, there's been all those awful Waiting for Compassion letters in the paper . . . and now this incident with the baby. I don't know how I'm ever supposed to win the support of my staff if I'm constantly joined at the hip to the legal department." She sighed. "I hate it."

"I'm not too impressed with lawyers myself." Wes frowned, picked up a rock, and hurled it toward the water. "There was a high-profile murder case in Dallas last spring. The body was found after a long search." He shook his head, remembering. "A defense attorney tore one of the search-and-rescue volunteers apart on the witness stand. Accused him of destroying evidence and tried to convince the jury that he joined the search to gain some sort of personal glory. It wasn't my team, but that sort of thing filters down." Wes chucked a second rock. "People don't realize the time, effort, and expense members go through to become volunteers. Extensive training, time away from their families. Money out of their pockets with no compensation. All of that because they care about their communities. They step up, do something to help. And then get ambushed by some attack-dog attorney."

Kate sighed. "Now I'm really not looking forward to meeting with Barrett Lyon again."

"No worries. His job is to protect the hospital."

"Plenty of worries," Kate corrected. "He represents the hospital first and foremost. Individual employees not so much." Anxiety flickered across her face. "A lot depends on what the police discover in the investigation." Her shoulders sagged. "I wish it could all go away. I'm . . . so tired."

Wes wanted to put his arms around her but made himself stay back. He was amazed she'd shared this much; no way was he going to risk looking like he was trying to rescue this dedicated and competent woman. Her worries were professional, not personal.

Kate was quiet for a long time, her eyes scanning the lights dotting the shore. A boat, passengers laughing, chugged across the dark water in the distance. When she turned toward him again, her expression was somber. "Your mother died in an accident?"

It caught him unaware. He took a breath, exhaled slowly. "She drowned. Her car went into the river. Record rainfall that year, flooding, and multiple deaths at low-water crossings. They searched for a long time. Finally found her body after nearly a year."

"Oh . . ." Kate's eyes were huge in the pale light. "You were seven?"

Wes nodded. He had no idea the last time he'd really talked about this. Didn't want to now.

"How . . . ?" She stepped closer. "How did you get through it?"

He should have continued with the Highland Lakes travelogue.

"I'm sorry." Kate touched his arm. "I shouldn't have asked that."

"No," Wes said quickly. "It's just nobody's asked that—it's been a long time. But after it happened, I prayed a lot." Somehow he expected the discomfort he saw on her face. "I kept telling myself that no matter what had happened, God wanted the best for me. And whenever I felt lost, he'd be there to find me."

"You honestly believe that? Even now?"

Wes nodded. "It's hard sometimes. Especially when so many things can't be explained. Like the other day. With that baby in the ER."

Kate shut her eyes, lashes inky dark against moonlit skin. The pain on her face made him wish he could take the words back.

"Kate . . ." Wes stepped closer.

"One of the churches is going to have a service, then bury him whenever the medical examiner finally releases the body." She shook her head. "And there was this other woman . . . standing on a busy corner near the hospital. Holding up a sign with a picture of her baby. She was asking for money for—"

"A funeral," Wes finished, wanting to spare her having to say it. "I saw her too."

"Lauren heard that she was visiting from out of state when the baby got sick." Kate sighed. "I don't understand how you can still trust God after those kinds of things. I used to, I think. But after my mother . . . and how things were with my father, and then . . ." Kate stared at Wes, her dark eyes as grief-stricken as they'd looked when she held Baby Doe. "I admire your faith. All that you have with your family. That must feel good, believing you'll never be 'lost.' But I can't see ever having that kind of hope. I'm not the kind of person that God—" She stopped, shivered.

In an instant he was holding her. She didn't resist but began to tremble painfully. He tightened his arms around her. "It's okay."

"I'm not crying," she insisted, her lips moving against the hollow of his neck. "I don't do that. Ever."

"I don't care if you are or aren't . . . whether you do or don't," he whispered against her hair. "I'm just holding you, Kate. Until you tell me to let go. I'm just here."

Her arms wound around him, small palms warm against his back. Her lashes brushed his skin, butterfly soft. "I think . . . I'm tired. That's all."

Tired of going it alone, Wes suspected, thinking of that house she leased. So empty. As if it was only a temporary perch and at any moment she'd fly away.

They stood there for a few moments in silence.

"I'm fine now," Kate said finally, slipping from his arms and taking her soft warmth away. "I'm sorry about that."

"Nothing to be sorry about." He watched as she sifted her hair through her fingers, squared her shoulders. As if she were brushing away, distancing herself from the baby funerals and the emotion she'd felt. *Distancing herself from me, too?*

Kate managed to scrounge up a smile and a shrug. "I always react that way to cupcakes. Allergic—I should carry an EpiPen."

*Right.* Wes shook his head. Then took a risk. He bent down, kissed her cheek.

"Um . . ." Kate's eyes were luminous. "What's that for?"

"A thank-you," he said, taking her hand. "Safer than a cupcake, I hope. Thank you for what you did for Dylan yesterday." He squeezed her fingers gently. "And for agreeing to spend the day with me."

"I'm glad I did. On both counts." Kate made no effort to slide her hand away. "And . . . thank you, Wes. Despite my embarrassing allergy, you've been nothing but kind. And honest. I appreciate that."

"You do?"

"Of course." Something in her expression—a surprising, approachable softness—gave him courage.

"Good." Wes reached out and touched his fingertips to the side of her face. "I'd like to be honest again. Okay?"

- + -

Kate's stomach betrayed her in a foolish dip. "Okay."

Wes's fingers traced her jaw, light and impossibly warm. The blue eyes held hers. "I want to kiss you again," he said, his voice deep, certain. "But not like a brother this time."

She wasn't sure if she indicated aloud that she was okay with the idea or merely thought it. She wasn't certain she nodded. She meant to. But before Kate could give it another thought, Wes's hands were cradling her face. His lips touched the corner of hers. A gentle brush warmed by a sigh. Her pulse skittered.

He leaned back a few inches, smiled at her. "You're amazing, Kate. Smart, tough when you have to be . . . funny, caring." His thumb stroked her cheek. "Beautiful."

She couldn't speak. Wasn't even sure she was breathing as Wes bent low and covered her mouth with his own.

His lips were warm and tasted of coffee and chocolate, the kiss somehow tender and profoundly dizzying at the same time. That he'd comforted her only moments ago made it all the sweeter. Her practical mind tried its best to wave a red flag, whisper caution, but that time was past. The moment was here. All Kate could do was close her eyes, hold on tight, and hope her legs wouldn't give way as she returned the unexpected kiss as best she could.

# 13

"**TRAILER FOOD?** You couldn't do better than that?" Gabe set the brake on his wheelchair. It was clear Wes's account—an edited version—of yesterday's outing with Kate was far better than hospital entertainment. "She's from California. Probably knows ol' Wolfgang personally."

"Wolfgang?"

"Wolfgang Puck. Famous LA chef—don't you watch the Food Network?"

"Not if I can help it. You *do*?"

Gabe grinned. "Mom. At the funeral home. Unless there's a visitation or viewing. Then it's Wolfgang Mozart."

"Yeah, well . . ." Wes pointed at his friend's leg, extended straight out from the hip in the wheelchair. "If you don't pull that robe closed, there'll be an unfortunate viewing right here." He laughed at Gabe's immediate scramble for modesty. "When are they springing you from this place?"

"Maybe tomorrow. Don't change the subject. You were telling me about this date."

Wes frowned. "It wasn't a date. I told you, I was thanking Kate for what she did to help Dylan."

"Nice try, Tanner. I got *shot*—I don't see you offering the Hey Cupcake! tour to my trauma surgeon." He raised his brows. "So?"

"I . . . don't know," Wes admitted. It had been a long time since he'd taken serious interest in any woman. "I get the feeling Kate's kind of a loner. And that she might not stick around long." He was surprised by the sudden thought, more so by the immediate discomfort it created. He hoped he was wrong. "The only 'dates' I've got planned are taking Dylan to the movies and Clementine out for training."

"How is Clem?"

"Fine. Bored as you are. I thought I should take her down to the Braxtons', though. Make her walk around that grove and near the trailer. Replace bad memories with good ones." For some reason Wes thought of Kate, talking about her mother's death. Her father's absence. Her loss of faith? Bad memories.

"The trailer still there?" Gabe asked.

"Empty."

Gabe's brows drew together, and it occurred to Wes that Clementine wasn't the only victim in that scenario who needed to replace bad memories with good ones.

Then Gabe's face lit with a grin. "You should take Kate with you."

"Where?"

"On your trail ride around Miss Nancy Rae's property. You said she can ride. So I'm thinking . . ."

"You think too much. I'll get Clem out there, maybe take Hershey with me. He won't talk my head off like you do." Wes tried to make his shrug nonchalant. "I doubt I could get Kate back on a horse. Besides, she works."

"Right downstairs." Gabe pointed over his propped leg in the direction of the elevators.

Wes narrowed his eyes. "Don't you have some cooking show to watch?"

"She's two floors down."

The truth was that Wes hadn't even talked to Kate yet. He'd sent a casual "Good morning" text from the barn while working on a pump motor, leaving a grease smudge on the keypad, then realized it was barely 7 a.m. So much for casual. He managed to avoid his parents' curious glances but caught his mom's barely concealed smile when Dylan asked him point-blank over a spoonful of Scottish oats, "Did you remember to tell Kate I think she's pretty?" His family was as interested as Gabe, but . . .

Wes hadn't called Kate because he wasn't sure what to say after last night. It had been only one kiss—a great one—followed by a somewhat-awkward walk back to his truck. They'd managed to fill the ride to Kate's place with a steady stream of disconnected conversation. Music, football, Pacific beaches vs. Gulf beaches, and crazy discourses on Texas-shaped tortilla chips and the nocturnal behavior of armadillos. Everything but the obvious: *We just kissed. Where do things go from here?*

She didn't invite him in; he didn't ask. She said she didn't need him to walk her to the door; he didn't press. And that was it. Except for the part where he lay awake rethinking it all.

"Wes?"

"Huh?"

Gabe was staring up at him. "Downstairs. It says *Emergency* in red letters. Can't miss it."

- + -

"He grabbed that cupcake paper right off the tablecloth." Kate demonstrated, swiping her hand across the visitors' table. "And then scurried underneath. I didn't actually see it. It was dark, and I was . . ." Her face warmed. "What?" she asked, watching Lauren's mouth sag open. "You've never seen a raccoon?"

"I'm still stuck at the part where you said, 'I went out with Wes Tanner yesterday.' Adding a masked rodent didn't faze me at all."

"No," Kate said as casually as she could, considering that she'd just noticed what looked like Wes's truck parked toward the rear of the lot, near the medical offices. "I don't think raccoons are rodents."

"I didn't think you liked Wes."

Kate opened her mouth. Closed it.

"Mmm. That's interesting." Lauren smiled. "Kate Callison speechless."

"No. Really, I'm . . ." Kate tugged at her wispy hairline. "I don't know how to explain it. Wes helped me with my father. I offered help when his brother choked on the brisket. It was more like mutual aid. We helped each other; we were grateful. Liking Wes Tanner—or not—doesn't fit anywhere."

"Ah . . ."

Kate rolled her eyes. "Don't do that to me. The whole peer counselor 'ah' thing. Where you sit there and 'actively listen' and I offer up deep emotion. It won't work." She glanced toward the parking lot again and saw two women in scrubs pushing a man in a wheelchair from the clinic toward the hospital. "I told you I'm not good with relationships. Meaning good relationships don't happen with *me*. Far from it. I have this ugly magnetic pull for the bad ones."

"The contractor in San Antonio?"

"Right." Kate wished he were the only one. Or even the worst.

"But Wes isn't like that," Lauren offered. "I think he's more the what-you-see-is-what-you-get type." She was quiet for a moment, then met Kate's gaze. "How do you see him?"

"Wes?" Kate's pulse quickened at the memory of the unexpected kiss. "Close to family, protective. Easygoing. Funny sometimes. Sort of solidly rooted, I guess. Religious." Her stomach sank with lead-heavy truth. "He's the exact opposite of me."

"I think you're selling yourself short."

"Oh yeah?" Kate nodded toward the parking lot. "Look over there. See the Mercedes pulling in? Barrett Lyon. Now that's my usual type. I told you: magnetic pull. What do you bet he'll walk this way?"

"Crum. I was just about to tell you—warn you. I had a call from him last night."

"Warn me?"

"He asked me about having coffee with you the morning the baby was left in the bathroom."

"I don't understand." Kate glanced toward the lot. The attorney was definitely headed toward them. Right behind the staff with the wheelchair. Its occupant flailed a bandaged arm, seeming agitated. Was that blood on his shirt? Kate turned her attention back to Lauren. "Why would Barrett Lyon care that we met for coffee?"

"We were on the security tape. Which also showed you talking to a young woman at the ER doors. Lyon said the police were asking questions."

*The girl.* An image of the teenager's pale face rose. Frightened, suffering, lost. "They think she's—"

"Ladies, good morning." Barrett Lyon moved briskly past the wheelchair, flashed his smile at Kate and Lauren. "I was on my way to find you, Kate. We need to—"

"Help! Oh, please, over here. We need help!" One of the women with the wheelchair waved her arms.

"Lauren, let's go." Kate leaped to her feet. "Barrett, run to the ER," she ordered, "and tell them we need a gurney out here!"

In seconds they were close enough to see that the man in the chair, gray with pallor and sweating, was rapidly losing consciousness—and soaked in an alarming quantity of blood. As was the nurse's aide trying frantically to keep pressure on his bandaged arm.

"What's going on?" Kate reached for the man's uninjured arm, pressed her fingers deep against his clammy wrist. *Pulse thready, rapid.* Footsteps thudded in the distance—gurney coming. "What happened to him?"

"He was drunk at the counseling office," the aide gasped, eyes wide and gloved palm flattened against the saturated bandage. "He yelled at the billing clerk, then slammed his fist against the office window. It broke. One of the doctors said to bandage it and wheel him to the ER." A thin stream of bright-red blood spurted into the air, speckling Kate's shoulder and the side of her face like a scene in a low-budget horror film. The man groaned, mouth pale and gaping wide. Then his eyes rolled back and his body convulsed.

"Here!" Lauren shouted, signaling the staff with the gurney. "Arm lac—arterial bleed, shocky. Let's get him flat and run 'im to the trauma room!"

"Quit jabbin' me, woman!"

"Stay still, sir," Kate instructed yet again, flinching against the alcohol fumes as much as the man's glare. Conscious barely three minutes and he was fighting. "I'm trying to get another IV in— you need it. Hold still. Please." *I liked you better passed out.*

She signaled to a tech. "Hold this gentleman's arm for me, would you?"

"Got it."

Kate slid the eighteen-gauge needle set into the vein, saw the flash of blood, advanced the needle a bit farther, and then slid the plastic catheter in to the hilt. "Okay, second line's in. Blood's off to the lab." She glanced at the monitors. "How are his vitals?"

"BP's 103 over 70," the tech reported. "Heart rate 112." He pressed his palm against the patient's shoulder. "Don't try to sit up, sir. We need you to stay still."

"I need to see my daughter!" the man growled, frowning at the physician assistant applying pressure to the deep avulsion on his right forearm. "Tell her to come in here." He raised his head off the gurney, pinned Kate with a threatening look. "Get my daughter!"

"Uh . . ." Kate glanced toward the ER physician. The thought struck her that her own father's drinking patterns didn't seem so bad right now. There was something to be said for absence. "Are we still planning to send him to the OR?" *Please . . .*

"Yes. Looks like it's the ulnar vessel, not brachial, but the wound needs to be explored. Vascular and neuro—and for glass fragments." The doctor shook his head. "And it's not like we'd have his cooperation here. We'll need to see the blood alcohol and tox—"

"Are you deaf?" the patient shouted at Kate. "I believe I told you to get my daughter. Hop to it!"

"Okay." Kate pasted on a smile. "I'll see if she's out in the waiting room, sir."

"I already told you she is. She's waiting to drive me home."

Risky time to mention he wasn't going home. "What's her name?"

"Trista," he grumbled as if Kate should have known. "Mopey face, glasses. Has that baby with her." He shook his head. "Named it Harley. Not married and has a baby named Harley. The girl can't do nothin' right."

- + -

"There was a messy case, an arterial bleed," Lauren told Wes as they stood in the hallway outside the ICU. "I bet Kate went to get cleaned up. She has a meeting off campus." A small frown pinched her brows. "Did you text her?"

"No." Wes shook his head. *Not since that idiot 7 a.m. rooster crow.* "It's not a big deal. I was visiting Gabe, thought I might run into her. That's all."

"Ah . . ." Something in her expression said his subtlety was wearing clodhopping boots.

"Not important." Wes glanced toward the ICU doors. "Have a good shift."

"Thanks. By the way, how is Gabe?"

"Doing good." *And as curious as you are.*

"Great." Lauren smiled. "Hope you find her."

Wes made a quick run to the cafeteria and bought an apple, telling himself it was a hunger quest and not a one-man hasty search for Kate Callison. Then he headed for the parking lot, munching the apple along the way. And getting back on track with his workday. There was a rainwater-catchment install at two o'clock and he still had to pick up some hardware fittings. Work. The best distraction.

By the time he reached the side exit to the parking lot, he'd stopped second-guessing everything—the cheesy trailer food, telling Kate about his mother's drowning, and that out-of-the-blue kiss. It was crazy to read anything into the fact that she hadn't texted him back. She'd been busy. Lauren said as much.

Wes pushed the door open, stepped outside, and—

"Oh . . . hi." Kate blinked at him with an expression of mild surprise. She seemed to take in his Got Water? shirt. "Visiting Gabe before work?"

"Right," he said, hoping his voice didn't sound like his breath was stuck in his throat. It was. She looked beautiful, wearing a trim-fitting jacket the same seal-brown color as her eyes. Her lips were shiny, rosy almost, like she'd just added some sort of gloss. Businesslike but feminine and touchable too. Definitely not dressed for the ER.

Wes realized he was staring. "Gabe's terrorizing the surgical floor," he added quickly. "My guess is they'll kick him out sooner than later."

"Good news." Kate glanced at her watch, then toward the parking lot.

"I'm keeping you."

"No . . ." Her lips pinched in an expression Wes couldn't read. "I still have a few minutes." She shifted her briefcase from one hand to the other.

Discomfort. That's what Wes saw on her face, in her eyes. Because of last night? He didn't want to think that.

"Look . . ." Wes took a cautious step closer. "I don't need to be at the work site until two. I have to pick up some supplies, but I could swing back by here. We could grab coffee, or—"

"Here's my ride."

He turned to look where Kate was looking, at the car pulling to the curb. A gold Mercedes roadster convertible. Driven by Barrett Lyon. The attorney sprang from his car like a big cat after a gazelle.

"All set?" Lyon asked, opening the passenger door after a dismissive nod at Wes. The sun glinted off his watch—same color as the car. "Got us squeezed in at Piranha Sushi. I'd rather it was Uchi, but they don't serve lunch." He smiled like one of those irritating guys in a dental office ad. "We should go, Kate. They won't hold that reservation. Even for me."

"Ready." Kate's eyes met Wes's for a split second. "I'll . . ."

"See you," he said as she walked to the car.

Lyon held her briefcase as Kate slid into the luxurious leather seat, then closed the door and gave Wes one last nod.

After they left, Wes stood there for a few moments, wondering if Kate's obvious distress had been because of what happened between them last night. Or because she was waiting to be taken to lunch by Barrett Lyon and Wes's presence made it awkward. He eyed the remains of his apple, frowned. Piranha—he knew the place. And he wasn't one of those men who had to haul his fish into a bass boat; he'd eaten his fair share of seared tuna and spring rolls. It was just that right now . . . Wes's teeth ground together. Right now, the thought of sushi turned his stomach.

He pitched his apple core at the waste can, hit it with a satisfying thunk, and started off toward his truck. He might just tell the day laborer to take a break. Then grab a shovel and pickax himself.

**14**

**"YES, OF COURSE IT'S ME."** Kate stared at the dark images on the attorney's iPad, her stomach queasy. The feeling had nothing to do with her barely touched sushi. This was like viewing herself in a police lineup. *And that poor girl is me ten years ago.* Kate swallowed, mouth dry. "Have they identified this girl as—?" Her eyes met Barrett's. "Have they found her?"

"Not yet." He tapped the screen to stop the video. "But her photo's being circulated to clinics and doctors' offices, and it's only a matter of time before the media has it. Much less time before the police question you again. There's a good reason you didn't mention this contact before?"

"No." Kate frowned, prodding a shrimp with her chopstick. "I mean I didn't need a reason because . . ." She wasn't any better at lying now than she had been a decade ago. "I didn't remember talking with her."

"Even after the triage nurse described her to you? This 'Ava Smith'?"

"Wait a minute. What is this?" Kate glanced at the nearby booths, glad they'd arrived before the crush of the lunch crowd. She leaned forward, lowered her voice. "Are you accusing me of something?"

"Of course not." Barrett's smile flashed. "I'm on your side, remember? I want you prepared for what the police might ask."

"Even if this girl is the mother of that baby, what does it matter if I saw her?"

"It matters a lot. Because of Safe Haven. In order for that law to protect her, she must have left her baby in the hands of a designated provider. Or at the very least have told someone where he was." He tapped his finger against his iPad. "This timed security tape could mean you had contact with her after Baby Doe was born. You might be viewed as that designated provider, Kate."

She stared at him, stunned.

"The police will undoubtedly want to know what Ava Smith said to you."

"Nothing really." *Except ask me if I'd help her.*

"It looks like the two of you talked."

"I don't know." Kate forced herself to stay calm. "If it's on the tape, I guess it happened. I don't remember. Patients and visitors come and go. I talk to a lot of people. We were in the same place at the same time; then Lauren arrived. I was hurrying to meet her."

"Good." Barrett leaned back in his chair. His grin spread like the Wonderland cat that had scared Kate sleepless as a kid. "That's what I wanted to hear. *If* you spoke to this girl, it was a few words of no consequence. Nothing at all that would keep you from meeting a colleague for coffee. A reasonable case could be made that this mother had an opportunity to do the right thing and didn't. Your actions support that." He shook his head. "No one would believe someone like you would walk off and leave a baby, Kate."

- + -

"Your father's been admitted?" Judith shook the tiny silver rattle for Harley. She'd seen it at Neiman's and couldn't resist. The infant's blue eyes followed intently, her little legs flexing in the car seat.

"He's having an operation—emergency surgery." Trista glanced at the clock on the waiting room wall. "In about an hour."

"Oh. I'm sorry to hear that." Judith wished she'd arrived earlier for her volunteer shift, been here to allay Trista's fears and help with the baby. She hoped to goodness the man hadn't sat in the waiting room long. "May I ask what type of—"

"He put his arm through a window. Cut a blood vessel, I guess. Maybe nerves, too." Trista grabbed a pacifier as Harley began to fuss. "The cut bled a lot. I've got all his clothes in this bag. His favorite shirt. The washing machine doesn't work so great anymore. I'll soak them, but I doubt the shirt's gonna come clean. He won't like it."

"You know—" Judith glanced around the waiting room, satisfied that the patients were being triaged and roomed in a timely manner—"there's a nice waiting room up near surgery. TV, hot cocoa, coffee, tea. I even know where they hide the graham crackers. Why don't I take you up there to wait? It's close to the post-anesthesia recovery room." She smiled down at Harley. "So when Grandpa wakes up and wants to see his beautiful little—"

"She won't be here." Trista pushed her glasses up her nose. A dark smudge on the lens blurred one of her eyes. "Neither of us will be. They're keeping him overnight. I'll get a message on my cell phone when I have to come pick him up."

"Oh." Judith watched as Trista reached for her purse. There was dried blood on her sleeve, which made Judith worry it was also the source of the smudge on her glasses.

"I've got the car. They locked up Dad's wallet, but . . ." Trista's brows rose ever so slightly. "There was $11.96 in the front pocket of his pants. He'd figure someone would steal it. So I'm thinking Chick-fil-A. Spicy chicken sandwich and—" the corners of her mouth tugged upward—"a peppermint chocolate chip milk shake." She wedged the bag of clothes under her arm and reached for the baby seat. "I'm going there now. There's one right at the end of my street."

"Here," Judith said. "Don't forget Harley's rattle."

She watched them go. Then realized it was the first time she'd ever seen Trista smile.

- + -

"This is better." Barrett studied Kate's face over the rim of his coffee cup. Somewhere in the distance, the cappuccino machine ended its gurgling in a steamy, fragrant whoosh. "As good as our meal was, it's hard to talk with the lunch crowd filing in. Better to finish up here. Agree?"

Kate didn't try to hide her frown. She glanced around the sparsely populated Starbucks; it was within walking distance of Austin Grace and more often than not filled with folks wearing scrubs. Mercifully not at this moment. "I'd rather be at the dentist for a root canal."

"Ha!" Barrett laughed, eyes glittering. "See? That's exactly what I like about you, Kate. No mincing words; you call them as you see them. You're not always out to win some popularity contest."

"Clearly." She tried not to think what he'd heard from the staff. Had he been asking about her?

His expression softened. "I meant it as a compliment. You are, without a doubt, most genuine and unique." He smiled a smile that could qualify as jury tampering. "In a culture of sweet tea and porch rockers, you are a delightful breath of fresh air—dangerously flirting with hurricane status. I like that." His eyes held hers. "Very much."

"Well . . ." Kate glanced down at her coffee, no doubt cooling in the breeze emitted by furiously fanning red flags. "I'm fairly sure 'unique' isn't going to help in my efforts to pull the emergency department together. My first clue was the 'Go back, California Girl' note left on my car."

"Not as bad as bits of ground pork sausage. Raw. Stuffed into the leather upholstery and under the seats of my leased BMW. Festering for a week in the summer heat." Barrett's smile turned rueful. "My ex-wife. The first in a series of colorful antics."

Kate wasn't going to ask.

"I've been watching you, Kate. You're not like the rest of the staff at Austin Grace. Lauren, Dana . . . Sunni Sprague."

"So I've been told." Kate wasn't all good with the idea of being watched. Especially by a man toting video evidence from the security tape. She reached for her coffee.

"Again," Barrett insisted, "you're different in a good way. You're more like . . . me."

"Excuse me?" She grabbed a napkin, squelched a near choke that burned her nostrils.

"I mean that you set a goal and do whatever it takes to accomplish it. I respect that." The smile was back. "Not at all unlike my father's old boys down at Granddaddy's hunting lease. Aiming at one of those big-ticket trophy bucks. Take your shot, bring down what you want, reload. In your case, move on." His brows rose.

"Ten hospitals in six years? Seven different cities, three states?" The confidence in his expression said he could tape a map on the Starbucks wall and follow her scurrilous path with a laser pointer. And probably knew she had an application for that traveling nurse agency in Dallas.

"Sounds about right." Kate shrugged, one foot beginning to wiggle under the table. "Is there some reason you bring that up?"

"Only to prove my point. You're different from the majority of the people on that hospital staff who think it all begins and ends with 'team spirit.' Folks who love it that their cousin's wife works in the cafeteria, that all four of their kids were born in the OB department, and who insist on every staff meeting including a potluck and doing a secret Santa in December. You know: the same people who like to gather in the chapel and pray for each other." Barrett shook his head.

Kate tensed at his mention of Lauren's hospital ministry. "Let me get this straight. You're saying I'm more like a deer hunter than a team player."

"I'm saying that you're too smart to let that stubbornly dug-in 'we are one' mentality keep you from making reasonable decisions. I'm saying that you're not likely to line up and hold hands with a hundred other kids playing Red Rover. Then consider it your honorable duty to fall down if they do. You're not like a Lauren or a Sunni or . . . some Eagle Scout well digger either."

*Well digger? He's taking a shot at Wes, too?*

"I'm not sure I like where this is going." Kate nudged her cup away. "Let's stop with the clever metaphors and cut to the chase, okay?"

"Absolutely." His smile said he expected nothing less of her. And liked it.

Kate spread her hands. "You take me to lunch to show me that security tape. You make a big point of telling me that I'm not like the rest of my staff. What exactly do you want from me, Mr. Lyon?"

"Barrett. And I want you to do what you do best, Kate." His expression went serious, his gaze direct. "Look out for number one—yourself."

"Meaning?" Despite the coffee, she fought a chill.

"Tell the police what you told me about that video. Your conversation with Ava Smith was minimal. Nothing to disrupt your social coffee with Lauren. And if they find that mother, stick to your story. Don't deviate an inch. If there's any question of liability, it's best that fault points away from hospital management. And to non-regular staff."

"Dana Connor?"

"Yes. As triage nurse, she accepted responsibility for that pregnant girl—and the safety of her unborn baby. She's likely to say everything she said before: it was a busy shift, and she was overwhelmed. She hadn't slept before coming to work because her husband's severely disabled and she has a young son. She worries about losing her home. She'll cry." Barrett steepled his hands. "And while that's admittedly sad, it's also Dana Connor's ace in the hole. People will empathize. The old 'There but for the grace of God.' You know the quote—and I'll probably use it."

"You really think it will come to that?" Kate hated the anxiety in her voice. "The hospital needing to mount a defense over Baby Doe?"

"It could happen if Ava Smith's future attorney tries to defend her using the Safe Haven law." He shrugged. "Despite the lead offered by the security tape, there does remain the possibility this mother will never be found. She could disappear like fireflies at summer's end. It happens all the time."

*I know . . .*

"But with that local church planning a memorial service," Barrett continued, "the media will keep the story alive. Baby stories are notoriously hard to bury—no tragic pun intended. And anything to do with innocent little children evokes strong emotion. Look at all those people who got duped into giving money to that woman waving a sign with a photo of a dead baby."

"What?"

"Just a few blocks from the hospital. I saw her myself. That grifter who claimed she needed money for—"

"Her baby's funeral?" Kate's throat squeezed. "It was a scam? I don't believe that."

"Cyber proof. Here you go." Barrett pulled out his iPad again, tapped the screen, scrolled down. "There it is. Fresh from this morning's *Statesman*." He turned the screen toward her.

And there she was—grieving expression, lit candle, and the baby's face on the huge poster.

"She got the photo from an online diaper ad, had it enlarged." Barrett shook his head. "Of course it's all secondhand from another panhandler; the baby-funeral entrepreneur has moved on. Now there's a practical team for you."

"I think I'm officially sick." Kate glanced at her watch. "And I should get back to work."

"All right." Barrett reached for his briefcase. "But I meant what I said, Kate. You're unique, a stand-alone, and in my opinion that's a good thing." He connected with her gaze. "I know you have issues with your staff and that administration will be making decisions regarding your permanent status." His smile spread slowly. "Maybe I can be of some help in that respect."

*Help?* "Got it covered," she said, breaking eye contact and reaching for her own briefcase. It was a lie. She knew it and Barrett Lyon knew it too. The way he obviously knew too many things about her. Kate wasn't sure which made her sickest: his snooping into her life, a heartless plan to destroy Dana Connor, the scam about the baby funeral, Barrett's derisive potshot at Wes, or—

"Just remember," he said, opening the door for Kate to exit, "don't hold hands with a team that's toppling over. Look out for yourself. And if you need backup, I'll be here. You might not see it yet, but it's true—we're a lot alike, Kate. Sympatico."

*That.* That's what made her the sickest.

- + -

"Hold up a second!"

Lauren slowed her jog, trotted a few steps, and then stopped. She looked back toward Kate. "Oops . . . sorry," she said, her words half chuckle, half gasp. "Finally got into the zone and forgot you were back there."

"So much . . . for . . . toppling over with . . . the team."

"What?" Lauren asked as Kate walked up the Barton Creek Greenbelt trail. She was glistening with sweat. "Toppling with the team?"

"You had to be there." Kate swiped her hand across her forehead. "Be glad you weren't."

"Sushi in the Lyon's den?" Lauren watched as Kate took a long swig of vitaminwater. "I figured it was the reason you suggested this run—you don't jog, Pilates Girl."

Kate stretched out her calf with a grimace. "Today felt like a good time to start. I needed to pound something. Safer if it's my shoes against this trail."

Lauren nodded. She waited, but Kate didn't offer more. "Well, I'm glad you asked me along." She scanned the lush foliage along the community greenbelt, burnished with autumn color. There was a botanical garden and natural pool not far ahead. "I've wanted to explore this part of the trail, follow it along the water into Zilker Park. But some of this is definitely a wilderness area. I'm not sure I'd want to go it alone."

"According to our esteemed hospital attorney, going it alone is what I do best."

"In reference to?"

"My ability to be part of a team. Or lack thereof." Kate shook her head. "To tell you the truth, he was encouraging it."

"Being a team player?" Lauren remembered the debriefing. Kate sitting as far from her fellow employees as possible.

"No. Not teamwork. Exactly the opposite. He told me to look out for myself." Kate was quiet for a moment while she stretched her other calf. "Have you talked with Dana Connor recently?"

"For a few minutes the other day." They began to walk along the trail.

"How did she seem?"

"She . . ." Lauren weighed how much she could divulge. "She hasn't accepted a triage assignment since that day with Baby Doe."

Kate's expression said she didn't know that. *You never checked on her?*

"Did she mention me?"

*Ranted more like.* "She mentioned that she'd talked to you . . ."

"And?" Kate's brows pinched together. "Oh, I get it. You can't tell me what she said because of the whole peer-counseling thing. Great."

"Okay . . ." Lauren decided Kate needed to hear this one thing. "She told me that if she had a chance to meet with you again, she'd want to ask a question this time."

"What question?" Kate stopped walking, concern on her face.

"Dana said she'd ask if *you* have ever made a mistake. You personally."

"Oh." Kate stood for a second, then started to walk again.

It was clear that though Dana's proposed question hit its mark, Kate was not going to respond. Lauren decided to change the subject. "Barrett didn't think the security tape was a problem? You talking with that girl?"

"Not really. He said that having coffee with you afterward proved that nothing significant had happened. And that . . ." Kate's voice thickened. "It wasn't like I'd knowingly leave a baby in danger."

"Are you okay?" Lauren asked, seeing the sudden pallor on her friend's face. "Want to sit down somewhere?"

"No. Fine. Completely." Kate tried to smile. "Leg cramp. Pilates Girl with delusions of runners' grandeur." She wove her fingers through her hair. "I heard our man with the severed arm vessel gave them a rough time upstairs when anesthesia wore off. It's incredible that he injured himself at a substance abuse meeting."

"I ran into Judith. She knows his daughter from the times she waits for him during those meetings. I guess she sits in the ER waiting room."

"Yes. With her baby. I think Judith's becoming surrogate family to that mother. She even took some photos of her baby. Harley."

"Harley? About two months old?" Lauren saw Kate's immediate nod. "I've seen her too. At least a couple of times now. Small world. That reminds me, did Wes ever find you?"

"I ran into him for a minute before . . . What do you mean did he 'find' me? He was looking for me?"

"He stopped me at the ICU and asked if I knew where you were. As in, he wanted to find you." Lauren smiled at the thought. "Search, find. What Wes Tanner does. Without the rescue this time."

"He did find me." Kate sighed. "Right as Barrett pulled up."

"Ouch. Rescue sounds like a better plan."

"Maybe, though now I'm not sure if . . ." Kate's expression was impossible to read. "Let's run this last stretch to the Zilker trailhead. My feet need some serious pounding."

## 15

+

"I'LL NEED YOU TO COMPLETE your portion of the performance review," Evelyn Harkin explained, sliding her glasses to the top of her head. Morning light spilled through the office window, hitting the purple frames and shiny lenses, making the glasses look like a dragonfly perched on her hair. "Standard questions about what you feel you've accomplished. Your strengths, areas that you feel need improvement, and your future goals here at Austin Grace."

Kate nodded. *One goal: to stay.*

"There's a place for special projects," the CNO continued. "Of course, you haven't been here long. Past managers have included projects like the fellowship group, organizing the Adopt a Family Christmas program, implementing a staff hardship fund."

"I see . . ." *that you're comparing me to Sunni.* Kate's special projects had been more on the order of damage control from the very first day. At least no one had stuffed pork sausage into her car upholstery—yet. She met Evelyn's gaze directly. "Do you plan to post the department director position? Actively search for other applicants?"

"We . . ." Evelyn hesitated for a moment. "The plan was that the interim director position would transition into a permanent one. Your education, clinical skill, and leadership experience—along with a stellar recommendation from a representative of the Hale Medical Foundation—was impressive, Kate."

*But . . . ?*

"I don't have to tell you that it's been a rocky few months," Evelyn continued, empathy in her voice. "The incident with Baby Doe and those anonymous letters to the newspaper aren't helping things. On top of that, team morale is low and patient surveys show dissatisfaction at an all-time high. None of which sits well with the hospital board. Unfortunately it points to management. All the way to the highest level."

Kate remembered Barrett Lyon's words: *It's best that fault points away from hospital management. And to non-regular staff.* Dana Connor had averted her eyes when they passed in the hall today.

"I understand, of course," Kate told Evelyn. "And I promise that I'll do everything I can to put the hospital in a better light. I'm working on that—an ongoing special project, you might say."

"I'm glad to hear it. I'm required to post the position, regardless. Even as a formality. If it reassures you, your application will be our first consideration." But Evelyn's smile seemed more rueful than encouraging. "I'd like to have your input back within the week. Then we can set up a meeting to go over your review. Perhaps the Monday following Thanksgiving. Would that interfere with your family plans for the holiday?"

"No. No problem there." Kate stood. "I can work around it."

"Good. We'll be in touch."

Kate retrieved her briefcase and said good-bye, then headed toward her office—and kept going. Along the back corridor, out the employee exit, and across the parking lot. She continued on toward her car, thinking of what she'd said to the CNO about the timing for their meeting. Laughable, if it weren't so pathetic. There were no Thanksgiving family plans to work around. The truth was that nothing was working the way it was supposed to. All Kate wanted was an end to the turmoil, a new start, with no reminders of—

She stopped fishing for her keys, grabbed her buzzing cell phone. A text message. From her father.

**Heading back to California. A few miles from you now. Austin Grace Hospital?**

Kate leaned against her car and closed her eyes, feeling the weight of the phone in her hands. Nothing, *nothing* was working out right. She took a slow breath and deleted the message. Then tapped the speed-dial number for the ER. It was only eleven thirty, but . . .

"I'm taking the rest of the day off," Kate told the clinical coordinator when she came on the phone. "You can leave a message in case of emergencies, but otherwise I won't be available."

There was a barely concealed sigh. "Dana Connor went home sick."

"Grab a nurse from the walk-in clinic. Take a few patients yourself. Call the staffing agency if you need to. I'm sure you'll handle it fine." *I can't stay here.*

Kate pulled out of the parking lot without looking back, made it through the afternoon traffic on autopilot, and was within a mile of Barton Springs when something caught her eye. A woman on the street corner, too much of a blur to make out for sure.

She made a quick turn, circled the block, waited for a Brownie leader to file her troop over a crosswalk, then slowed and pulled to the curb. Her eyes scanned the street. Where was she?

There. *Unbelievable!* Kate slammed the car into park and cut the engine. Blood rushed to her head, pounding in her temples. No way. There was no way she was going to let this happen.

"You!" she yelled, sprinting down the sidewalk. "You there!" Kate shoved past pedestrians and came to a breathless halt in front of the young panhandler. She jabbed her finger into the space between them. "How dare you! I should call the police right now!"

"Excuse me?" The young woman, maybe Kate's age, took a step backward and held her *Hungry—God Bless* cardboard sign to her chest like a battle shield. Her expression was a mix of fear and streetwise bravado. "I'm not on anyone's private property. I'm—"

"Lying!" Kate hissed, beginning to tremble. "I saw you with that poster of the baby. And the candle. Looking so sad. Collecting money for a funeral. Lying about all of it. You got that photo off the Internet, used it to scam people. Other mothers—" She choked on the painful tumble of words. "People who have lost their own children. Who continue to suffer because of that." She jabbed her finger again, her fingernail poking into God's name. "What gives someone like you the right to—"

"Dude, hey." A bearded young man in a knit cap stepped close, palms raised in an attempt at peacemaking. "Leave her alone. C'mon now."

"Yeah, ease up, lady. Chill."

"Whatsa matter, sister? You never had no bad times?"

*Bad times?* Kate's brows drew together as she glanced at the handful of people gathering close. Two men held similar cardboard signs. An elderly woman with missing teeth cradled a small, shivering dog against her chest. The troop leader, in a protective gesture, moved the Brownies closer to the line of buildings.

The young woman lowered her sign. "I was only trying to get by. Survive." She brushed her fingers across her nose ring, sniffed. "Things are bad all over—I'm not making excuses. But I do what I have to. It's all I know right now. I'm hoping for better someday. I hear it's possible. You know?" The look in her eyes was like she could see right into Kate's soul. "But I'm guessin' I should say I'm sorry. About *your* baby, ma'am. I'm truly sorry for your loss."

*Please, God, don't do this to me* . . . Kate turned, ran back to the car. She pulled away from the curb and into traffic, only vaguely aware of the unforgiving blare of horns.

- + -

"Have you signed the patient registration log, sir?"

"No." Matt Callison smiled at the pretty woman in the pink volunteer smock; he'd seen her minutes before, drawing a smiley face on a balloon made from an exam glove. "I'm not a patient. My daughter works here. I'm on my way home to California and I'm hoping to catch her for a few minutes. Sort of surprise her."

"Oh." The woman's smile reached her blue eyes. There were silver angels dangling from her ears. "How nice. I'm Judith, with the Ladies Auxiliary. I'd be happy to help you, sir. What's your daughter's name?"

"Kate Callison. She's the emergency department director. The clerk is checking; she wasn't sure if Katy was still in her office."

"Oh, dear. I'm sorry," Judith said, her expression sincere, "but Kate left word that she's taking the rest of the day off. Perhaps if you call her? I know how disappointed I'd be if my daughter dropped by to see me and I missed her by a smidge."

"Yes." Matt was sure that was true. He wasn't about to tell this gracious woman that Kate hadn't returned his text. And had never given him her home address. "I'll call her. Thank you."

"You're more than welcome, Mr. Callison."

"It's Matt," he offered as she batted the glove balloon back to the giggling child. He thought of Juliana playing with Kate. "They keep you busy here, Judith."

"Always. I like it that way." She met his gaze. "And I like your daughter. She's working hard. In some trying times. I'm sure she told you that our previous department director went missing—so tragic."

*Missing?* Matt's heart squeezed. He knew only too well how that felt.

"Your daughter's doing her best to pull the department together. I support that effort, absolutely. And I admire her moxie in light of the challenges." Judith offered her hand. "Nice to meet you, Matt. Glad you're visiting Kate. Encouragement from a father can make all the difference."

Matt took her hand. *From your lips to God's ears, Judith.*

It would take that sort of miracle if Kate was ignoring his calls.

- + -

"Don't let him climb into your lap, Gabe. He's too—" Wes broke off the useless words of caution, laughing instead as Hershey began licking his friend's face. "At least keep your leg out straight. I've got the seat back all the way. The goal here is to get you home. Not mauled in the hospital parking lot." He turned to the nurse's aide helping Gabe squeeze into the passenger seat. "Excuse us. Rescue dog gone wild."

The bearded aide grinned. "Totally understand. We have a yellow Lab. A hundred pounds of lapdog—don't even try to eat popcorn with your Netflix." He checked his patient's leg position once more. "Looks good, pal. You're set."

Wes thanked him, closed the door, and was jogging around the truck to the driver's side when he thought he saw—"Matt?"

"Hey, Wes, good to see you." Kate's father walked over.

"Here to see Kate?"

"Tried." Matt shoved his hands into his pockets. "The ER volunteer said she took the rest of the day off."

Wes hated that his imagination went immediately to Barrett Lyon. "You called her?"

"Text message. Haven't heard back." He raised his brows. "You've seen her?"

"Not since yesterday." *The day after I kissed her . . .* Wes pushed the thought away.

Matt looked as if he were choosing his words. "I don't know if Katy told you, but we've had sort of a rocky go of it. Some family troubles."

"She said her mother died."

"Yes." Matt released a breath. "And I wasn't there for Kate when I should have been. I'm not proud of that." His expression was raw, honest. "I'm doing everything I can to make up for those years. Finally get my priorities straight. One day at a time." He glanced up at the sky. "Thanks to God's grace. You know what I'm saying?"

"Yes, sir." Wes thought of Kate's doubts, wondered if her father's faith would only widen the chasm between them. *Lost . . . found.* Was everything that way?

"I don't mean to keep you," Matt told him. "You need to get your friend home and settled. And I should be on the road back to California. It's a long drive. I'll try Kate's number again." There was no mistaking the pain in his eyes. "Maybe she had her phone turned off. Or the battery ran out or—"

"Stop by her place."

"I don't have her—"

"Near Barton Springs and Zilker Park. You're like ten minutes away." Wes shook his head. "I can't tell you how many times I've kicked myself for not storing addresses in my phone. It's 803½ Creekview, the guesthouse."

"I . . ." Matt cleared his throat. "Thanks." He extended his hand, gripped Wes's firmly. "You're a good man, Wes."

"Thank you, sir. I hope you find her." He watched Matt Callison walk away, then headed back toward his truck, glad that Gabe and Hershey—and full-volume bluegrass—would fill the drive home. It would distract Wes from thinking about what he'd just done. Completely invaded Kate's prickly wall of self-protection. Meddled, big-time.

Though Matt hadn't voiced it, Wes was certain Kate hadn't shared her address with him. She was avoiding her father with the same stubborn determination she used to dodge God himself. And Wes had sent one of them to knock on her door. Maybe both, considering Matt's reference to grace. Either way, Kate wasn't going to like it. But he had to believe he'd done the right thing. Even if it meant that his first kiss with Kate was also his last.

- + -

Kate slowed her jog to a walk, breath still heaving. Lauren had been right; running even this short stretch of the greenbelt trail was far different from working out to a Pilates video on the living room floor. But for the second time in a week, she'd had an angry need to pound something.

*Oh, brother.* She cringed, remembering how she'd screamed at the panhandler a couple of hours ago. Yelled, threatened, and sent a Brownie troop running for cover. She'd never intended it to go that far, but . . .

She sank down onto a bench, wiped her sleeve across her perspiring neck. Jogging truth was less gentle than Pilates truth: her tirade against the funeral scammer was only the tip of the iceberg. She knew that now. The meeting with the CNO and her father's text had her bailing today, sure, but Kate had been at the helm of the *Titanic* for months. She'd described it that way to Lauren before: a doomed voyage. And it had only gotten worse. These past few days the deck had begun to tilt dangerously. Baby Doe's death, the Waiting for Compassion diatribes, a debriefing, her father's sudden visit—and that miserable lunch with Barrett Lyon. Kate was queasy at the possibility there was truth in what he'd said. That she was someone who looked out only for herself, had no need for a team . . . or for God.

She shivered as the late-afternoon breeze moved over her damp shirt. Evelyn Harkin had compared her to Sunni Sprague, whether she'd admit it or not. She'd cited Sunni's special projects, like the hospital fellowship that Lauren now headed. Implying perhaps that faith was a missing puzzle piece, and if Kate found it, her staff would rally round and support her. She frowned. How many prayers had been breathed into that icy air from the decks of the *Titanic*? It still went down. Lost.

Very soon there would be a performance review. Then Kate's application for a permanent position as department director would be discussed by the hiring committee. Meanwhile, according to Barrett Lyon, it was entirely possible that Baby Doe's mother would be found and the hospital embroiled in litigation. Kate squeezed her eyes shut, remembering what the attorney had suggested: to point blame at the baby's mother or at Dana Connor.

Could Kate do that? Blame either or both of them to deflect liability from the hospital and protect her job? Could she make herself believe the desperate young woman she'd spoken with on that dark morning wasn't pleading for help? And could she forget Dana Connor's question: *"Have you ever made a mistake?"*

Kate started off along the path again. She'd force herself to put one foot in front of the other despite how her muscles and lungs complained. No matter the struggle, it felt better than most things did these days. Running was something she knew well. And it was no secret to Barrett Lyon, apparently. *"Ten hospitals in six years? Seven different cities, three states?"*

Kate clenched her jaw, pushed her speed. Smug as he was, Lyon didn't know the half of it. Running away . . . and mistakes. But the point was that she'd left all that pain behind and wasn't going to let anything or anyone make her relive it. Not the hospital attorney, the ghost of Sunni Sprague, well-intentioned inquiries by Lauren, a horrible woman waving a fake photo of a dead baby . . . not even the promise of comfort in Wes Tanner's arms. Kate had to put the past behind and move on. It was the reason she'd ignored that text from her father today. She simply couldn't risk . . . *going back.*

Fifteen minutes later, when her feet were tired and her heart finally calmed, she walked up the tree-lined driveway. Then saw the car parked near her guesthouse.

"Kate." Her father stepped down from the porch. "You're back."

**16**

+

"**THANK YOU.**" Matt took the mug from Kate's hands, reminding himself of what the hospital volunteer had told him. *"Encouragement from a father can make all the difference."* He prayed it was true—but his daughter's expression said otherwise. Still, he had to take this chance. It could be his last one. "Good coffee," he said after taking a sip.

"Instant." She wiped a dishrag at a nonexistent spot on the blue-tiled breakfast bar that separated them. It might as well have been the Grand Canyon. "We could have met at Austin Java."

*If you'd answered my text.*

She hadn't asked how Matt found her house. He didn't offer the information. They both knew it would point out the obvious: she didn't want to see him.

Matt rubbed a finger over the enameled daisy on the chipped

mug—from the set Juliana had found in Carmel long before Kate was born. Her favorites—she'd sipped herbal tea from one when she was in early labor with Kate. And much later, when she was sick and achy from chemotherapy. Kate had taken two of the three remaining daisy cups with her when she'd completed her GED and left for college. Eleven silent months after she returned home from . . . *where?* He still didn't know how she'd spent that year of her life.

"You had a good visit in Fort Worth?" she asked, walking in stocking feet toward the small living room. He followed, choosing an ottoman across from where she settled on the couch. "With your college friend, Phil?"

"Yes. I got to see his granddaughter baptized." Matt watched as an orange cat appeared from nowhere and jumped up onto the couch beside Kate. It had at best half of a tail.

"Cat versus ambulance," she explained, stroking his white-washed chin.

Matt hid his wince, hoping Kate wasn't remembering how he'd run over her cat all those years ago. Angry, drunk. It was a reminder of why he was here. *Thank you, Lord. I hear you.*

"I wanted you to know," he began with his heart in his throat, "that I've been attending services at the church where the AA meetings are held. Good Shepherd. It's been a help for me in a lot of ways. I've been sober for nearly eight months now—237 days as of this morning, to be exact." He held his breath, watched his daughter's eyes.

"I'm glad for you," she said, clearly uncomfortable. "But you don't need to tell me any of that."

"I do." Matt tightened his fingers around the solid warmth of the daisy mug. Reminded himself that by unexpected grace he now had a father's encouragement. All things were possible. "I do need to tell you, Katy. That's why I came to Texas."

"If this is part of that twelve-step make-things-right pledge, skip me. I don't need to hear it. We're good."

Matt sighed, said the words that pierced his heart. "We're not good, Katy. We're strangers. It's killing me that I caused it to happen."

She closed her eyes, but he kept talking. Had to.

"When your mother got sick, I couldn't handle it. She was the strong one, the one with faith. The heart of our family. I didn't trust myself to fill that void." Matt set his coffee down and leaned forward, hands clasped. "It's no excuse. Worse than that, it was deeply wrong—because of you. I checked out and left you to deal with it. Sixteen years old and forced to be the adult because I wouldn't step up."

Matt saw Kate hug her knees, eyes downcast. Curled up like a lost child. His vision blurred with tears. "And afterward, when you needed me most, I drank myself numb. I was selfish, heartless, and undeserving." He swallowed, realized his hands were trembling. "I'm sorry, Katy. It's no wonder you ran away."

Her chin lifted—a lost child finding strength in familiar defiance. "I can't talk about that. I won't."

"I'm only trying to say that I understand—"

"You can't possibly." Her defiant expression twisted with pain.

"I . . ." Matt scrambled for words. *Please, help* . . . "I only meant that I'm sorry I caused it to happen. And I regret not telling you that after you came back." His voice choked. "I searched for you, Katy. I drove every street in Sunnyvale and then streets in every town within a hundred miles. I knocked on doors, made calls. Posted flyers. Hounded the police. And when you finally called to say you were fine and not to look for you, I checked the number and flew to Las Vegas. Searched there. You're my only child. My *baby*. I couldn't stand the thought of leaving you alone somewhere—"

"I can't do this." Kate stood, her face drained of color. "I *can't*."

"Kate . . ." Matt rose, walked toward her. "I love you, honey. I want a chance to be part of your life. I want to be there for you if you need—"

"No." She raised her palms. "Don't. I'm sorry, but this isn't going to happen." Kate's eyes met his, the raw misery in them ripping at his heart. "It's good that you're better, Dad. That you're sober and you've found . . . God. It's good, I guess. But it's too late for this. I don't need anything from you now. Can't you see that? I don't need anybody."

- + -

"Yes, ma'am," Wes told Amelia Braxton, hoping his finger wasn't permanently stuck in the handle of the dainty flowered cup. "Best tea I've ever had."

The elderly woman's barely visible brows rose, and he hurried to amend his compliment. He turned to Nancy Rae, sitting on the porch swing, wearing a cherry-print dress and something that looked like an old Pilgrim hat. Only faint scratches gave evidence to her near miss with the business end of a shotgun. "Thank you, too, Miss Nancy," Wes said, fairly sure that Hershey, wriggling beside him in hopes of a cookie, would laugh out loud if he could. "It was very nice of you to invite me to tea."

Amelia giggled. "She thinks you have beautiful eyes. So do I. And good manners." She peered at Wes through lenses finely dusted with powdered sugar. "Your mother did a fine job of raising you up. Manners, Sunday school, music lessons. Yes indeed. . . .

But we hardly see Lee Ann these days. You must tell her to come by for tea. We miss her."

"I'll do that," Wes promised, wondering if anyone really did miss his mother. Twenty-seven years was a long time.

Framed photographs of his mother had been gradually stored away at the Tanner home. They were replaced by images of Miranda and Paul, Wes with his adopted brother and sister, the grandbaby, countless snapshots of foster children—and horses, of course. But there were still some remnants of Lee Ann. A redbud tree she planted when they were laying the house's foundation, and the *Bless this Home* stencil she'd sponged over the kitchen sink. Miranda had carefully taped it off and brushed around it the times they repainted the walls. After all these years, there wasn't much of anything left. Except the questions in Wes's heart.

"Excuse me, Mr. Tanner." The newly hired caregiver smiled at him from the screen door. The scent of cookies wafted onto the porch. "Mrs. Braxton and Miss Lily have doctors' appointments at two thirty—" she glanced at Amelia—"and Nancy Rae wants to stop by the grocery."

"Of course." Wes twisted his finger in the cup handle, freed it. "I promised I'd have a look around the grove to see that things are cleaned up. I'll make sure the horse trailer isn't blocking your car, and—"

"'Mary Had a Little Lamb.'" Amelia raised a finger. "That's what you played for your mother at the recital. She sang along to help you when you forgot that last verse. 'Why does the lamb love Mary so?'" Amelia sang, her voice thin, quavery. "'Why, Mary loves the lamb, you know.'" She sighed, shaking her head. "It made her cry."

Wes stared down at his fingers, heart in his throat. He'd forgotten.

- + -

Kate ran her fingers through her damp hair, stubbornly wayward after a shampoo, and then frowned at her image in the foggy mirror. Even scrubbed clean, she looked like someone who'd just sent her father packing. After he'd poured out his heart, saying what she'd yearned to hear for so many years. *"I searched for you, Katy."*

She turned away, sick of what she saw reflected in her own eyes. Sick at heart . . . *of who I am.*

She zipped her jeans and reached for her thermal tee with guilt hissing in her head. How could she let her father talk about newfound faith and family—*"You're my only child. My* baby.*"*—after what she'd done? He'd searched Las Vegas for her. Kate's stomach twisted. What if he'd seen her that desperate day she was seven months pregnant and snatched a half-eaten cheeseburger off a casino's smoky bar? No father could love a daughter like that.

He said he wanted to be part of her life. What if he knew . . . *I walked away from my baby?*

She pulled on her boots, grabbed a quilted vest, then yanked her purse from the vanity, avoiding her reflection.

She couldn't stay in this house whether Roady was here or not. Right now his company wasn't enough. There were two daisy coffee mugs on the counter and a cross hidden in the closet. Oil and water. Honesty and lies. They didn't mix. And Kate couldn't stand the way they made her feel.

She opened the door, car keys in hand. She'd gone AWOL from work and it was well past lunchtime. Chuy's, Shady Grove, veggie empanadas at Flipnotics? Her Austin neighborhood promised an endless supply of food . . . to fill a hole in her heart?

Not everything was possible. But she was going. She'd slid into the Hyundai when her phone buzzed in her purse. She wouldn't talk to her father. But she'd told the hospital to call if there was an emergency. She pulled the phone out and her eyes widened.

"Barrett?"

"Hi," he said, somehow making a two-letter word stretch to a syrupy drawl. "I hear you escaped from the workaday world."

"Appointment," she fibbed.

"I thought maybe we should have dinner tonight."

Her heart froze. "Did they find Ava Smith?"

"No." His careless laugh made her skin crawl. "Nothing like that, Kate. You're far too serious."

Too serious? An abandoned baby was too serious? A threat to her job was something to be taken lightly? Her fingers clenched the phone. "Then why should we meet?"

"Because I like you."

She pulled the phone away, grimaced.

"Kate?"

"I'm here," she managed despite a troubling memory of that ill-fated date in San Antonio. With a man currently wearing a jailhouse jumpsuit.

"Officially I make it a rule not to become personally involved with anyone even remotely connected to a case. But—" the unnerving chortle repeated—"you are far too tempting, Kate Callison. I'm betting that you feel the connection too. We should pursue this."

*Pursue?* "No. I don't think . . ." She flailed, wanting to stomp him like a scorpion but terrified by what he could do to her career—and her flimsy hope for a new beginning. "I'm not feeling well," she said finally. Truer than anything today. Other than in Las Vegas, she'd never felt more ill. "I can't go to dinner."

"Ah, I'm wounded. Rain check, then."

Kate sighed. The continuing Texas drought gave further proof that God had no mercy for her.

When she finally put the car in gear and pulled out onto the road, her appetite was gone but not her need to run away. Kate had no clue where she was going. Or what she needed. She only knew that going back—even to a house that had begun to feel like home—wasn't something she could do right now. She needed comfort beyond what food could offer; she needed to feel that she wasn't the woman Barrett Lyon thought she was. She wanted to feel . . . *"Smart, tough when you have to be . . . funny, caring . . . beautiful."* The words came back, washing over her like a balm.

She pulled to the curb. Then lifted her cell phone from her purse and scrolled to the number.

"Kate?" Wes's voice sounded more than a little surprised.

"I took the day off," she told him as if that were reason enough for calling.

There was a pause. "Did your father find you?"

She'd guessed it, of course. "Yes."

"I meddled."

"Yes." Kate heard him sigh. "Look . . . I get that your sense of family would have to be skewed. You're all so close-woven, this fuzzy-warm blanket that's, like, generations thick. I'm not angry that you gave my father the address. Since he didn't have it, you can guess that it's not a Hallmark movie on our side. But you were probably still hoping for that."

"I—"

"Admit it," she pressed. "You were. You were hoping for a scene where he shows up and I fling my arms around him and cry. And then he calls me 'baby girl' and I call him 'Daddy' . . ." She swallowed past a sudden lump. "And all is forgiven and we start making Thanksgiving plans."

"What did happen?"

"I gave him instant coffee and told him to drive safely. And I told you I don't cry." Kate watched the cars pass by for a moment. "I'm not like you, Wes. Or Sunni Sprague."

"I don't expect that. Hey, don't you remember, that night at the lake . . ." His voice lowered and he sounded so close she expected to feel the warmth of his breath. "When I said that I think you're amazing and—"

"Where are you?"

"At the Braxton ranch. Why?"

"I was going for a drive." Kate's heartbeat began to thud in her ears. "I thought maybe I'd come out your way. If it's okay, I mean."

"Sure. The caregiver took the ladies to an appointment and I promised to check the fences while they're gone. It'll take another hour or so."

"I'll come there."

"This is out in the middle of no—"

"I have GPS."

She swore that his laugh tickled her ear.

"So you'll need to give me the address . . . ," she prompted.

Once he had, Kate disconnected from the call. She sat there for a moment, stunned by what she'd done. Then she began tapping the Braxton address into the GPS, a gift from her father when she left California. He'd preloaded it with the Sunnyvale address designated as "Home." Though neither of them really expected she'd be back.

She watched the colored map come up, the display of the route to the rural destination and her expected time of arrival. Kate shook her head. There was no map that could tell her where she was going with this unexpected meeting. She didn't know that herself. She only knew that hearing Wes's voice had erased some of the pain of her day. And that she'd needed the response he gave when she said she wasn't like Wes or Sunni: *"I don't expect that."* It made Kate feel almost like she was okay. Acceptable. Despite everything. And that she wasn't like Barrett Lyon, no matter how many times he told her she was.

Dinner with the hospital attorney or checking fences in the middle of nowhere—with the man he'd dismissed as an "Eagle Scout well digger." She smiled at her choice. Then started the engine and let the GPS lead her to Wes Tanner.

# 17

**"HEY THERE."** Wes watched as Kate negotiated the rock path to where he sat at the wheel of the Braxtons' old Jeep. She was wearing boots, jeans, a green quilted vest over a thermal T-shirt—and yet another inscrutable expression. Still, Wes wasn't sure he'd ever seen anyone who looked more in need of a hug. Was that why she'd come? He wasn't about to risk a guess.

"Is that an old Willys?" she asked, eyes widening.

"A 1950. Original dust." He glanced to where Hershey, tongue lolling, had wedged himself behind the Jeep's seats. "Dog hair's more recent."

"Amazing." Kate shook her head. "It looks like something out of an old *M\*A\*S\*H* rerun."

"Climb in." Wes patted the sun-worn passenger seat. "I still have one more thing to check. Ride along with me." The image

of Kate climbing into Lyon's Mercedes rose. *And now she's here.*
Despite the irony, he wasn't going to question it.

"I'm game," she said, hauling herself into the seat beside him.
She reached back to give Hershey a pet; then her eyes met Wes's.
There was discomfort in her expression. "I needed to get away.
The walls were closing in."

"No walls here," he said, flattening the clutch pedal as the Jeep's
engine rumbled to life. "Or doors either. That's a warning. Hang
on." Wes jiggled the gearshift, shoved it into first as Kate took hold
of the grab bar. No luxury ride. He could imagine Lyon's smirk.
The Jeep lurched forward, tires grinding the chalk-soft caliche rock.

"I saw the horse trailer." Kate raised her voice over the engine
noise.

"Only Clementine. I tied her down in the grove and left her
with a bucket of sweet feed. After what happened down there, I
figured she needed to replace those memories with some good
ones." *Maybe we all need that.*

"You come here a lot?" Kate touched a fingertip to the faded
black-and-white snapshot that had been tucked into the Jeep's
windshield frame for as long as Wes could remember. A wedding
photo of Amelia and her late husband. "To help the Braxtons?"

Wes nodded. "I do what I can. They're neighbors. But we train
here too—search and rescue. I did my survival night here."

"Survival?"

"Part of the FUNSAR training—fundamentals of search and
rescue. The trainee is left alone in a wilderness area for a full day
and night. With his twenty-four-hour pack—" Wes pointed
toward his pack, now serving as Hershey's pillow—"and nothing
else." He saw the concern on Kate's face. "Monitored from a distance by the team, but no contact. It's a confidence builder; you

learn to trust that you have everything you need to survive." Wes smiled. "All the right stuff."

Kate's stomach rumbled. She laughed. "I'm guessing there's no cupcakes in there."

"Sorry. GPS, Leatherman tool, headlamp, whistle, space blanket, rain cover . . . tape, hand and foot warmers, water bottle, sunblock, first aid kit."

"So did you?" Kate asked. "Have the 'right stuff'?"

"Guess so. I'm here now," Wes told her, suddenly hoping he had the right stuff for what today held as well. What did Kate expect from him? He returned his gaze to the road in time to avoid a clump of prickly pear cactus. "We're almost there now."

"Where?"

"Right . . ." Wes slowed the Jeep, pointed toward a stand of scrubby trees and the tumble of stones that was once a cattle shed. "There."

"What is it?"

"An old abandoned well." Wes paused, then added, "And the site of a rescue."

- + -

"But it's just some old boards on the ground." Kate watched as Wes tested the sun-bleached wood with his boot; it responded with a hollow thunk. "I thought wells were sort of . . ."

There was amusement in his expression. "Stone wishing wells with a wooden bucket and shingled roof?"

"Maybe." Kate decided he didn't need to know that the Callisons' elderly neighbor had one exactly like that in Sunnyvale. Guarded by a tacky garden gnome—not too effectively, since the well was always filled with pennies, Popsicle sticks, and probably some LEGOs, tossed in by every kid on the block. "But I will bow to your obvious expertise. Given the Got Water? shirt and engineering degree." She watched as Wes knelt down, inspected the well cover. The afternoon sun splashed over his silky dark hair. "What did you mean when you said it's the site of a rescue?"

Wes stood. "This well was drilled way back, one of the few that wasn't my grandfather's. There was a cattle shed here once, a watering tank." He tapped the toe of his boot against the wood again. "The Braxtons built the ranch house where it is now, with a new well. This one was covered up—or so they thought."

"Oh no." Kate's stomach tensed. "Someone fell in?"

"A three-year-old girl, Chrissy Faraday, back in 1991. I was twelve. The whole town was out here. National TV news teams too. Our family was called first, of course—Grandy, Dad, Mom. The old shaft had been filled, but the fill dirt settled with time and years of rain. The well cover rotted and—"

"Chrissy fell down it." Kate winced, imagining her parents' terror.

"About twenty feet. She tried to grab the rope the fire department lowered, but the dirt would fall and she'd get scared. It was getting dark, starting to rain. Nightmare situation."

"So . . . ?" Kate watched Wes's face as he recalled the details.

"They had a harness. But the hole was narrow. None of the firefighters or volunteers would fit. I was a skinny kid back then. Shoulders like a wimp. I hated it. Until that moment."

Kate's mouth sagged open. "They asked you to go down there?"

"No. They tried to talk me out of it—didn't work. I'd latched on to the idea like a tick on a dog." Wes shook his head. "My nose plowed dirt the first few feet. Then I was scared I'd step on the poor kid. Or cause a cave-in and bury us both. But the hole widened out toward the bottom and I was able to get a flashlight focused."

"You saved her."

"I got Chrissy into the harness and they pulled her up."

"You saved her life." Kate realized that she'd stepped close to him, laid her hand on his arm.

"When I was buckling the harness—" Wes's voice softened—"she kept saying this one thing over and over: 'I'm not lost anymore. . . . I'm not lost.' I couldn't forget that."

"That's why you do what you do. Search and rescue."

Wes swallowed. "Partly, I suppose."

Kate was quiet for a few moments, thinking of what he'd told her. This man had been kindhearted and unselfish . . . heroic even as a youngster. Despite his modesty, Wes Tanner had the right stuff all along. For some reason it made her think of Barrett Lyon. And all the wrong stuff he was certain he and Kate had in common. Then she thought of the disappointment on her father's face when she sent him away.

"I don't . . ." Kate cleared her throat. "I don't think I could have done what you did. I'm not that kind of person. I'm selfish and . . ." She took a step, felt the wooden well cover beneath her feet. Solid as truth. "I've made so many mistakes. Even today. With my dad."

"Kate . . ." Wes said nothing further. He simply held her gaze.

Kate couldn't stop herself from trembling—or continuing. "After my mother died, I ran away from home. I was gone for almost a year. It hurt him. I knew it would. And when I came back, we never talked about it. He wanted to . . . today." The familiar threat of tears rose, but Kate shoved them down. Wes had taken hold of her hand, his tenderness compelling her far beyond her comfort zone. "The year I was gone was a terrible time in my life. I can't talk about it any more than I could climb down a well. Or believe that God hears prayers. I know you believe that, Wes. But I can't." She shivered. "I'm not the kind of person God would listen to. Should listen to. I've made too many mistakes. Unforgivable ones."

"Kate, no. It doesn't work that way. We all make mistakes. We're human. We're flawed. That's where grace comes in. That's the beauty of it—an undeserved gift." Wes took a slow breath. "When I saw your father at the hospital, he told me he regretted the way he'd handled things when your mother was sick. I saw how much that bothered him. But I also got the feeling that he's found some hope. I wanted him to share that with you. It's the reason I gave him your address." Wes's thumb brushed the back of her hand. "And took the risk of making a mistake myself." His lips tugged toward a smile. "Meddling. I'm a repeat offender. So—" He stopped short as his cell phone began beeping. "Rescue tone. Excuse me."

Wes hauled it out of his pocket, checking the screen. "Amber Alert."

"Do you have to go?" Kate asked, torn between regret that he would leave and relief that it would mean the end of this unplanned conversation. She'd driven out here today because the walls were closing in, but if Kate kept talking, she'd demolish every wall she'd put up to protect herself. She couldn't risk that. Someone like Wes would never understand the truth about Kate. "Do they need you?"

"No." He reread the message, pocketed his phone. "It's in Austin. An eight-year-old. The majority of these are school bus mix-ups; it's that time of day. I ask for all the alerts because I like to be prepared."

*Because you've got the right stuff.* Everything Kate didn't have. What was she doing here with a man like this?

"So . . ." Kate felt suddenly awkward in the wake of her un-expected babbling. "The well cover's good?"

"Yes. We'll take the Jeep back. I'll leave a note for Lily Braxton, then go get Clementine." Wes glanced at his watch. "Hey, maybe you can help me out. Save me some time?"

"Sure. How?"

"Go to the grove with me. Drive the Jeep back and I'll ride Clem." Wes's brows rose. "Or you ride Clem, and—"

"I'll drive." Kate wrinkled her nose. "I want to be able to sit down."

"Good point. Because I want to take you to dinner tonight." He waited. "This is where you say yes."

"Yes," she told him finally, promising herself she'd be more careful with further conversation. She'd missed lunch and was starving. And regardless of the fact that Wes was out of her league, there was something almost redemptive—if only temporarily—about saying yes to him on the heels of saying no to Barrett's din-ner invitation. She'd picked a man who risked his life for others over one who was unapologetically proud of his ability to "look out for number one." Choosing the hero felt like a significant first.

She hung on tight as the old Jeep bumped along the rocky ter-rain toward the grove. And tried not to question why a man like Wes would choose someone like her.

- + -

"Kate? Are you there?" Lauren glanced at the parked Hyundai, then rapped on the lacquered green door again. "It's Lauren. I—"

The door swung inward.

"I'm here. I'm sorry it took me so long." Kate rolled her eyes. "I thought it was the police again."

"Police? What do you mean?"

"Here, come in." As Kate led her inside, Lauren noticed she'd done some things with the house: packing boxes gone, sweater-knit pillows on the couch, and a framed photo on the mantel. Lauren sniffed. *Potpourri? What prompted all this?*

"A detective came by. They have the security tapes," Kate explained as they sat on the couch. She had cotton balls tucked between her bare toes, protecting freshly painted nails. A polish bottle sat on the coffee table next to her cell phone. "Barrett said they'd be asking me more questions."

*Lyon?* Lauren hoped the potpourri and polish weren't for his benefit. After everything Kate had said about her poor choices when it came to men . . . "What did the police want to know?"

"A detailed description of the girl. Everything she said to me. What I said to her." Kate plucked at her hair; her fingernails were polished too. "Barrett said it was important that it didn't appear as if this girl was looking to me as a Safe Haven provider."

"They found her?" Lauren's brows scrunched. "I didn't hear anything about—"

"No. No, they haven't found her." Kate rubbed her neck. "Barrett's just doing what he does."

*Barrett.* Again. Lauren decided she liked it better when Kate didn't call the hospital attorney by his first name. "Strategy in the event that Austin Grace faces a lawsuit over the baby's death?"

"Yes. But I don't want to believe it will come to that."

Lauren pulled a couch pillow into her lap. "Dana Connor went home sick today."

Kate's lips pinched. "I heard."

"I've talked with her a few times as a peer counselor. She has a lot on her plate even aside from her nursing career." Lauren ran a fingertip over a row of cable knitting on the pillow cover. "Dana has to be worried that she could be targeted for blame in the Baby Doe incident."

"Yes, well . . ." Kate glanced away, let her words trail off.

*You wouldn't do that. Would you?* Lauren dismissed the thought. She knew her friend better than that.

"I stopped by because I heard you left early; I wanted to be sure everything was okay." Lauren's eyes connected with Kate's. "You're good?"

"Yeah. Now I am. Rough morning: meeting with Evelyn, a humiliating skirmish with a Brownie troop . . ." She smiled at the confusion on Lauren's face. "Nothing worth talking about. Then my dad showed up again."

*Ah.* "How'd that go?"

"Not so well." Kate flexed her toes and a cotton ball dropped to the hardwood floor. "He's on his way back to California. We're better via e-mail."

"Family," Lauren commiserated. "Not always easy."

While Kate reached down for the cotton ball, Lauren glanced toward the framed photo on the mantel. A woman with dark hair and Kate's eyes. Her mother, without a doubt. "I understand family drama, trust me. I may need to go home to Houston before Thanksgiving. To check on things."

"Jessica?"

Lauren nodded, worry pressing down like a weight. "She's been missing some school—I think I told you she's pre-nursing. Anyway, Jess hates it when I go big sister on her. But . . . it's a fine line. So—" She stopped short as Kate's phone signaled a text message. "Go ahead. Really."

"Thanks. I should check. I was expecting . . ."

*Barrett Lyon?* Lauren watched Kate's face as she read, caught the fleeting smile she tried to conceal.

"Sorry 'bout that." Kate set the phone back down on the table. "You were saying?"

"Nothing really. Another time." Lauren pushed the pillow aside. "I need to get going. I only wanted to make sure you were good." She pointed to the nail polish. "In my professional opinion, nail polish is always a positive sign. Even better if you were wearing a killer dress and heels."

"Black jersey. Italian pumps. Laid out and waiting."

"Seriously? For what?"

"Dinner. With . . ." Kate's pause was merciless.

"Tell me now, or I'll pitch a fit." Lauren held her breath, tried not to think of the gold Mercedes.

"Wes Tanner." Kate's smile returned.

- + -

"All settled in?" Wes asked, noting the half-eaten plate of food next to Gabe's recliner, a cafeteria array of entrées from his neighbors and church family. He spotted one of Lily Braxton's powdered-sugar cookies.

"Snug as a bug in a rug." Gabe pressed the remote to lower the volume on the TV. Then nudged his dog's nose away from the dinner plate. "Thanks for taking Hersh out today; he'd have been bored to tears playing nurse. Clementine did okay with the grove?"

"Yeah. That old trailer's scheduled for haul out on Friday, I think."

"The sisters must be relieved." The compassion in Gabe's voice reminded Wes once again how unselfish and good-hearted this man was. "Nancy Rae will sleep better too."

"I expect." Wes rolled his eyes. "You sure you don't need me to bunk on the couch tonight? Give you a hand?"

"Nah." Gabe pointed toward the mounded plate. "I've got more food than I need; the crutches are no problem. And Mom's insisting she's going to stand by—covering her eyes—when I navigate the shower tomorrow morning." He shook his head. "In our line of work she's seen a lot worse."

Wes snorted. "Don't count on it." He glanced toward the door. "Hey, did I see a county car pulling away when I drove up?"

"Yeah." Gabe nudged Hershey's nose again, then caved and tossed him a piece of Lily's cookie. He turned back to Wes. "Corey, from the sheriff's department; you remember him. Wife's doing K9 training. Anyway, he stopped by to say hey . . . and give me a little inside information on Sunni's case."

"Like?"

"Like there could be another park search. Didn't we both predict that?"

"Which park? When?"

"Not sure when. Sounds like the DA's pushing for more information first. But the inmate mentioned the Barton Creek Greenbelt." Gabe caught Wes's gaze. "All hush-hush, of course. Which probably won't keep you from heading in that direction again."

"Tonight." Wes smiled at the thought.

Gabe's brows rose. "I was kidding. In the dark? You wouldn't."

"I would. I'll be heading toward Zilker Park tonight." Wes stalled, enjoying the look on his friend's face. "But not for the reason you think."

"Don't torture an invalid. I'll throw a crutch."

Wes grinned. "Kate lives near there. I'm taking her to dinner."

**18**

+

"IT'S AMAZING," KATE SAID over the soft clatter of glassware and distant strains of guitar. She peered through the restaurant's window and across darkened Lady Bird Lake toward the glowing cityscape. "The horizon does look purple now that the sun's set."

"Violet, officially. Or so they say." Wes smiled at her across the linen-topped table. Candlelight played over his freshly shaved jaw and the shoulders of his navy twill jacket, creating smoky shadows beneath his dark lashes. "City of the Violet Crown. Supposedly it was O. Henry who gave Austin the nickname. Back in the late 1800s. Could be a tall tale, though." His smile stretched. "Folks claim we Texans are prone to that sort of thing."

*Tall tale.* Kate hated that his words made her think of what she'd said to the police scant hours ago. Or rather, what she hadn't said. *That poor girl was asking me for help. . . .* Had Kate lied?

Was she willing to shift blame to Dana Connor? Do exactly what Barrett Lyon expected of her . . . because she was like him?

"You're lost in thought," Wes said, bringing Kate's attention back.

"No," she said in a hurry. "Only remembering how much of this amazing city I've discovered, thanks to you." She glanced toward the window again. "That shoreline down there—with Stevie Ray Vaughan himself—the capitol, those crazy food trailers, and Lake Austin." *Where we kissed.* His eyes met hers and Kate felt her face flush. "And now this spot," she added, glancing across the casually upscale oak-and-brick dining room toward a lively bar offering spotted cowhide stools. And in summer, apparently the city's best view of the famous Congress bridge bats. "It's great."

He pointed to her empty salad plate. "You were just surprised to find Humboldt Fog goat cheese this far from California."

"True." Kate smiled at him, feeling again the persistent quiver that had begun with Wes's arrival on her doorstep tonight. It wasn't so much that he'd looked different, though he certainly did: jacket and dress shirt paired casually with nice jeans and boots, and an enticing hint of a scent that had nothing to do with horses. It wasn't that he'd left his Got Water? truck behind in favor of a comfortable sedan—something she greatly appreciated with her clingy dress and heels. The quivers didn't even spring from the way Wes kept a protective hand at the small of her back when they crossed the street to this restaurant. The truth was that they came from the sense that tonight was different. *Because I've never known a man like him.*

Kate blinked, realizing Wes had said something else.

"And if we get the sort of rain they're predicting this week, you might wish you were eating your salad in California. There's a good reason we call them gully washers."

"Will that kind of rain affect your work—the well-drilling business?"

"The drought's affected it more. We've had almost more business than we can handle: extending wells, drilling in new sites, and installing rainwater-catchment systems. Austin needs this rain." He traced a finger down the condensation on his water glass, his expression sobering. "Though flash floods are possible. Which would affect my other business."

Kate gave him a puzzled look.

"Search and rescue," Wes explained. "Travis County has an impressive swift-water rescue team. Central Texas is known as Flash Flood Alley—it's our number one natural disaster threat. And we've had some, trust me. Back in 2001, a supercell thunderstorm, combined with tornadoes, hit Austin during rush hour. Fifteen inches of rain, high winds. Eight of the ten deaths from the storm were vehicle related. Two feet of water will carry away an SUV." Wes's blue eyes darkened and Kate suspected he was thinking of his mother. Her death in that river.

He shook his head. "Sorry. Never give an engineer an opening to quote statistics." He glanced toward the sound of the guitar. "How about I settle up with the waiter and we go enjoy the music? Take back what we lost to that raccoon at Lake Austin."

"The cupcake wrapper?"

"No." Wes smiled. "The dance. Let's finish one this time."

- + -

They stood and Wes stepped aside, allowing Kate to weave through the tables ahead of him. Which also offered yet another glimpse of how great she looked in her dress and heels. He'd been nearly speechless when she opened the door at her house. From jeans

and boots and handily navigating that rusty old Jeep, to . . . *this.*
He took a slow breath. Right now Kate Callison would look completely at home on the arm of some Dallas banker, but she was
with Wes. *With me . . . not Barrett Lyon.* It felt incredibly good.
If only he could manage not to botch things by boring her with
more weather statistics. Or mentioning the greenbelt and its possible connection to Sunni's disappearance. Kate didn't need to add
that to her list of problems. Wes didn't want to worry her; he just
wanted her back in his arms.

Kate stopped at the edge of the small, darkened dance floor. A
few yards away, a solitary guitar player leaned toward his microphone in a soft pool of light, eyes closed as he sang.

A bittersweet look flickered across Kate's face. "That song . . ."

"Van Morrison. 'Brown Eyed Girl.'"

"My father would sing it to my mother," Kate explained. "She
had these big eyes."

"Like yours," Wes said, noticing how bottomless they looked
in the dim light. *Big, sad eyes.*

"I suppose that's true." Kate glanced away again. "People have
said I look like her."

*Then she was beautiful too.* "Let's dance," Wes said, taking her
hand.

In moments they'd joined the other couples on the dance floor,
Kate managing elegance with the somewhat-awkward twirl Wes
attempted in the impossibly small space between other elbows and
shoulders. The singer continued the familiar love song:

*"Standin' in the sunlight laughin'*
*Hidin' behind a rainbow's wall . . ."*

Kate laughed as Wes barely missed stepping on her foot, and she insisted that he attempt the twirl again, her eyes glittering. He twirled; she spun, stumbled, and recovered. Then returned to his arms, nearly collapsing against his chest in laughter, as if she had no cares in the world, no painful past and no uncertain future. Only laughter and music . . . He held Kate, laughing along with her. And then realized something: maybe more than he'd ever wanted anything, Wes wanted to keep the sadness from ever returning to Kate's eyes.

He raised her arm and twirled her again.

*"You my brown eyed girl . . ."*

The singer held the last note and then smoothly transitioned to a slower song. Even more smoothly, Kate moved back into Wes's arms. As before, it felt like she belonged there. Her small hand curled inside his, her chin at his collarbone and that soft hair brushing his cheek. It smelled of shampoo, maybe some kind of flower or herb. Wes breathed it in.

"Safe," she said, leaning away. A smile tugged at her lips. "No raccoons."

"I noticed." A bald-faced lie, of course. Wes wouldn't have noticed if there'd been a flash flood through the restaurant. All he knew was that Kate was in his arms, and even as she moved close once again, all he could think of was that the song would soon end. And then the evening, too. He didn't want that to happen.

- + -

Judith crossed the ER waiting room to where Trista was settling her baby's car seat on a chair. One look at her face and Judith was glad she'd decided to return for a few hours on the evening shift; the girl's father had been causing quite a ruckus upstairs.

"They said he signed himself out," Trista told her, eyes anxious behind her glasses. "I don't get it. He was supposed to stay two more days. They kept saying something like MAA. What does that mean?"

"AMA, dear." Judith glanced down at Harley; she was wearing a lavender knit hat and her cherub lips puckered in her sleep. The silver rattle Judith had gifted her was wedged under the car seat's shoulder strap. "The abbreviation stands for 'against medical advice.' Meaning that your father has chosen to leave the hospital against the advice of his physician. Even if it poses a risk to his health. They had your father sign the papers so that he would understand the seriousness of his decision."

Trista frowned. "And to avoid being sued if he dies at home."

Judith winced, looked down again as Harley began to whimper.

"I talked to his nurse last night," Trista continued. "Two thirty in the morning and he was wide awake. Shaky, she said. Talking out of his head for a while. They had to give him a pill. She called it sundowning and said it happens sometimes to older people in strange surroundings."

Judith bit her lip. Though he was certainly an older parent, Trista's father wasn't much older than Judith herself was.

Trista pushed her glasses up her nose and let out a withering sigh. "He wants to come home so he can get drunk. Period. It doesn't take a doctor to figure—"

"There you are!" A wheelchair appeared at the door to the waiting room. Trista's father wore a bulky bandage, an arm sling, and a very sour expression. "Let me out of this chair," he barked to the nurse's aide, who didn't appear much happier.

"I need to wheel you all the way to the car, sir," he said, resting a hand on his patient's shoulder as he tried to rise. "That's policy, so please—"

"I don't give a—Trista!" her father hollered, rising from the wheelchair. "Grab that baby and get me out of here."

A woman near the door pulled her toddler protectively into her arms; another patient stood and walked to a seat farther away.

"I'll carry Harley," Judith offered as Trista's father shrugged off the aide's help and started toward them. "And I'll wait at the curb with your father if you want to go pull the car up."

Trista held Judith's gaze for a moment. Long enough for Judith to clearly understand that the young mother most certainly didn't want to go get the car if that meant taking her father home. So sad.

Still, it wasn't realistic to think that all family relationships were happy. She thought of Matt Callison, sitting here this afternoon. Hoping to see his daughter. The love and pride in his eyes were unmistakable. A lot like Judith's husband and Molly. Something to be treasured.

Life was fragile. You never knew when something wonderful might be lost. She was glad Kate still had that.

- + -

"You do look like her," Wes said, standing in front of the framed photo on Kate's mantel.

"I like to think that," Kate told him, carrying the daisy mugs to the coffee table. She felt a pang of guilt. The favorite photo of her mother, wearing a floppy beach hat and a sprinkle of summer freckles, had been snipped in half from top to bottom. She'd left the piece with her father's face on the sink the day she hoisted her backpack and walked out. No note, just a pair of kitchen shears and a cruel gesture that said, *I've cut you out of my life.*

Kate set the mugs down, glanced up to see Wes looking at the printed card beside the framed photo. "Engagement announcement," she explained. "A trauma chaplain I worked with at Alamo Grace. She's marrying an ER physician in March. In a Fredericksburg peach orchard." Four months away. The thought came without warning: Would Kate still be in Texas then?

*"Ten hospitals in six years? Seven different cities, three states?"* Barrett's words echoed. He'd pegged her in an instant. Did Kate honestly think Wes wouldn't? Was she foolish enough to hope it could be different this time?

As Wes walked toward where she'd settled on the couch, she wondered briefly if quivers were a sign of hope. They were still here.

"It's good," Wes pronounced after taking a sip of the coffee—brewed this time, not instant. She'd made a quick stop at Austin Java on her way home from buying the nail polish. His thumb brushed the flower on the mug. "This cup looks old."

"My mother's. She bought them in Carmel on a spring break during college."

Wes smiled. "About the same vintage as 'Brown Eyed Girl'?"

"Probably not long after." Kate slid off her shoes, seeing Wes glance discreetly at her polished toes, and reached for her coffee mug. "There used to be a set, but there are only three left now. They were her favorite mugs." Kate clucked her tongue. "I remember them filled with my paintbrushes and once with an avocado seed. I poked it with toothpicks and tried to get it to sprout in water on the windowsill. And . . ." Her heart cramped. "I fixed Mom's herbal tea in those mugs when she was getting chemo."

"You must miss her."

She nodded, afraid to trust her voice. Or imagine what her

mother would think of her mistake-riddled, vagabond life. "We didn't have the big, close family that you have. But she was sort of the glue, you know?" Her father's words, just today, drifted back. *"The heart of our family . . ."*

Wes's expression said he understood.

"The house is on Happy Hollow Lane," Kate continued with a smile. "Mom got the biggest kick out of that; she said it made us sound like a family of chipmunks. She'd puff out her cheeks and make this goofy face." Her smile faded. "Afterward . . . I wanted to rip that street sign down. *Happy* didn't fit anymore." She set the mug on the table.

"Your father still lives in Sunnyvale?" Wes's voice was gentle.

"Happy Hollow Lane." *Except I only use his e-mail address.*

Wes took another sip of his coffee and was quiet for a moment. The coffeemaker burbled in the kitchen and Kate wished she'd switched on her iPod for music. She still could. . . .

"It's funny," Wes said, his voice low and soft, "the things that stick in our minds. My mom—my stepmom, Miranda—has been in my life for much longer, but I still remember my mother making pancakes. The way you do it to make them into shapes: hearts and Mickey Mouse faces. And a *W* for my name. You've seen that?"

An ache filled Kate's throat. She nodded.

Wes shook his head. "I had tea with Amelia Braxton today. She reminded me about my piano recital way back when. And about my mother being there, rooting for me. Coaching me when I got lost with the verses. I'd forgotten." He set his coffee down, met Kate's gaze. There was vulnerability in his expression. "My stepmom would say it was a blessing. A good thing to hold on to."

Kate wished she hadn't just thought of the cross hidden away in the closet, only yards from where she sat with a man who was comfortable talking about blessings. And grace and hope. She didn't want to think about how nothing about her fit with any of that.

"And I think *you* are too, Kate." The blue eyes met hers.

"What?" she asked, hearing her voice emerge in a whisper.

"A good thing." He reached for her hand. "A good thing I'd like to hold on to . . . if that's okay with you."

"I . . ." Kate struggled, the quivers robbing her of speech. "Yes. It's okay."

"Great." He raised her hand to his lips.

"It's . . ." She heard herself chuckle. Knew it was because she was nervous. And because she was having a ridiculous time breathing now that he'd moved close, cradling her cheek in his big palm. She blinked at him, warmth flooding through her. "The nail polish, right?" Her heart skittered as Wes leaned closer. "You can't resist this great nail polish."

He laughed, lips against her cheek. "No. It was the Jeep. Drove me crazy the way you handled that old Jeep." Wes nuzzled Kate's neck, a trace of beard growth tickling her skin.

Then he leaned away just enough to smile at her. "And?" he asked.

She smiled back at him. "And what?"

"You can't resist me because . . . ? C'mon, it's only fair."

"Okay. Your eyes, then."

He chuckled. "Nancy Rae said that too. Just today."

"She's too old for you." Kate's breath caught as Wes leaned close again. "Too short. Bad hair. And—" She sighed as his lips touched the corner of her mouth and raised her arms, eased them around his neck. He slid his around her, strong but gentle, then brushed his lips lightly across hers. A promise of another kiss to come.

"I'm serious," he whispered. "I think it's good that we found each other. Don't you?"

"Mmm." Kate nodded, but she didn't really want to think at all. Right now she only wanted to feel. To be in this good man's arms even if it was only for a short time. Hope beyond that was too risky. But it was the closest thing to happiness she'd known in so long. It did feel different, safe . . . *wonderful*.

She buried her fingers in the softness of Wes's hair, drew him closer. Then closed her eyes and tasted his tender warmth more deeply . . . beginning a kiss he seemed only too willing to continue.

# 19

+

**"WHAT'S THAT TUNE?"** Wes's mom covered the serving platter with a cloth napkin and settled opposite him at the porch table.

"Hmm?" He realized he'd been lost in thought.

"That song." She gazed at Wes over the rim of her coffee cup. The morning breeze wafted scents of sausage and country-fried potatoes—a testament to Mrs. Tanner's kitchen. "You were humming. It sounded like 'Brown Eyed Girl.'"

"Probably was." He smiled, warmth spreading through his chest at the memory. "Heard it last night. In Austin." Wes picked up his coffee, knowing she'd wait forever. Patience could have been Miranda Tanner's middle name. He released the breath he'd been holding. "I like her, Mom."

"I figured." She left it at that, respectful of his privacy as always, though her caring expression was as effective as the huge welcome mat outside the Tanners' door. And a walloping dose of truth serum.

"Kate's different," he told her. Then was at a complete loss for words. How could he explain Kate to his mom? He wasn't sure he understood any of this himself. "I mean, she's pretty, of course— that's obvious. Smart. And funny, too." He shook his head. "I don't know. Maybe I like that she's so determined and independent. Strong. And tries like the devil not to need anybody. But . . ."

"But you think she might need you?" There was something in his mother's eyes that Wes had seen before. That day she watched him slide down the Braxton well to rescue the little girl.

"I'm not sure." He suspected Kate's admitted "mistakes" had something to do with her relationships with men. That she'd been disappointed, maybe even hurt. He hated the thought of it. For that reason alone, Wes was determined to take things slowly where Kate was concerned. Be completely respectful. And protective? He had no doubt she'd prickle at that. "Kate's pretty stubborn. I told you what she said the first day we met: 'No one here needs to be rescued.'"

"If I recall—" his mom glanced toward the sound of a horse's whinny—"you told me she was like 'brushing up against a cactus.'"

"Uh . . ." The warmth returned. "Not so much." Wes shrugged, knowing that if truth serum were actually on the breakfast menu, he'd admit in a heartbeat that he'd never held a woman as soft and sweet. "She's had some tough things to deal with in her life."

His mom waited, the gentle concern in her eyes saying, *As have you, Son.*

"Kate's mother died when she was a teenager." Wes stopped himself from mentioning that she'd run away from home. And been gone for a year. The thought staggered him, but he wasn't about to betray Kate's confidence. "She and her father had some issues related to all of that. Still do."

"I liked Matt. I had a sense he was on a much bigger journey than a drive out here from California. And that his daughter was an important part of it."

"Hmm." So had Wes. It was the reason he'd risked giving Kate's father her address. So the man could share his newfound hope. And faith? Wes couldn't deny that he'd wanted that for Kate too.

But she'd sent her father away. *It's not a Hallmark movie . . . I gave him instant coffee and told him to drive safely.*

"More coffee?"

"No thanks. Let me help you clear these dishes; then I'm heading to the drilling site. Dad's going directly there after he drops Dylan at school. I'm hoping to get that job done early—have to go into Austin later."

"Kate?"

"Travis County Search and Rescue meeting. We're going over water-rescue plans."

"Ah yes. The storm that's coming." His mom glanced up through the pecan branches.

"Right." He stacked the breakfast plates.

"That's fine, Wes. I've got the rest of this. Go to work."

"Thanks." He stepped close, gave her shoulder a squeeze. "Great breakfast, Mom."

"You're welcome." Her quick smile was replaced by that same look he'd seen earlier. The familiar careful-Son-it's-a-deep-well expression of motherly concern. "When you said that Kate tries hard not to need anyone . . . does that include God?"

- + -

"You're smiling," Lauren told Kate over the din of the hospital cafeteria. She paused as an overhead page for an OB department visitor repeated a second time. "And considering that your fork is hovering over a dubious-meat-source enchilada, I'd say that look on your face indicates . . ."

"That I'm really hungry?" Kate was unable to stop the spread of her smile or the betraying flush she felt at the neck of her scrubs. Lauren had phoned and texted at least a half-dozen times last night, starting around 9 p.m., about half an hour after Wes drove away from her house. He'd left her reluctantly; she'd seen it in his eyes, felt it in that last lingering kiss.

He'd made a joke of not wanting her landlord to see a car sitting late in her driveway, then said he had to be up early for work. She knew Wes was being respectful of her. The way he'd been when he opened the car door, pulled out her chair, and stayed protectively on the side of traffic every time they walked. That he'd willingly gone home early left her feeling both relief and a pang of regret. It confirmed everything she'd started to believe: *This man is special.*

"I did send you a text," Kate said, wrinkling her nose as she cut the enchilada—it was an iffy entrée. Not anything like last night's amazing dinner. The flush reached her ears.

"'All fine. CU tomorrow,'" Lauren quoted. "You call that a post-date recap? You could never write scripts for *The Bachelorette.*"

Kate laughed. "I didn't call you back because I was still talking to Wes. On the phone. He called as soon as he got home and we talked until way late."

It was Lauren's turn to smile. "That can only be good."

"I guess." Kate prodded something with her fork; she hoped it was an olive. How could she explain that she wasn't sure she could recognize "good" for certain? The words *good* and *man* had never linked up in Kate's life experience. She only knew that today—everything today—felt better after last night. She took a slow breath. "Yes. I think it could be. Good." Her mouth was dry. She stabbed the olive and popped it in.

"I'm not going to pry. Don't worry." Lauren pressed the edge of her fork against her own enchilada. "I only needed . . ." Her eyes met Kate's. "I wanted to be sure my pal was okay. You know?"

"I know." Kate's throat tightened. *Where were you ten years ago, my friend?*

"Great. So I was thinking if you're not going to California for Thanksgiving, maybe—" Lauren grimaced suddenly, pointing her fork over Kate's shoulder. "Hunker down. Look at your plate. Barrett Lyon's sniffing the air. Oh no, he's heading—"

"Kate." Barrett arrived beside them, flashed Lauren a smile. "Lauren, good to see you." His gaze connected with Kate's for longer than was comfortable.

"Was there something you needed?" Kate asked, thinking her friend was holding her fork more like a weapon than a utensil. "I'm grabbing a bite of lunch, and then I'll be back in the office if you have business to dis—"

"I only have a few minutes. I'm due at the courthouse." He shot a glance at Lauren. "If I might interrupt and speak privately with you, Kate?"

Kate let herself imagine how he'd look with a cafeteria fork stuck between his well-groomed brows. "Lauren, I—"

"No problem." Lauren set her fork on the tray and stood. "I wanted to say hello to Dana anyway."

"Thanks. Sorry." Kate's gaze returned to Barrett as he claimed Lauren's chair. In a room dotted with scrubs, his beautifully tailored suit made him look like a foreigner.

"I'm glad you're feeling better." His lips quirked at the confusion on her face. "Yesterday, when we spoke on the phone. You said you weren't feeling well."

When he asked her out to dinner. Saying, *"We should pursue this."*

"But now . . ." Barrett's gray eyes seemed to note her new nail polish like it was evidence in a fraud case. "You look fully recovered."

Kate refused to feel flustered. "Thank you. Never better." She lifted her chin. "That is, unless there's some new problem?" She noted the leather briefcase he'd set on an empty chair.

He leaned forward slightly. "I spoke with Austin PD this morning."

Her throat constricted.

"The detective who came to your house," Barrett explained. "He said you gave a limited description of the young woman on the tape. It was dark, obviously. He said it seemed clear to him that your conversation with her was brief. And that she offered nothing to indicate she was in serious distress."

*Other than grabbing my arm . . . asking if I'd really help her.*

"Which supports any defense the hospital may have to present." Barrett smiled. "You did well, Kate."

"Has there been progress in locating that girl?"

"Nothing from the photo sent to doctors' offices and clinics. But I expect the police will get responses now that the local media has it." He raised his brows. "You probably saw the mention on the news. Last night?"

"No. I missed it."

"At any rate, the police are doing what they can to find Ava Smith. And as I explained before, the best-case scenario liability-wise is that it doesn't happen. She stays lost, the church buries Baby Doe, and it all dies down." He tapped the tabletop like he was banging a gavel. "Second-best outcome is that she's found negligent in her baby's death."

Kate fought a wave of nausea.

"If that doesn't happen and the hospital's backed into a corner," he continued, "the optimal defense would be—"

"To put the blame on the triage nurse," Kate whispered, unable to stop herself from stealing a glance at Dana Connor. Lauren was still at her table.

"I hope it doesn't go there. But yes." He glanced at his watch. "I have to get to the courthouse. I wanted to bring you up to speed. And say thank you."

"There's no need."

"I'm playing golf this afternoon. With Dub Tarrant," he added, dropping the hospital board chairman's name like a winning putt. "I'm sure he'd like to hear that his emergency department director is doing a fine job."

Something in his eyes made the statement seem more like a question. Her application for a permanent position would soon be under review. Barrett knew that.

"Later, then," he said, reaching for his briefcase. "Enjoy your lunch."

Kate managed a weak smile. Then pushed her tray away with a groan. Was Barrett Lyon so sure of her? Confident she'd root for that troubled girl to stay lost and alone with her pain and guilt? Or face arrest and conviction for her baby's death? Did he think Kate was the kind of person who could point a finger at a fellow nurse and accuse her of negligence? She glanced Dana's way again, remembering what Lauren said about the question Dana wished she'd asked Kate the day that baby died: *Have you ever made a mistake?*

Did Barrett really think Kate could do any of those awful

things? Still . . . for the first time in so long, there was finally some hope. And so much to lose. If Barrett put in a good word—

"Hi there!" Judith Doyle set her folded newspaper on the edge of the table. "I'm sorry. I didn't mean to startle you."

"You didn't, really. I was just thinking." Kate wrinkled her nose. "And avoiding this enchilada."

"Probably wise," Judith agreed. "I wanted to tell you that my volunteer shift ends at three today. You'd mentioned going for coffee. Is that a possibility?"

"Not today, unfortunately," Kate told her with regret. "I have to come back for a budget meeting tonight, so I'm leaving a little early to go over some notes at home. Maybe get a short jog in before it starts to rain." She pulled out her cell phone. "But let's exchange numbers. And check our calendars—plan for that coffee. Okay?"

"Sounds good." Judith paused. "You haven't seen Trista and her baby, have you?"

"No. I heard her father signed out of the hospital AMA."

"Yes. I'm a little concerned because she usually drives him for those rehab appointments. Brings Harley, sits in our waiting room. She's not here today. But maybe he's taking a break because of the surgery."

"Could be," Kate reassured, touched again by the woman's kindness and dedication. "I wouldn't worry, Judith."

They exchanged numbers, made a tentative date for coffee. As the volunteer left in a swish of pink, Kate noticed she'd forgotten her newspaper. An *Austin American-Statesman* folded to the editorial page. Kate picked it up, frowned: another commentary from Waiting for Compassion. She skimmed the well-written letter alleging unsafe practices in a local ER. Kate sighed with relief. At least it didn't appear to be Austin Grace this time.

- + -

Wes found Kate exactly where her text indicated she'd be. On the greenbelt near the trailhead in Zilker Park. Next to a bench under the trees.

His breath snagged. Could she have any idea how beautiful she looked right now?

"You found me." She smiled, her face dappled by shadows from the boughs—and by dark clouds overhead. Her hair had gone wavy from the building humidity, her skin almost glowing. "Such as I am." Kate glanced at her jogging attire: blue-and-gold San José State University T-shirt, shorts over dark running tights. "Pretty grubby. I warned you."

"So you did," he managed to say, though his pulse had taken off as if he'd been the one jogging. "And . . ." Wes closed the space between them in a heartbeat, wrapping his arms around her. She giggled, breath warm against his neck, then clung to him as his hug lifted her nearly off the ground. "I missed you," he whispered hoarsely with his lips pressed to her hair. "I know I told you I wouldn't be able to see you today. Then you said you'd be home early . . ."

"And you . . ." Kate regained her footing and leaned back just enough to blink up at him. Her expression was like a child reaching for a soap bubble let loose from a wand, not sure it would last if she touched it. The look blossomed into a smile that warmed his heart. "You couldn't stay away?" she asked.

"No." He reached out to rest his hand along the side of her face, brushing his thumb over her moist skin. "I couldn't."

There was a sharp crack overhead and then a huge rumbling roll of thunder.

"Oh, wow." Kate stared at the sky.

The ground trembled.

"I think the temperature just dropped like a rock," she said, hugging her arms around herself.

"Texas." Wes shook his head. "There's a saying: 'If you don't like the weather, wait five minutes and it'll change.'" He took hold of her hand, wanting the connection again. "I've been following the reports. Dust storm in Monterrey, Mexico, blowing into south Texas. And a band of showers headed in from the west. We could see some strange weather." He glanced away as a pair of joggers passed them, heading through Zilker Park.

"I'm glad I got most of my run in, anyway." Kate's warm fingers moved inside his, making him very aware that talking about weather was a big waste of time.

"I'll drive you home."

"It's like five minutes away. Less." Kate shook her head. "I could walk there before I climbed into that big truck and got my seat belt fastened. Besides, we both have meetings to get to. If the weather doesn't interfere."

Wes eyed the trail that headed toward the greenbelt, thinking of its trees and dense stands of shrubbery. Kate had just come through there, and Gabe thought the inmate was going to reveal the area as a crime scene.

"Wes?" She smiled at him, that bubble-wand look back on her face. As if she weren't used to someone being concerned for her safety. "I'm fine walking. It's all good."

"I'm driving you," he insisted, drawing her into his arms again. "Right after—" Wes cast a discreet glance at the mercifully vacant trail, then sighed and dipped his head low—"this."

- + -

Kate lifted her face for Wes's kiss, not sure if the insistent thrumming in her ears was her heartbeat or another roll of thunder. The first splash of rain hit her forearm just as his lips met hers. She didn't care. He was tender, thorough, and—

"Oh! Water down my back!" She laughed against his lips as rain streamed between her shoulder blades. Her laugh turned to a sigh as Wes pulled her closer to kiss her again. And again. Her lips, cheek, neck . . . Rain trickled along her scalp, dribbled from her ear, its cool contrast making the warmth of his skin against hers even more wonderful.

"It's pouring!" Kate leaned back, breath almost catching at the sight of his handsome face soaked with rain. She blinked as drops wet her lashes. Then glanced down at the puddle forming around her feet. "You said two feet can carry an SUV away," she continued, raising her voice over a humid gust of wind. "I'm a lot smaller."

There was another flash of lightning, and thunder rumbled.

"My feet are soaked through to my socks. I think we should—" Kate gasped as Wes hoisted her high into his arms.

"Hey, wait," she protested, half-laughing as he began to stride toward the road, carrying her under the darkening sky. "What—?"

"Consider yourself rescued," he told her as she squirmed in a weak show of resistance. "Like it or not."

*I do,* she decided, smiling. Not that she'd tell him, of course.

They were at her house in five minutes and he'd driven off to his meeting in less than seven, time for one more kiss—two if you counted the one that happened when she ran back to grab the water bottle she'd left on the seat. They'd managed it with impetuous acrobatics, Kate on her tiptoes and nearly doing a chin-up on the driver's window and Wes leaning out. Both of them dripping from the rain.

She wasn't sure if she'd run or floated on air to the shelter of the house.

Kate decided she'd shower and fix something to eat before heading back to the hospital. She grabbed the TV remote and gave it a click, laughing when she saw the puddle she was leaving on the hardwood floor. She'd get a towel to wipe it up. Hopefully the weather would clear before she left the house again. It didn't really matter because even a Texas "thunder bumper" couldn't dampen how she was feeling right now. Warm despite her soaking clothes. Cared for, safe . . . hopeful? Yes, maybe even that.

She looked at her mother's photo on the mantel, feeling her throat tighten. "Mom, I've met someone," she whispered. "I think it's good. I think—"

The TV news blared, interrupting her.

"Police are asking for anyone who might recognize this young woman—" Ava Smith's shadowy image filled the screen—"in connection with the death of a newborn infant abandoned in the emergency department of Austin Grace Hospital," the newscaster continued. "Any information should be—"

Kate switched off the TV, shuddering against the chill of her sodden clothing for the first time. She glanced toward the window as rain continued to pelt even more heavily. Thudding like a lumberjack's boots now. She squinted and walked closer, confused at what she was seeing. The window glass was brown with . . . *mud?* It looked like mud, streaks of it. But the windows had been cleaned a week ago. What on earth was happening?

She walked, clothes still dripping, to the front door. Then out onto the porch, her mouth sagging open in confusion. She stepped onto the driveway, felt the sloppy brown grit splash her skin. It really was—

"Raining mud!" her landlord shouted over the rosemary hedge and another menacing rumble of thunder. He raised his golf umbrella, splotched with the sludge. "Mexican dust storm hit that west Texas front. It happens." He pointed to her car. "Don't wipe it down. It'll scratch your paint. Use the hose."

"Oh. All right. Thanks." She stepped back into the house, stunned. Mud from the sky? Strangely, she thought of fireflies. One of her favorite things about Texas. Bright, magical, hopeful. What happened to fireflies when it rained mud?

She stared at the blank TV screen, remembering Ava Smith's face on the security camera clip. And Barrett Lyon's comment that Kate had done well when questioned by the police detective, his unnerving confidence that she would continue to do as he dictated. Kate glanced once again at her mother's photo. Only moments ago she'd been giddy and hopeful enough to risk saying out loud that this new relationship with Wes could be good. Then it rained mud.

Her cell phone played its text ringtone. She walked to the coffee table, picked it up. Her father.

Arrived in Phoenix. Home tomorrow. Seeing you was good, Katy.

She closed the message with a sigh.

If her landlord hadn't said that raining mud wasn't unheard of in Texas, Kate would have thought it was some sort of awful sign. From God, maybe. That her unforgivable mistakes doomed her like fireflies snuffed out by muddy rain. She'd have thought hope was impossible. But now . . .

She hugged herself, remembering the warmth of Wes's arms. Lauren's friendship. And this newest proof that things were okay: her father's text. Tomorrow he'd be in California. Before long Kate could forget that he had sat in this room and bared his soul.

Yes. Things were back to normal. Better than that—they were bordering on "good" for the first time in forever. She took a slow breath. *Right?*

## 20

**"A NEAR DROWNING FROM THE STORM?"** Kate peered at the ER tech from under her umbrella, raising her voice over the insistent drumming of rain on the ambulance bay overhang. She saw him nod confirmation.

Until yesterday, Kate wouldn't have believed such a thing was possible. But the downpour hadn't quit except for a few hours around dawn. Last evening's budget meeting had been canceled, and Kate lost count of how many times she'd been awakened in the night. By thunder, howling wind, and incredible flashes of lightning so bright she could see them through her closed eyelids. She glanced up at the sky—at least it was standard-issue rain, not muddy sludge.

A handful of gathered staff hoisted a rainbow of umbrellas and awaited the Code 3 ambulance arrival. Kate caught sight of Dana Connor, saw her adjust her umbrella to avoid eye contact.

Kate turned back to the tech. "This homeless woman was swept away by rushing water?" Sirens wailed as the ambulance pulled in behind the hospital.

"From a group camping under a bridge," he explained, raindrops beading on his rust-colored beard. "Water rose and grabbed her sleeping bag and tent." He shook his head. "A teenager. Runaway, I'd bet."

Kate's stomach shuddered.

"She was probably dragged down by the wet sleeping bag—like the proverbial cement overcoat—and hauled downstream," the tech continued. "Then got tangled in an uprooted cedar tree, facedown. Good thing someone had a working cell phone." He stepped forward, rain sluicing over his surgical cap as the ambulance pulled to a stop and began its backing-up beeping. "Here we go."

The ambulance doors burst open, and through a humid blur of rain, Kate saw the young girl on the stretcher. *Very young.* A paramedic hunched over her, one hand holding a face mask and the other squeezing a plastic Ambu bag. No cardiac compressions, but—

"Trauma room one," Kate directed above the din of voices, then closed her umbrella and trotted alongside the hustling stretcher shoulder to shoulder with Dana.

"Carly Udall. Near drowning," a paramedic reported as they clattered into the trauma room. "Sixteen-year-old, no available medical history. Underwater for unknown time; Glasgow Coma Scale 9 or 10. Glucose check 78. Some abrasions, no obvious head or neck injury. BP 100 over 60. Monitor shows sinus tach at 108. Respirations 32 and shallow. Lips dusky. Wheezes, crackles—pulse ox 87 percent on high-flow oxygen with bag assist."

The girl's face was pale behind the rescue mask, her chin tucked into a protective cervical collar. She groaned and tried to raise her arm. A second medic lowered it, checked the tape on the IV, then gently plucked a twig from her soaking blonde hair. "Easy, Carly . . ."

The paramedic squeezed the Ambu bag, supplementing her breathing efforts.

"Let's move her," the ER physician instructed. "On my count. One, two . . ."

"I've got it," Dana said, moving alongside. Her eyes, unreadable, connected with Kate's. "I can handle this."

"Right." Kate stepped away from the stretcher, glancing to where the respiratory therapists were preparing for ventilatory assistance. BiPAP, probably, to enhance breathing through bi-level positive pressure. They'd also opened the intubation tray and laid out both the standard and fiber-optic laryngoscopes, as well as an assortment of endotracheal tubes—just in case. Kate moved to the crash cart, pulled out the necessary drugs for emergency intubation. Sedation and a paralyzing agent—this doctor called himself old-school in his preference for Versed and vecuronium.

"Let's cut these wet clothes off." The tech looked toward the warming unit being wheeled into the corner of the room. "Good, the Bair Hugger's here. We'll have her temp reading in a minute."

"X-ray's standing by for a portable," Kate reported, her throat constricting as the young patient's eyes met hers. *So lost and alone.* She caught the doctor's attention. "Think you'll have to intubate?"

"She's tired but still making a fighting effort." The physician, a father of teenagers, looked at the girl's face and sighed. "With her Glasgow well above 8, I'm going to give her some time on

BiPAP while we run arterial gases. I expect her $PO_2$'s will be low—we can support that. But if her $PCO_2$'s are high, there's a ventilatory problem, and she'll get that tube." He nodded at Dana. "We'll get her dry and warm. Let me know as soon as you have a temp. Start another IV line, pull blood for labs—I'll write those orders. Tox screen too. Pregnancy test. Put in a Foley cath. We'll want to x-ray her neck, clear it before we get complete chest films. Once I have a better look at her, I'll be able to tell you what else I'll need."

"Yes, sir," Dana told him, getting the monitoring equipment ready as the techs cut away the girl's multiple layers of soaked clothing. She glanced at Kate, her expression wary.

"Good," Kate said, not entirely sure who she was addressing. "I'm going to see what the social worker's found out about contacts and family." She took another look at the pale girl battling to breathe. If this had happened to Kate in Las Vegas, they would have notified her father. *And he'd have discovered my pregnancy.*

Kate stepped into the outer corridor, surprised to find Lauren.

"I'm filling in for Dana for a couple of hours," Lauren explained. "Didn't she tell you?"

"She barely looks at me these days. But I'm always glad to have you. What's going on with Dana?"

"Baby Doe. That church is having a memorial service today. She wants to be there."

"Oh."

"One of the ICU nurses is married to a PD officer; she told me undercover detectives would be there too."

"In case the mother . . ." Kate's voice caught. "Shows up."

"Sad business all around."

"Yes," Kate agreed, remembering what Lyon had said about the optimal outcome for all of this. That the mother "*. . . stays lost, the church buries Baby Doe, and it all dies down.*"

"Miserable situation. This morning's not much better. I'm on my way to find the social worker—" Kate nodded toward the trauma room—"for our near drowning. A teenager from a homeless camp. They rescued her from a flooded creek."

"I heard." Lauren's lips hinted at an incongruous smile. "From your rescue man."

"My . . ." Kate tried to deny the sudden quiver. "You mean Wes?"

"You have more than one?" Lauren teased, hitching her thumb over her shoulder. "He's nursing a cup of scalding coffee in the ambulance bay. And he's drenched. Someone should put plastic caution cones around that man."

"I'll see about that," Kate told her, hoping her face didn't look as pink as it suddenly felt. Caution cones? She smiled. It was too late for that.

- + -

"Will you mention it again, please?" Judith peered through a narrow opening in the window separating the waiting room from the emergency department registration office. She wanted to be sure Beverly understood the seriousness of the situation.

The clerk stared back at her, holding a phone receiver protectively against her shoulder. Likely a personal conversation Judith had interrupted. They were all too frequent.

"I'm certain the triage nurse would want to know that Mr. Beck has begun to perspire," Judith explained. The sixty-year-old truck driver's face had gone suddenly pale, maybe even gray. Something was definitely wrong. Judith searched for the word she'd seen in her Internet medical research. "Tell the triage nurse that Mr. Beck has become . . . diaphoretic."

Beverly frowned. "I get it. He's sweating. I'll check the thermostat. People complain it's cold. Then it's too hot. This humidity is making things all wonky. All I can do is—"

"No. Wait," Judith insisted. "That's not what I meant, Beverly. He's not sweating because it's hot in here. He's sicker."

The clerk leaned toward the window, stared into the waiting room. "Is he having chest pains? It doesn't say chest pains on his admission note."

Judith was tempted beyond reason to lie. "Not exactly. He told the nurse it's his gallbladder. He ate chile rellenos last night. He knew it was a bad idea. But some people can't tell the difference between indigestion and cardiac pain. And with this sudden heavy sweating, I think—"

"Sure. I understand, hon." Beverly's patronizing smile pointed to an essential truth: Judith was a volunteer. Her role was to fetch coffee, direct patients to the restrooms, work puzzles with the children. And push wheelchairs . . . with careful supervision. Medical diagnosis was not part of the deal. "I'll tell the triage nurse what you said."

"When?" Judith jutted her jaw and felt her angel earrings rally. "How long will Mr. Beck have to wait? It's been close to forty minutes now."

The clerk's smile vanished. She held up a finger, whispered something into the phone, and disconnected. "The nurses in the back are busy with that girl who almost drowned. That is a priority. Meaning they probably won't have time for Mr. Beck right now." The barely tolerant smile returned. "But as soon as the triage nurse is finished with the baby she's seeing now, I'll tell her that Mr. Beck's gallbladder situation is worse. No worries, hon.'"

Judith bit her lip, made herself nod patiently despite rising anger.

No worries? It was Beverly who should worry. That woman was sadly mistaken if she believed Judith would put a patient at risk so she could resume her personal phone call. And nibble on that warehouse-size bag of cheese puffs she kept in the desk drawer. Judith would do what was right. She'd check on Mr. Beck again and take whatever actions were necessary to—

Except that he was gone.

Judith stood at the vacant chair, her anxiety rising. "Where's that man who was sitting next to you?" she asked the woman who'd injured her wrist in a fall at a grocery store. "Balding. Wearing a blue jacket with a trucking company logo. You were talking to him . . ."

"He went to the bathroom." The woman pointed her ice pack toward the far hallway. "He looked like he was going to vomit."

"How long's he been gone?" Dread made Judith's mouth dry.

"Quite a while. Poor man—he said something about bad Mexican food."

*Oh, please . . .*

Judith jogged toward the hallway bathroom, heart pounding.

- + -

"You found me," Wes told Kate, remembering that she'd used those exact words yesterday. The prelude to some very memorable minutes in the rain at Zilker Park. She had raindrops in her hair right now. His pulse quickened and he reminded himself that it was completely inappropriate to pull her into his arms. "You must have seen Lauren."

"Yes." Kate stepped closer to the sheltered visitors' bench, the Bambi eyes moving over his rescue attire: rain suit, boots, vest, radio. "She said you were drenched. I'd say she has accurate assessment skills." A smile teased her lips, quickly replaced by a flicker of concern. "You went into the creek after that girl?"

"Climbed out on the fallen tree mostly. The swift-water team provided the real expertise. How's Carly doing?"

"Awake, still confused. On BiPAP by now. We'll know more when we see the blood gases. But . . ." Her eyes held Wes's long enough to make his breath snag. "You got to her in time."

"The team—"

"You saved her life, Wes." Her fingers brushed his shoulder. It took all he had not to capture her hand, raise it to his lips.

He cleared his throat. "I'm glad we found Carly. She's just a kid."

"Social services will try to locate contacts, phone numbers—family."

"That group she was with is familiar to PD. Transients." Wes hesitated, knowing the impact the scenario must hold for Kate personally. "She's probably . . ."

"A runaway." Kate crossed her arms, rubbing the sleeves of her scrub jacket as if suddenly chilled. "The tech thought so." She gazed at the continuing rain. "Lousy time to be on your own."

*"The year I was gone was a terrible time in my life."* Wes recalled the pain on Kate's face when she shared that confidence. He hated to imagine what she'd endured.

"Are the counties anticipating more flooding and rescue calls?" She looked toward his truck parked nearby: tailgate still down, his twenty-four-hour pack, helmet, and the rest of his gear inside.

"The rain's supposed to continue until tomorrow sometime. But lighter, I think." Wes reminded himself to check the weather feed on his phone app. "Those west Texas cells are moving through. TV and radio stations are broadcasting the usual warnings about low-water crossings."

"'Turn around; don't drown.' I've seen the ads. And those videos. Scary."

"You'd be surprised how many people take the risk anyway. Drive right into the water."

Wes saw Kate flinch and knew she was thinking about his mother. He was glad she didn't know the whole story.

"I suppose the greenbelt is flooding too." Kate frowned. "There goes my jogging. Such as it was."

"For a while probably. Reports say there's at least one major sinkhole on the trail. Near the Zilker trailhead. And mudslides, trees down. Lots of debris. They brought bulldozers in during the break this morning, started some of the cleanup. The rest will have to wait a few days. Meanwhile it's all behind barricades."

Wes had heard something else. A grid search for evidence in the Sunni Sprague case was indeed being organized. The area would include the greenbelt trail not far from Zilker Park—after the rains let up and they could get volunteer teams in. There was already some covert discussion between crews eager to clear the park and law enforcement intent on preserving evidence. But bottom line: jogging and searching were both on hold for now.

"I'll be doing Pilates," Kate said with a sigh. "DVD in my living room with no risk of flash flooding or—" She stopped short, peering toward a buzzing crowd of people near the doors to the emergency department waiting room. "What's happening?"

"Nurse!" a man shouted, waving frantically at Kate. "Some

guy's passed out on the floor in the bathroom and the volunteer lady needs help—hurry!"

- + -

*Oh, please . . . help . . .*

Judith told herself not to panic, to keep on until help came. It would, wouldn't it?

A crowd had gathered. Knees, feet—she couldn't see more from down on the lavatory floor. Couldn't take the time to try. Voices, shouts. Her own heartbeat pounding in her ears.

"What's happening?" someone shouted.

"That lady's doing CPR—tell somebody. Get some nurses over here!"

*Press down on his chest; count.* Judith rocked forward on her knees again, lowering her full weight onto her palms. Flat against the center of Mr. Beck's breastbone. She counted each compression out loud, a fearful quaver making it sound like a foreign language. "One and two and three and four and—"

Her gaze darted toward the man's face, too much like a death mask already: gray skin, blue lips, eyes glazed and unseeing. It had been terrifying to find him like that and a miracle he hadn't taken time to lock the bathroom door behind him. She'd yanked the emergency call cord, shouted for help, then dropped to the floor to check his breathing and pulse. It had only been a minute or two since then, but it felt like forever. "Fifteen and sixteen and seventeen and eighteen . . ."

Nervous sweat dripped from her chin, splashed onto the trucker's shirt now stained and sour with vomit. He wasn't breathing. There was a froth of mucus on his lips. She couldn't have done mouth-to-mouth without gagging. But rescue breathing wasn't necessary in cardiocerebral resuscitation, just the chest compressions, so—

"Judith . . ." A deep voice, someone crouching beside her.

She looked up, her hands still trembling on the man's chest. There was a commotion at the lavatory doorway. Nurses, a security officer, a technician . . . gurney wheels, a squeak as it lowered to the floor. Was that Kate Callison?

A hand tugged her gently. "Judith, it's okay. Help's here. Come away now. Let them in."

She rose, legs weak, and staggered backward as the staff converged in a rush.

"Lift him. One, two, three—okay, let's go!"

"Stand back, folks. Everyone back!"

Judith watched as Mr. Beck disappeared through the door to the emergency department corridor in a surreal blur. So horrible. The whole thing—fighting to get him reexamined, discovering him missing, finding him collapsed. Judith felt her legs losing strength, her vision dimming. *Don't faint . . .*

"Here, lean on me." An arm slid around her waist. Strong, solid. "Let's get you sitting down, Judith."

She blinked up, recognized him. That rescuer. The man who'd found the lost woman with Alzheimer's and helped with Baby Doe. He'd been here again when his friend was shot and needed surgery. She couldn't recall the man's name right now, but she'd never forgotten that look in his blue eyes, each of those times. It was there now, for her. Compassion.

"Your first time doing CPR?" he asked gently as he guided her toward the lounge a merciful distance from the still-buzzing waiting room.

She nodded, already feeling an arthritic twinge from kneeling on the cold floor. "I tried to get him help. His wife dropped him off and then went to check on her elderly mother. Mr. Beck was waiting by himself. All alone." She shivered and the rescuer's arm drew her closer to his side. "It shouldn't have happened."

- + -

Kate added more warm water to the tile-topped tub and then stretched out, letting the frothy bubbles swoosh over her like meringue. She closed her eyes, breathing in the scent. Sweet pea, her favorite fragrance—favorite flower. Blossoms in ballerina-skirt colors, smelling like still-warm angel food cake. The way her mother made it, drizzled with pink glaze and topped by maraschino cherries.

But it wasn't only the flowers' scent that amazed Kate. It was also that sweet peas started out so humbly. Rock-hard, unlovely seeds—nicked with a knife to encourage sprouting and then submerged in water overnight. She sighed, remembering them in a jelly jar on their Happy Hollow Lane kitchen sink. Wounded seeds poked unceremoniously into cold, inhospitable, and barren soil. As if they were some sad sacrifice to the loneliness of winter. Gone. Forgotten. And then suddenly, in spring . . . Kate smiled, remembering. There they would be: pale green and arching from the ground, reaching for support. Then climbing, twining, turning toward the sun. Fairy-tale flowers that smelled of birthday cake. And hope? Was that what felt so good about them?

Kate slid lower in the tub, letting the bubbles beard her chin. Even after all that had happened at the hospital today, there did seem to be room for hope. Carly Udall, the near-drowning victim, showed improvement and hadn't required the ventilator. She was in the ICU, receiving antibiotics and vigorous respiratory treatments. While awaiting the arrival of her family, divorced parents united in the relief of finding their daughter. Her pregnancy test, mercifully, had been negative. Kate had held her breath reading the lab results.

Mr. Beck's lethal heart rhythm resisted the first two jolts from the defibrillator, converted successfully on a third try, and was maintained via drug infusion. By the time Mrs. Beck returned to the hospital, he was in the capable care of the cardiac cath team. And reportedly able to squeeze his wife's hand. With tears sliding down his face.

Kate had reviewed his chart with some anxiety. But Mr. Beck had no known history of heart disease. Vital signs were normal on arrival to the ER and he'd rated his abdominal discomfort low on the pain scale, insisting it was food related. He'd been adamant in his denial of chest pain. The triage nurse's first inkling that the stoic trucker felt worse was a message via the clerk; she'd been on her way to check him when . . . Kate sighed. Things had been done according to policy, fully documented. Bad things couldn't always be predicted. Thanks to Judith Doyle, the man was found right away.

Kate's cell phone buzzed on the edge of the tub: Lauren.

"Catch you at a bad time?" her friend asked.

"Up to my neck in a bubble bath—definitely good."

"I thought maybe you'd be out with Wes."

Kate smiled, remembering the discreet hug they'd shared before he left the hospital. "He had plans with Dylan. Brothers' movie night. We're doing something on Sunday."

"Good. I wanted to let you know that I called Judith at home, checked on her again."

"How did she seem?"

"Quiet. But okay, I think. Considering. She said again how appreciative she was of Wes's help. And she was glad I could give her at least a general update on Mr. Beck's condition. I'm going to talk to the Ladies Auxiliary about nominating her for volunteer of the year."

"That's a great idea. Judith is such a hard worker, but this went far beyond the call of duty. It had to have been awful for her."

"For everyone in that waiting room too. I vote for a lot less drama out there. Which reminds me—did you see that piece on the news? After the service for Baby Doe?"

"No." Kate reached for her terry robe with one hand. The water was getting cold.

"It was really short. Just a few words from the pastor and from a representative of a women's clinic regarding Safe Haven."

Kate stood, slipped an arm into her robe. "Could you tell if there were many people there?"

"Quite a few apparently." There was sadness in Lauren's voice. "The camera caught people leaving the service. I'd wager a few of those were detectives. I saw Dana. And . . . this was sort of strange . . ."

"What?" Kate asked, moving the phone from hand to hand to tie her robe. She was shivering now. Enough to make her teeth chatter.

"Barrett Lyon was there too."

## 21

"**LOOKS LIKE YOU'RE PREPARING** for a callout, buddy." Wes straddled a chair in Gabe's kitchen, a safe distance from the oak table piled high enough to risk avalanche: twenty-four-hour pack, three GPS units, open laptop, maps, helmet, Gabe's extra-large rescue vest, and Hershey's little orange one. Plus a Costco-size bag of dog biscuits, a case of Dr Pepper, and what appeared to be a half-eaten breakfast burrito. "Or maybe you're auditioning for an episode of *Hoarders*."

Gabe snagged a balled pair of socks and hurled it at him. "I'll be ready and I'll be there." He frowned at his injured leg, propped dutifully on a chair. "In the command trailer. I can do that much." He nodded decisively. "Zilker Park, as soon as they give us the green light weather-wise. It's probably going to be delayed for several days. I heard they aren't allowing any cleanup past the trailhead until after the search. They blocked off the sinkhole and left the dozer sitting there. Everything at a standstill until law enforcement gives the go-ahead." He sighed. "Weather's really playing havoc with our chances here."

"But the rain's easing up." Wes scratched Hershey's chin. "And sometimes weather works for us—stirs up things we missed last search." He retrieved the sock ball and tossed it back and forth between his hands. "Sounds reliable, that tip from the inmate. Everything he heard from the man he thumbed a ride with outside Waco."

Gabe's expression was solemn. "If our inmate hadn't been in an Oklahoma lockup the week Sunni disappeared, he'd be a prime suspect himself. A nickname and a description were all he gave about the driver, but it was enough of a lead for law enforcement and the FBI to beef up their manhunt." He nodded. "This was a solid tip. No police reports mentioned that turquoise cross she wore. One of a kind, and the inmate described it to a tee."

"I remember Dylan looking at it, that time Sunni stayed over-time to sit with him in the ER. Sunni said her grandfather made it from a stone he found when he was doing missionary work in Colorado."

Gabe was quiet for a while. "Jenna's going to handle Hershey on the search."

*And Hershey is human-remains certified. . . .* Wes reminded himself that finding nothing, not ever knowing, was far more painful.

A slow grin spread across Gabe's round face. "The Nancy Rae hotline says you've been seen around town—and in a certain Jeep—with Kate Callison."

"Nancy has always been the jealous kind."

Gabe dangled a biscuit for Hershey, peered sideways at Wes. "The Jeep ride, then a dinner date? Sounds serious."

"Uh . . . not sure." Wes wondered what Gabe would think if he knew Wes had also stood like a fool in the pouring rain because he didn't want to stop kissing Kate. And today he'd felt an irresistible urge to send flowers. Did that mean "serious"?

"Maybe," he admitted finally. "I'm glad Kate's in line for a full-time management position. I want her to stay. So I can get to know her better." He smiled at Gabe. "Don't tell Nancy Rae."

Gabe traced a finger over his heart.

- + -

"Praise for our efforts with Mr. Beck?" Kate set her coffee on Evelyn's desk before the giddy whoosh of relief made her spill it. She'd been certain the summons to the CNO's office spelled doom.

"High praise. From his wife, along with a visitor who stopped me outside the ICU and then a phone call I received only half an hour ago." Evelyn played with her purple reading glasses, beaming at Kate. "He's a newspaper reporter who was here to cover the near drowning case." Her smile found a hidden dimple. "He was impressed with the department's 'immediate and skilled response' to a critical situation, like a 'well-oiled team.' This could lead to some good press."

"I hope." Kate smiled. *Hope.* The word slipped out like it was the most natural thing in the world.

"You were commended personally," the director continued, "for your skill in directing your staff and for the way you handled things with the people in the waiting area. 'Efficient, calm, and caring.'"

*Thanks to Lauren and Wes.*

"It was a tough situation," Kate agreed.

"That you handled well." The director leaned forward in her chair. "And apparently you've made some other good impressions. Dub Tarrant stopped by to say hello early this morning. I'm sure you're aware that he's chair of the hospital board of directors. He mentioned the hiring committee's meeting next month. Said he'd heard good things about you."

*On the golf course. From Barrett Lyon.*

"He's eager to see the management of the emergency department stabilized. Under the leadership of a permanent director who makes it a priority to present this hospital in the best possible light."

*And?* Kate held her breath as Evelyn took a sip from a can of Diet Coke.

"Anyway," she concluded, "I wanted to pass along the compliments. And tell you that I appreciate your efforts."

Kate knew it was foolish to think the CNO would—or could— say more at this point. But hope was indeed blossoming . . . like a fistful of sweet peas. She'd take it.

"I appreciate your telling me all this." Kate retrieved her coffee, stood.

"I'm sure you're as relieved as I am that the media focus on Baby Doe seems to have abated," Evelyn added, bridging her palms. "I understand that a local church had a service for him yesterday. I have to believe that will help. On all counts."

"I'd like to believe that too."

Kate slipped through the doorway, wishing the conversation had stopped a few moments earlier. When unexpected compliments showered down and hope began to float. Before the mention of Baby Doe's tragedy, which still felt too much like muddy rain.

- + -

"It sounds good." Lauren scooted over to give Kate more room on the bench. The rain had lightened to a drizzle, making ticking sounds on the roof of the hospital gazebo. "The boss giving you an official 'attagirl' so close to your performance review." She could tell Kate thought so too. There was something new and beautifully hopeful on her friend's face lately. If they could market that, Lauren would be first in line. *Jessica* . . . No, she wasn't going to dampen Kate's happy moment with her family concerns. "I'd say it's a good sign."

"Hard to know." Kate shrugged, but the hopeful look remained. "Plenty of balls still in the air. Lyon's a pro at reminding me of that. I don't know what to make of his being at the baby's service."

"Maybe it was his expression of sympathy for—" Lauren caught the look on Kate's face. "Okay, I don't believe that either. He was probably curious to see if the mother really would show up like the detectives speculated. A traumatized teenager lurking in the back of the church. Knowing that her baby . . ." She sighed, feeling for the troubled girl. And her family. "It's all so sad."

"Yes." Kate was quiet for a few moments, then turned to Lauren. "How's your sister? You said something about having to go home to Houston."

"She . . ." Lauren was startled by an unexpected sting of tears.

"Lauren?" Kate slid closer. "What is it?"

"I'm probably making too much of it. I hope I am," Lauren whispered around the ache in her throat.

"You've said she's had trouble with depression."

"Only one bad episode. But . . ." Lauren made herself say words that frightened her still. "Jess ran away last spring. After an argument with a friend, Eli; he's a PA at Houston Grace ER. She didn't say anything to any of us. Just disappeared. We found out one of the docs at the hospital had given her a prescription for sleeping pills. We were afraid . . ." Lauren met Kate's gaze through a prism of tears. "Eli found her and brought her home."

"And now?"

"Some erratic behavior." Lauren swiped a tear. "Higher than a kite for weeks. Aces her classes, charms the pants off her coworkers at the hospital—Jess is an admitting clerk in the ER. And she gets really irritable sometimes, at least with the family. Then sort of slows down, like she's knee-deep in bayou mud. Won't show up for classes, misses work."

"Drugs?"

"I asked. You don't want to know how that went over." Lauren sighed. "She denied it, of course. And I believe her. I know it sounds naive, but I don't think my sister would do drugs. Mom says Jess is simply high-strung, which 'runs in her side of the family.' Dad blames it all on Eli's influence, says she was fine till she met him."

"This guy is still in the picture?"

Lauren tensed. There it was again, the miserable snarl of emotions Eli always stirred. Anger and . . . "Off and on, I think. It's not a romantic relationship; they were both on the hospital softball team, did some group things together." She shook her head. "Trust me, Jess runs through friends pretty quickly—people get tired of a roller-coaster ride. Eli's been more patient than most, I guess. He's older, a single father. And a little too free with helpful advice, if you ask me. He really knows how to push Jess's buttons. We all wish he was out of the picture completely. Still, if Eli hadn't found her last spring . . ."

Kate was silent for a while. "It must have been awful when your sister ran away."

"Beyond awful. I thought I'd never see her again."

"I'm surprised you took the Austin Grace position. So far from Houston."

"Jess wants to prove she can make it on her own. School, her apartment, relationships. Faith, too—on her own terms, whatever that means. She asked the family to give her space. And truthfully, I needed some distance too. I love her with all my heart and I worry. It's hard either way."

"She's lucky to have you." Kate slid her arm around Lauren's shoulders. "You're a good person, Lauren."

*A good person?* Lauren prayed that was true. But more and more she felt like she'd taken the selfish way out. That offering Jessica "space" by moving to Austin was no more noble than blaming her troubles on high-strung genes or the influence of Eli Landry. It felt too much like . . . *I'm looking the other way while my sister gets lost.*

- + -

Kate parked her car in the driveway, careful not to block the gardeners' van; they were clearing away branches and debris from the storm. Weather reports said the worst of it had passed. Apparently her landlord believed it. He'd told Kate to expect a team of window washers today or tomorrow. Ladders, hoses, scaffolding, men with overalls and squeegees—better than detectives with questions any day. She guessed the window washers would come tomorrow, since the afternoon was stretching on. Regardless, Kate liked the way it made her feel. Washing away the mud and starting fresh. For some reason it added to that sense of hope she'd started to feel.

She clucked her tongue as she slid from the car; now if only she could get back on that jogging trail. There were barricades across the Barton Creek trail entrances clear to Zilker Park. Kate had seen a giant earthmover making its way into the park. Mud, a sinkhole, and uprooted trees, Wes had said. Fortunately, the Texas sun dried things out fairly quickly.

"Kate!"

Her landlord stepped through the hedge, walking briskly toward her. He was carrying a flower bouquet. A beautiful autumn mix: gerbera daisies, black-eyed Susans, miniature mums, Queen Anne's lace, and what appeared to be tiny wild roses. All wrapped in tissue, with sticks of cinnamon bark tucked under a sheer lavender ribbon. Simple and woodsy, but elegant, too, and romantic.

He held it out to her.

"For me?"

He nodded and she took it from his hands, eyes wide.

"Who . . . ? How?"

"The florist didn't want to leave them on your porch, so . . ." His eyes twinkled behind his rimless bifocals. "Lovely flowers for a lovely young lady. As for who, I'll leave that part to you."

"Well . . . thank you."

"My delight, Kate."

*Wes.* Kate knew it even as she closed the door behind her and sank onto the couch. And was even more certain when she slid the little envelope from under the cinnamon sticks. It had to be Wes. She knew it because of the way her heart was behaving. As if it would leap free from her chest and soar around the room in the hands of a silly cupid. Her fingers trembled on the card he'd signed, right below the words . . .

*Just because.*

Kate was still smiling when her cell phone rang. She didn't need to check the caller. She could join the circus as a fortune-teller now.

"Hi," she managed, despite a giggle that could not have been hers a week ago. "'Just because' . . . what?" she teased.

His laugh sounded close enough for his lips to tickle her ear. "Just because they reminded me of you. Black-eyed Susans are sort of 'Brown Eyed Girl.'" He groaned. "Skip all that. I sound like a fool."

*You sound like I feel.* "Thank you," Kate told him, smelling cinnamon on her fingers. "They're wonderful."

"I'm glad." There were background sounds of voices, a dog barking. "You saw the barricades keeping joggers out of the green-belt and Zilker, right?"

"Right. And a bulldozer as big as a house. Don't worry." She glanced at the grimy windows. "I've had my fill of mud. It will take more than the lure of a runner's high to get me out on that trail."

"Good."

"I hear dogs. Where are you?"

"K9 meeting. I'm filling in with Hershey. Helping Jenna get ready for . . ." Wes seemed to hesitate. "Training."

"Hiding or searching?"

"Huh?"

Kate smiled. "That's what Dylan said when he explained the K9 demonstration out at your parents' ranch, remember? He asked me whether I'd be hiding or searching."

"Ah, right." She heard a warbling whine that had to have come from Hershey. "I should go. But I want you to think about something."

She shifted, floral tissue rustling. "What?"

"Thanksgiving. It's next week. Smoked turkey this time, probably hickory. Mom's already shelling pecans for pie. I've been the potato man since I was eleven. Peeling duty, as long as I don't carve on the barn. My sister and her family will be at the in-laws' this year, but the Braxton ladies are coming. Amelia isn't supposed to travel, so they'd be alone. Which means we can expect Nancy Rae in a booster chair and that Pilgrim hat."

Kate laughed. "It sounds like you'll be having a full day."

"Always. Dylan's captain of the annual pasture football game. He recruits every able-bodied person. General warning: there have been cows in that grass. We have Team Tanner shirts in all sizes. So . . . ?"

Her throat squeezed. "You're inviting me?"

"Yes. Unless you changed your mind about going to California."

"No." She closed her eyes against the memory of her father in this room.

"You aren't working that day."

Kate glanced toward the muddy windows. "You're inviting me like you invited the Braxtons. Because I'm alone."

"I'm inviting you . . . just because." Wes sighed against her ear. "I want you there, Kate. You. With me."

"Oh." The thieving cupid made a grab for her heart.

"Think about it?"

"I will," Kate promised.

"Great." Wes's good-bye was smothered by Hershey's eager whine.

Kate disconnected, once again catching the scent of cinnamon on her fingers. She smiled. Not the birthday-cake scent of her ballerina sweet peas, but still . . .

*"You. With me."* She cradled the autumn bouquet in her arms

and let herself imagine wearing one of those football jerseys. And spending a day with the Tanners, good people who gathered family and friends around their table and joined hands, giving thanks for blessings.

Her throat tightened at the memory of that other time. Her hands linked with Wes's and her dad's. The love in Paul Tanner's voice as he spoke of their expected grandchild and the wistfulness in her father's when he said, *"I'd love to have grandchildren."* Kate had taken that from him. No blessing there. If her father knew the truth, would he still want . . . *"a chance to be part of your life"*? For that matter—she shivered, rustling the tissue again—how eager would Wes be to see her in a Tanner football jersey?

No. Kate sat upright, put both feet squarely on the wood floor. She wasn't going down that remorseful path any more than she was going to hit the greenbelt jogging trail before it was safe. The only truth that mattered now was that she was starting a new life. Today had proven it. She had flowers in her arms, an invitation to Thanksgiving dinner, and—Kate smiled at Lauren's words—*"an official 'attagirl'"* from the Austin Grace CNO. As well as a nod from the chair of the board of directors. Tomorrow Kate would have sparkling-clean windows, the mud washed away, starting fresh. And if Evelyn predicted correctly, maybe even some good press for her department. Everything was finally looking up.

- + -

Judith peered through her reading glasses and scrolled down the list of e-mails again: reverse mortgage information, a discounted cruise vacation, free muffins at Mimi's, and a fourth "final notice" that she'd inherited millions from a stranger in Nigeria. All typical mishmash aimed at a fiftysomething widow. Except for the

cute animal video forwarded from her daughter in San Antonio—
penguin babies. But nothing at all from Trista Forrester.

*Nothing* . . . Only that read receipt last week for the e-mail that
Judith sent with the shots she'd snapped of Harley at the hospital.
Including one that caught a rare, precious smile from the tiny girl.
Trista had received the photos, yet there had been no response.
Judith had planned to send the photos she'd taken of the Barton
Creek trail too, along with information on activities at the park.
But maybe she should wait. . . .

She reached for her flowered Spode teacup, swiped her other
palm across a moisture ring on the cherrywood desk. She'd finally
stopped shivering yesterday; Lauren said it was an expected reaction from the adrenaline rush during her effort to save Mr. Beck.
But her fingers trembled again as the image of his face returned:
gray, eyes vacant, froth on his lips—lying still as death on the
bathroom floor only moments after she'd pleaded his case to the
ER clerk.

Judith gripped her cup, took a deep swallow of the honeyed
brew, and made herself recall Harley's smile instead. Innocent,
trusting. A life beginning. She looked at a silver-framed photo
on her desk of her husband holding their daughter when she was
near the same age.

Trista was clearly distressed the last time Judith saw her. The
night her father signed out AMA. And she hadn't been back. It was
troubling. There was no phone listing for a Trista Forrester; she'd
checked. But this morning when Judith helped in the mail room,
there had been a card marked for forwarding to Trista's father. *Blue
Meadow Way.* She couldn't remember the house number, but she
knew she'd recognize that Dodge sedan Trista drove. Crumpled
rear quarter panel and an old gubernatorial campaign sticker on

the bumper. Would there be any harm in just driving by? And taking a little something for the baby?

Judith made herself stop, get back to what she'd been doing when she let e-mail interrupt her. She opened the medical book she'd borrowed from the library, scanned the notes she'd made in the spiral pad that she kept in her uniform pocket. Then she closed her e-mail screen and brought up the Word file. She was nearly finished. And in the long run, this part of her volunteer work was even more important than what she'd tried to do for Mr. Beck.

She took a slow breath, remembering what she'd said to Wes Tanner the day that baby died: *"If more folks took the responsibility to help where they could, this would be a healthier community—and a kinder world."*

Judith felt the truth of that clear through to the marrow of her bones.

## 22

**"IT COULDN'T BE WORSE, LAUREN,"** Kate told her, expression anxious as she stared at the *Statesman*'s editorial page on her digital tablet. She lowered her voice as visitors passed by the hospital gazebo. "Not only does it condemn our handling of the Beck case, but it compares it—apples to apples—with what happened to Baby Doe." She tugged at her bangs. "Did you see how many people have shared this on Twitter and Facebook? This horrible person has a cult following."

"Mr. Beck's stable after his stent placement," Lauren offered like an eye-watering whiff of smelling salts. She hated to see Kate so distraught. That she was here at the hospital on a Saturday was proof of her level of concern. "His wife brought huge boxes of Lammes chocolates. For the ER, too—you're eating one now."

Kate lowered the half-nibbled Longhorn cluster. "She hasn't seen this letter yet. She'll be throwing pralines at our heads. While she's phoning a cutthroat attorney." She traced her finger down the screen. "I quote: 'Insensitive neglect that required a hospital volunteer to initiate resuscitation for a cardiac victim. An effort that took place on a lavatory floor, the exact location where a night custodian recently discovered an abandoned newborn. The infant boy who subsequently died. Both this heart patient and the laboring young mother waited, suffered, worsened—unnoticed and unattended. Where was the professional staff in each of these instances? Where was their compassion? Who is to blame?'"

Lauren groaned with empathy. "Warm fuzzies from administration, followed immediately by a public lashing in the paper. That has to feel awful." She smiled grimly. "A little like spending a rough week with my sister. But seriously, the hospital's name isn't mentioned."

Kate pinned her with a look. "I remember arguing that same point with our favorite attorney. Who made a sarcastic remark about the possibility of so many other ERs finding a newborn wrapped in paper towels in an emergency department bathroom." She pushed the device aside, lifted the piece of candy. "I may as well have a last meal."

"You really think there will be repercussions from that letter?" Lauren asked. "All signs point to Mr. Beck having a good medical outcome."

"Thankfully. And strictly speaking, guidelines were followed in his early care. Prompt triage, appropriate assessment, good documentation of history, normal vital signs—not even an excessive wait time. He didn't tell staff he was feeling worse. He just crashed."

"And Judith found him."

"Yes. It's not so much that this Waiting for Compassion letter criticizes all that," Kate said, anxiety on her face again. "But it dredges up the Baby Doe event. I can't tell you how many times I've heard administration voice hopes that everything related to that incident will—" she grimaced—"die down."

"Hate the choice of words. But it will. Eventually. The local stations will stop showing that photo from the security camera. That baby will become another sad abandonment statistic that proves the importance of early intervention and the value of Safe Haven. It will end, Kate."

Misery flooded into her friend's eyes. "Unless they find her. That mother."

"Right." Lauren sighed. "I don't know which would be worse: finding that poor girl or having her stay lost. She needs help, support. I can't even imagine how awful it would be to live with that burden on my heart. Some things don't ever die down. You know?"

"Mmm." Kate glanced at her watch, reached for her things. "I need to get back to the office."

"Wait. I wanted to talk with you about Thanksgiv—" Lauren's phone buzzed and she held up a finger. "Let me just check this." She scanned the message, then clucked her tongue. "Looks like it's finally happening."

"What?"

"It's from my friend in ICU. There was an announcement on TV a few minutes ago. About a multiagency ground search. Early next week." She met Kate's gaze. "On a 'reliable tip' regarding new evidence in Sunni's case."

- + -

"Careful, Son. No grease on my baby things." Wes's mom smiled at him over a pile of Target shopping bags, sharing table space with her Bible and a huge bowl of half-shelled pecans. "Big preholiday sale."

"More things for Kyra, Bridget . . . Chelsea?" he asked, proud he'd remembered the narrowing list of names for his newest niece.

"A few." She touched a fingertip to the train embroidered on a blue terry sleeper. "But most of these are for the nursery here. My stock of Onesies is looking a tad worn. I've given so many things away."

"And you're hoping you'll have another foster baby to rock." Wes wiped his hands on an old towel, then straddled the oak chair beside her. The air in the kitchen smelled of coffee and the faintest hint of baby lotion. It could easily be Miranda Tanner's signature perfume. "You can't fool me. I recognize that look in your eyes."

"Hoping?" She sighed. "I can't call it that. Not when these babes come to us out of so much tragedy. Neglect, abuse, abandonment. This is the time of year when those cases rise. The holidays. Such a sad irony. A time when most families gather and there's opportunity for unexpected blessings. But—"

"Life isn't a Hallmark movie," Wes finished, echoing Kate's words. He let new warmth dissolve the troubling memory. "I went ahead and invited Kate for Thanksgiving. With a disclaimer about cow-pie football."

"I'm glad. She accepted?"

"I didn't push, told her to think about it. I'm seeing her Sunday night." He frowned. "Unless they decide to start that search earlier."

"I saw the announcement on the news. Do you know anything about this new evidence in Sunni's case?"

Wes's jaw tensed. "Only that they're asking for dogs. Hershey will be there."

"Human remains." His mom brushed her hair back, released a deep sigh. "I can't be surprised by that. But my heart hurts for her family."

"Yeah. Still, it's better to know. Waiting for months and months is . . ." He shook his head.

His mom was quiet for a while. "Besides worrying about you, that was the hardest thing for your father. Waiting and not knowing during that long year before they found your mother. Not understanding why she went out that night. He used to go over and over the possibilities: she needed milk for your cereal, got a call from a friend in trouble. Had cabin fever from all those rainy days. Or it was one of her 'blue days' . . ."

Wes hated the deep tremble in his gut. "None of that explains why she left me in the woods."

She reached over her Bible, found his hand. "Your mother loved you, Wes. You were the center of her life."

He swallowed, ashamed of the anger that bound his pain like baling wire. "I don't understand how a mother can abandon her child." His eyes moved over the soft pile of baby clothes to the face of a woman who only wanted more and more children to gather close. "What gets messed up in her head?" Anger choked his voice. "'Center of her life'? I'm sorry, Mom, but if I was the center of her life, she wouldn't haul me out of bed in the middle of the night and leave me lost and crying in those woods."

"Son . . ." Tears shimmered in his mom's eyes. "We can't always understand. Good people have desperate moments. Make mistakes."

"Mistakes?" Wes hated that he'd made her cry but couldn't stop the words from tumbling like a child down a well. He plucked at the tiny foot of the terry sleeper. "Tell me you didn't wonder if you might be rocking Baby Doe if his mother hadn't abandoned him on that bathroom floor."

"Wes . . ."

"It's true."

"Yes. But being angry and placing blame don't help."

"I know," he managed around the ache in his throat. "I'm sorry, Mom." Wes leaned forward, pressed a kiss to her forehead. "I love you—you're a huge blessing in my life. It's just that . . ." His sigh puffed her hair. "It's hard to get past this."

- + -

"What are *you* doing here?" Kate asked, not caring that she sounded curt. This man had no right to be standing on her porch unannounced.

Barrett Lyon's amused smile said, *"Feisty. I like it."*

"So . . . ?" Kate hoped her anxiety didn't show.

"Are you going to invite me in?"

"No." She fought a ridiculous memory of a fairy tale. *"I'll huff, and I'll puff, and I'll . . ."* This house was made of stone. She stepped onto the porch, closing the door behind her. "I was on my way out. To jog."

His gray eyes skimmed her Pilates tank and leggings. A little too slowly. She wished she were wearing a jacket.

"Those flood barricades are still up if you were thinking of the greenbelt or Zilker Park."

"Right now I'm only thinking, *What's so urgent that you had to come to my house?*"

He was quiet for a few moments, an unnerving silence that felt rehearsed. Kate knew she'd never want to face him in court. "Dana Connor walked off her shift thirty minutes ago."

"What do you mean?"

"She arrived for the p.m. shift and refused a triage assignment. The clinical coordinator insisted. Then someone mentioned today's letter to the editor, suggested it referred to her." He shrugged. "Or so I heard; I make it a point not to speculate on workplace gossip."

The words in the letter came back with a vengeance. *"Where was their compassion? Who is to blame?"*

"She went to the p.m. supervisor," Barrett added, "to say she'd be canceling her scheduled shifts and terminating her contract with the nursing registry."

Kate leaned against the wall of the house, stunned. "How do you know all of this? It's a Saturday—you don't work weekends."

He smiled. "I have contacts. People who know what information might interest me."

*Staff you're pressuring?* Kate's stomach churned. "She has a small child and a husband with serious medical needs. You don't mean she's leaving nursing altogether?"

"I have no idea. Frankly, I don't want to know that much. I'm looking at this from a legal perspective. Right now, I have to say it's an encouraging view."

"Encouraging?" Kate couldn't believe her ears.

"You need to remember that my job is not to look at these things personally, Kate. I see the facts. Sort them for what benefits a legal case. Or potential case. The facts are that Dana Connor abandoned her duties today. And very recently took time off from her job to attend the memorial service for a baby who died at the hospital where Dana works. After she quite possibly neglected to properly assess—and assign emergent priority—to that baby's laboring mother."

"The girl Dana triaged, Ava Smith . . ." Kate's voice cracked. "She never said she was preg—"

"Was never asked, according to the electronic record."

Kate pressed her shoulder harder against the stone wall, hoping to stop her trembling. "No one knows for sure that Ava Smith really is that baby's mother."

"But I think we will. Soon."

Kate could hardly breathe. "What does that mean?"

"Tips in response to the TV photo. Dozens. And information gleaned from video surveillance at the church."

"She . . . That girl was there?"

"It's possible. Everything's being processed as we speak. Which brings me to the reason I stopped by." His expression assumed courtroom seriousness. "It's important that you stay consistent with the story you told the detectives. The truth as you know it."

*Truth.* Kate was afraid she was going to be sick.

"If they locate Ava Smith," Barrett continued, "you stick to that story no matter what. You saw her in the dark and exchanged a few words. She said nothing to indicate she was in distress. You went for coffee with Lauren." He tipped his head. "Kate?"

"I hear you."

"And if we need to use Dana Connor . . ." Barrett shrugged. "I'll deal with that. First things first." His eyes took uncomfortable liberties again. "Like your application for department director. I hear Dub Tarrant dropped a good word."

- + -

Lauren stood next to her Volkswagen in the hospital parking lot, listening to Jess's apartment phone ring. For some reason she wasn't answering her cell. Lauren had left a message on it, but—

A beep heralded her sister's newest greeting: "It's Jessica. I'm not here. Y'all know what to do. Be advised: If you're a telemarketer, my minimum rate for listening is thirty-five dollars an hour, so . . ."

Lauren rolled her eyes and decided to leave another short message, but then the recorded greeting was interrupted by a click.

"Lauren?" The voice was deep, too familiar.

"Eli . . ." She leaned against the car, her legs suddenly unsteady.

"I thought I recognized your number," he said. "It's been a long—"

"Is my sister there?" she asked, cutting him off.

"You missed her by a few minutes."

"Oh . . . uh, I wanted to ask her about Thanksgiving." Lauren frowned—there was no need whatsoever to explain herself. She resisted the urge to disconnect. "She's at the hospital? School?"

"I have no idea. But I'd skip asking her about Thanksgiving if I were you." There was a short huff and she could easily imagine his dark smirk. "We were having that discussion right before she stormed out. She said something about not being able to get on board with a holiday that's all about people gorging themselves 'like pigs at a trough.'"

"She . . . Jess isn't eating?"

"I suspect it. Baggy clothes, canceling on friends to avoid going to restaurants. She looked thinner today than I remembered." He sighed. "Truth is, I don't see that much of her outside of work. My schedule, hers . . . life. I was having a look at her cupboards and refrigerator when you called."

Lauren tightened her fingers on the phone, torn between hating his intrusion on her sister's privacy—loathing that he was even there at all—and woozy relief that at least someone was doing something. Guilt jabbed. *It should be me.*

"It's not that bad," Eli continued in his maddeningly clinical tone, as if he were merely dictating a note on a wart removal. "Rice cakes, nut butter, ramen . . . some of those fruit and vegetable drinks, a frozen slab of that redfish I caught in the Gulf last spring."

*The fishing trip you postponed to go find her.*

"And a couple pounds of vitamins," he added. "So there is food. And overall she's getting along at work, from what I can see." She heard a sound like the closing of a cupboard door. "So . . . how are *you*, Lauren?"

She frowned. Apparently Eli hadn't finished his inspection. "I'm fine."

There was a short silence. "Not beating yourself up over Jessica's meltdown last spring?"

Lauren's stomach knotted. "Of course not."

"Good." Eli's voice softened ever so slightly. "I thought maybe it was the reason you moved to Austin. Your sister's problems . . . and what happened between you and me."

Lauren hung up.

- + -

"No. You're not interrupting." Wes cradled the phone to his ear, sat back on the workbench. And returned his father's knowing grin.

"Where are you?" Kate asked. "I hear a TV."

"In the shop. Dad's got the news on the big screen." He laughed, glancing at the ancient portable TV and the duct-taped remote in his father's hands. "Perks of a home-based business. That and Mom's grilled Reuben sandwiches. Where are you?"

"Home. I was starting my Pilates workout. Before I review some staffing hours."

There was something strange in her voice. "Is everything all right, Kate?"

"Sure—fine."

Now he was certain something was wrong. "Word about your job?"

"Not really. . . . Hey, is it true there's going to be a big search for Sunni Sprague in a few days?"

"For evidence," he clarified, remembering his mother's words: *"Human remains."*

"Here in Barton Springs?"

*In the greenbelt where you jog* . . . "Yes. Though they haven't released the exact site. So—"

"I'm not asking. I just wondered if you were going to take part."

"I'll be there." He frowned. "Are you sure everything's okay?"

"It's been a long day, that's all."

Wes wanted to jump in the truck and drive over there to hold her. "I have a few hours' work here. We don't usually work Saturdays, but there are some emergencies because of the storm. I could come by later if you want. Bring some burgers. And do my impression of Nancy Rae as a Dallas Cowboys cheerleader. Guaranteed prescription after a rugged day."

Her short chuckle was something, at least. "Thank you for the thought, but I'm good. I'm going to do my workout, tackle that paperwork, then curl up on the couch with Roady."

New low: he was jealous of a stub-tailed cat.

"We'll plan on tomorrow evening, then. I'll—" He stopped as his phone buzzed with a text message. "One second, Kate. I need to read an Amber Alert." He scanned the details, noted the time. "Okay, got it."

"Will you be called for a search?"

"Probably not. Unless they need volunteers to knock on doors. Law enforcement handles kidnappings. This one's a baby."

Kate's distress was audible.

"Yeah. Two months old. A girl," he added, sharing her sentiment, "named Harley."

- ✦ -

Judith shut off the shower and made a hasty reach for her robe. She'd been right; she hadn't imagined the sound. Thumps, pounding. Shouts too. The TV was on, but it was too loud for even that. *What on earth?*

She tightened her belt, glanced in the foggy mirror, and walked toward the living room. Scant steps into the hallway she realized someone was pounding on her front door. Then she heard the shout.

"Judith Doyle? Austin Police Department. Open the door, ma'am!"

# 23

+

"**I DON'T BELIEVE THIS.**" Kate sat cross-legged holding her phone, glued to the TV and reeling from the second shock in fifteen minutes. "The police actually suspect Judith—our Judith? Are you sure? The news isn't saying anything about that. Though I think this is taped from a little earlier."

"I don't want to believe it either." Lauren sounded as stunned as Kate felt. "But I heard it from my friend who's married to a PD officer. And there's only one Austin Grace volunteer named Judith that I know of. Apparently the police asked Trista if anyone had been showing unusual interest in the baby. She told them Judith took photos of Harley and bought her a gift."

"Judith showed me the photos, but I can't believe she's capable of something like this. It doesn't make any sense." Kate shook her head; Judith had asked her about the mother and baby only recently, expressed concern about not seeing them. The day she and Kate exchanged phone numbers and made plans to have coffee. *Judith, a kidnapper?*

"I remember them both, mom and baby," Lauren told her. "Trista left Harley alone in the ER waiting room once, and—never mind, it doesn't matter. But I talked with her, offered to help her with some pamphlets. She'd picked up the new Baby Moses brochure by mistake, so I made sure she knew there was information on baby care, immunization safety, all that. The mother's a kid herself."

"I thought that same thing the time we treated Harley in the ER. Trista looked undone. It wasn't easy to convince her it was safe to take the baby home, and—"

"Do you see that, just now?" Lauren interrupted. "That's the grandfather they're interviewing."

"I see it. Still has a bandage on his arm." Kate watched as the scowling man wedged in front of his daughter to talk to the reporter. He aimed a finger toward the camera lens. "I didn't know Trista and the baby lived with him."

Kate and Lauren were quiet for a while, listening as he recounted the story.

"No way," Lauren said finally. "Judith wouldn't crawl through a nursery window in broad daylight and snatch that baby out of her crib. But, dear Lord, someone did. Trista looks an inch from catatonic. I can't imagine anything more horrible than having no idea where your child is."

*Except ten years of it . . . and knowing I'm to blame.*

"I have this urge to call Judith and check on her. But . . ." Lauren sighed.

"What do you think is happening with her right now?" Kate

slipped the Pilates DVD back into its case. "Would the police just show up at her house?" She grimaced; they'd shown up here. Police, Barrett Lyon . . .

"I'd think so. Without warning. Search her home. Everything. I hate the thought of it, but they have to check every lead. Harley's welfare depends on it. Maybe even her life. I don't want another tragedy with a baby."

"No." Kate fought a wave of dizziness. "It can't happen again."

- + -

Wes hurled his twenty-four-hour pack into the truck, slid behind the wheel—and made himself stop for a moment. As angry as he was right now, he'd flip this rig over in a ditch before he got to Austin. He bit back a curse, taking a breath instead. *Please, Lord, let this end okay. Use me.*

He reached for the ignition and then remembered Kate. She'd been distraught when he'd talked to her earlier; she needed to hear this newest update. He pulled out his cell, tapped her number.

"What is it?" Her voice was anxious. "You've heard something?"

"We haven't found the baby," he reported quickly. Anger whitened his knuckles on the steering wheel. "But don't worry about Judith. She's not involved. This isn't a kidnapping."

"Where's Harley, then?"

"That mother—" Wes's teeth ground together—"dumped her baby off somewhere. Abandoned her and drove away."

"I don't understand."

*I don't either . . . all my life.* Wes shoved the anger down. "Apparently the mother's had some kind of breakdown. Babbling about the Bible and milk shakes—not much that's helpful or even coherent. She claims she drove around all day, then left the baby 'somewhere.' She can't remember exactly where. Only that she left her in her car seat, with her favorite white blanket. They're trying to compile a list of possible sites. I'm leaving now for the staging area. There's not much time before it gets dark and cold."

"I want to help," Kate said in a rush. "Pick me up. Let me—"

"Can't." His heart tugged at her offer. "They aren't using citizen searchers yet. I'm meeting Jenna. I'll call you when I know something. Promise. Gotta go."

Wes said a quick good-bye, set the truck's engine to roaring, and took off. There was barely an hour of daylight left and then it would be flashlights and headlamps. He prayed Trista Forrester had dressed her child warmly or at least tucked that blanket around her and hadn't left the baby at the mercy of the elements in some remote location, and . . .

*No.* The memory rushed back, unfolding before Wes could stop it.

That awful night. Running. Pajamas, bare feet, and inky darkness. Chest heaving, throat raw, his heart threatening to explode. Gulping air, stumbling over tangled roots and ankle-deep in sucking mud. Straining to see—to find her. The sharp scent of the cedar whipping across his face, its laden boughs soaking his skin with icy water. Bringing cruel shivers that trapped his tongue between his teeth and brought the salty taste of blood. Running, trying to find her—lost. Every moment like no nightmare or bogeyman he'd ever dared to imagine.

But nothing compared to the terrifying confusion of being abandoned. Left without explanation in blackness and cold, silent except for the rush of the storm-swollen river somewhere in the distance. And his own sob-choked shouts, hoarse and foreign to his ears.

"*Mommy! It's dark. I'm scared. . . . It's cold, Mommy. Please come back!*"

Wes pressed his boot flat on the gas pedal. He'd find that baby.

- + -

"You're pacing." Lauren sighed through the phone. "I can feel it."

"No, I . . ." Kate stopped the dizzying circuit she'd been making around her living room since the call from Wes. She was still in her workout clothes and her stomach had started to growl with hunger. But there was no way she could eat. "I can't just wait here for Wes to call back." She glanced toward the muted TV screen. "Or for something awful to show up on the news. Waiting isn't something I do well. It's—"

"Because we work in a hospital," Lauren finished, voice full of the understanding only another nurse could offer. "We jump in when there's a crisis. We act; we fix. We don't wait. Waiting is like hobbling a racehorse. . . . Which is why I called Judith a few minutes ago."

"You did?" Kate sank onto the arm of the couch. "How is she?"

"In shock, I think. I offered to meet her somewhere to talk, but her daughter was on her way up from San Antonio. She's a lawyer. Though, thank heaven, it doesn't sound like Judith needs one."

"The police have completely backed off?"

"Yes. But the media managed to follow the police on the initial call. Judith said it looks like wild pigs were rooting in her dahlia bed. She sort of rambled from one subject to another. But mostly she sounded truly frightened for Harley. And Trista. Upset with herself, too."

"Why?"

"For 'crossing the line of professionalism.' She said that at least three times."

"Because she gave a gift to the baby." Kate hated that this volunteer's kindness had brought her so much trouble.

"And because she took those photos of Harley." Lauren clucked her tongue. "The police still have Judith's camera. She'd uploaded almost everything to her computer. Except for three photos of Harley. And some of the Barton Creek Greenbelt. She was planning to send them to Trista with a link to information on the trails. They spoke about taking the baby there in the spring."

"I saw those photos too. They showed the greenbelt near the Zilker Park trailhead." Kate stood, her heart starting to pound. "They talked about the park?"

"Yes. Because Judith took her daughter there when she was a baby. And Trista said she wanted to walk somewhere along the water."

"Wait." Kate pressed her hand to her chest, her mind whirling. "Didn't you tell me that Trista had one of those Safe Haven brochures?"

"Yes. She didn't understand what that meant. So I explained the story from—"

"The Bible." The words left Kate's lips with a gasp. "The Bible and milk shakes."

"Huh?"

"Something Wes told me," Kate said, dashing to where her running shoes sat beside the front door. "When Trista finally told the police she'd abandoned Harley, she was babbling incoherently about the Bible and milk shakes." Kate slid a foot into her shoe. "I have no idea about the milk shakes. But unless I've forgotten everything I learned in Sunday school, Moses was left by his mother—"

"At the water's edge," Lauren finished. "Oh, dear Lord . . ."

"Call the police." Kate reached for her other shoe. "Tell them what Judith said about the park."

"You really think Trista left her baby there?"

Kate yanked her jacket from the coat peg. "I'm going to find out."

"What? No way. It's going to be dark soon. It's flooded out there. It isn't safe, and—"

"And I'm minutes from there. I'll only go as far as the trailhead, take a quick look around; that's all. I'll be in and out before dark. The police can take over from there. I'm going, Lauren."

**24**

+

KATE WEDGED A HIP between the wooden flood barricades, grimacing as a nail caught her tights and jabbed the skin beneath. She wrestled with the fabric in the deepening dusk; it would have been smarter to have taken the time to pull on her jeans. More protection, warmer, and—

She gave the barricade a shove, heard it collapse with a clatter, amber caution beacon still flashing. There was no time. Not even minutes to spare. It would be dark far too soon.

She broke into a trot, anxiety rising. If she was cold, what would happen to a baby left down by the water's edge? With just a little blanket. She tried to recall Harley's sweet face, but the only thing that came was the constant loop of Wes's words in that last phone call. *"That mother . . . dumped her baby . . . abandoned her . . ."*

Kate pushed her pace, heading toward the trail and trying to out-run a painful intrusion of images: Baby Doe limp in her hands, her newborn son wrapped in that sweatshirt . . . *"dumped her baby . . ."*

She stumbled, lurched forward, fell to her hands and knees in a mix of mud and gravel. She clambered upright, wiping her stinging hands on her tights. Then pulled the mini flashlight from her jacket pocket. Switched it on, focused the beam—and gasped.

The flat terrain she'd jogged only days ago was now a minefield of mounded mud and water-sluiced ruts. As if the devil himself had delighted in scraping cruel fingers across this family park. Could Trista have actually chosen this place to leave her baby? Kate's stomach sank, the ugly truth making her shiver. *Ava Smith picked a darkened bathroom. I chose* . . . Panicky decisions, unfor-givable mistakes. Kate started forward again, hustling as best she could as the flashlight beam bounced over the pocked terrain in cadence with her thoughts. *Dumped, dumped, dumped* . . .

She tried not to think of her chances of finding the baby. She couldn't. Kate only knew that she wasn't going to let this happen again—a baby left alone in the dark. She'd find Harley.

- + -

"We're stopping to listen for a minute," Wes said, signaling to Jenna in the darkness.

"Gotcha." She halted, just yards away, her headlight beam hit-ting a tree in the distance. Her whisper sounded like it rose straight from her heart. "I've never prayed for a baby to fuss. Until now."

He nodded, grateful again that he'd been paired with her on the hasty-search team. It was easy to see that even as a rookie, Jenna had the dedication it took for this kind of work. Wes closed his eyes, concentrated. Heard a single whine from a live-search dog.

And the thud of boots of the other team members also coming to a halt. A cough. The droning chug of a boat motor out on Lady Bird Lake. Traffic over the Congress Avenue Bridge. But no baby. It was dark now, the temperature dropping. There had been no concrete response to the news coverage. Nothing.

The searchers were following every convoluted lead they'd gotten from Trista Forrester. Every place she'd remembered being today: Chick-fil-A, a Walmart, and here, by "that big, ugly statue in the park." Stevie Ray Vaughan. It seemed so long ago that he'd been here with Kate. Her silly air guitar, their first date. He reminded himself to call her as soon as he got a chance. It had to be killing her to sit and wait.

"Two minutes," Jenna whispered, checking her watch. "No crying. Do you think . . . ?" She cleared her throat. "Could Harley have cried herself to sleep?"

*Or can't cry anymore.* A baby blanket wasn't near enough protection from the chill. Wes recalled what he knew of hypothermia symptoms in infants: reddened skin that was cold to the touch, drowsiness, cardiac disturbance. *Death.* What kind of mother did something like that?

He swallowed the anger down. Signaled to Jenna. "Let's go."

- + -

"Stop blaming yourself, Mom. You didn't do anything wrong."

Judith set her teacup on the table, looked at her daughter. Molly's eyes were so like her father's and filled with worry now. "They told us in volunteer training that we should keep an emotional distance. Avoid personal involvement with patients. And with visitors. They warned it could lead to problems, for volunteers and for the hospital as well. And now . . ."

"Now the mistake has been cleared up—that poor, misguided teenager's confusion in accusing you." Molly slid her arm around Judith's shoulder. "You only did what you always do, Mom. Throw your heart into helping other people. There's no mistake in that."

No mistake? Judith shivered against a chill she hadn't been able to shake since the Austin police burst through her door. She glanced toward the TV, showing a repeat of footage outside the Forresters' Blue Meadow Way house. The photo of Harley and a mention of the favorite white baby blanket and car seat. Then new clips of a search-and-rescue command trailer and a close-up of a waiting ambulance. Judith's throat squeezed. "That poor baby. This shouldn't be happening."

Molly sighed. "No. It shouldn't. But right now all we can do is pray that they find her quickly."

*Pray?* Judith glanced toward the Bible lying on the table near her wingback chair. What would Molly think if she knew that her mother rarely prayed anymore?

Her daughter slid her arm back and was quiet for a moment. "I've been wondering if you should maybe try something else, Mom."

"Try . . . ?"

"With your volunteering. I'm not sure that being around a hospital is a good thing for you. Especially emergency—"

"No." Judith sat taller on the couch. "That's not true, Molly. It's the best possible thing for me. And for the hospital, our patients."

*Our.* Judith didn't think she'd ever said that before.

"They're fortunate to have you. But I wonder if you're investing too much of your time. It seems like whenever I call, you're at one hospital or another. There's more to life than carrying vases of flowers and filling balloons for kids in waiting rooms."

And doing cardiac compressions on the floor . . . What would Molly say about that?

Judith met her daughter's gaze. "They need me."

"Mom . . ." The concern in Molly's eyes increased. "I see how this situation with the baby is affecting you. I watch you putting your life on hold to be at those hospitals day in and day out. All times of the day and night now—at Austin Grace."

"Yes. Because I'm needed there," Judith repeated, beginning to feel too much like she was being interrogated again. "There's no reason for you to be concerned, darling."

"No reason?" Molly's brows pinched together. "Daddy died in that hospital."

- + -

"Harley? Sweetheart, where are you?" Kate trotted a second circuit of a slushy swath made by bulldozers near the trailhead, her light beam bouncing along the water's edge like a firefly. Her eyes stung from staring into foliage and peering—breath held in fear—out across the shallow water. Her running shoes had to be carrying a pound of sludge in their waffled treads. "Haaaarley . . ."

She walked on, skidding, then catching her balance, her flashlight on a grove of trees. Possibly near the bench where she'd met Wes that day. Nothing looked the same now. She swept the beam across debris, searching for landmarks, and glimpsed what was probably the reported sinkhole, surrounded by a circle of barricades. Then she raised the beam—higher, higher still—to capture what she could of an immense yellow-and-green earthmover, its claw bucket poised like a scorpion. Behind it, earth and rock and debris were mounded like the aftermath of a volcanic eruption. *How can I find anything here?*

Kate let the beam sweep over the mess, telling herself that though she ached to cover every square inch of this park, it was impossible. If Trista had come here, she would've been limited by the flood damage too. Kate was doing only what she could until the police got here, and—

What was that?

She stopped, held her breath, and swept the beam back over the course it had just followed. Up there, on the hill mounded by the earthmover and near a huge uprooted tree. A glimpse of white? Where was it? There . . . Yes, something white. Tucked among the debris. Hadn't Wes said that Harley's blanket was white? She started forward, beam bouncing and mind tumbling. Had Trista wrapped her baby in the blanket and . . . *dumped, dumped, dumped* . . .

Kate told herself she was being foolish; Trista would have chosen an easier place to leave her baby. She tortured herself with a memory of that abandoned Vegas car wash and the darkened doorway of the fire department. There had been no "easy" in those choices. She knew better than anyone that panic didn't give rise to rational decisions. And if the baby was really up there and Kate didn't check—

"Harley!" There was no cry, no sound as Kate started up the muddy mound. It was impossible to focus the beam as she climbed, so she jammed the flashlight into her jacket pocket. Then slid backward, her mud-packed soles like skis. She grabbed a branch of the downed tree, hauling herself upward to where she'd seen that glimpse of white. Awkward, but possible. And she had to be sure. She grabbed another branch, tried to get better footing.

"Harley?" she called again, hearing sounds in the distance. The police or searchers—both, Kate hoped. She'd check this out, then meet them down on the path. She stopped, breath heaving. Pulled the flashlight from her pocket. Focused the beam.

*What is that? Not a blanket . . .*

Kate's beam moved over the white object she'd spotted. A canvas tarp. And other whitish things. Long, short, and several tiny pale bits as small as shells. But they weren't shells.

"No," she whispered, reaching out. "It can't be . . ."

*A leg bone?*

Trembling, she picked it up, and her stomach confirmed the horrifying reality: *a human leg bone.* Kate gagged and then held her breath as the light picked out what were undeniably ribs and a hand and . . . She began to tremble more, the bone clutched in her hand and a hideous truth making her legs weak.

"Sunni . . . it's you."

She took a step backward, senses reeling, and in an instant her left leg dropped out from under her, sinking knee-deep into mud. She grasped frantically for a tree root, then struggled to free her leg. She yanked it loose at last, the momentum sending her staggering backward. Kate fell, bone and flashlight flying from her grasp. She fought to sit up, right herself, but continued to slide and roll. Downward over rocks, wood debris . . . *and more bones?*

The awful thought was followed by a scream—her own—as Kate's body slammed into the earthmover torso-first, causing a whiplash that drove her head against metal. There was an explosion of pain. Then merciful blackness.

- + -

"Tanner! Over here, by the pagoda and the lily pond," the radio voice squawked.

"What have you got?" Wes glanced at Jenna in the darkness as he waited for the searcher's response.

"Dog's alerted on a scent."

"On our way," he confirmed, beckoning to Jenna.

They took off at a run and within seconds heard the crescendo of barking that could only mean one thing.

*Please, Lord. Let this be a live find.*

# 25

**HARLEY FORRESTER WAS UNDER A SHRUB** near the lily pond, still strapped in her blanket-draped car seat. Despite the glaring lamp beam, the baby's eyes remained ominously closed, her head lolled to one side.

"Oh no," Jenna gasped. "Is she . . . ?"

"Leash your dog," Wes told the K9 handler who'd called them with the find. He dropped to his knees beside the baby. "Jenna, make the calls." He grasped the car seat and pulled it clear of the shrubbery, fighting a growing sense of foreboding when the baby made no response to the movement. *Please, baby girl.*

"Harley, wake up." He lifted the blanket away. The baby's skin was pale but not blue. He traced a fingertip down her cheek. Cold to the touch. Scary cold. "Hey there . . ." Wes jostled the car seat, reached for the restraint buckles. Impossible to see if her chest was moving. He needed to get her free of the seat, in case . . . Wes ran infant resuscitation guidelines in his head, praying he wouldn't need them. "C'mon, little babe. Give us a cry."

Sirens wailed in the distance.

Wes's headlamp beam bounced over the baby's tiny chin as he released the last buckle and—

Harley whimpered. Her lids fluttered.

"She's breathing," Wes announced, finding his own breath. "Her eyes are open."

"Awesome." The handler grinned, giving his whining dog a pat.

"Medics on the way," Jenna reported, still manning the radio.

"Good." Wes lifted Harley from the car seat and cradled her against his chest, feeling the chill of her skin through her pajamas. "Grab those hand warmers from my pack; we'll tuck them under the rescue blanket. Let's do what we can to get her body temperature moving up."

"Here you go."

"Thanks." Wes patted Harley's back as she began to cry. "No sweeter sound, guys."

In mere moments only Harley's cherub face was visible in a voluminous nest of foil blanket—a space-age papoose. Startlingly blue eyes peered up at Wes as he held her. He said a silent prayer, grateful he could whisper his favorite words. "It's okay. You're not lost anymore."

"Wes . . ." Jenna stepped close as police, rescue, and medical personnel began converging on the scene. "I heard part of a radio report. There's something strange going on near Zilker Park."

"Already looking for more action?" Wes teased, shifting the baby in his arms. His smile faded as he read the concern in her expression. "What is it? What's wrong?"

"It's Kate Callison. She's been hurt."

Wes's breath caught. "How—where?"

"She fell at the trailhead. Near that big sinkhole. Paramedics are on scene. Police too." Jenna's brows pinched together. "The strange thing is that they said it happened after she found some human remains."

- + -

"What . . . ?" Kate moaned as pain knifed her side. Her immediate shivers caused a second stab. Radios squawked over a rumble of voices. She squinted, trying to see past a beam of light that made her head throb. There was a rigid cervical collar under her chin and oxygen tubing in her nose. They'd started an IV line in her left forearm. "Lauren?"

"I'm here, darlin'." Her friend's face, etched with worry, loomed overhead. "I've got you," she reassured, her hand warm on Kate's. "I'll save the ranting 'told you so' for later."

"What happened?"

A paramedic's face displaced Lauren's. "You're in Zilker Park, Kate. You fell and hurt your ribs." He clucked his tongue. "And bought yourself a brain CT."

"What?"

Lauren's face returned. "You've asked, 'What happened?' a least a dozen times. Concussion probably. Looks like you climbed—" she glanced over her shoulder—"up that mound of dirt and then rolled to the bottom like Jack and Jill." She patted Kate's forehead. "I'm not allowing you to have a broken crown, though." Lauren pulled the rescue blanket higher as Kate shivered again.

"Make room! Medical examiner's here," a voice boomed in the distance.

"Bones . . ." The surreal memory surfaced. Kate stared at Lauren. "I found those bones."

"There's an army of folks interested in that sad discovery. Trust me."

"Lauren . . ." The visceral certainty came back as strongly as when she'd held that leg bone in her hand. "It's Sunni."

Her friend winced. "It will take a while to do the testing, and—"

"It's her."

The stretcher jiggled, clattering as the medics moved Kate toward the ambulance.

"Well, first things first," Lauren told her, walking alongside. "We're taking you to Austin Grace. Don't worry; I'm sticking to you like a chigger. You won't be alone."

*Alone.* Details came back in a rush.

"The baby." Kate raised her shoulders, hindered by straps and a skewering pain in her ribs. "Harley. They need to find her."

"Stay down." Lauren pressed her hand against Kate's sternum. "Harley's on her way to the same place you're going. She's cold. And a bit dehydrated, sounds like. But I think she's going to be okay."

"Where was she?"

"The lily pond at Lady Bird Lake. Your handsome hero found her." Lauren winked. "I'll bet you're next on his list."

- + -

Wes followed Lauren toward the ER. The last time he'd taken this route was when Gabe was shot. Judith Doyle had ushered him through the security-protected doors. An angel of mercy. Today she'd been a kidnap suspect. An innocent woman accused and a helpless baby abandoned. He'd had his fill of reckless—*criminal*—irresponsibility today. Even before those actions landed Kate in the hospital.

"Kate . . ." His throat tightened as he caught sight of her on an ER gurney. Swathed in blankets, IV hanging overhead, and a bruising welt across her cheekbone. "Hey," he said, moving to her bedside.

She gave him a wan smile. "You're here to read me the riot act."

"No." He ached to kiss her, simply brush his lips across her forehead. Except that this was her hospital, her staff. Lauren had stepped away, but several other people had already cast curious glances his way. He took her hand instead. "Lauren said your ribs are bruised, not fractured. And—"

"You found Harley." The dark eyes were huge against her pale face.

"Team effort. Jenna was there. The dog was really the one . . ." A lump in his throat squelched his words. "She's safe, Kate. Right now I need to be sure you are." He tried to smile. "There's mud in your hair."

"Everywhere." Her chin began to tremble. "You found the baby. And I . . . f-found Sunni . . . Sprague."

Wes grimaced, still rocked by what he'd heard of her unbelievable experience. He'd fended off a dozen reporters outside the hospital. A baby. A body. A media feeding frenzy. "I'm sorry." He wasn't going to lie to her. "I wish it hadn't been you. But it probably is Sunni. We were planning to search not far from that spot."

She groaned. "I had her leg in my hands, Wes. I never met her and then I was standing there h-holding her bones." Kate took a breath, flinched.

"Pain in your ribs?" Wes glanced toward a nurse at the trauma room computer, then decided he didn't care what anyone thought. He brushed her hair back and touched his lips to her brow. "Should I get the nurse?"

"No." Kate moaned again softly but shook her head. "I'm okay. They can't really give me anything until after the—"

"Excuse me, sir." A nurse with a soul-patch beard moved the IV bag to the pole on the gurney. "We need to get Kate down to radiology." He glanced at her. "Did you want him to follow us down there?"

"No," Kate said quickly, her gaze moving to Wes. "Brain CT. I'll be there awhile." She sighed. "They're going to admit me overnight. You go on home."

"Nice try." Wes looked at the nurse. "When is she going to her hospital room?"

"Directly from CT."

"Okay." He nodded, met Kate's eyes. "Your dad knows you're being admitted?"

"No."

When she glanced away, Wes knew she hadn't contacted him at all. *Ah, Kate.*

"I'll be waiting in your room when you get back from CT. No arguments. You're stuck with me."

"Like a chigger." Kate gave a short chuckle. "That's what Lauren said. She'd stick by me like a chigger."

He smiled. "Chiggers and sinkholes. We'll toughen you into a Texan yet."

Wes watched her disappear down the hallway, then headed for the stairs; he'd pick up some food from the cafeteria. At the first landing, his cell phone rang.

"How's Kate?" his mom asked.

"Pretending she doesn't hurt as much as she does." Wes leaned against the wall, a delayed rush of relief making his legs weak. Food, definitely. "But so far so good. No rib fractures. Or signs of internal injuries. Her neck's been cleared. She's having a brain scan now."

He heard his mom's soft gasp.

"A precaution," Wes assured her. "It looks like a concussion. Kate's coherent now. Enough to remember finding the bones."

"I can't even imagine how awful that was. They've got TV crews reporting from the site right now. My heart goes out to the Sprague family. Wondering, waiting."

Wes knew she was thinking of his father, when they found his mother's remains at last.

"How's the baby?" she asked softly.

"I haven't seen her. But I hear things are improving."

"They keep repeating this tragic news clip on TV. That young mother, looking dazed and saying all she wanted was for her baby to be safe. It's so sad."

"Yeah, well . . ." *Sad* wasn't the word Wes had in mind.

"Anyway, I'm glad to hear Kate wasn't seriously hurt. And that the baby is doing all right." She sighed. "Such a rough day for so many people. I'll be bending God's ear with prayers tonight."

"I have no doubt."

"Come by for dinner? Dylan's helping me make spaghetti with the ground venison from his weekend at Grandpa's hunting lease. It will be served with breadsticks and tall tales."

"Thanks, Mom. But I'm going to stay here for a while."

"I thought you'd say that." There was a knowing smile in her voice.

Wes said good-bye and started down the stairs again, thinking of what she'd said about praying for those people. He knew she didn't mean only Kate, Harley, and the Sprague family. His mom would include Trista Forrester in her prayers. A woman who dumped her baby and drove off without a backward glance. A heartless mother who left her child crying in the dark—cold, confused, and lost.

There was no way Wes could dredge up an ounce of compassion for someone like that.

## 26

**KATE FOUND SUNNI.** Judith switched off the eleven o'clock news and sat in her darkened living room, truth making her head pound as effectively as the police officers' fists against her door. They were Sunni's bones; she had no doubt of that.

She grabbed a couch pillow and hugged it, closing her eyes against the news images that refused to switch off: Trista Forrester's dazed expression, eclipsed by the face of her blustering father; Harley with the silver rattle and the smile Judith had captured with her camera; grainy footage of the lily pond at Lady Bird Lake, a hand pointing to the shrubbery where they'd found the baby; photos from outside the emergency entrance to Austin Grace. And then that horrible clip of Sunni Sprague's mother at her front door, squinting into camera lights. A reporter's shout: "Mrs. Sprague, do you believe it's your daughter?" The pain on the woman's face— like a scabbing wound reopened.

"Oh, dear God," Judith groaned into the pillow, staggered by the events of the day. Harley missing, Judith accused, Trista's breakdown, Wes Tanner finding the baby, Kate discovering those bones—then ending up as a trauma victim in her own emergency department. A head injury. She could have been killed. Just as that poor, sweet, innocent baby might have died in the park. Judith shivered and felt the sting of tears as the full-circle sense of the tragedy struck her again. Along with the miserable truth that had been whispering from deep down all day. Like bones unearthed by a storm.

"Help me, God," she whispered in the darkness. "I think I've made an awful mistake."

- + -

Matt Callison finished his voice message and disconnected from the call; it was two hours later in Texas and Kate was probably asleep. *Or not answering because it's me.*

According to the short clip on the national TV news, she'd had a full day: an abandoned baby brought to the Austin Grace ER and then that grisly discovery of human remains in a location that sounded somehow familiar. Possibly near Kate's place. He'd wanted to check on that and ask if Wes had been involved in the search for the infant. Matt sighed at the truth: excuses to talk with his daughter. And tell her he sold the house. Would she want to know?

He grabbed a piece of packing tissue and lifted the daisy mug from the cupboard. He ran his thumb over the design. It matched the two Kate had with her in Texas, the mugs she'd fixed their coffee in. He'd so hoped there would be a different ending to the conversation they'd had that last day, that his apology, sharing about his faith, would change things. Heal what was broken between them. It had done neither. And then Matt returned home to finish up with the sale of the house. With no promise of a job, he'd had no choice but to sell. Still, he was finding it harder than he'd imagined. Another good-bye that left a chink in his heart.

He set the mug back in the cupboard. He'd wrap it up later, add it to the growing list of tasks he kept finding excuses to put off. Like that touch-up painting. Matt glanced at the can of gloss enamel on the kitchen table, then at the doorway to the laundry room. Marks on the trim paint—pencil, pen, felt marker—measuring Kate's growth from preschool age. Far from engineering perfect, since she'd cheated by rising on tiptoe more than a few times. *I'm a big girl, Daddy. How big does it take to drive a car?* On her way, even then.

There was no need to tell Kate about the house. She wasn't coming back.

- + -

Kate awakened in the dark, confused. She moved before she remembered not to and felt a merciless jab of pain in her ribs. The hospital. She squinted at the wall clock, barely illuminated by a shaft of light through the partially closed door, and struggled to get her bearings: third-floor medical wing. She'd been admitted, after—

"You awake?" The voice was deep, sleepy, and accompanied by the squeak of a chair.

"Wes?"

"Yes, ma'am." The chair scraped on the floor, and his hand found hers atop the woven cotton blanket. "How are you feeling?"

"Sore. Everywhere." She shook her head, causing an ache deep in her eye sockets. "It's after 3 a.m. You're still here?"

"Yep." His chuckle merged into a yawn. "Better than some places I've slept—no cactus."

She smiled, thinking of what he'd told her about his search-and-rescue training. The wilderness test for twenty-four hours with only his pack and his instincts. To see if he had the "right stuff." His thumb brushed the back of her hand, warm and gentle. It struck her that she'd never met a man who had so much of the right stuff. Wes was the kind of man . . . *I could love.*

Her eyes widened. Where had that come from? It had to be the concussion. "Have you heard anything more about Harley?"

"Temperature's normal. Eating like a champ."

"Good. It was so cold out there." Kate grimaced, remembering her own search for this baby. Running in the night, shouting her name, needing so desperately to . . . *make up for what I did to my own son?* "I'm glad you found her in time."

"She was strapped in the car seat and sort of limp. She didn't blink at my light and her skin was really cold. Almost like with Baby Doe. You know."

*I know.* Kate closed her eyes against a wave of queasiness.

"I thought she was dead." The chair squeaked again as Wes leaned forward. Kate felt the warmth of his nearness more than she saw his features. "Two months old. Helpless. And her mother dumps her." His hand slid away from hers.

Kate's head began to throb.

"I don't understand how someone can do that," Wes continued. "I never have."

There was something in his voice that frightened her. Hinted at things she couldn't bear. Kate wanted him to stop, wished he hadn't stayed.

"That night with my mother. When she drove into the river . . ." He exhaled and cleared his throat. "I was with her."

*No.*

"My dad was in Fort Worth on business. She woke me up in the middle of the night and herded me to the car. I was barefoot and it was muddy. I remember worrying that I'd get the upholstery dirty. She said it didn't matter." His shadow moved like he was shaking his head. "I was never allowed to eat in the car because of crumbs, and all of a sudden mud didn't matter. We drove a long time. The radio was playing a Reba McEntire song. 'How Blue.' I don't know why I remember that song so clearly. Anyway, I guess I fell asleep. I woke up to the sound of water and saw our headlights on the river. Whitecaps. I'd never seen it like that. I asked her why we were there. She didn't answer. I remember the low-water crossing sign. Our wheels spinning in the mud. Then the car sort of lurched forward. I started to cry. I think she was crying too."

*Oh, dear God.*

"The front tires were in the water. I climbed over the seat, begging her to turn around. I said everything I could think of. I remember telling her that Dad had to help me finish my pinewood derby car. That I'd be the only Scout in the troop who didn't get to race. I think I knew we weren't coming back."

Kate's stomach roiled.

"Then all of a sudden she backed up and turned the car around. Followed an overgrown hunting trail for a ways and told me to get out. To be a good boy. That was it. She left me in the dark and drove away."

"That's . . . so awful," Kate whispered. "Wes, I—"

"When I talked to Mom earlier," he continued, his tone different now, "she told me she would be praying for everybody. Harley, you, the Spragues. She'll be praying for that baby's mother too. It's the right thing to do, I suppose. I wish I could, Kate. But I know what it feels like to have your mother dump you like you're so much trash. I don't understand it and I can't make it right no matter which way I look at it. How can I forgive something like that? It's all the same: my mother, Trista Forrester, that girl who left her newborn on the bathroom—"

Kate retched. "I'm sorry. . . . I feel sick."

Wes sprang up, grabbed an emesis bag. "I'll tell the nurse you need something for nausea."

The IV medication took the edge off Kate's headache and painful ribs. It settled her stomach too but made her light-headed and woozy and slurred her speech enough that it was impossible to talk. It blurred the broad-shouldered shadow that remained when Wes once again fell asleep—so close that his head touched the edge of her bed. She could feel him breathe.

Despite the medicine, Kate couldn't sleep. Not because of pain or nausea or even because of the horrific events of last night. She was sleepless because even with her eyes closed, she saw images of a frightened Scout abandoned in the dark woods. And heard, over and over, the heart-wrenching question posed by that boy grown into a man. The only man that—if even just for a delirious moment—she'd ever imagined loving: *"How can I forgive something like that?"*

There was no medicine strong enough to erase the truth: Kate had done the one thing that Wes Tanner found unforgivable.

She stretched out her hand to touch his hair. Her heart cramped. It felt silky and soft against her fingers. And a lot like . . . good-bye.

## 27

**"YOU'RE SURE I CAN'T DO SOMETHING MORE, DARLIN'?"** Lauren peeked through the doorway of Kate's steamy bathroom. "Maybe dab a little concealer over that bruise on your cheek? So you won't look quite like—"

"I fell in a sinkhole?" Kate stopped rubbing the towel over her hair and squinted into the mirror. The bruise was ugly, but she knew it was far from the worst of it. *My entire life is a pathetic sinkhole.* Makeup wouldn't fix that.

"I've got some mineral powder in my purse," Lauren continued. "We'll blend the edges real good."

"Thank you, but no." Kate tightened the belt on her chenille robe and took a step, felt the pain of a wrenched knee. "You brought me home, stood by while I got the mud out of my hair, laid out my clothes, put food in my fridge, and made coffee. That's more than enough."

"And I led reporters right to your door. I had no idea they'd follow my car, Kate. I'm so sorry."

Kate summoned a smile. "My landlord's handling it. He may look like something out of a Rockwell painting, but I know for a fact that man has an Alaskan bear mounted on his family room wall. He'll keep the media away."

"Good." Lauren stepped aside to let Kate limp through the doorway, then followed her to the living room and helped her settle on the couch.

"You know—" Lauren handed her a mug of steaming cinnamon-laced coffee—"the hospital staff is singing your praises. Saying how brave it was of you to go looking for Harley." Her voice dropped, soft and tentative. "And they think finding the bones was the next best thing to a flat-out miracle."

"They believe it's Sunni too."

"Everyone does. They're sad, but it could mean some emotional closure." Lauren glanced toward the window. "That's probably what those reporters want. To hear firsthand what it felt like to find the remains of what could possibly be a fellow nurse." Her blue eyes were filled with compassion. "I can't even imagine."

Kate took a sip of her coffee, hoping it would still her shivering. "I didn't have time to feel anything," she said, avoiding her friend's gaze. "It happened so fast and then I fell."

Lauren's patient silence was a reminder that she was a peer counselor as well as a friend.

"I hear Harley's doing well," Kate said to fill the pause.

"They'll probably keep her another day, then release her to emergency foster care. It doesn't sound like there was any stability in that home. And now Trista's under psychiatric evaluation." Lauren shook her head. "The most horrible thing occurred to me today."

*Join the club.* "What?"

"Remember when I told you that I first met Trista because she'd left Harley alone in the ER waiting room?"

"Yes . . ."

Lauren pressed her hand to her chest. "Kate, she was outside . . . and looked nervous when I spotted her. What if Trista was trying to abandon her baby even then?"

Wes's words prodded. *"She left me . . . and drove away."*

"I didn't catch it," Lauren whispered. "Even with that Safe Haven brochure in her hand. I completely missed it."

*"It's all the same: my mother, Trista Forrester, that girl who left her newborn . . ."*

"Kate?" Lauren leaned forward. "Are you okay, sweetie?"

"Headache. Queasy. It'll pass." *If only that were true.*

"Well . . ." Lauren reached for the knit throw and tossed it over Kate, tucking it gently around her painful knee. "I don't think you should push it. I think you should do what Evelyn said when she came by your hospital room this morning. Take next week off."

"Maybe I will." Kate saw the surprise on her friend's face.

"Good. Thursday and Friday are holidays anyway."

*Thanksgiving.* She wasn't going to think about Wes and his family.

"I'm going now. So you can get some rest." Lauren stacked the coffee cups. "You sure you don't want me to help you with that bruise? And maybe a dab of lip gloss? It always makes me feel better. Plus, I just know Wes's truck is going to pull into your driveway any min—"

"No. I'm fine." Kate made herself smile despite a debilitating wave of sadness. "I'm going for the natural look. California girl."

*And Wes won't be coming here anymore.*

- + -

"There you are." Wes sat on a step of his parents' porch, cell phone to his ear, and stretched out his legs. "I was getting worried. You didn't answer my texts. I was about to climb in the truck and—"

"I was asleep," Kate interrupted. "I took one of those pain pills. I guess it sort of zonked me."

"Good," he told her, remembering her bruised, lost-waif expression when she left the hospital this morning. "Get some rest. Don't worry; I won't expect you to twirl on a dance floor tonight."

"Tonight?"

He smiled. "It's Sunday. We hadn't firmed up our plans yet, but—"

"I can't. My face is all bruised and I'm limping now. There are reporters outside. I . . . can't."

"No problem. I'll come there. You can let me in through the back door if that's better. I'll bring whatever you feel like eating. Plus Blue Bell ice cream. And a movie. Your pick—even that new tearjerker romance my sister's raving about. I'm swallowing my pride here, so take advan—"

"I don't think so."

He got a bad feeling. "Action film?"

A sigh. "I meant I don't think you should come over, Wes."

"Why not?" he asked, torn between the bad feeling and a new concern. "Are you feeling worse? Your knee?"

"No. It's . . . I don't feel like seeing anybody."

I'm "anybody" now? What was going on?

"I'll call you later," she said, the tone in her voice too reminiscent of when she'd admitted to sending her father away.

"Look . . ." Wes stood, glanced toward the house. "I told Mom

I'd help her set up the crib. I'll be finished in half an hour. Then I'll swing by your place. I won't stay long. I want to make sure you're okay, and—"

"A crib?" There was something seriously wrong with Kate's voice.

"For Harley," he explained. "I told you in the text; my parents are taking her in for emergency foster care."

There was a sound like a small, wounded animal.

"Kate?"

"Of course," she whispered. "You rescue her. And your family takes her in. It all makes perfect sense. So . . . perfect."

Wes checked his watch. "I'll be there at—"

"Don't come."

He struggled to make sense of it. There was none. "Kate . . ."

She was silent so long he thought they'd lost the connection. "Please, Wes. Stay away."

"Why? What's wrong?"

"Us."

His heart stalled. "What does that mean?"

"I can't see you. . . . I can't do this."

- + -

Kate limped to the window, thinking how odd it was to have the glass shiny-clear when everything felt so sodden and dark. Her landlord was still on the lawn pretending to rake leaves while he watched for invading reporters. The car in the driveway was his daughter's; she'd brought the grandkids for a visit, no doubt. The news vans were gone for now.

Kate shook her head, remembering what Lauren said about the staff praising her failed search for Harley. And the "miracle" in finding the unearthed remains. Lauren guessed the news reporters were eager to hear how it felt to make that unimaginable discovery. Kate told her that it had happened too fast to feel anything at all. She'd lied.

What Kate felt in the horrid moment she realized it was Sunni was a dizzying flash of anger. The same confusing rage that sent her railing at the homeless woman scamming for a baby's funeral. Soul-deep, humiliating anger. That's what she'd felt, all she'd felt. What would the reporters do with that ugly truth? What would her staff think? The grieving Spragues? Lauren? *Wes?*

Kate squeezed her eyes shut, remembering the darkness and the cold and her shoes heavy with mud. How the flashlight beam bumped across the dark earth and debris in her almost-visceral need to find a baby—not abandon one this time but find one. Save one. And then in some cruel twist, she was holding a bone in her hands. Sunni Sprague's. The skeletal remains of the perfect person Kate could never measure up to. The compassionate, self-sacrificing, and much-loved woman who'd made Kate's life beyond miserable from the first day she'd arrived at Austin Grace. A sainted ghost who reminded her how very much she was lacking. Every . . . single . . . day.

Kate limped back to the couch and pulled the blanket over herself again, cold despite her jeans and sweater. She let her gaze travel the room and told herself that she'd never belonged here. She'd been fooling herself about the sense of home she'd felt in this little house—in Austin, the city Wes called the Violet Crown.

She pushed the memory aside. Kate was no more of a nester than Roady. And true to form, the stump-tailed cat was gone again. As for her tenuous position at Austin Grace . . .

Kate jumped as her cell phone buzzed: Barrett Lyon.

"How's the pretty noggin?" There was a leer in his tone.

"I'm okay." Kate wondered if it was possible to despise him more than she did this very minute.

"More than okay, I'd say. Now that you've delivered the goods."

"Goods?"

"The lovely bones."

Kate decided it was very possible to despise him more.

"Everyone thinks you're amazing," Lyon told her. "And I could kiss you."

"No, you can't."

He laughed. "I meant that your adventure has provided a perfect distraction. The media's all over it. No one has time for pointing fingers on behalf of Baby Doe."

*"How can I forgive something like that?"* Wes's words whispered.

"Was there something you needed?" Kate asked. "I'm supposed to be resting."

"I only wanted to let you know that there's no news regarding Ava Smith. The lead from the memorial service didn't pan out. The little girl's still out there somewhere, keeping her head down. So we're good."

*Good?* Kate closed her eyes.

"I heard another intriguing bit of information today." Barrett paused, letting his news dangle like he was teasing a dog with a table scrap. Kate would rather starve. "The medical examiner's report isn't complete, but my source tells me there are signs Baby Doe may have died several days before his birth."

Kate's breath caught. "Stillborn?"

"Not yet official. But that conclusion would certainly take pressure off the hospital. Of course, I'm prepared to handle it any way it falls. Meaning we still have Dana Connor as our bird in the hand. But so far so good." Barrett gave a low chuckle. "And along those lines, I'd say the amazing Kate Callison is looking awfully good for our permanent emergency department director. Trust me on that. I think a celebration will be in order. When you're feeling better, let's get together for that din—"

"Bye." Kate disconnected, then took a moment to delete the recent flurry of unread text messages. Her father, Lauren, the ER. And the three Wes sent earlier—she hadn't had the heart to read them. Still didn't.

*"I can't see you. . . ."*

She'd deleted the last message when the phone buzzed and its preview screen lit with Wes's name and four words:

`I'm on your porch.`

# 28

WES STEPPED OVER THE THRESHOLD, grateful Kate was letting him in. He'd felt like a fool sending a text when she was yards away but figured she might think it was a reporter if he knocked.

"You *are* bruised," he said, closing the door behind him. "It looks sore."

"I'm okay." Her dark eyes avoided his. "I really wish you hadn't come, Wes."

"I had to." He wanted to tell her to deal with it, wanted to grasp her shoulders and make her look at him straight on. He'd rather have her stubborn and prickly like the first day they'd met than like—

"What is this, Kate? Did I say something wrong? Do something?"

"No." She took a step backward, still refusing to meet his gaze. "It's not you."

Wes nearly groaned at the worn-out cliché. "Well then, we're even, because this isn't you either, Kate. You're like a different person since—" A thought struck him; he was an idiot for not considering it before. "It's the head injury," he said, taking hold of her hand whether she liked it or not. New concern warred with selfish relief as he attempted to tug her toward the couch. "Let me look at you. Is your headache worse? Vision blurry? Have you vomited?"

"No. None of that." She planted her feet, refusing to budge further. Her eyes lifted to his, a hint of the old prickle in her expression. "If you want me to, I'll recite the neuro checklist: It's Sunday, November 18. Thursday is Thanksgiving. I ate pancakes for breakfast. With a plastic spoon because there was no fork on my hospital tray. Lauren drove me home." Kate slid her hand away, crossed her arms again. "My brain CT was normal. I'm fine."

"I'm not."

"I don't want to talk about this."

"I do," he lied. She was going to shred his heart. He knew it without a doubt now. A frisson of anger rose, protective as his safety gear. "On the phone I asked you what was wrong, and you said 'us.' What was that supposed to mean?"

She swallowed. "I think we need a break—I need a break. From everything. I'm taking a week off. I thought I'd pack up the car. Go somewhere."

"Where?"

"I'm not sure yet. I . . ."

"What the—? You're running away?" He stared at her, anger besting confusion. "You are. And you weren't going to tell me." He bit back a curse but couldn't stop the next words. "Why do I suddenly feel like your father here?"

He saw her flinch and hated himself. *God, please. She looks so lost.*

"I'm sorry." Wes took a step toward her, desperate to take her in his arms. "That was wrong; I shouldn't have said it. But I don't understand." He glanced at the vase of flowers he'd sent, still fresh, still perfect. "We were making plans, and . . ." *I think I'm falling in love with you.* The thought sent his brain staggering like a punch-drunk boxer.

Another thought slammed him square in the gut. "Is this about Lyon? Are you and he . . . ?"

Kate grimaced. "Of course not."

"Then what? What's the reason for shutting me out?" Her expression was as unreadable as a trail after a storm. All he could tell was that . . . *She wants me gone.* "Look, if you want to jam out of here and leave me behind, I'll get out of the way. I'll do that. But I think I deserve the truth first. Can you give me that much?"

Her shoulders sagged, and when she finally nodded, Wes wasn't at all sure he wanted to hear what she had to say. He reminded himself of what he believed about searching: better to find something—even a bad outcome—than nothing at all. It didn't help this time.

"We're too different," she began. "You and I. And that can't change, Wes. Not by putting me on a horse or making me laugh around a mouthful of cupcake or twirling me on the dance floor. Or telling me I'm beautiful and caring . . ." She closed her eyes, pain on her face. "Or even inviting me to wear a Team Tanner jersey on Thanksgiving—the nicest thing that's happened to me—" her voice choked—"in so long."

"Kate . . ." He moved toward her and she raised her palm. It was shaking.

"But I don't belong there at your family table," she continued. "Not anywhere with someone like you, especially after what you told me last night."

"What I told you?"

"You said your mom was praying for Harley and the Spragues . . . and me. *Me.*" Kate shook her head as if the idea was somehow ludicrous. Then she hitched her thumb toward the hallway. "Know what's on the top shelf of that closet?" she asked, her eyes fixed on his. "A cross, Wes. I yanked it off the wall of this house. And I hid it away. I didn't want to see it here. Couldn't bear to because—"

"Wait," he interrupted, sudden relief nearly choking him. "Is that what this is about? My faith? The 'mistakes' you said you made—your doubts about God? Everyone makes mistakes, Kate. We all have doubts. I think I told you that last night. About myself. About—"

"Forgiveness," she finished, staring at him hard. "You said you didn't understand how a mother could abandon her child. You said it was something you couldn't forgive." Kate blinked up at him. "You said that, didn't you?"

"Why does that matter now?"

"Because I can't forgive it either," she whispered, her whole body trembling. "And I can't believe God ever will. I put that cross in the closet so it wouldn't remind me that I'm not beautiful, not caring. I hid it so I could try to forget that I'm exactly like . . . them."

"Like who?" He had no idea what she was talking about; he only knew something was very wrong.

"I'm Trista," she blurted, eyes riveted to his. "I'm Ava Smith. . . . I'm your mother, Wes."

- + -

Kate was afraid she was going to be sick, scared her legs would give way. More frightened than she'd ever been in her life, even that awful day when—

"I did the same thing they did," she told Wes, feeling the words slice like a scalpel into a festering wound. "Eleven years ago, when I ran away. I trusted the wrong person. A man I worked for. He assaulted me." She dropped her head, sucked in a breath. She was suffocating. If she looked at Wes, she'd never be able to do this. "I got pregnant . . . couldn't let myself believe it, even after taking a pregnancy test—even when I was in labor. A baby boy . . . this tiny boy." She clutched at her stomach, moaned. "Before he was fifteen minutes old, I wrapped him in a dirty sweatshirt and I left him in the dark. Dumped him off at a fire station and walked away. I have no idea where my son is today."

Kate doubled over, her shoulders convulsing with the struggle to stop tears that had threatened for a decade. If she started to cry, she knew she'd never stop. "Don't you see? That's the kind of person I am."

"God . . ." Wes's gasp ended in a groan.

Kate raised her head, teeth chattering. Wes's mouth was slack with shock. The blue eyes she'd come to trust . . . She couldn't make herself look into them, couldn't risk it. It was there; she knew it: the same revulsion she saw in the mirror. *How can I forgive something like that?*

Somehow she made it across the room to the door.

"I don't know what to say," he whispered, following her. "Or what . . . I should do. Kate . . ."

"I don't expect you to do anything." She reached for the door, opened it. "Except go. Please."

He did . . . and it broke her heart.

Twenty minutes later there was a knock on the door. Hope wedged Kate's heart into her throat. Maybe it would be okay; maybe—

She pulled the door open, then dropped her gaze to the eager face of the young boy on her porch.

"Hello, ma'am—oops." He yanked a knit Longhorns cap off his head, his immediate grin revealing dimples. The boy's dark eyes were fringed by lashes that probably got him teased at school. A few freckles dotted the bridge of his nose. "Grandpa said I should ask if it's okay. I kicked my soccer ball really high and it went over the fence into your yard. I climbed up. I can see it. I was gonna jump down and get it, but . . ." He shook his head and Kate spotted a lipstick print next to one dimple. A badge of love. "Anyway, Grandpa said to ask you first, ma'am."

"Sure," she told him, the boy's dutiful manners touching her. "The gate isn't locked. Help yourself."

"Cool. Thank you." He pulled the cap over his unruly hair and started down the steps.

"Hey, wait," Kate said in a rush. "How old are you?"

"Ten." He stretched taller. "And a half. Almost."

*Ten.*

Kate closed the door and leaned against it, sank down until she was sitting on the cold floor. Then finally let the flood of tears come.

**29**

+

**"KATE?"** Judith held a cardboard coffee carrier in one hand, the scent of Starbucks wafting upward as she tapped on the door. "It's Judith Doyle, from the hosp—Oh, hello." She tried not to gasp as morning sun revealed the swollen bruise on Kate's face. "I hope this is all right. That I'm here. Your address was on the thank-you card you sent after the auxiliary fund-raiser. . . ."

"Of course it's fine. I almost didn't recognize you without your pink uniform. Come in. The place is sort of a mess. I haven't felt like doing too much since I got home yesterday."

*And haven't slept either?* There were shadows under Kate's beautiful eyes. Judith could relate; she'd been awake most of the last two nights herself. Thinking. Then praying, at long last.

"The way you like it," she said, lifting Kate's coffee from the carrier after they settled on the couch. "And there are scones, too—maple oat nut and a blueberry. We never got a chance to meet for coffee last week. And now so many things have happened." Her throat tightened at Kate's expression. Her eyes were red like she'd been crying.

"It must have been awful when they thought you were a kidnapper, Judith."

"Yes." Oddly, it seemed long ago now. And completely insignificant compared to—"I came here to apologize," she said in a rush. Tears rose; she thought she'd cried them all. *God, please help me.*

"Apologize? I don't understand."

"How could you possibly?" Judith made herself smile. "I should have known about Trista," she explained. "I should have seen all of it. Her father's abuse and—"

"Abuse?"

"You didn't see the news last night?" Something in Kate's expression said she hadn't wanted to. Judith could understand that. "After Trista was more lucid, she reported she'd been abused by her father for years. A broken jaw, a ruptured eardrum another time. None of it reported to authorities. He became more violent after he learned she was pregnant. She wanted an abortion. He was dead set against it, though he beat her so badly once she almost miscarried." Judith winced. "Trista said she wished she had. She didn't want a baby then. She doesn't now."

"So she abandoned Harley."

Judith nodded. "She said if she'd known about Safe Haven, she'd have turned her over after birth. She wanted to do it now but was afraid Harley was too old. Her father has been going to rehab counseling, but he's still getting drunk and abusive. Trista was sure it was only a matter of time before he started hurting the baby, too. She doesn't want her baby, but she doesn't want her hurt either."

"She wanted to keep her safe." Kate's face paled. "I heard she'd said that."

"I guess Trista figured someone would find Harley in the park and give her a home. It was a safer bet than what she could offer at her father's house." Judith's stomach tensed. "She came to the waiting room once with her face bruised. She told me she tripped over the dog. And then when her father was admitted, all Trista could think of was taking the money from his pocket and buying fast food. It was the only time I ever saw her smile. The only time. Even with that sweet baby. She never held her, never took any pictures. I should have put it all together. I missed it, and that baby could have died." Tears filled her eyes. "You could have been killed too, Kate. You were out there in the park because of Harley, and she was out there because I made an awful mistake."

"Judith, hold it. Wait." Kate reached for her hand. "You're taking too much on yourself. Lauren and I saw Trista and Harley too."

"A few times. I saw them almost every day. I made it my business to check on them even though they weren't hospital patients. I should have seen the signs. I could have prevented all of this. I'm sick over it."

"You're a volunteer, Judith. The best volunteer we have—incredibly dedicated. Still, no one would ever expect you to foresee every possible outcome."

"I do. I expect that of myself, Kate. Every day, every minute I'm at the hospital. It's why I'm there. I know the name of every patient who comes into the ER. I make notes on their conditions. I keep track of waiting times and pester the registration staff. I stay up at night to search the Internet and medical books. That's how I knew to start cardiac compressions on Mr. Beck." Judith forced herself to say the painful words. "I do all of those things because my husband died at Austin Grace—collapsed in the ER waiting room."

Kate's eyes widened.

"He had headaches. Tension headaches. A shot always fixed them; I'd drive him home and put him to bed. Simple as that. A small pothole in a wonderful life. The ER was busy that day and the triage nurse apologized for the wait. My husband had his golf magazine, and his pain wasn't severe. He knew I'd fidget waiting. There was a one-day sale at Macy's and he insisted that I go. He said he'd be fine." A tear slid past her nose. "While I was waiting in line to pay for a sofa pillow, my darling husband was bleeding in his brain. Dying. He had a seizure in the waiting room and was in a deep coma by the time I got there. A massive stroke. He never woke up."

Kate's eyes held hers. "And you became a volunteer. To help other patients, other families."

"Yes." Judith sighed, dreading what she had to say next. "And to keep my eye on the staff. I've made it my business to keep tabs on inefficiency and lapses in professionalism. And potentially dangerous mistakes. I've tried to intervene before a tragedy happens. Again. Like with my husband. He was waiting an hour and a half, got worse, and no one checked on him."

"The triage nurse—"

"Was Sunni Sprague."

Kate's lower lip sagged.

"They were short staffed that day. Sunni was filling in everywhere. She was kind and polite, a jewel. Except that she let my husband collapse in the waiting room." Judith shook her head. "I lay awake last night, thinking about it: Sunni, Trista, Harley, and you. And now Sunni again, if those were her bones in that park. A tragic circle. Please believe that I never wished Sunni any harm. I was as distressed as anyone when she went missing. She's human; she made a mistake. And—" Judith winced at the truth—"I did too when I left my husband's side. I know that now. But I've been so wrapped up in preventing everyone else's mistakes that I didn't see it. I realize now how very lost I felt after my husband died. I think the hospitals, Austin Grace especially, became my new family. The nurses, doctors . . ." She sighed again. "Even Beverly at the registration desk with her cheese puffs and her personal calls. I know her. I care about her problems even when she aggravates me. I was riding herd on the staff like a mother would. I only wanted to help everyone do the right thing. But I made my own dreadful mistakes."

"I still don't think you should blame yourself for Trista."

Judith cleared her throat. "I did something else, Kate. Something that caused you problems. And probably made Dana Connor quit—maybe staff at other hospitals too. I was self-righteous and judgmental. Such a sad hypocrite."

"What are you talking about?"

"The newspaper." She met Kate's gaze. "Waiting for Compassion. That's me."

- + -

"Hold it," Gabe warned. "That's dog kibble you're about to eat."

"What—?" Wes growled, dropping the crunchy bits back into the bowl. He wiped his fingers on his shirt, then glared across the funeral home's mahogany desk. "What's it doing there?"

"I'm picking the green pieces out." Gabe scratched his dog's ear. "Hershey won't eat 'em. Some kind of omega fatty stuff. And probiotics, whatever that is. Can't blame him. He's like me; someone ought to make dog food that tastes like chicken-fried steak."

Gabe raised his brows. "But maybe those green things will improve your mood, pal."

"Nothing wrong with my mood," Wes grumbled, glancing toward doors flanked by tall vases of white chrysanthemums. There were strains of classical music somewhere in the distance, no doubt chosen to be comforting and soul-soothing. It wasn't. The only thing worse would be a mouthful of dog kibble, followed by a chorus of "Brown Eyed Girl." The painful confusion that had left Wes tossing and sleepless returned with a vengeance. *Kate* . . .

He turned his attention back to Gabe. "Is there a funeral today?"

"Not till four." Gabe's eyes filled with questions that he wouldn't ask outright. And that Wes couldn't answer. "Jenna's going over to Zilker Park; she's hoping to find out something about the bones. We could join up with her."

*Zilker. Close enough to see Kate's car drive away . . .*

"What do you say?" Gabe patted his leg, free now from the bulk of bandages. "I'm not ready to hike, but we could hang out and get a feel for how things are going there."

"Don't think so," Wes said. "They're not going to reveal anything until the medical examiner gives the word. If it's Sunni, we'll know in a few days." Where would Kate be when that happened? No. It did no good to think about that. Or talk about it either.

"It must have been awful for Kate. Finding the remains."

"Right." Wes's throat tightened at the memory of her on the ER gurney, the tremble in her voice when she talked about holding Sunni's bone in her hands. He glanced down at his own; they'd been holding Harley not long after Kate had done that.

"Of course, you know more about the effects of that kind of trauma than I do."

"Effects?" Wes met Gabe's gaze, confused. Lack of sleep was making him brain dead.

"Traumatic stress. I'd think accidentally finding the remains of a fellow nurse would be a fairly emotional sucker punch. But then you're the expert."

Posttraumatic stress. He hadn't even considered it. Baby Doe, Harley, Sunni. It would impact anyone emotionally. He remembered Kate's expression as she held Baby Doe's limp body in her hands. Grief-stricken. He'd recognized it even when he knew nothing about her. And then she'd run out of the conference room at the ER debriefing. Because . . . it was personal. Wes saw that now.

"I guess—" Gabe dropped a piece of yellow kibble on Hershey's tongue—"if they identify the bones as Sunni's, there will be another round of counseling at Austin Grace. You said Kate wasn't on board with the idea last time, but maybe . . ."

*Maybe she won't even be there anymore.*

"Wes?"

"I'm leaving," Wes said, standing. "You have a funeral and I need to go."

In ten minutes he'd passed the cemetery and then the Braxton and Tanner ranches, gripping the steering wheel like he had hold of someone dangling from a cliff. In three more minutes he passed the freeway sign showing the distance to Austin. And then—

Wes hit the brakes and jerked the truck's wheel, felt the big tires scrabble off the road and crunch against the gravel shoulder as he came to a jolting stop. Dust swirled across the windshield, making his vision as blurry as his thoughts. His mouth was dry, head pounding. He closed his eyes, listening to the whoosh of passing traffic. Then pulled out his cell phone and tapped the contact number. He held his breath.

"I'm not able to take calls right now," Kate's recording said in the voice he'd begun to hear in his dreams. "Leave me a message and I'll get back to you."

*Will you?* He disconnected before the signal could sound.

No. *I can't . . .* He told himself he was too wrung out to make rational decisions. It was Kate who'd opened the door and asked him to leave. She intended to go away, very likely was gone already. There was nothing he could do about that, the same way there'd been nothing he could do about the pain in her eyes yesterday. Or her obvious suffering when she told him she couldn't see him anymore, because . . . *"I'm Trista. . . . I'm Ava Smith. . . . I'm your mother, Wes."*

Guilt rose, burning his chest like bile. He should have found a way to comfort her, should have at least tried. Any man with a heart would have. But . . .

Kate's words came back as clearly as if she were sitting next to him in the truck: *"You said you didn't understand how a mother could abandon her child. You said it was something you couldn't forgive."*

She'd asked him if that was true. He'd hedged, asking her why it mattered.

*But . . . it is true. It does matter. How can I forgive something like that?*

He was the son of a woman who left her child in the woods. Unchangeable as DNA.

Wes rested his forehead against his arms on the steering wheel. "Help me, God," he whispered aloud. "You brought Kate into my life when you know who I am. I don't understand. What do you expect from me now?"

**30**

+

"I SLEPT OKAY," KATE FIBBED, looking down at the rumpled sweater and jeans Lauren had pulled from the closet yesterday morning. She nestled the phone against her ear as she reached for a second pair of socks and stuffed them into her travel duffel. "A little hard to get comfortable with the bruised ribs." *And my whole world blown apart.*

"I'm not trying to be a mother hen, sweetie," Lauren assured her. "But you haven't answered my texts."

"Sorry. Pain pills make me groggy." Or would, if she took any. Kate rolled a sweater and wedged it into the corner of the bag.

"Did Wes come by after I left?"

Kate shut her eyes against a wave of pain no pill could ease.

"Kate?"

"Yes." She set the duffel on her bed, limped in the direction of the living room. "He was here. But not long."

"Because of the whole 'groggy' thing."

"Right." *And because I told him something completely unforgivable.*

"Hey, I saw Judith a few minutes ago—here at the hospital. I'm off today, but I wanted to check on how the staff was doing. Because of the bones. You know."

*I know.* Over the last two days, Kate felt more and more like her own bones had been unearthed and scattered.

"She brought in food for the entire ER staff," Lauren continued. "Breakfast tacos, *chilaquiles*, chorizos, pastries, and this huge mountain of fruit. Beverly was beside herself. No one could believe it."

Kate glanced at the untouched coffee and scones on the table in front of the couch. She wasn't going to say anything. Enough bones had been laid bare.

"And now Judith's in the nursery rocking Harley." Lauren sighed. "I think that's incredibly brave considering she was accused of being a kidnapper."

Kate nodded. Brave and responsible, too. Trying to fix a mistake. While Kate's could never be made right.

"I'm sure you know that the Tanners are providing emergency foster care," Lauren added.

"I . . ." Kate was unable to stop the image of Wes helping his mother assemble a crib. A family with love to spare. And share. She limped to the couch, eyes brimming. "Mmm . . . yeah. I know."

"You sound . . . Are you having a lot of pain? I can finish up here and come over."

Kate's first instinct was to say no. Her bag was nearly packed, the urge to run never so strong. But all at once she wanted to tell Lauren everything. How frightened she'd been that year in Las Vegas. How worthless and lonely she'd felt all these years since.

"It'll take me twenty minutes, tops," Lauren promised.

The trembling was back. Kate hugged her arms around herself, dared to imagine how it might feel to have Lauren listen to her story. The relief it could bring. Her voice emerged in a hoarse whisper. "Okay."

"Is there anything you need me to bring?"

"Only yourself." Kate swiped at a tear, almost smiled.

"You got it. I'm going to run by the ICU and then—Hang on. I've got a text popping up." There was a gasp. "Oh no. I'm putting you on hold."

When Lauren spoke again, her voice was breathless. "I've got to go to Houston. It was Jess. . . ." Her voice broke. "She tested positive on a random drug test at work; it was a prescription med, but Jess thinks they don't believe her. She's scared and—"

"Go," Kate interrupted. "You belong there. Not here. Go!"

She disconnected and sat on the couch for a few moments, rubbing her knee and thinking that it was just as well. In truth, things were exactly as they should be. Despite the circumstances, Lauren would be with a family that loved her. Judith was back at the hospital. The Tanners would have a baby to fill their crib. And Wes . . . he'd finally accepted that Kate was beyond rescue. She'd known that all along. And now she could do what she did best: leave all this behind.

In twenty minutes Kate had showered, pulled on fresh clothes, and finished packing her duffel. She stopped at the hallway closet to find a jacket but didn't allow herself to look up at the newspaper-wrapped object on the top shelf. She went through a mental checklist, decided she had everything, and headed toward the front door. Then stopped. She returned to the kitchen and grabbed the daisy mugs, then crossed to the mantel for the framed photo of her mother. Kate tucked them in her duffel and opened the door. She told herself it felt more comfortable to have them with her even though she'd only be gone a week.

But by the time she pulled out of the driveway, she'd reminded herself that her position at Austin Grace was as an interim employee. Then accepted her initial suspicion that the heavens raining mud had been a sign. She knew without a doubt that her landlord's beautiful ten-year-old grandson would love to take in a stub-tailed cat.

When Kate passed Zilker Park, she averted her eyes so she wouldn't see the barricades, county cars, and news vans. But she couldn't stop the whisper in her head. Wes's voice: *"You're running away?"*

It was probably true.

- + -

There were flowers planted around the grave—his stepmother's quiet, ongoing effort. Sprigs of spent summer alyssum bordered a few stubborn marigolds, but there were new fall plantings too. Wine-colored snapdragons, blue pansies. And those yellow-orange blooms with dark centers called black-eyed Susans. Like in the bouquet he'd sent to Kate. It seemed a lifetime ago.

Wes glanced down at the pink granite headstone. *No, this was a lifetime ago.*

He crouched, one knee on the autumn-brown grass. The late-morning sun lit the headstone's carved epitaph:

**Lee Ann Tanner**
1951–1986
*Devoted wife and mother*
*Loving memories last forever*

Wes swallowed against a familiar and confusing mix of feelings. *Everything that keeps me from coming here.* Guilt, always a part of that mix, nudged. How long had it been? And why had he stopped here today? It was the last place he wanted to be after all that had hap—

"Hello, Son." His father's voice behind him, deep and gentle. "I saw your truck at the gate."

"Hi." Wes stood, dragged a hand through his hair. His father was dressed in his work clothes. "I thought we didn't have anything on the schedule until tomorrow."

"I told the Phillipses I'd take a quick look at that flood damage on my way into town."

"Want me to come along?"

"No need."

His father's gaze dropped toward the headstone for a moment, and Wes realized that he couldn't recall the last time they'd been here together. Maybe not since Wes reached adulthood.

He wished he'd had the good sense to drive past those gates today. Lack of sleep had him too ragged to trust his instincts. Or keep his guard up. And . . . *Lord, please. I don't want to remember.*

"Dylan missed you at breakfast this morning. He couldn't stop talking about that clip of you on the news. His brother, the hero." His father's smile crinkled the edges of his eyes, a shade Miranda had dubbed Tanner blue. She'd had Home Depot do a paint match for the guest room. "He wanted to ask you for your autograph."

Wes was grateful for the laugh. But he sensed the unspoken question. "I had some thinking to do. It's been a rough couple of days."

"We expected that was the case." There was concern in his father's eyes. "Searching for the baby couldn't have been easy. And we all thought you wouldn't be involved, since the Amber Alert went out as a kidnapping. But . . ."

"Right." Wes expected the usual prod of anger about the reason for the search, but strangely it didn't come. Instead, something too much like sadness filled his chest. "I saw her on the news last night. The mother. She said she left Harley because she wanted her to be safe."

"We heard that too. The mother was an abuse victim." His father sighed. "Her judgment went haywire for sure. But I want to believe she meant that. About keeping her child safe."

Wes stared at his father. "You do?"

"Yes. Don't you?"

"I . . . don't know." Wes shook his head. And then it was there: anger, grabbing the earlier sadness by the throat. "What about my mother?" he heard himself ask. "What am I supposed to believe about what she did?"

His father flinched slightly, drew in a breath.

"That night . . . ," Wes continued, suddenly helpless to stop himself from voicing the painful questions he'd never asked aloud. "When she put me in the car, did she know where she was going? Did she realize she was taking a risk? Or . . ."

Wes's gaze darted to where it always did. Since the first time he'd come here, holding his father's hand at the funeral: the empty plot beside his mother's grave. "Am I alive today because she changed her mind about taking me into that river with her? Was she going to drown us both?" He dropped his head, his stomach churning. Then felt his father's strong grip on his shoulder.

"I wish I had the answer, Son. I can't count the number of times I've asked that myself. Though I—" His voice broke, his thumb moving against Wes's collarbone like he was willing a fracture to heal. "I never had the courage to say it out loud like you just did. But God got tortured earfuls from me for a lot of years. Your stepmother too."

Wes raised his head and tried to speak but couldn't.

His father's eyes shone with tears as he continued. "When I scraped bottom for every possible reason she'd left the house that night, I started to beat myself up. I told myself she was unhappy because I wasn't a good enough husband. That I was too absorbed in the business and overlooked reckless behavior that proved she was having problems. I hated myself for staying in Fort Worth that night. I knew a decent man with any shred of a heart would have stayed close, paid more attention, questioned her 'blue days.' Taken her to a doctor. Taken us both to church. A man worth anything at all would have done *something*."

"Dad, I'm sorry," Wes said, remembering the sound of his father crying in the darkened house all those long months. "I shouldn't have—"

"No. You should ask. You have every right to answers. But . . . sometimes it's not for us to know. It's taken me a long time, but I've accepted that. And now I have far more gratitude than questions." A smile tugged at his lips. "I'm a blessed man. I still have you, Wes. A son who makes me proud every single day of my life. I have a loving wife I don't half deserve. And because of her big heart, we've built a beautiful family—" his smile widened—"that's about to grow again."

Wes watched his father, lifelong respect for him growing even deeper.

"Yes," his father went on, "I believe that you were left in the woods that night to keep you safe. Your mother loved you, Wes. Even before you were born. You were everything to her." He clucked his tongue. "I'll never forget how proud she was when you played the piano at Amelia Braxton's spring recital. 'Mary Had a Little Lamb'—you'd have thought it was Mozart. I could hardly keep her off the stage."

The ache in Wes's throat was relentless.

His father glanced at his watch. "I'll call Steve Phillips. Tell him I'll be by tomorrow instead."

"No," Wes told him. "Go on. I'm going to hang around a little longer. Do some of that thinking. I'm fine, Dad."

His father studied his face. Then stepped forward and hauled Wes into a bear hug.

"Okay then," he said, adding one last thump on his back. "Call your mom later. She's concerned."

"Yes, sir. I will."

"You know . . ." His father glanced toward the headstone. "Your grandfather chose that wording. After all those months and finally finding her . . . I couldn't think. I told him to pick something. I know now that they're exactly the right words. Good memories are God's mercy, Son. Remember that."

Wes nodded. "I'll try."

"Do that. Because otherwise it's hard to see the hope. Or find the peace that comes with forgiveness." He shook his head. "And living that way is the worst kind of lost."

# 31

**"IT'S FRESH."** Dana Connor handed Kate the coffee. "I'm sorry, but the only cup that wasn't in the dishwasher was my son's Superman mug. My husband's new therapy aide started this morning. It's been a busy day already." She glanced toward the adjacent room filled with medical equipment. Only a chandelier—shortened to be out of the way—hinted that the space had once been a dining room. There was no table. No chairs except the wheelchair. A man in scrubs squatted beside it. Somewhere down the hallway were the sounds of a TV and childish giggles.

"Some of the exercises require two helpers," Dana explained. "So my housework gets pushed aside—like dishwashing."

"The coffee smells wonderful," Kate assured her, noticing a cluster of framed photos on the end table next to the couch. A shot of a young man in football gear, baby portraits, and a candid of Dana in a swimsuit with her husband—tanned, muscled as that superhero—both grinning as they hoisted a canoe overhead. Happier times. Kate recalled her conversation with Dana the day Baby Doe was found. *"I didn't get a chance to sleep before my shift. . . . I need to work if we're going to keep the house. . . ."*

Dana's teeth scraped across her lower lip. "On the phone, you said this wasn't about the incident with the baby. Then . . . ?"

*Why am I here?* Good question. Kate had been asking herself the same thing. One minute she'd been on the freeway barreling toward Dallas; the next she'd turned off and headed back to Austin, found Dana's number stored in her phone. "I heard that you canceled your shifts at Austin Grace."

Dana looked down. "It's a closer drive, but . . ."

"You didn't want a triage assignment," Kate said gently.

"No. I can't do that yet. After . . ." Dana glanced toward the dining room, then lowered her voice. "I keep second-guessing myself. I think about those newspaper letters. I know it sounds crazy, but I feel like everyone's watching and waiting for me to make another mistake."

"It doesn't sound crazy. But if it helps, I think we've seen the last of those letters." Kate read the skepticism on Dana's face. "Trust me," she added, then regretted the choice of words. What had she ever done to earn this woman's trust? She set her coffee down. "I'm certain we won't hear any more from Waiting for Compassion. I'm also sure that a big part of the reason you're leaving Austin Grace has to do with me."

Dana looked like she was going to deny it, then lifted her chin instead. "I've never been a manager of any kind. I can imagine that it's hard. But it's not easy from my side either. Being a temporary employee, having to straddle shift assignments, get used to new routines, different personalities—and being the appointed scapegoat. It happens. It's even understandable, I suppose. I'm not regular staff; it makes me a safer target. I'm not complaining." Her eyes held Kate's. "But I do my best. Every minute. And I *am* compassionate. To a fault sometimes. Ask my husband how many times I've called the hospital in the middle of the night to check on a patient. All the times I've cried or how often he's had to tell me to 'let go and let God.' He always reminds me that I can't fix it all no matter how much I want to." She glanced toward the dining room again, her voice breaking. "I can't . . . fix it all."

"No," Kate agreed, thinking of Dana attending Baby Doe's memorial service. A sad, late attempt to fix her part in the baby's tragedy. Like her own frantic search for Harley . . . *because of my son.* Kate's fingers found the bruise on her cheek. "And I know I can't fix all the worries you've had since that incident at the hospital. But I wanted to tell you that I'm sorry."

Dana's eyes widened.

"When I called you into my office that day, I handled it poorly," Kate said. "You were trying to explain the chaos of that night, how hard it was to function given the patient acuity and the staffing. I cut you short. I should have listened instead of pointing a finger." A groan escaped her lips. "It's not like I don't remember how it feels to be in the trenches. I do. You shouldn't have to remind me."

"Sunni used to say something like that when someone would grumble about a bad day or a difficult patient." Dana shook her head, a faint smile on her lips. "She'd put her hands on her hips and say, 'You're preachin' to the choir—I've been in that foxhole.' Then she'd ask what she could do to make it better."

*Sunni.* Kate glanced down at her hands, feeling that weathered bone. Then remembered Judith's words: *"She's human; she made a mistake."*

"Do you think . . . ?" Dana's voice was tentative. "Do you think it was Sunni's bones that you found?"

"Yes," Kate said, feeling the certainty even more deeply. "I do."

"I think that will help make things better at Austin Grace."

"And I think—" Kate caught Dana's gaze—"it would make things even better if you stayed, Dana. I'm asking you to do that. I'll talk to the CNO about finding you a permanent staff position. With full benefits and—"

"Wha . . . ?" Dana's voice choked. "But what about Ava Smith?"

"We'll handle that if we have to," Kate told her. "I'll vouch for the job you had to perform under very difficult circumstances. But I don't think that's going to be an issue." *Because she's long gone. Hiding somewhere.* Kate knew it with the same certainty she felt about the bones.

Hope began to replace the bewilderment on Dana's face. "Why would you do all of this?"

"Because we need nurses like you," Kate said simply. "And because . . ." Somehow the words began tumbling out of their own accord. "I'm sure you know the security cameras caught an image that might be Ava Smith. I was in the film too. I saw that girl when she was leaving the ER. It was dark, but I could tell she was pale and shaky."

Dana stared at her.

"I told the police that we exchanged only a few words," Kate continued, "and that's true. I asked her if she needed help. She said she was fine. I gave her my name and tried to point her back to the registration desk. But then Lauren came and the girl ran off." She swallowed against a sudden ache in her throat. "What I didn't tell the police is how frightened she looked. Desperate. I think she really wanted our help. I . . . should have done more."

Kate met Dana's gaze. "I made a mistake too. I intend to add that to my statement. From what I've heard, there may be no case against the hospital. But I promise if anything further happens, you are not in this alone."

*And that's why I came here today.*

Ten minutes later Kate pulled away from the Connors' cul-de-sac with a gift from Dana's four-year-old son: a ziplock bag filled with Texas-shaped tortilla chips. She shook her head, watching as the GPS powered up. Dallas or . . . ? She still had no clue where she was going.

There was a buzz and Kate glanced at her cell phone, lying on the passenger seat next to the bag of chips. A call from . . . *Great.*

She pulled to the curb and yanked the phone from the seat. Heat rose in her neck as she tapped the button to connect. "Barrett—perfect timing."

"Really? I *liiike* the sound of that, pretty lady." His familiar chuckle was deep, seductive.

"No," Kate told him, narrowing her eyes. "I don't think you'll like what I'm going to say at all."

"Meaning?"

"Meaning that I've been a fool to play this cat-and-mouse game with you. No, wait. I should have said deer-hunting game—isn't that what you told me? I'm like one of those deer hunters on your granddaddy's hunting lease. And I'd do whatever it takes to bring down a trophy buck?"

"A metaphor, darlin'."

"Don't. Don't call me darlin'. And don't tell me *ever* again that

I'm like you." Kate knew she was close to shouting and didn't care. "I'm nothing like you. And you're sadly mistaken if you think I'll throw one of my nurses under a bus to help you win a court case. Even if you got one of your golf buddies to grease my way into that director's position."

"Kate, Kate. You've had an accident—a concussion, for heaven's sake." The slick courtroom voice was back. "It's only natural to feel confused, emotion—"

"What's *your* excuse?" Kate blurted, realizing she'd somehow smashed the Texas chips.

"Excuse?"

"For unprofessional, inappropriate behavior toward a female employee—of a hospital your legal firm represents." She hoped she'd heard a gasp. "Coming to my home uninvited. Making personal remarks, inviting me out to dinner on several occasions, along with offers to be of 'help' with my employment situation, and—"

"What are you implying?"

"Not implying. Promising," she told him calmly, snapping another chip with her fingertip. "If you do anything to hurt Dana Connor or any other member of my staff, I'll be filing a harassment complaint. I'll make you feel like you sat on a hill of fire ants, Mr. Lyon. It may be the last thing I do as interim director, but I will *so* enjoy it. Count on that."

There was a short silence.

"Well then." Barrett's voice was cool, detached. "I won't keep you . . ."

*No, you won't.*

Kate disconnected. She sprinkled some of the smashed tortilla chips into her palm and lapped a few salty bits, then prodded a less demolished chip. Not a bad representation of the state map, considering that it was cut from cornmeal. Gulf Coast, panhandle, east Texas . . . *Where am I going?*

She stared at the GPS. The truth was, Kate had no idea where she was headed, and she'd already hit two major speed bumps: the detour to Dana Connor's house and that long-overdue conversation with Barrett Lyon. Each completely unplanned. Yet, strangely . . .

Something about them made her feel a little less lost.

# 32

**KATE AWAKENED SEVERAL TIMES** in the night, heart pounding in the dark, confused by the pain in her ribs and again by the unfamiliar hotel surroundings. *I'm in Dallas.* Her mind tumbled through a disjointed recap of the past week before she slid back into fitful slumber. Only to awaken and have the cycle repeat without mercy. *Where am I? What happened?*

Dawn found her staring at the ceiling, and it wasn't until hours later—to the distant buzz of Tuesday morning commuter traffic—that Kate finally found a few hours of dreamless sleep. The muted TV news showed that it was after ten when she stumbled barefoot to the shower.

Afterward, she wiped the steam from the mirror and studied her reflection. The face could have belonged to a stranger; she traced damp fingers across her cheek in a foolish reality check. Too real: etched shadows—like artist charcoal—smudged her eyes, the bruise on her cheek going green around the edges. Her always-wispy and wayward hair now begged for a trim. Kate dropped the hotel robe enough to see her ribs, gasped at the mottled purple bruising. Too much like flog marks against her pale skin. She leaned closer to the mirror and stared into her own eyes, the truth making her groan. She looked exactly like she felt: battered, body and soul.

Tears welled. *Where can I run . . . to leave you behind?*

- + -

Wes's mom stilled the rocking chair, meeting his gaze over the sleeping baby's head. Her smile was dreamy soft. "Have you ever seen a more beautiful face?" she whispered, her lips against Harley's curls.

"No," he told her honestly, feeling the ache that was now a permanent part of his throat. He drew in a breath scented by baby lotion and freshly stacked Pampers. "She looks . . . content."

He'd almost said *safe*. It seemed like the right word. His father's word. *"I want to believe she meant that. About keeping her child safe."* It was a confusing possibility Wes had never considered before. Trista, Ava, Lee Ann Tanner, and maybe . . . The ache was determined to choke him senseless. *Safe?*

His mom set the rocker to creaking softly against the wood-plank floor. "I heard that they've arrested Trista's father. And after things have been determined by the court, she's hoping to go live with a cousin in Oklahoma. Go back to school. Start fresh."

Wes watched as the pink bundle stirred, murmured, then burrowed her face against his mom's neck, relaxing again. "She's planning to take the baby?"

"No. Even if Harley were allowed to return to her, Trista made it clear it's not part of her plans." She sighed. Then smiled in the way Wes had seen for as long as he could remember. Peaceful, trusting. Certain. "I'm so relieved God has plans too."

*God's plan.* Was it possible . . . ?

"Dylan said something this morning before he left for school." His mom's eyes captured his. "He told me, 'Wes looks sad.'"

"Mm . . ." Wes dragged his fingers through his hair, knowing the importance of what she'd said. Reading emotions—empathy— was a big accomplishment for someone with autism. Wes was proud of his little brother . . . and Dylan was right.

"Kate's gone," he said, heart lugging.

"Gone?"

"She asked for a week off to recover from the accident. But . . ." The choke hold squeezed tighter. "She's running away, Mom." He saw the compassion in her eyes. And questions she wouldn't ask out of respect for his privacy. "I think she's bothered by all that's happened lately. The baby at the hospital, Harley, and finding those bones." His stomach churned as the truth hit. "I think it's stirred up some of those 'tough things' she said she had to deal with in her life."

His mom nodded, her silence speaking more eloquently than words. *"Like it has for you, my son. I'm so relieved God has plans too."*

"I should go," he managed. He stepped close, pressed a kiss to the top of her head, then stroked a fingertip along the sleeping baby's feather-soft cheek. "I'm glad Harley's safe."

He'd reached the nursery door when his mom called out, "Your cell phone." She pointed to where he'd left it on the edge of the baby's changing table. "You wouldn't want to miss a rescue call."

- + -

Kate pushed the room service tray aside. Despite the fact that she'd had nothing to eat since yesterday, breakfast had been as appealing as those tortilla chips she'd pulverized during her conversation with Barrett Lyon. She'd forced herself to eat, but somehow it only made her feel emptier. How was that possible? And why—when it had always worked before—hadn't she found the relief that came when she packed a bag and jumped into her car?

*"You're running away?"* Wes's words rushed back, bruising her further.

She'd been alone for so many years. Needed that protective solitude, stubbornly clung to it. And now, inexplicably, being alone felt . . . *lonely. I'm so lonely.* How could that be?

*Wes.* She closed her eyes, remembering the awful moment when she told him about her son. His gasp of shock and that look in his eyes. She'd seen it, hadn't she? Revulsion, loathing, unforgiveness. It had to be there. Because it was exactly the way she'd felt about herself all these years.

She drew her knees up, resting her face against the terry fabric of the hotel robe. Then let herself recall the conversation she'd had with Wes at the old Braxton well. The day he'd told her about his training, the test to prove he had the "right stuff." She'd revealed that she'd run away from home and hinted at that terrible year. She told Wes she didn't think God would listen to her prayers because she'd made so many mistakes.

And then . . . Kate squinted her eyes, remembering. He'd talked about grace. He'd said, *"We all make mistakes. We're human. We're flawed. That's where grace comes in . . . an undeserved gift."*

What if that were really true?

Kate stared at the muted TV, then reached for the remote. It was a national news broadcast with a ticker banner that read, *Bones identified as missing Austin TX nurse.* She hit the button just as the cameras zoomed in on the faces of a middle-aged couple.

"We're heartsick," the man said, putting his arm around his wife. "It's been such a long, painful journey. No parent wants to hear this kind of news." He glanced at his wife, his voice thick with emotion. "But we're grateful, too. For everyone who has searched, for all the prayers. And for our daughter's friends—all the good folks at Austin Grace who never gave up . . ." He hung his head.

Kate held her breath, trembling inside as Mrs. Sprague continued for her husband.

"Sunni was blessed by that team; she was grateful every day to be part of it. Being a nurse was her calling. Even the times it broke her heart . . . and . . ." She swiped at a tear, then smiled. "It was a nurse who found her. The same nurse who filled in when Sunni went missing—she's the one who found our girl. And now she's keeping our daughter's legacy going forward." She nodded as her husband drew her closer. "We have to believe that God planned it that way."

Kate listened for a few minutes longer as a law enforcement spokesman gave updates on the renewed search for Sunni's killer. He sounded cautiously optimistic. Kate switched off the television and stared at the blank screen for a long time. She let it all tumble, mix, sort . . . and tumble again. She struggled to find the connecting thread she knew was there. Something that linked so many tragedies, so many losses: her mother, Baby Doe, Harley, Judith's husband, Sunni Sprague . . . Kate's son. And caused people to make so many mistakes: Ava, Trista, Judith, Wes's mother. Even that homeless woman holding up the fake sign for a baby's funeral.

What was it the woman had said when Kate confronted her? She said she was "only trying to get by." That it was all she knew right now. And she was hoping for better someday. That she'd heard it was possible.

Kate hugged her arms around herself, unable to stop the trembling as the truth finally settled around her: Desperate people. Painful mistakes . . . tragic losses. And a plan? Was it also true what Sunni's mother said? That God had a plan to connect all these things?

Kate closed her eyes. "God," she breathed, "you know I've made one mistake after another. I'm not even close to having the 'right stuff'—maybe I did once, but I threw it away. Or wrapped it up and hid it in a closet. I don't know. All I know right now is that I can't live like this. I can't go on feeling so lost. I want to stop running." A tear slid onto her lips. "I want you to point me in the right direction. I need you in my life. Please help me."

By 3 p.m. Kate had cleared Dallas security and slipped her shoes back on. There would be just enough time to hit Starbucks and send Lauren a short text message; that would have to do for now. Though she ached to know how her friend was faring in Houston, Kate wasn't ready to talk yet. Everything that was happening seemed too new and fragile. She needed to focus on what lay ahead. It felt more important than anything she'd done. Even so, Kate couldn't remember ever feeling so free, so much at peace. And strong, too—like anything at all was possible now. She smiled. *Thank you . . . oh, thank you.*

She hitched her duffel over her shoulder, new hope warming her heart. No GPS needed for this trip. Kate knew exactly where she was going.

## 33

MATT DISCONNECTED FROM THE CALL. Leaving a message was futile. Kate wasn't answering her phone. And she hadn't replied to the message he'd sent on Saturday asking if she'd been affected by what had happened with the abandoned baby and that ugly discovery in the park. From what he'd seen on the news today, he was sure of it now. It had to be Kate who'd found that nurse's bones. His throat tightened as he recalled the image of the murder victim's parents; he knew only too well how it felt to have a missing child. Matt was so grateful that Kate had come home— so to speak.

He set the phone down. He'd be at an AA meeting tonight, and according to her habit, Kate would very likely leave a message then. *"Work's great. . . . I'm fine."* Messages left in place of conversation. He prayed for so much more.

With a pang, Matt reminded himself that the Sprague family would never have even that much. *Thank you for this blessing, Lord.*

He glanced toward the Crock-Pot on the kitchen counter, sniffing the air with appreciation. Chicken with carrots, red potatoes, and a package of frozen peas waiting to be stirred in later. He'd added a few stems of the rosemary bush that had taken over Juliana's vegetable patch. Sadness nudged again, whispering that he'd lost so much more than his job. It was good there was a meeting tonight. He'd find fellowship, offer hope to another lonely and desperate person.

The doorbell rang once, twice. Followed by rapping on the wooden door. Light like the small knuckles of a neighbor child or—

A voice from the porch. "Daddy?"

Was he imagining it?

Another knock. "Are you there, Dad?"

Matt raced to the door, barely able to breathe, and flung it wide. "Kate . . ." His heart stalled at the sight of her bruised face.

"Hi." Tears welled in her beautiful eyes. She blinked up at him with a tentative smile. "I was in the neighborhood and . . ." Kate pointed to the sign on the lawn. "You sold the house?"

"I—"

Before Matt could say another word, his daughter dropped her bag and flung herself into his arms.

- + -

"I'm okay," Kate reassured her father for the third time in twenty minutes. She sat back against the chenille couch pillow. "Really. Just bumps and bruises. Nothing that won't heal." *The broken heart will take longer.*

"It looks like a lot more," her father said as if reading her mind.

Kate's throat constricted at the concern in his eyes—all for her. He hadn't said it outright, but she suspected that it was debt from her mother's medical care combined with Kate's college that had stressed her father's finances. Even before his retirement plan took a huge hit. Now he'd lost his job, his house. *And a grandson. How do I tell you this, Daddy?*

"Well . . ." Her father gave her hand a squeeze. "I'll feel better after I feed you. The kitchen's pretty well packed into boxes, but I have a couple of plates, forks, and a chicken in the slow cooker. The way your mom did it, with a can of mushroom soup." He rose to his feet. "The rice is only the kind you heat in the microwave and we might need to use paper towels for napkins, but—"

"Wait." Kate caught his hand as he turned toward the kitchen. "Can we just have tea right now? I need to talk with you about something, Dad."

The look in his eyes said he'd been expecting it. There was no backing down now.

Kate hugged the pillow close, heard the water in the kitchen, the dings of the microwave. *Grace . . . an undeserved gift. Please help me find the words, God.*

Her dad returned, handing her the daisy mug, the one she'd left behind all those years ago.

"When you came to Texas," she began as he settled beside her on the couch, "I told you I wouldn't talk about the year I was gone, that I couldn't. But I need to now." She met his gaze. "I should have told you this a long time ago. Maybe it would have changed some things. I don't know. I only know that I want things to change now. Between us and in my life."

He took the mug from her trembling hands, waited.

Kate closed her eyes. "There was this man in Las Vegas, a manager at a casino. He said I was too young to work there, but that he and his wife needed a nanny for their children. They let me stay with them, drive their cars . . . even made me a birthday cake. I thought it was all good. But then his wife went away for the weekend, and—" She shivered.

"Kate . . ." Her father reached for her hand. "I'm listening. It's okay."

She met his eyes and forced herself to continue. "He drugged me, I guess. I only remember feeling sick. And crying. Begging him to please let me go home. Nothing after that."

Her father's jaw clenched.

"Dad . . ." Kate took hold of his hands, captured his gaze. "I had a baby. I couldn't even let myself believe I was pregnant . . . and then I was in labor. I didn't get to a hospital in time." Her father's face blurred through her tears. "I was s-so scared. It was dark. And I was alone. So alone. And then there he was—this tiny little boy. I panicked." Tears began streaming down her face. "So I wrapped him up and left him at the fire department. I rang the bell and ran away. I hid behind a car until I saw someone take him." A sob tore loose from Kate's throat, but she kept the connection with her father's eyes. He had to understand. "I took him there . . . so he'd be okay . . . safe."

"Dear God . . . Oh, Katy . . ."

In an instant, her father's arms were around her, warm, strong, holding her like he'd never let go. She burrowed her chin into the hollow of his neck, her cheeks wet with tears—whether they were hers or his, she didn't know. "I'm sorry," she whispered, unable to stop her trembling. "I'm so, so sorry. You said you wanted grand-children. I took that from you. I—"

"Wait," he said, grasping her shoulders and leaning back. "All that matters now is that you're here—that I still have you." He stroked her hair gently. "I don't feel like I've lost anything. I feel like . . ." His voice choked. "I've finally found a missing part of my heart."

Kate couldn't speak. She could only nod and settle into her father's arms again. He gently rocked her, and soul-soothing peace came at last.

- + -

"You're sure you'll be okay here?" Matt smiled as Kate used a fingertip to nudge rice onto her fork the same way her mother used to do. He shifted the Bible under his arm, finding it hard to believe that an hour had passed. He wanted time to slow down. "I'd skip tonight, but there's a young man I'm sponsoring and he's been through some tough things this week."

"Go." The empathy in Kate's eyes melted his heart. "I'm good, I promise. Full of chicken and tired enough to sleep for a week. Between the time difference and not sleeping last night . . ." A yawn swallowed her smile. "Go."

"Okay." He watched her for a moment, almost afraid that if he left, she'd be gone again. But he knew that wasn't true. So many things had changed for Kate, giving far deeper meaning to her "I'm good" quip. She'd told him she prayed last night. And that it was what led her here today. "Good" couldn't begin to describe that; Matt knew it only too well. But the peace in her eyes said it all. Or almost all.

Matt had a feeling there was something else she hadn't told him, something less momentous, but that it weighed on her heart. An unspoken sadness. He wouldn't intrude. She planned to stay through Thanksgiving. It might be Chinese food on paper plates, but there would be time to talk. And to listen. One step at a time.

"There's a blanket in the hall closet if you want to curl up on the couch." He fished his keys from his pocket. "And a fresh pint of Chunky Monkey ice cream." He smiled at her raised brows. "Can't give up everything."

He told her he'd be back by nine and headed out the door. The streetlights were on, a welcoming glow in the darkness. He smiled to himself, thinking that for the first time in so very long, Happy Hollow Lane's name actually suited—

"Mr. Callison?"

Matt heard a car door close. Watched as a man strode past the nearest streetlamp and began heading his way. Tall, broad-shouldered. It couldn't be, but he looked like—

"It's Wes Tanner, sir."

# 34

**"UH . . . THANKS,"** Wes managed as Kate shooed her father back down the porch, then led him into the living room. He'd blame his suddenly weak legs on the cramped flight from Texas, but it was relief, plain and simple. And deep gratitude. The last time they'd been together, Kate had sent him out the door; this was a second chance. It felt more important than anything he'd known. If only he could somehow unscramble his brain, find the words he'd come to say. *Please, Lord . . .*

"Thank you," he repeated as she settled into a corner of the pillow-back couch, leaving him more room than he needed. Or wanted. His gaze did a quick sweep of the room, taking in the packing boxes, a paint tray, and stripped-bare walls, all at odds with a mantel packed like an overbooked jetliner with framed family photos. Evidence of a man holding tight to what was important; Wes understood that, absolutely.

"I can't believe you came all this way." Kate's voice was soft. She'd pulled a pillow into her lap, fingers kneading the plush fabric. She looked exhausted, bruised. Still beautiful but different somehow. Her dark eyes held his. "How did you know I was here?"

"Lauren. At least she told me you'd gone to see your dad. She didn't have the address, but I knew it was Sunnyvale." He wished his heartbeat would stop hammering the side of his neck. "I remembered you saying it was Happy Hollow Lane. Followed a map. It's a small cul-de-sac, and I'd seen your father's car in Texas, so . . ." He shrugged, attempted a smile. "I find people; it's what I do."

"Yes. It is." Kate's fingers plucked at the pillow, her expression still so unreadable. She glanced toward the kitchen. "I could get some tea. Or water or—"

"No," he interrupted, despite the fact that his mouth had never been drier. "Don't get up—don't go. I came out here because I need to talk to you, Kate." He cleared his throat. "I hate the way we left things between us—I mean, the way I left it. I hate that I left at all that day. I know you asked me to, but I shouldn't have gone."

Compassion he didn't deserve filled her eyes. "I'm sure it was hard to hear what I told you."

"Not nearly as hard as it was for you, Kate. Awful when it happened and all these years since. Then these past weeks, with the Baby Doe incident at the hospital. And now Harley. And Sunni . . ."

Kate said nothing, but her eyes shimmered with tears.

"On top of that," he continued, "you get saddled with a jerk who spouts off about having faith but still can't get a grip on forgiveness. As if people's decisions . . . mistakes . . . can be looked at like an engineering plan. Black-and-white, good and bad. Or—" Wes swallowed—"as if they can even be fully understood by anyone but God himself."

Kate nodded. And there it was again, the sense that something was different about her. Peaceful somehow.

"I'm ashamed," he told her. "I've had things wrong for so long."

"Are you talking about your mother?"

He nodded. "After you left, I spoke with my dad, finally talked with him about that night. He said . . ." Wes cleared his throat. "He said he spent a lot of years being confused and angry. But now he remembers the good things. He said good memories are God's mercy, that they give us hope. And not having hope is 'the worst kind of lost.'"

- + -

Kate swallowed hard, feeling Wes's pain—his discovery—as deeply as her own. "Your father's right. I've been running away all these years, trying to find something I knew was missing. But I carried all my mistakes with me, telling myself I didn't deserve real happiness." She summoned a grim smile. "Bad road. No map."

He smiled back at her, the understanding in his blue eyes making her heart ache.

"Last night," she continued, "I ended up in a hotel room in Dallas. I had no idea where I was going from there. I'd never felt so alone in my life. And then I saw Sunni Sprague's parents on the news this morning. You could feel their heartbreak. But Sunni's mother said something about . . . *me*." Kate shook her head, feeling goose bumps rise. "She said they believe my finding Sunni was God's plan. It stunned me. I switched off the TV and sat there for the longest time. Thinking about everything that's happened. All of it. I told myself it could have been my father on the news. My bones instead of Sunni's."

Somehow Wes had taken hold of her hand. His warmth spread through her.

Kate cleared her throat. "I thought about Ava Smith and Trista, your mother . . . and me. And then I knew—felt it so deeply—that we'd all done those tragic things out of desperation. Bad mistakes, but not bad people. I thought about what you told me about grace." She felt a tear slide down her face, though she'd begun to smile. "So I closed my eyes and I prayed, Wes. This woman who stuffed a cross in her closet, talking with God. Can you imagine?"

He nodded, tears in his eyes, and drew her hand to his chest. "And you came home," he said, his voice husky and low. "To talk with your father about what happened to you." Pain flickered across his face. "I'm so sorry that you were hurt like that. I'm sorry I did all the wrong things when you had the courage to tell me. I should have been there—"

"Shhh." She pressed her fingers to his lips. "You're here now."

"I want to be," he said, his expression raw and vulnerable. "Not just for now. I want us to have a chance at a lot more. I want you with me, Kate."

She smiled. "I sort of guessed that. Tracking me down. Jumping on a jet . . . Taking that risk with the security checkpoint."

"Huh?"

"That UT belt buckle." She laughed. "Big belt buckles, big trucks, tortilla chips shaped like your state. Texans! Why I'd want to live there . . ."

"But you do." He nestled her face against his palm, his thumb stroking her cheek. "You're coming back."

She tipped her head, snuggling into his touch. "I have to— I left my car at the Dallas–Fort Worth airport."

His lips brushed her bruised cheek very gently. "And . . . ?"

"And I promised to go to bat for my triage nurse."

He groaned, his lips on her forehead. "And . . . ?"

She smiled, warmth flooding through her. "And I want to be with you, Wes."

"There . . ." Wes leaned back, still cradling her face in his hands. "Now there's my brown-eyed girl."

"Yes."

He bent low to brush her lips lightly with his. Then grabbed the pillow from her lap and tossed it to the floor. "Better." He tucked his fingers under her chin and kissed her more thoroughly.

"Much better." Kate wound her arms around his neck, returning his kiss.

His arms moved around her, careful of her ribs but bringing her closer. Closer still, until she could feel his heart beating against her. His strong arms held her securely there. As if he was thinking just what she was: that it was a flat-out miracle they'd found each other, and they weren't ever letting go.

- + -

Matt smiled at the young couple on his old couch. He'd returned from his meeting to find Kate rosy cheeked and chattering, her eyes filled with something that looked every bit like love—even if she didn't know it yet. And Wes, though respectful as always, couldn't take his eyes off Kate. It seemed like only yesterday Matt had felt that new and hopeful in his life with Juliana. He envied them a little bit, but his gratitude overshadowed it by far.

"So," he said with all the seriousness he could muster, "you're saying you don't think a Chinese Thanksgiving is such a great idea? We could go Mexican . . ."

"Uh . . ." Wes looked at Kate.

Her eyes shone. "We were thinking more along the lines of hickory-smoked turkey, corn-bread stuffing, mashed potatoes, pecan pie, sweet tea . . ."

"Ah." A lump rose in Matt's throat, though he wasn't at all surprised. She was leaving him already. "Let me guess. At a wooden table under a big tree and a Texas sunset?"

"Yes, sir." Wes slid his arm around Kate's shoulders. "Is that all right? We checked the flights and it's doable."

"Of course." Matt nodded.

"Thanks, Daddy. Then there's only one other thing we need to know." Kate nudged Wes with an elbow.

"Right," he agreed. "What size jersey do you wear, Matt?"

"Jersey?"

"Football." Kate rose from the couch, walked over to where Matt stood. She blinked up at him, eyes teasing. "Team Tanner. There's always a game on Thanksgiving Day. You're invited."

"I . . ." Matt glanced around his living room full of half-packed boxes, remembering the feeling of linking hands at that table in Austin. The next job interview wasn't for another week. "Great— terrific." He grinned, warmth spreading through him. "I accept."

Wes strode forward and offered his hand to seal the deal.

"Thank you," Matt told him, responding in kind to the firm handshake. "I appreciate your including me. It's been a while since I shared a turkey dinner with my daughter. And I have a lot to be thankful for this year."

- + -

"We all do," Kate said, leaning against her father. She glanced between the two men, not sure her heart would hold the sudden rush of feelings. Then she winked at Wes. "Should we break it to him?"

"What?" Her father feigned a wary glance.

"The seating arrangement." A slow grin spread across Wes's face. "You'll be sitting next to Nancy Rae."

"Nancy?" Matt raised a suspicious brow. "Eligible widow, I suppose."

Kate bit into her lip, a spasm of laughter bringing tears to her eyes.

"What?" her father asked again. "Tell a man before he straps himself into a plane."

"C'mon." Kate pointed toward the kitchen. "If there was ever a Chunky Monkey moment, this is it." She took hold of her father's hand. "Just remember that no matter what, I do love you, Daddy."

"That's good to know," he told her, giving her fingers a squeeze. "I've got plenty of ice cream, but I'm not sure about the bowls and spoons."

"I'm not worried." She smiled at Wes. "I think we have all the right stuff."

# Epilogue

**MAY**

"You're not interrupting. The party's winding down." Kate ducked under a pecan branch while holding the phone to her ear. The Tanners' resident squirrel chattered somewhere above, adding his voice to a medley of laughter and distant strains of Taylor Swift. With the temperature in the high eighties and the trees in bloom, the air was as humid and fragrant as a greenhouse. "Although as long as there's still cake, Dylan won't be calling it quits."

Lauren laughed. "I love it that Miranda threw an adoption party. Harley must be holding court like a princess."

"Wait till you see the photos. Her little sundress matches Molly's—hot-pink roses on robin's egg blue, ordered from Lilly Pulitzer. They both have pom-pom sandals. And the cake frosting is done in the same colors."

"Grammy Judith. No one would doubt she'd throw herself into that project. Heart and soul." Lauren's tongue clucked. "The same way you've been making things happen at Austin Grace. I saw the article in the *Statesman* about Sunni's memorial nursing scholarship. I know you got that ball rolling."

"It was a team effort. And now that the FBI has connected her murder to that medical-supply salesman they arrested in Atlanta . . ."

"It's like a sad chapter is finally closing," Lauren finished. "For you, too, Kate. Working on the new educational workshops for Safe Haven providers—that has to feel so good." The compassion in her voice wrapped Kate like a hug.

"It does," Kate agreed, grateful again she was no longer hiding from her own painful past. "I'm going to do everything I can to protect babies. And to keep women from making tragic mistakes that will destroy their own lives as well." She sighed. "Ava Smith is out there somewhere. And even if she knows the autopsy report showed her son died before birth, she won't believe she's worthy of forgiveness for abandoning him. If sharing my story helps someone like her, I'll do it in a heartbeat."

"Amen, my friend. I know you will. There are such good folks willing to offer foster care and adoption."

"Yes." Kate's gaze returned to Harley in Molly's arms. A few yards away, a beaming Judith was busy snapping photos of her daughter and new granddaughter. Miranda Tanner stood next to them. She slid her arm around Dylan's shoulders as he teased a giggle from the baby, a dab of blue frosting on his chin.

Grateful warmth flooded through Kate; these days when she thought of her son, she imagined him in a loving scene exactly like this one. Though Wes had offered to help her search for him—and though she yearned to finally know her son—Kate couldn't bear the possibility that her sudden appearance might cause him even a moment of painful confusion and turmoil. Because of that, she'd put the generous offer on hold for now. She also had a deep and peaceful sense that she shouldn't rush, that she should wait—trust God with this, too. Something told Kate that perhaps one day her lost but dearly loved son would find her.

"Well, it sounds like you've had a great day," Lauren told her. "I wish I could have been there. But Houston Grace ER has me in new-employee chains; thank heaven they come in colors that coordinate with my scrubs."

Once again Kate sensed undercurrents of trouble Lauren had yet to confide. Being closer to her sister had helped on some levels, but the complications were taking a toll. "I really miss you, Lauren."

"Sure . . ." Her friend chuckled. "Like you have time. With two men clamoring for your attention now, and—Oh, rats. Have to run. The triage light's flashing and I'm on the hot seat today. Love you, girl!"

"Love you back." Kate disconnected and turned to see Miranda walking up. Her auburn hair was piled high on her head, her face flushed and dewy in the humidity.

"I brought you tea." She handed Kate a glass mounded high with ice.

"Thank you." She caught the wistful expression on the woman's face. "It must be hard to let Harley go after all these months."

"I won't pretend it isn't." Miranda's gaze drifted toward the guests. "But I'm happy she's found such a wonderful family." She shook her head slowly. "That first day she came to us, I remember talking to Wes and telling him how—even after what had happened with Harley's birth mother—I was relieved to know God has a plan."

"Yes." Kate was sure of that now.

"Right now *my* plan is to help Molly and Judith gather up

Harley's gifts." Miranda glanced toward the barn. "Do me a favor and go check on those men down in the drilling shop. I told them to grab some sandwiches—man cannot live on cake alone—but when you get two engineers brainstorming . . ."

*"Two men clamoring for your attention . . ."* Kate smiled. "Dad's so happy about working with the business. And living in Austin and—"

"About finding Judith?" Miranda asked, her eyes teasing. "The way things have been going, I expect to see two new sets of initials carved into the side of that barn—remind me to hide my kitchen knives. On the other hand, it does lend itself nicely to the possibilities of seeing Harley a lot more often, her new grandmother having developed such a keen interest in well drilling."

Kate's smile widened.

Miranda's brows rows. "Speaking of plans, Wes said something about you and him taking the horses out this evening. On some kind of search?"

"Well . . ." Kate laughed, her stomach shivering the same way it always did when she thought of him. "It's not an official search. He knows I have this thing about fireflies."

"They'll be there." Miranda gave a quick nod.

"You sound sure—part of that 'plan'?"

Miranda laughed. "More equal parts Texas heat and humidity. Paul and I spotted a few from the porch last night right around dusk. There should be more down closer to the creek; Wes will know." She gave Kate a quick hug and headed back toward the other guests.

*"Wes will know."* Kate didn't doubt it for a moment. He'd known where to find her when she ran to California. And in these last months he'd awakened her heart, helped her heal and trust

again. And nurtured a blossoming faith that would sustain Kate for the rest of her life.

She smiled, remembering the first time she'd come to this beautiful ranch, that day she'd brought her father for the search-and-rescue demonstration. And how Dylan had asked her if she was "hiding or searching." She hadn't known how to answer. But she did now: she'd been hiding, absolutely—from family, from love, and from God. What a search it had turned out to be. And oh, how very much she'd found. Fireflies could never compare.

- + -

"Down there." Wes pointed toward the creek, thinking he'd rather keep watching Kate's eyes. Far more beautiful than lightning bugs any day. He settled close to her on the blanket he'd spread on the grass. "The sun's dropping behind the hills, and they like the water. We'll see them in the cedar along the creek. It won't be long now." He draped an arm across her shoulder, felt the kitten-soft brush of her hair against his bare arm. Wes stifled a chuckle at the thought that he'd ever considered this woman prickly.

"What's funny?" Kate asked, peering up at him in the near darkness. "You're laughing."

"Not really." He bent down, pressed a kiss on the tip of her nose. "Just happy."

"To see fireflies?"

"To see them with you." *And because* . . . Wes realized that he was nervous. After all his care and planning—his absolute certainty—he was flat-out nervous.

The horses snuffled in the distance, tied to a tree and nibbling at the grass.

"I can't believe you brought your rescue pack," Kate said, glancing to where it sat beside him. "It's not like you haven't mapped every inch of this property."

"You never know." He smiled in the darkness.

"And it's good to have all the right stuff."

He bit his lip to keep from laughing. "Absolutely."

She gasped, hunching forward. "I think I see—Oh, Wes. There!"

"Where?" he asked, mesmerized by the childlike delight on her face.

She snorted. "Not in my hair—look where I'm pointing. See? They're so pretty. Oh, I'll never get used to that! Do you see them?"

"I see," he said, wrapping both arms around her, inhaling her scent. *I see you.*

They were quiet for a few minutes, watching the tiny light displays arcing and dancing along the creek bed like embers launched skyward from a campfire. He thought about what he'd come here to do. Hoped he had it right.

"They're pretty interesting insects," he murmured against Kate's hair. "Want to know what makes them—"

"No!" Kate blurted, aghast. "Don't go all engineer on me. Please. I want them to stay magical. I don't want to know how they blink."

He laughed. "Then do you want to know *why*? Why they light up like that?" Wes smiled as her wary gaze met his. This fit right into his plan. "They're searching . . . for love."

"Love?" She grinned. "Thank you. I'm sure as a science guy that was tough."

"Not as tough as you'd think," he said, the nervousness coming back. Wes reached for his pack. "Here," he said, digging around in it. "Put this on."

"What is it?"

"A headlamp." He donned his own and switched on the beam, saw her blink. "Your turn." He tipped the light away but still saw the look on her face that said he was crazy. "Please. I want to show you something."

"Okay. I'm humoring you," she said, adjusting it over her hair. "But if we're here to see fireflies, adding light seems more than a little at odds with the search."

"I'm glad you said that."

"What?"

"'Search.' Because we are—you are, anyway." He fumbled with the pack again. Found what he was looking for, his heart in his throat. "Turn on your light."

She did, blinding him. "Oops. Sorry."

"Okay now," he said. "I'll show you how to use this. Point your nose where you want to see. Here." He gestured. "Spot that tree."

She turned her head. The live oak lit.

"Good job. Now that boulder over there."

The granite shone, Kate's aim hitting it with accuracy.

"The horses . . ."

Clementine's eyes blinked back at them.

"You're a natural." Wes smiled, his fingers busy with their covert task.

"I still don't see why we're doing this," Kate said, shaking her head and causing the beam to bounce like a silent movie. "Unless we're trying to look like a couple of demented fireflies ourselves. So why don't we—"

"Now," he instructed, "look here."

"Where?"

"At my hands."

"Wes, really . . ." Kate's beam hopscotched across the blanket, found the knees of his jeans, his shirt, and—

She gasped. "Oh, what . . . Wes!"

"Like it?"

The brilliant round-cut diamond glittered in the light.

"Oh . . ." Kate picked up the velvet box. "It's so . . ." She stared at him, eyes wide.

"Here." He pulled off his headlamp, reached for hers. Not before he saw tears and then the smile that said they were from happiness. His heart thudded. He left one of the lights glowing atop his pack, just enough to see her.

"I love you, Kate," he said, cupping her sweet face in his hands. "Remember a long time ago, not long after we met, when I told you I thought there was a reason we found each other?"

She nodded, the tears spilling over her dark lashes.

"It was true. I've been searching for you all my life. And I don't ever want to lose what we've found. Say you'll marry me. Please, Kate. Be my wife."

"I . . ." She nodded, cleared her throat, nodded again. "Yes, yes!" She flung her arms around him, one hand still clutching the ring box. "I love you so much. I do—so much."

Then he was kissing her. The side of her neck, her tear-dampened cheek, her eyes, a corner of her lips. And then her mouth. Tenderly and very, very thoroughly.

When they finally broke away, they started to laugh. Howled at his corny ring search, his suggestion of Nancy Rae serving as maid of honor alongside his best man, Gabe, and then Kate's come-back that Hershey would be ring bearer. He parried with a suggestion that Roady man the guest book. Kate giggled that her father should play air guitar for the reception—and then Wes admitted that he'd asked Matt's permission to propose. She stopped laughing, happy tears welling again, and told him she loved him even more for that.

Wes slipped the engagement ring on Kate's finger. And they simply sat there, holding each other in the languid silence of a warm Texas night.

The fireflies blinked, looped, and zigzagged. Then, one by one, finally disappeared. The way Wes's love for this amazing woman never would. He knew that without a doubt. The same way he knew that, despite the odds, it was Kate who'd done the rescuing after all.

*Thank you, Lord, for planning it that way.*

# About the Author

**CANDACE CALVERT** is a former ER nurse and author of the Mercy Hospital series—*Critical Care, Disaster Status,* and *Code Triage*—and the Grace Medical series—*Trauma Plan* and *Rescue Team.* Her medical dramas offer readers a chance to "scrub in" on the exciting world of emergency medicine. Wife, mother, and very proud grandmother, Candace makes her home in northern California. Visit her website at www.candacecalvert.com.

# Discussion Guide

Note: If you would like me to "attend" your book club's gathering, please e-mail me at Candace@candacecalvert.com. I'll try to arrange a speakerphone or Skype visit to join your discussion.

1. In the opening scene of *Rescue Team*, Wes Tanner plunges down a gully to rescue a missing woman; he is soon joined by a team of volunteers that includes a local funeral director, a coffeehouse barista, and a dog named Hershey. Throughout the story, we see that Wes is proud of and grateful for his team—folks united in a calling to serve others. In your personal experience, have you ever had a strong sense of team? What were the circumstances? How did it make you feel?

2. On the flip side, at the beginning of *Rescue Team*, we find Kate Callison struggling to hold her emergency department team together. She blames her problems on the fact that she's "stepping into the shoes of a saint," replacing a much loved and tragically lost ER director. Do you think she's correct in

that assessment of the problem? Could she have done more to unify her team? Discuss.

3. Tireless hospital volunteer Judith Doyle is dedicated to her own rescue plan. What was valuable about seeing the story from her point of view? Were you surprised by the turn of events that brought the police to her door? Did you suspect Judith's secret identity?

4. *Rescue Team* is set in and around Austin, Texas, and readers get glimpses of both rural settings (the Tanner and Braxton ranches) and colorful cityscapes, from famous music clubs to quirky tastes of Austin's famous gourmet trailer food. What imagery added to your enjoyment of this story? Have you ever traveled to Austin? If you were to visit, which of Kate and Wes's destinations would you want to see?

5. The story's more serious moments are balanced by small bits of humor, often from walk-on characters—even those who can't actually walk, like vintage doll Nancy Rae. What did the tea-and-cookie scene with Nancy Rae and Amelia Braxton tell you about our hero, Wes?

6. In a scene at the Braxton ranch, while standing at the site of an abandoned well, Wes describes his first rescue to Kate. Struck by a sense of Wes's good and heroic heart, Kate says something to him about her own flaws—that she's "not the kind of person God would listen to." Wes responds by talking about the undeserved gift of grace. How important was this conversation to Kate's overall journey? What similarities do you see between this exchange and the Bible story of the woman at the well (John 4:1-42)?

7. Both Kate and Wes join the search for missing baby Harley. Finding her feels both urgent and very, very personal for each of them—for far different reasons. Did you understand their feelings? Empathize with them? Discuss.

8. After her painful confession to Wes, Kate feels confused and hopeless. So she does what she's always done: runs away. Yet something prompts her to stop by triage nurse Dana Connor's house, and afterward, she feels "a little less lost." Why do you think that was?

9. Though Kate wanted desperately to find baby Harley, she instead found Sunni Sprague's bones. At a pivotal point in the story, Sunni's grieving mother says she believes it was God's plan that Kate found her daughter. Would you agree? Why? Have you ever found yourself in a role that seemed crafted by God but wasn't your plan? How did you respond?

10. The broken relationship between Kate and her father, Matt, was an important part of this story. How did you feel when Kate went home to Happy Hollow Lane? How important was that resolution to her healing?

11. How satisfying was *Rescue Team*'s ending for you? Were any of your questions left unanswered?

Please visit my website at www.candacecalvert.com for more information on upcoming books in this series.

Thank you for reading *Rescue Team*.

Warmly,
Candace Calvert

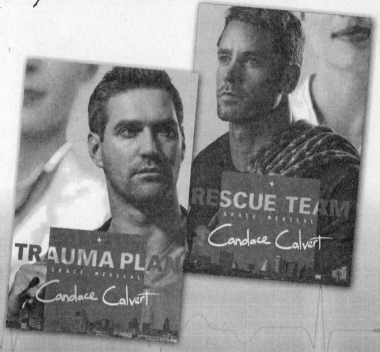